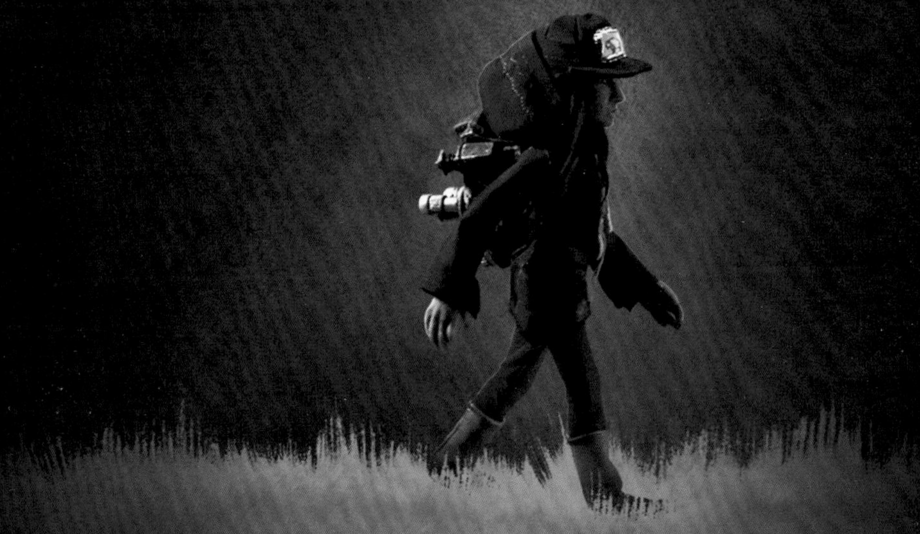

FOUR FACES OF THE MOON

WRITTEN AND CREATED BY

AMANDA STRONG

annick press
toronto berkeley

Cover art and design by Maya McKibbin, Dora Cepic, and Paul Covello
Edited by Mary Beth Leatherdale
Copyedited by Adrineh Der-Boghossian
Proofread by Mary Ann J. Blair
Interior design and typesetting by Paul Covello

Annick Press Ltd.

We acknowledge the support of the Canada Council for the Arts and the Ontario Arts Council, and the participation of the Government of Canada/la participation du gouvernement du Canada for our publishing activities.

Canada

ONTARIO ARTS COUNCIL
CONSEIL DES ARTS DE L'ONTARIO
an Ontario government agency
un organisme du gouvernement de l'Ontario

Library and Archives Canada Cataloguing in Publication
Title: Four faces of the moon / Amanda Strong.
Other titles: Graphic novelization of (work): Four faces of the moon (Motion picture)
Names: Strong, Amanda, 1984- author, artist.
Description: Adapted from the stop-motion animated film of the same name, written and directed by Amanda Strong.
Identifiers: Canadiana (print) 2020021084X | Canadiana (ebook) 20200210874 | ISBN 9781773214542 (hardcover) | ISBN 9781773214535 (softcover) | ISBN 9781773214573 (PDF) | ISBN 9781773214559 (HTML)
Subjects: LCSH: Indigenous peoples—Canada—History—Comic books, strips, etc. | LCSH: Indigenous peoples—Canada—History—Juvenile fiction. | LCSH: Indigenous peoples—Colonization—Canada—Comic books, strips, etc. | LCSH: Indigenous peoples—Colonization—Canada—Juvenile fiction. | LCGFT: Graphic novels. | LCGFT: Graphic novel adaptations.
Classification: LCC PN6733.S77 F68 2021 | DDC j741.5/971—dc23

Published in the U.S.A. by Annick Press (U.S.) Ltd.
Distributed in Canada by University of Toronto Press.
Distributed in the U.S.A. by Publishers Group West.

Printed in Canada

annickpress.com
spottedfawnproductions.com

Also available as an e-book. Please visit annickpress.com/ebooks for more details.

For Olivine

—A.S.

TABLE OF CONTENTS

Adapted from a stop-motion animation, *Four Faces of the Moon* is a story shared across generations. It will continue to ripple forward well beyond my lifetime. I share this story with my ancestors and with my grandmother Olivine Bousquet, who I dedicate this story to. We attended ceremonies together and I often sat and listened to her retell the history of our family. My grandma had a fighter's spirit and a presence that woke up the room. Spending time with her gave me the spark to carry our story forward.

Photography was one of my earliest forms of expression. I built a makeshift darkroom in my basement when I was a student. It became a portal between past and present, a place where time stood still. When inside I felt grounded in the present with my heartbeat and the timer as steady reminders, but I was also able to exist within time in a way that I hadn't previously experienced. In this story, the darkroom becomes a place between time and space.

In the settling of Canada and the United States, the slaughter of the Buffalo, the building of the railway, and the many tactics used to control and starve Nations left many families without land, shelter, or food. Many were forced into assimilation and survival. We come from families that resisted and went underground to keep our culture alive. The complexity of this experience cannot be told in one telling. Stories like this will continue to crack the earth like a Prairie lightning storm.

When I am feeling discouraged I remind myself that my grandma Olivine is at my side and all of my family are with her. They fought to keep ceremony, language, and our connection to the land and the Buffalo alive. *Four Faces of the Moon* is a personal story, yet it is also shared among so many. I offer it to you as space to create further discussion around the disenfranchisement and displacement of Indigenous Peoples and the original beings of the land in order to make way for the current colonial reality.

CHAPTER ONE
NEW MOON

WE WALK WITH OUR ANCESTORS,
TRACING THEIR STEPS WITH OUR OWN.
WE COME TOGETHER AND
CARRY THE STORIES FORWARD.

KI PIMOHTÂNAW KÂNAKATASKÎTWÂW
KIWAHKÔMÂKANAK AHCI,
Î PIMT'SAHAMA OTAHKISKÎWINOWÂWA.
KIMÂMAWINTONAW MÎNA
ÂTAYOHKÊWINA KIKANAWIHTÎNAW.

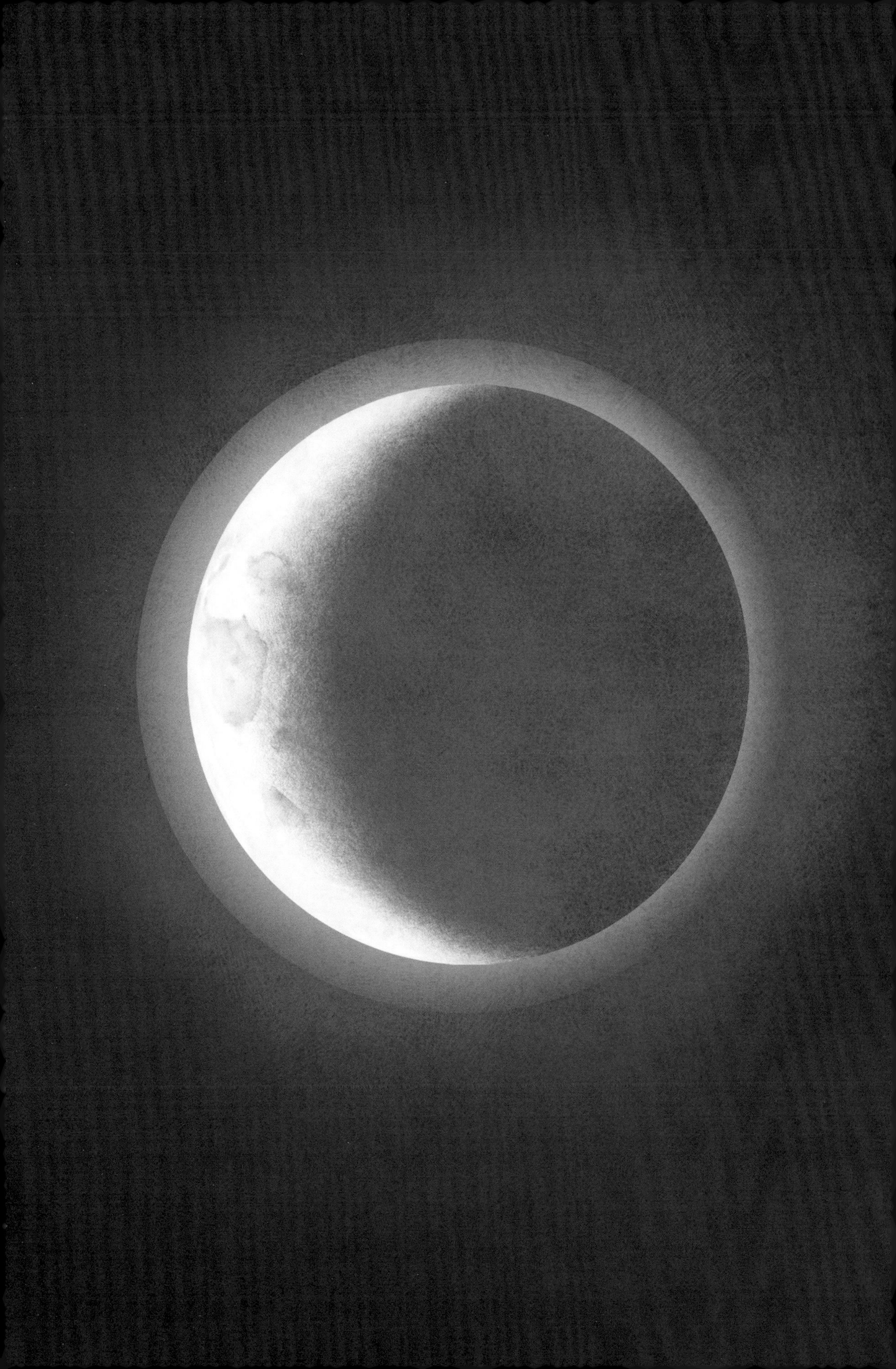

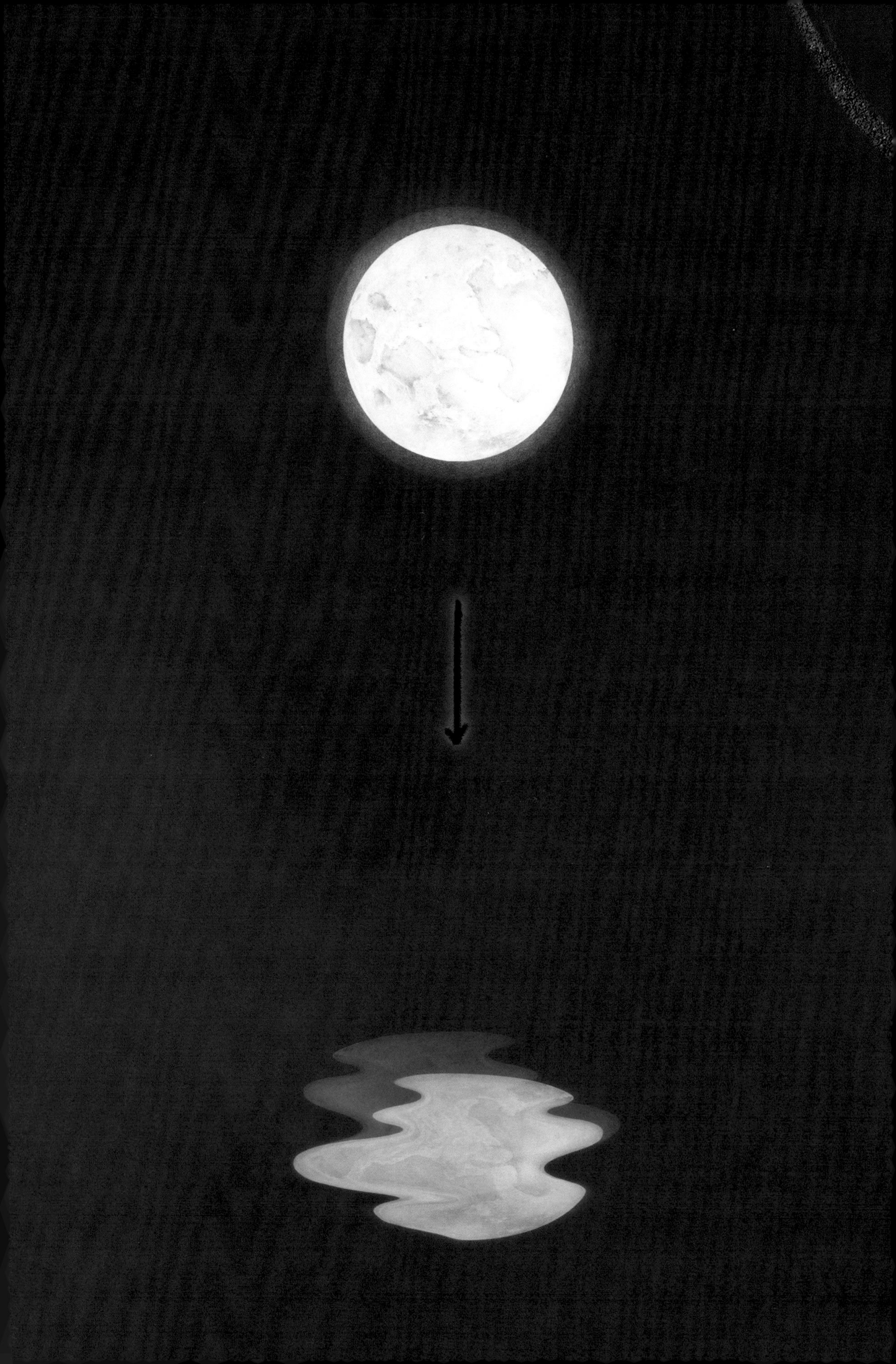

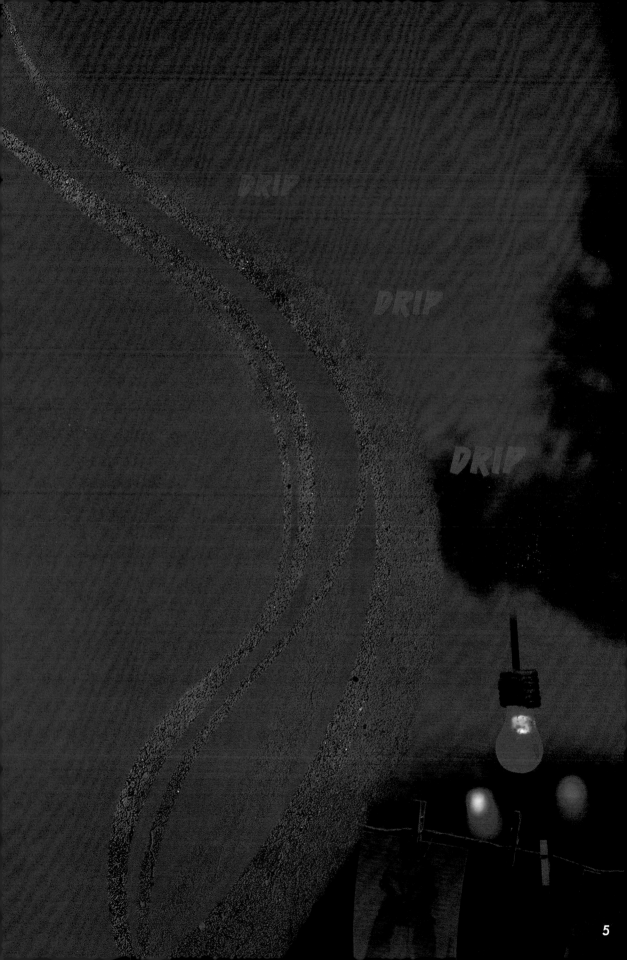

DRIP

DRIP

DRIP

5

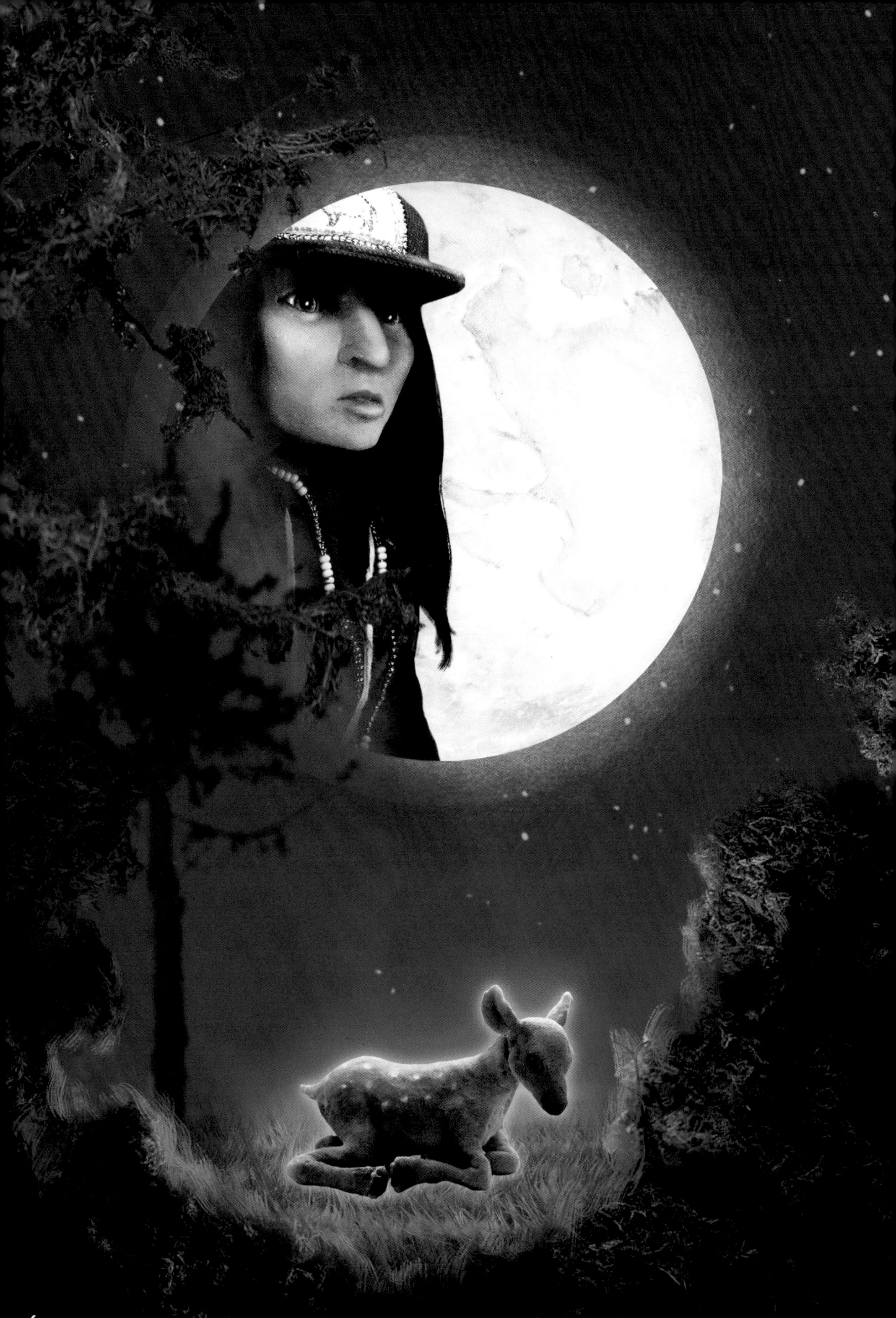

WHEN I WAS 14 YEARS OLD,
I WAS GIVEN THE NAME
GIDAGAAKOONS
IN A CEREMONY.

IT MEANS SPOTTED FAWN.

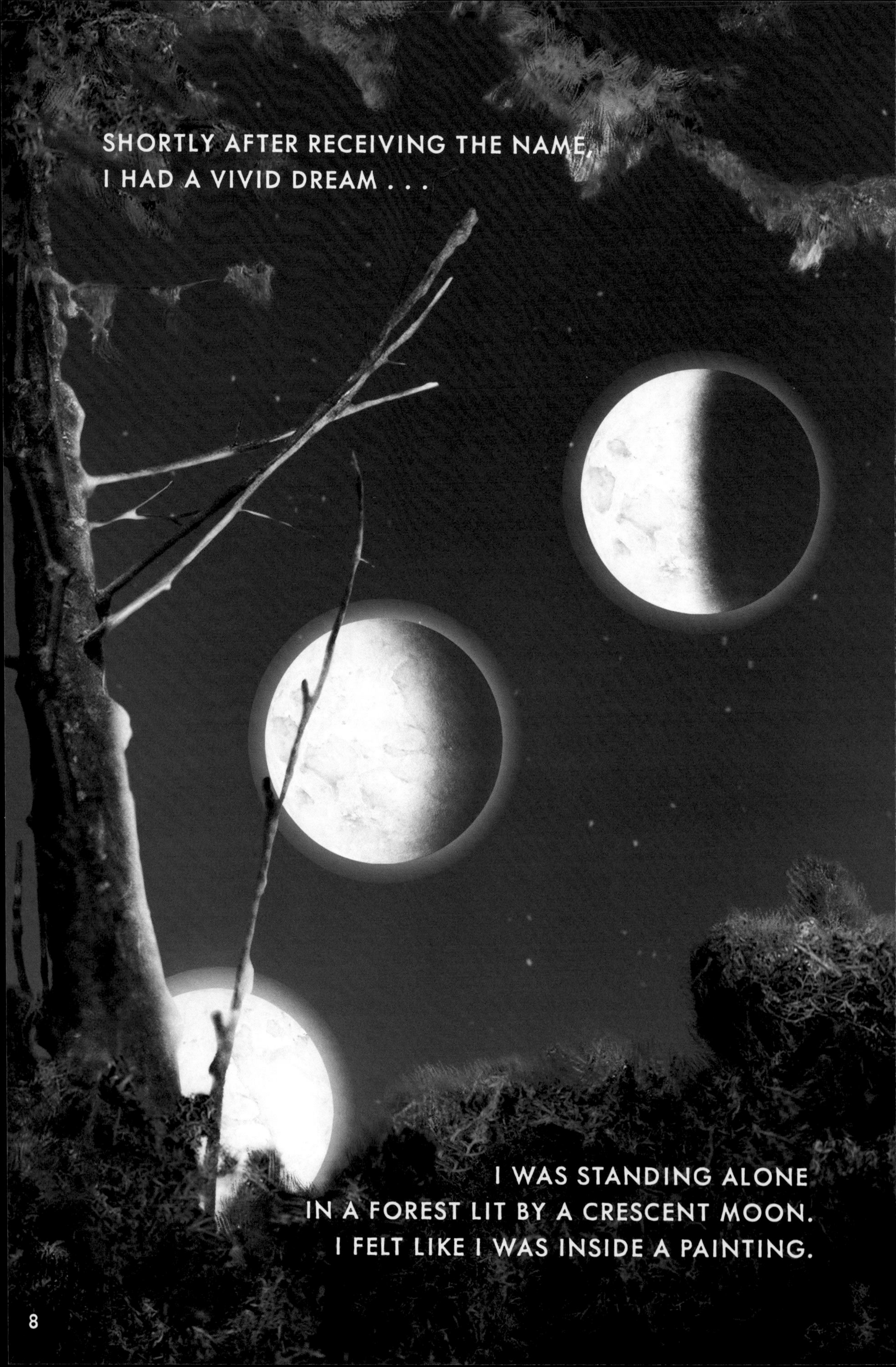
SHORTLY AFTER RECEIVING THE NAME,
I HAD A VIVID DREAM . . .
I WAS STANDING ALONE
IN A FOREST LIT BY A CRESCENT MOON.
I FELT LIKE I WAS INSIDE A PAINTING.

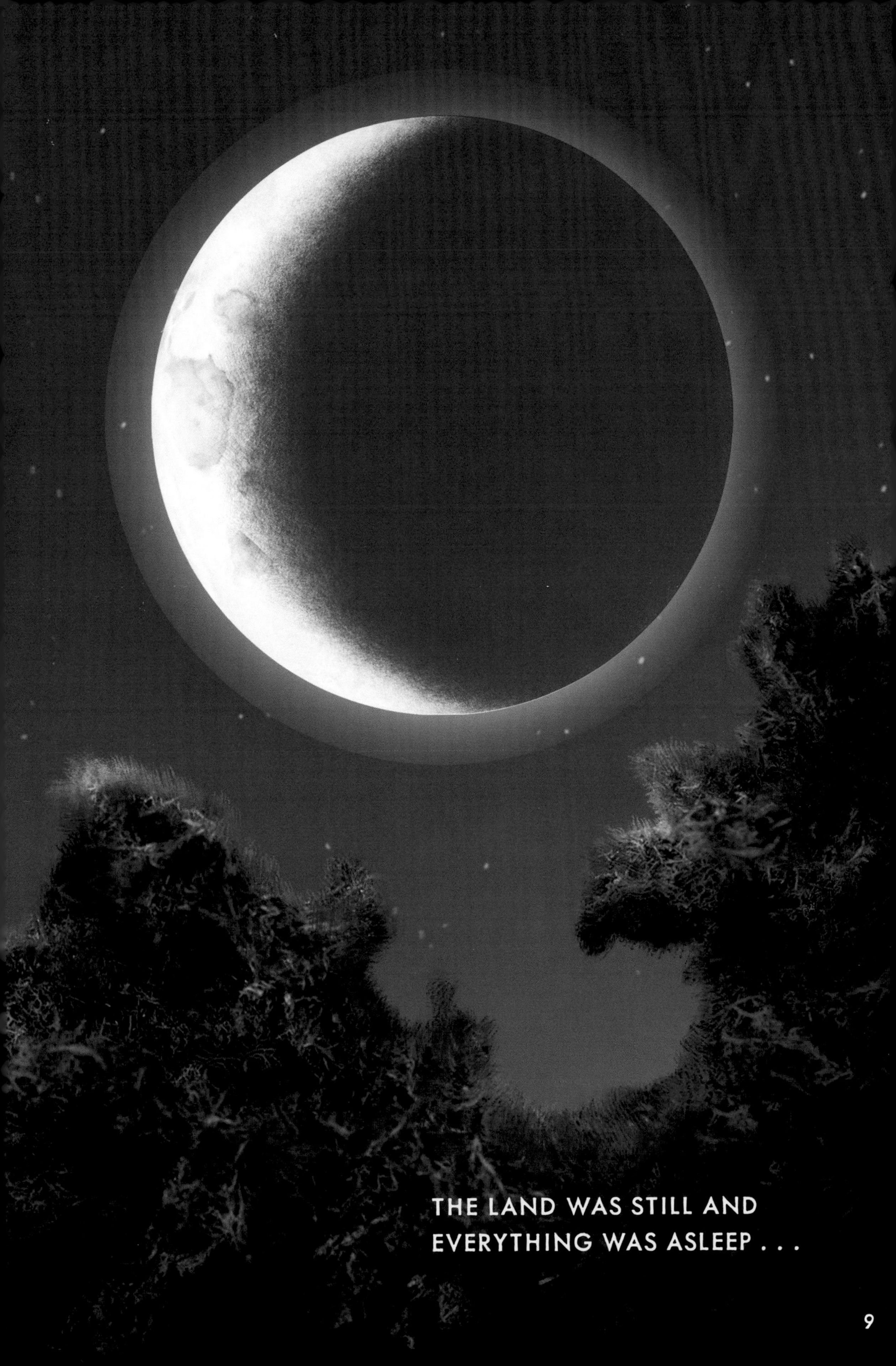

THE LAND WAS STILL AND
EVERYTHING WAS ASLEEP . . .

THEN, THE CALM WAS BROKEN
BY A SMALL FAWN
CRASHING THROUGH THE FOREST.

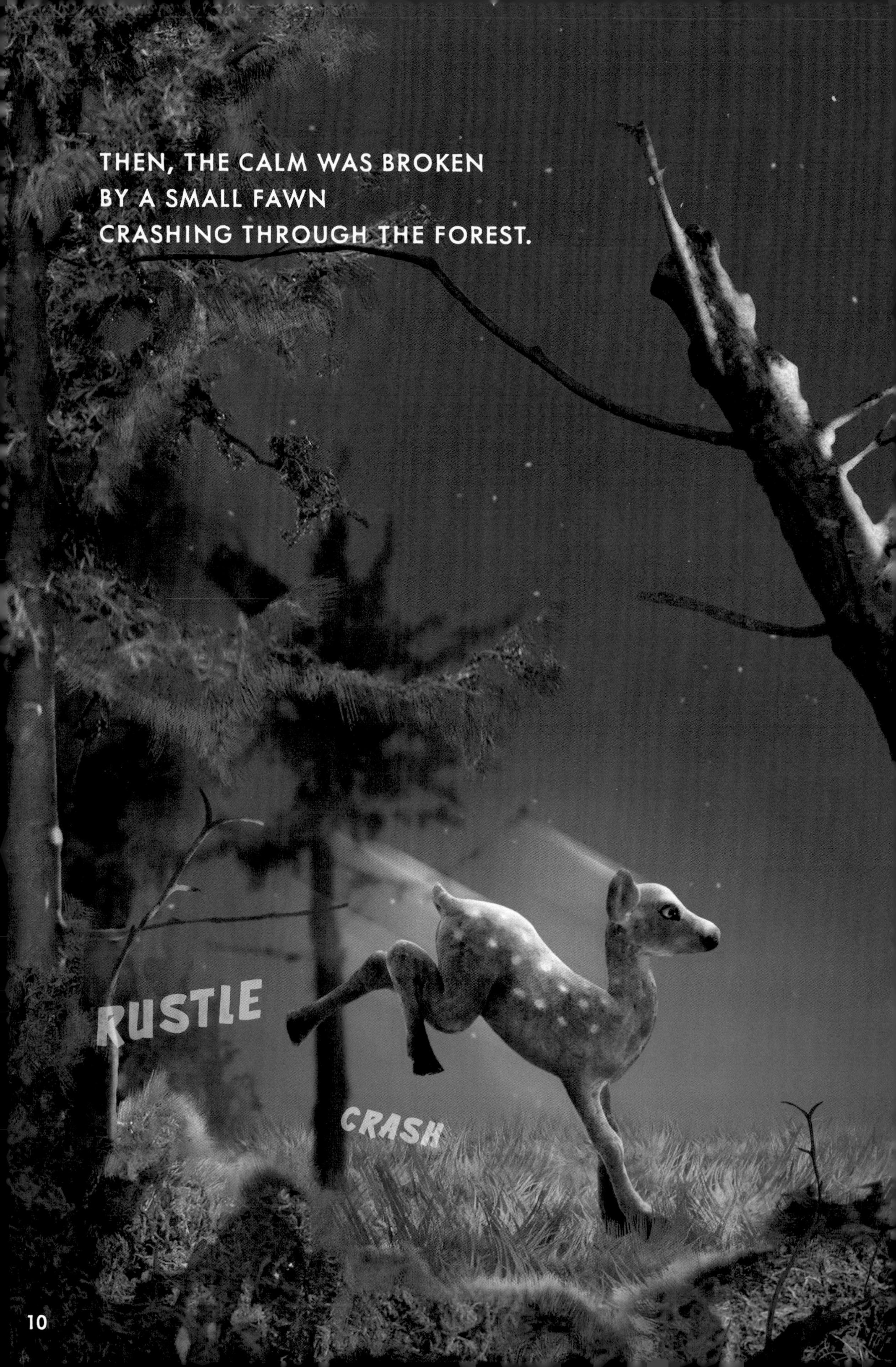
RUSTLE
CRASH

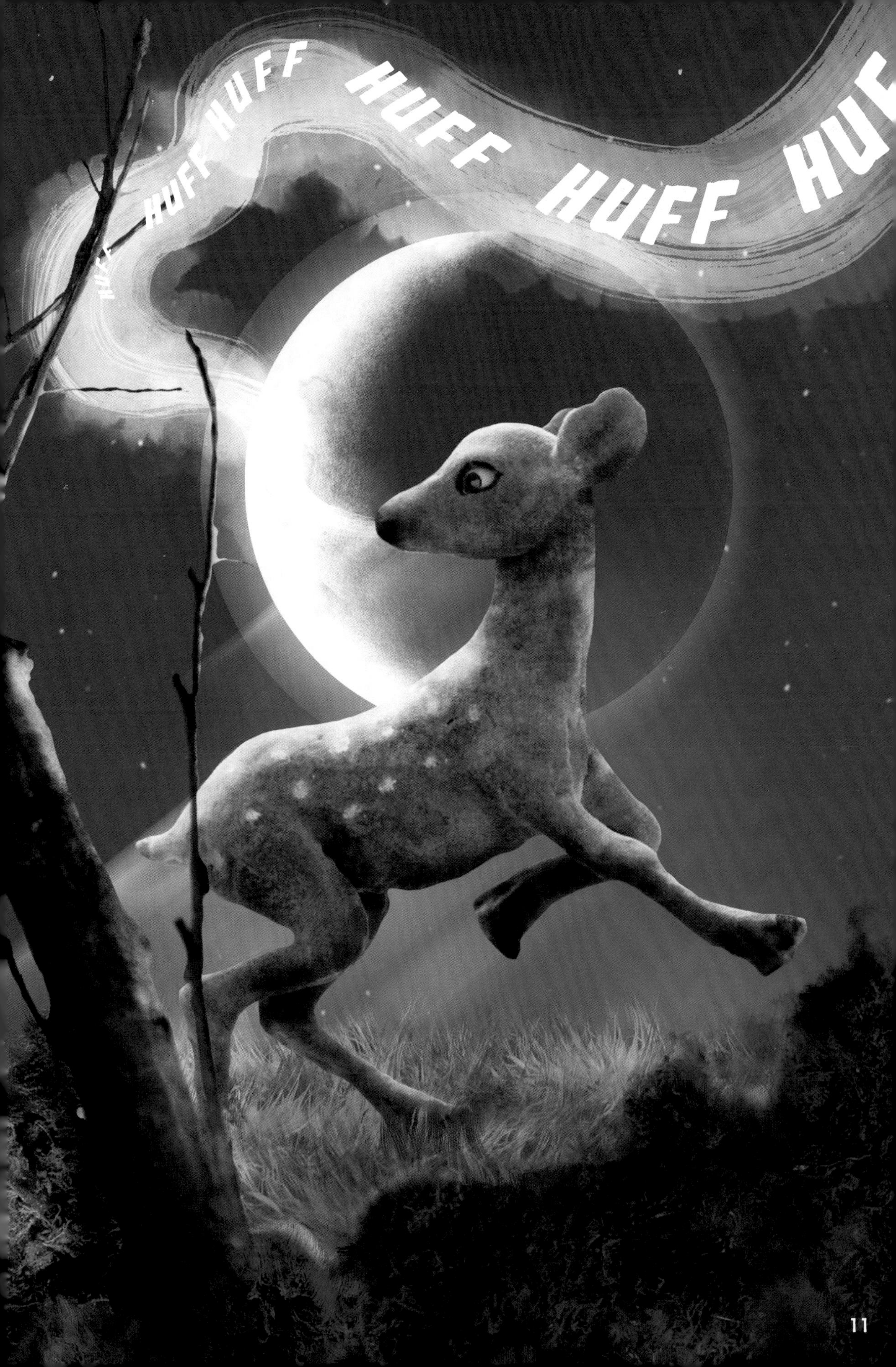
HUFF HUFF HUFF HUFF HUFF HUFF HU

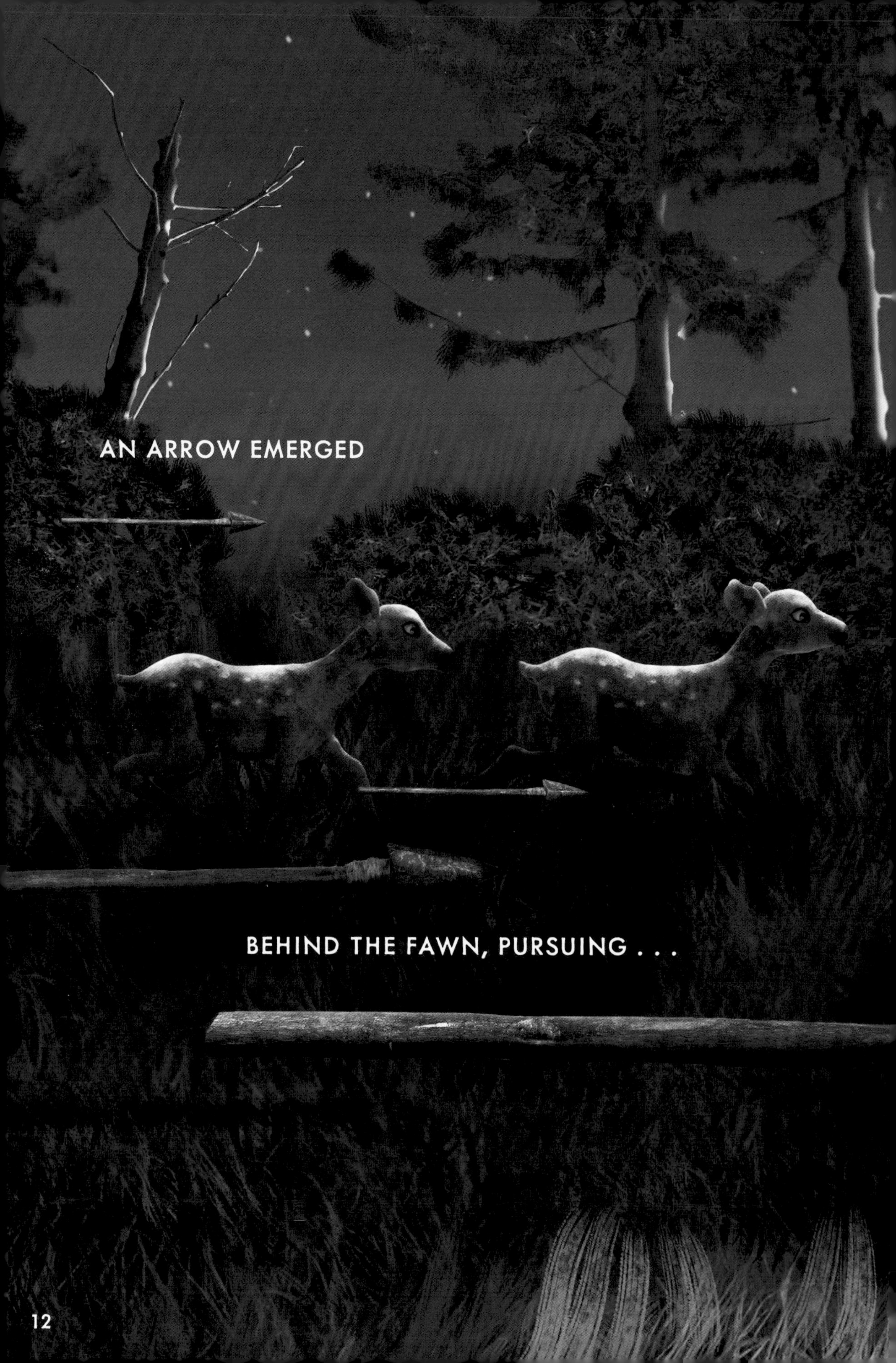
AN ARROW EMERGED
BEHIND THE FAWN, PURSUING . . .

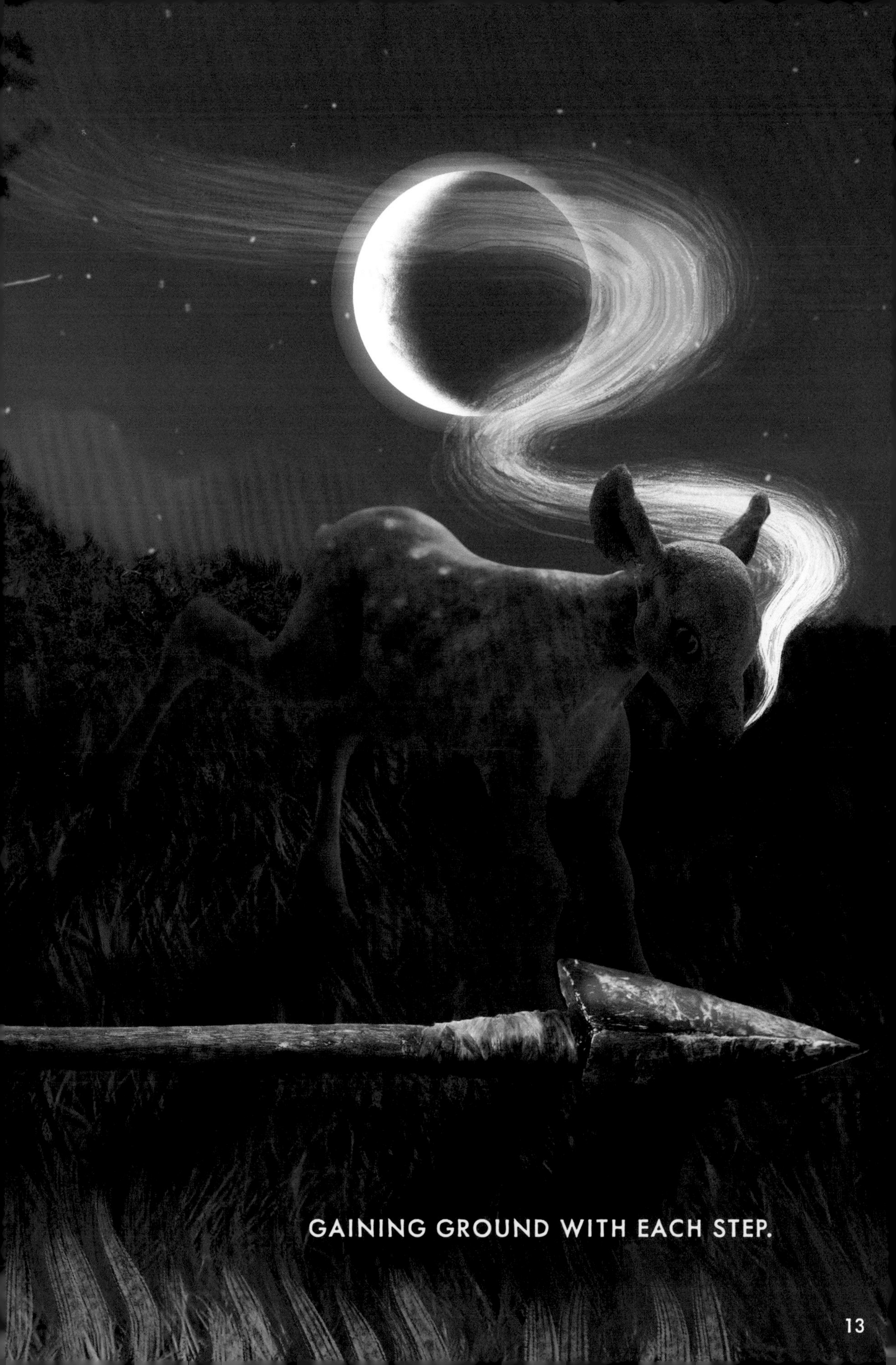

GAINING GROUND WITH EACH STEP.

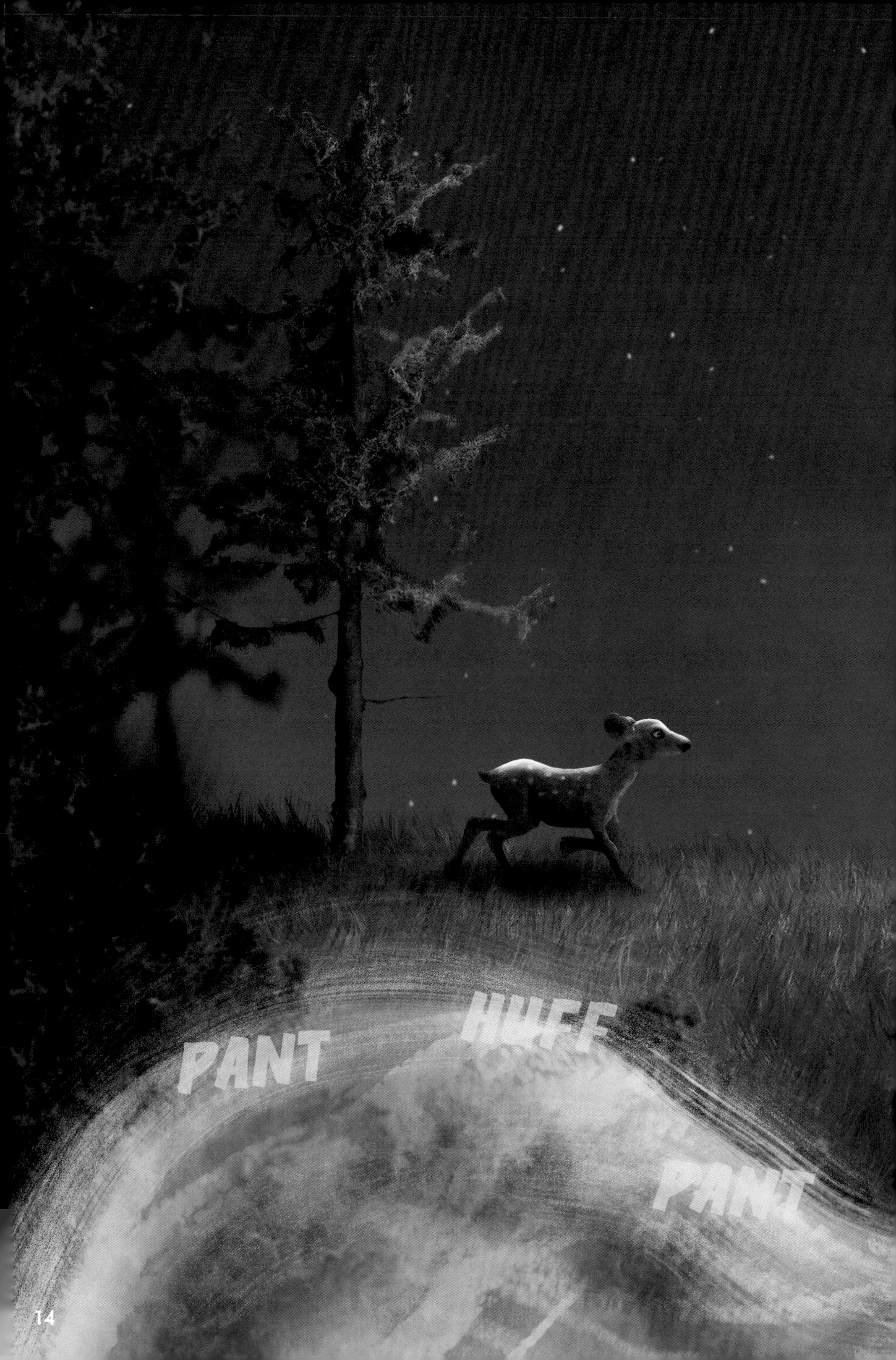
PANT
HUFF
PANT

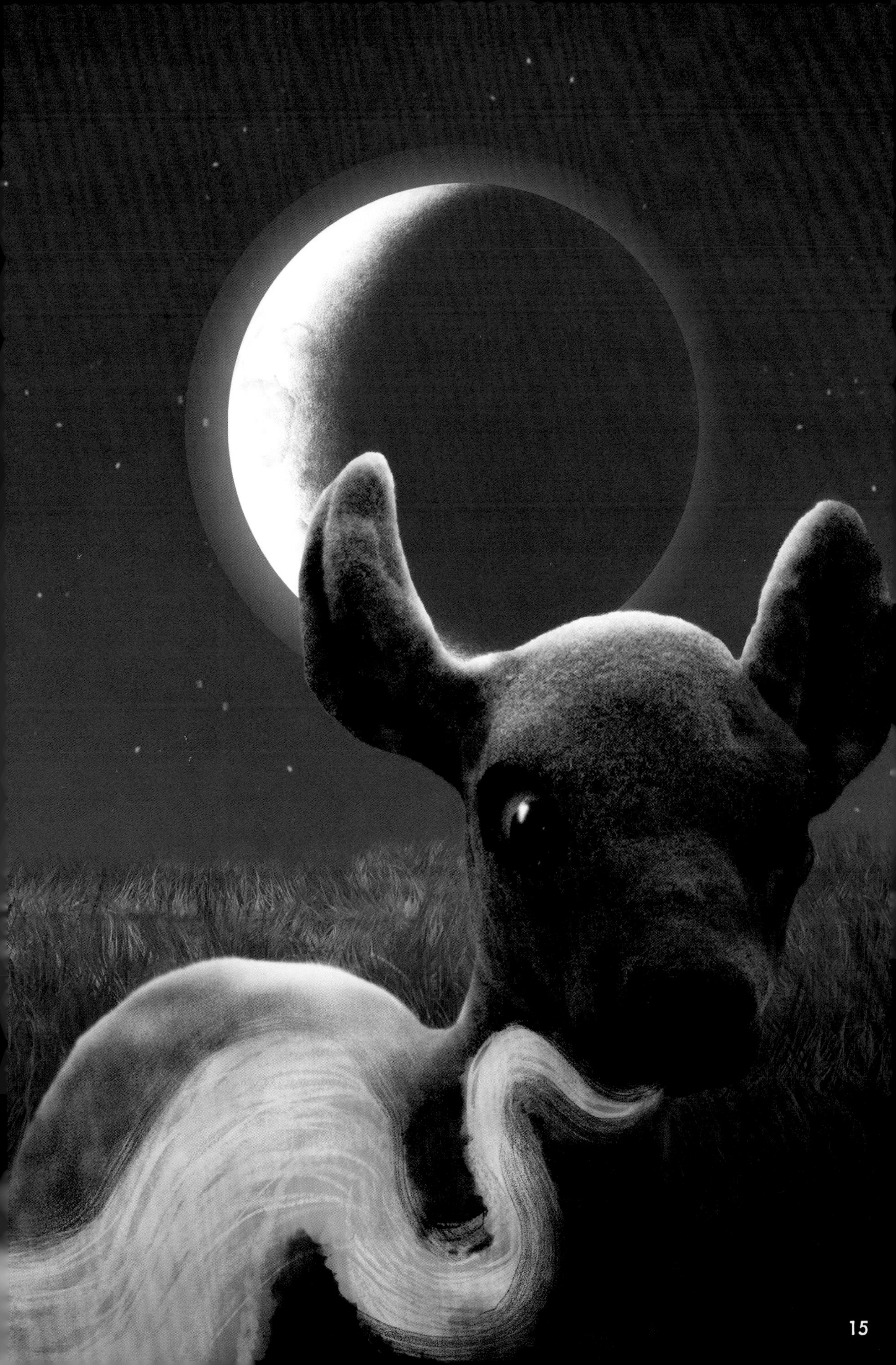

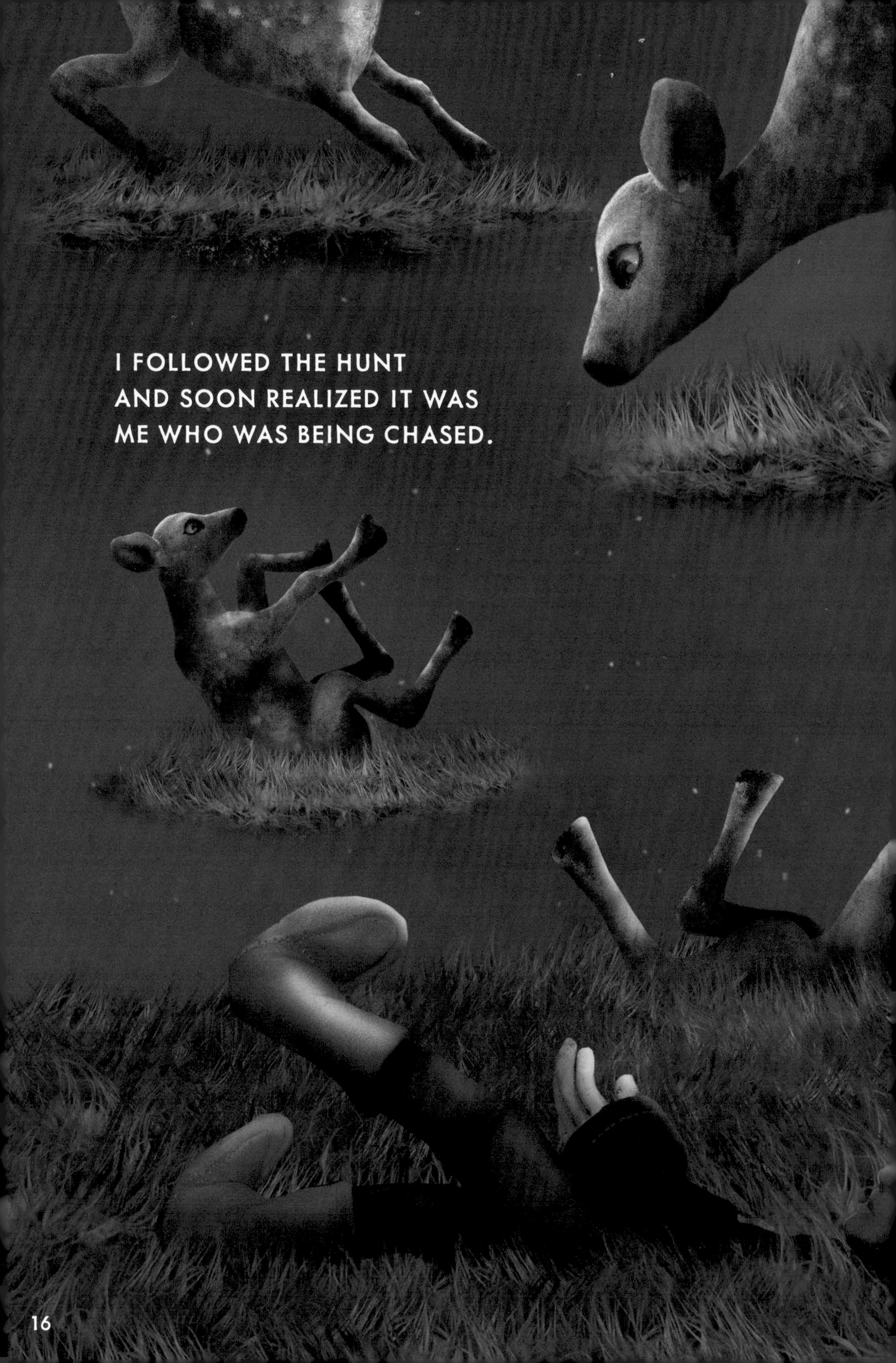
I FOLLOWED THE HUNT
AND SOON REALIZED IT WAS
ME WHO WAS BEING CHASED.

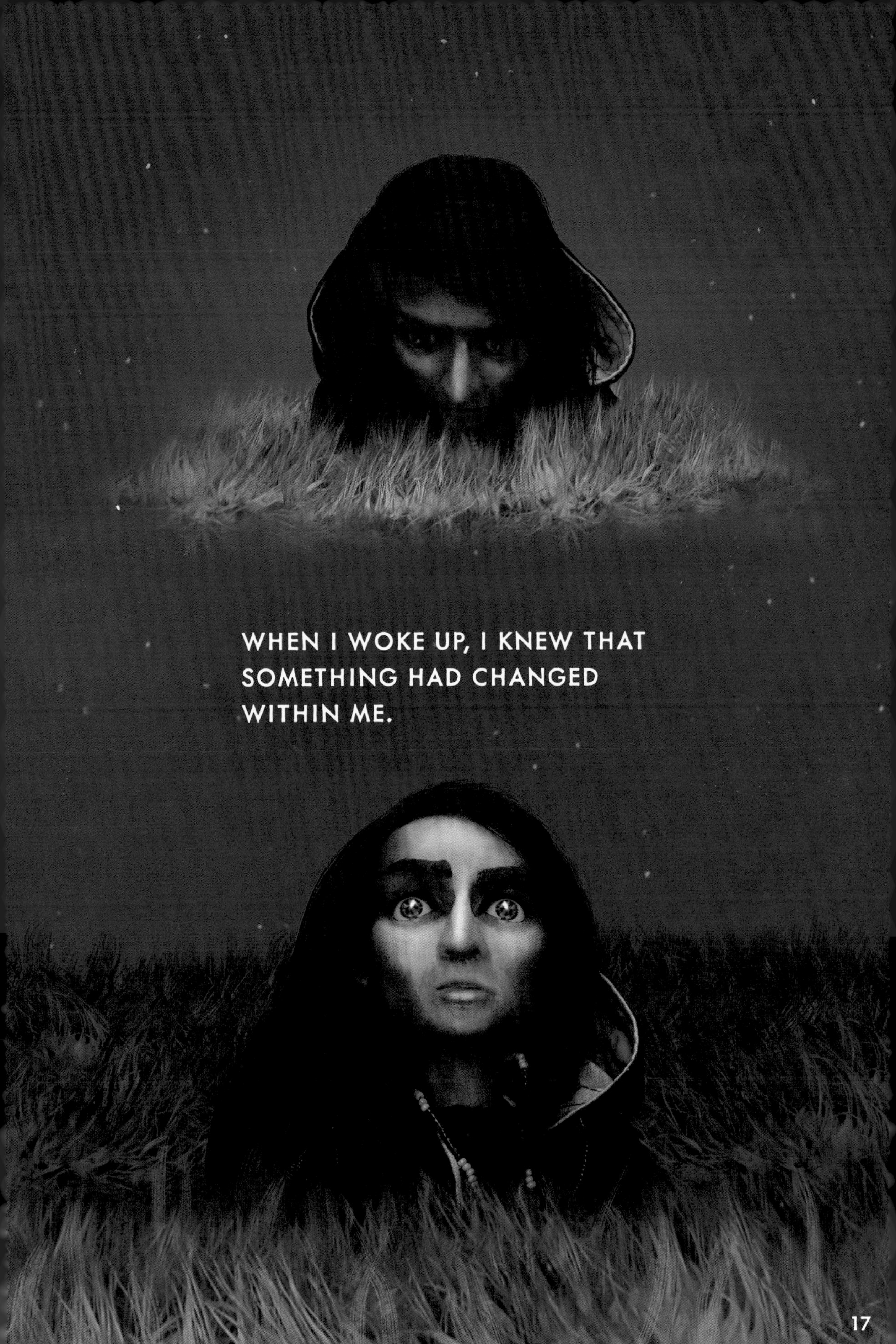
WHEN I WOKE UP, I KNEW THAT SOMETHING HAD CHANGED WITHIN ME.

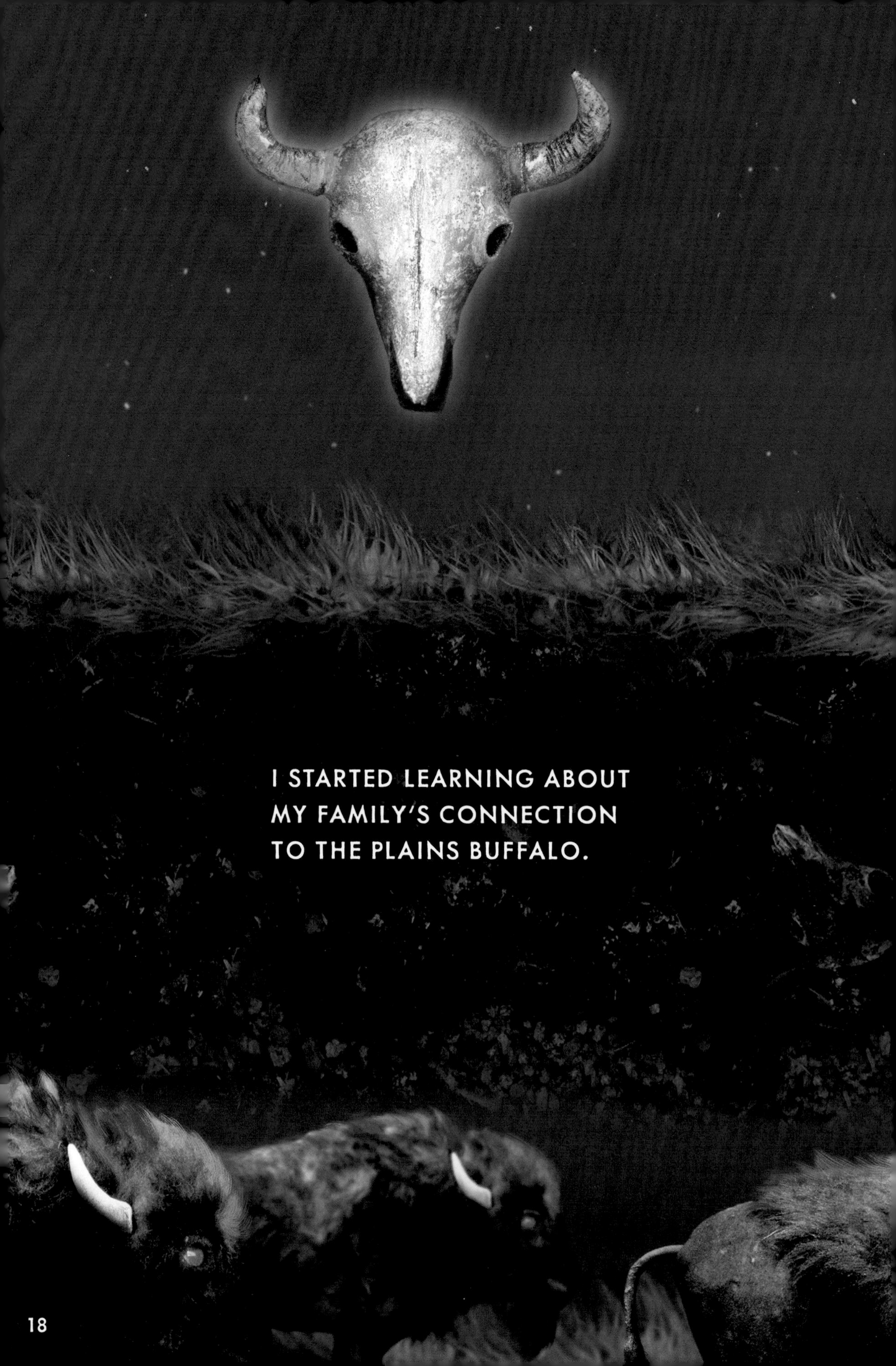
I STARTED LEARNING ABOUT MY FAMILY'S CONNECTION TO THE PLAINS BUFFALO.

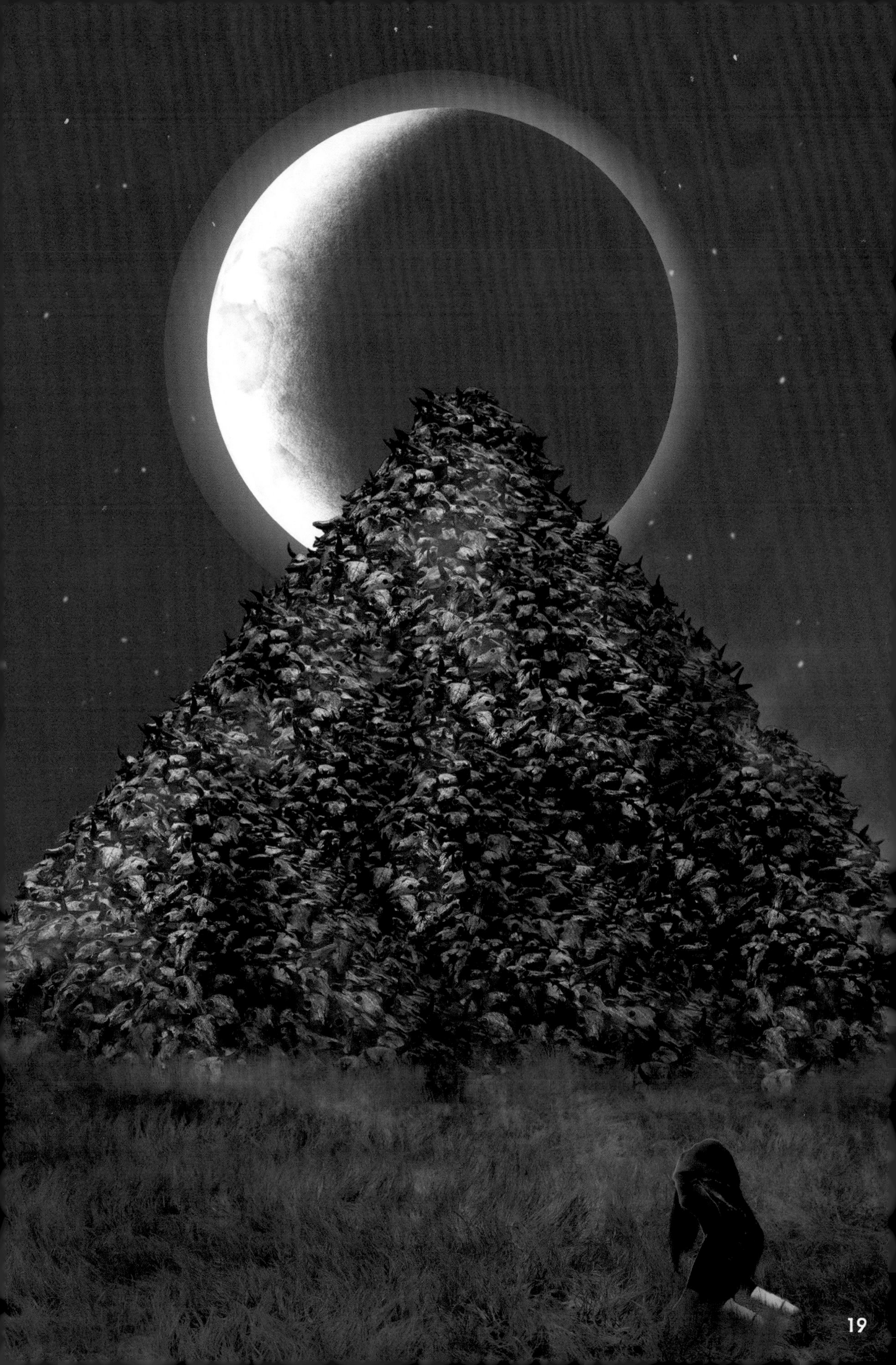

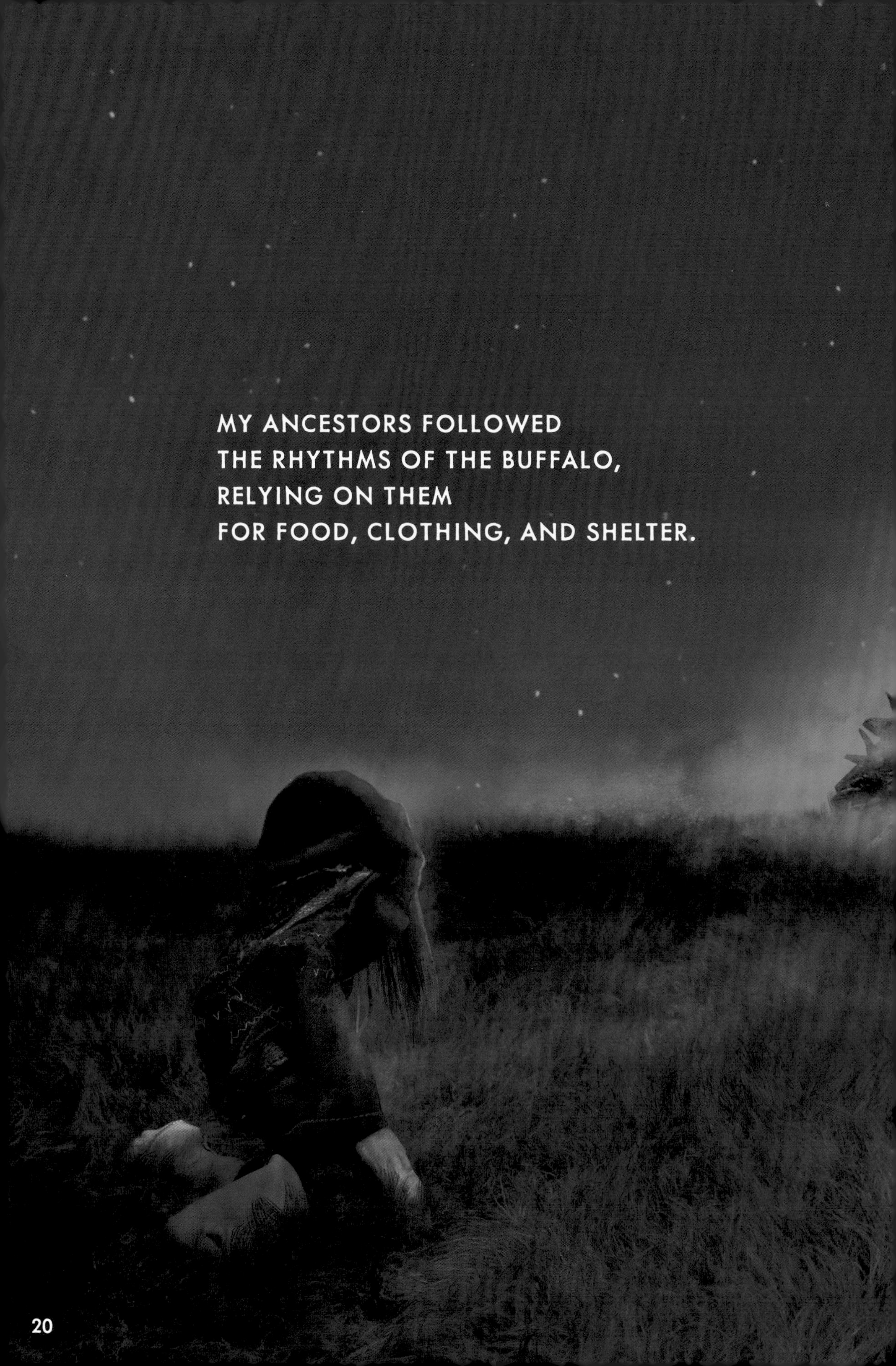

MY ANCESTORS FOLLOWED
THE RHYTHMS OF THE BUFFALO,
RELYING ON THEM
FOR FOOD, CLOTHING, AND SHELTER.

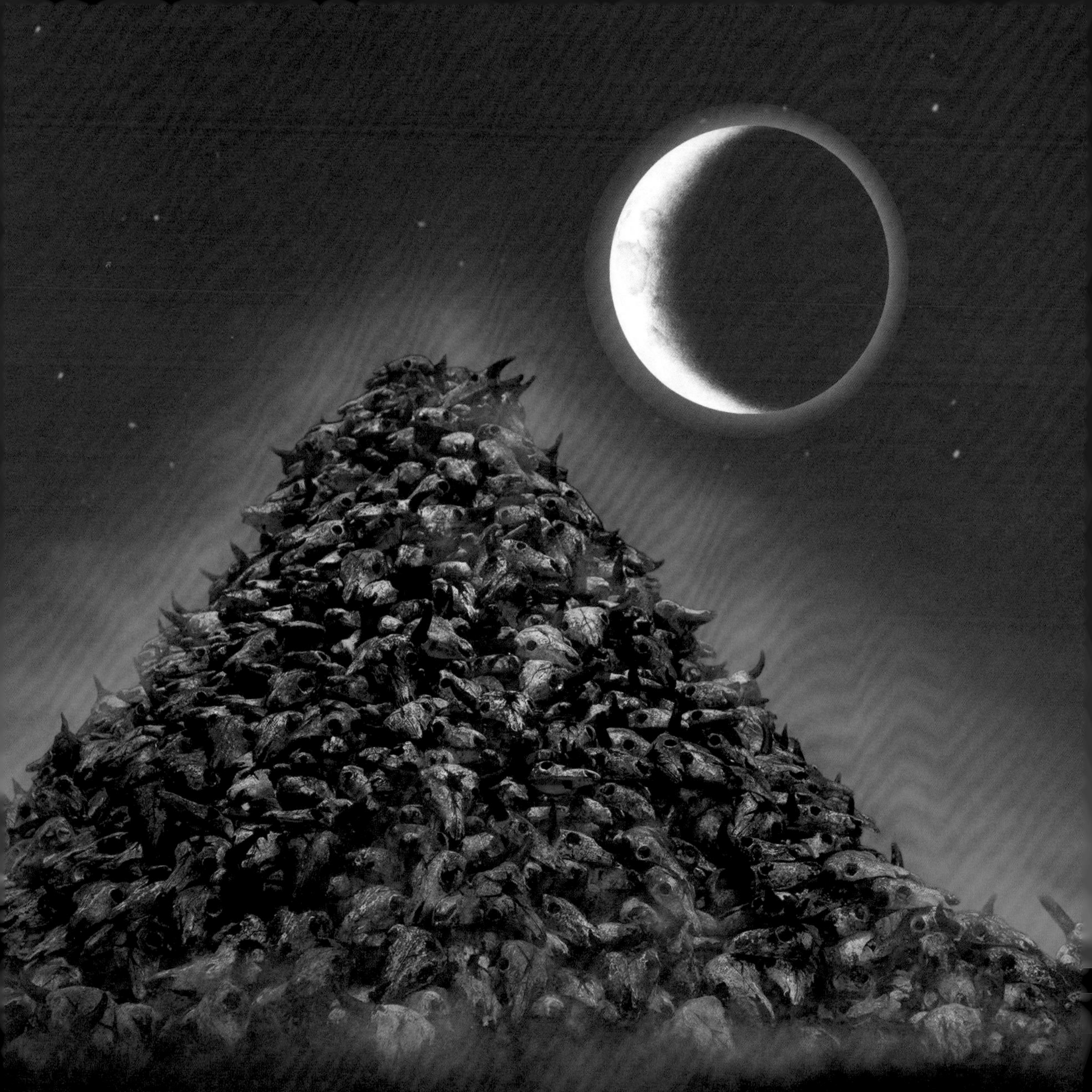

AS SETTLERS ARRIVED ON THE LAND,
THEY SAW THAT OUR CONNECTION
TO THE BUFFALO WAS STRONG.
THEY BELIEVED THAT IF THEY COULD
DECIMATE THE HERD, THEN
THEY WOULD BE ABLE
TO CONTROL US AS A PEOPLE.

THEY MADE MOUNTAINS WITH THEIR SKULLS.

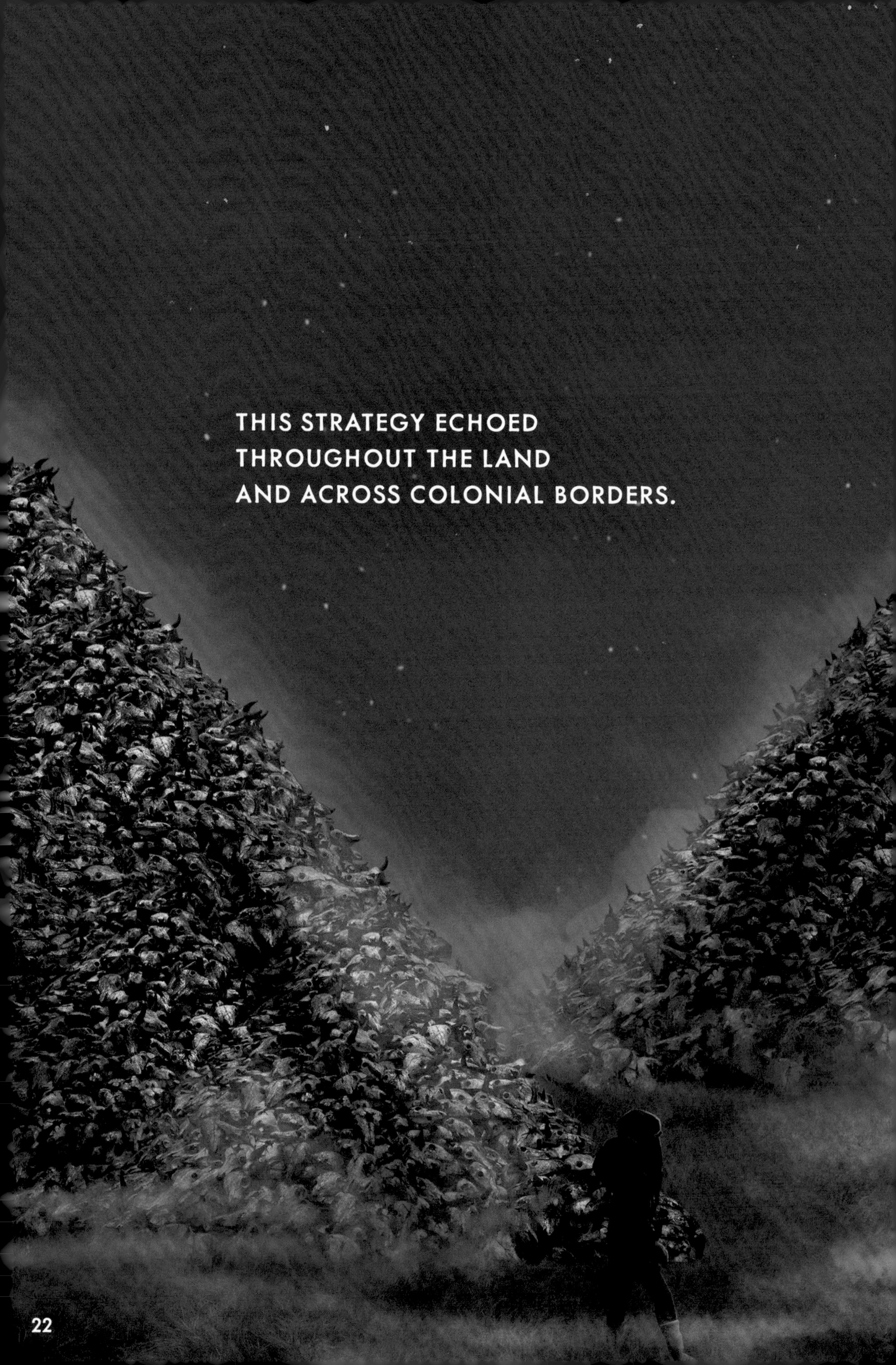
THIS STRATEGY ECHOED
THROUGHOUT THE LAND
AND ACROSS COLONIAL BORDERS.

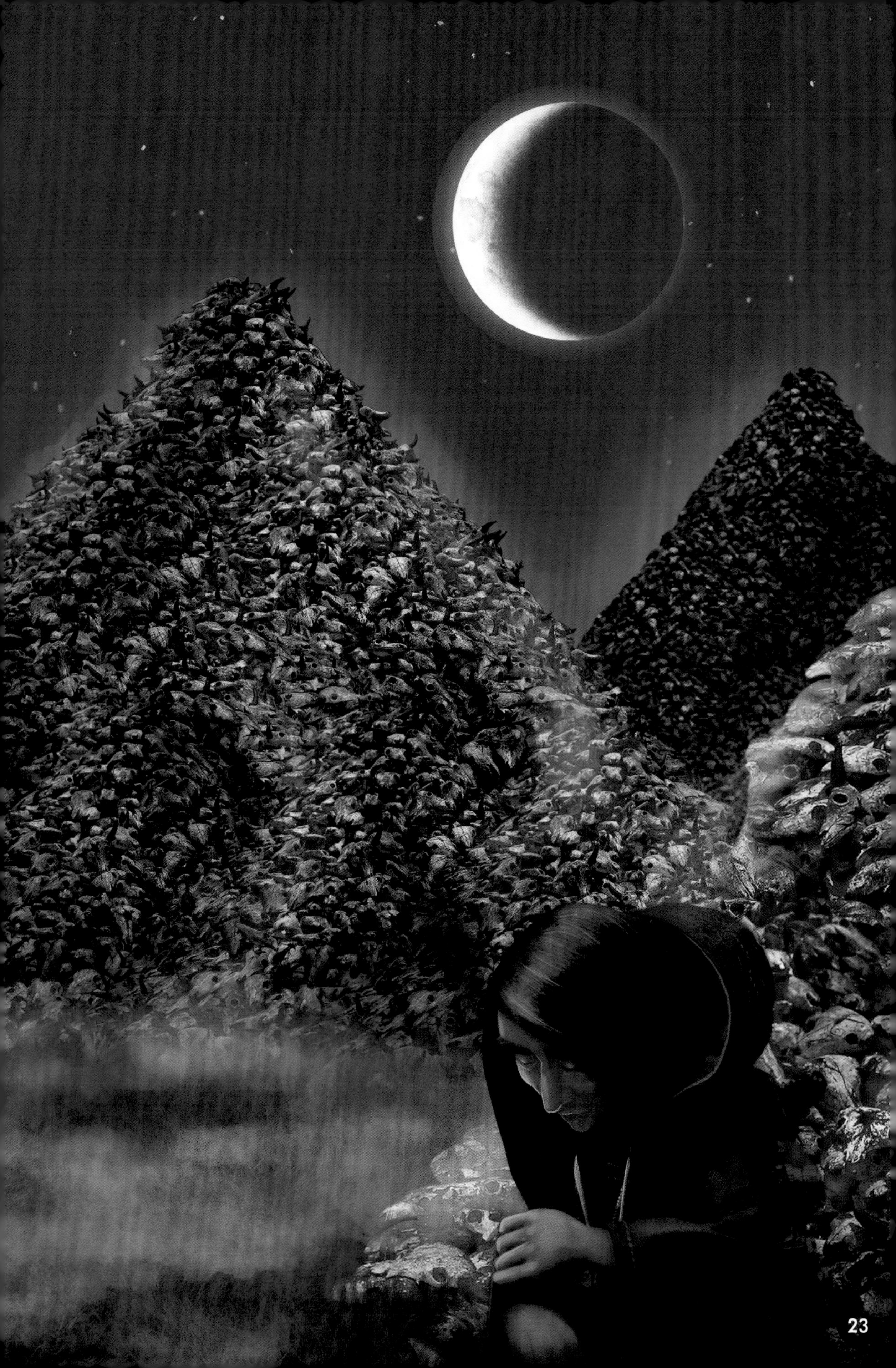

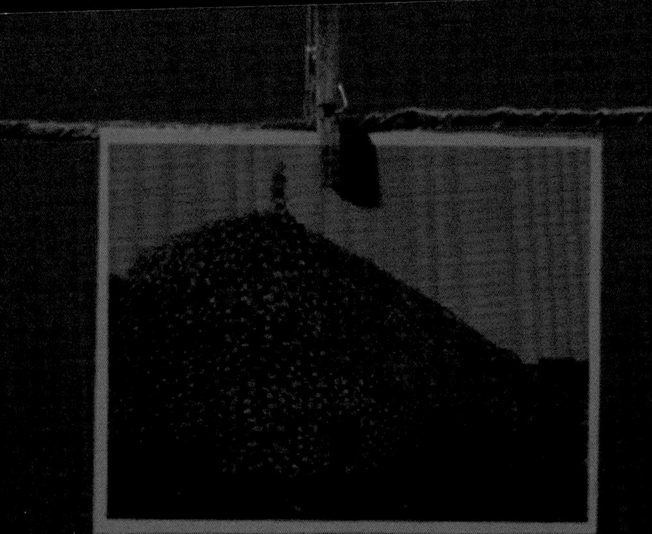

THE BONES PILED

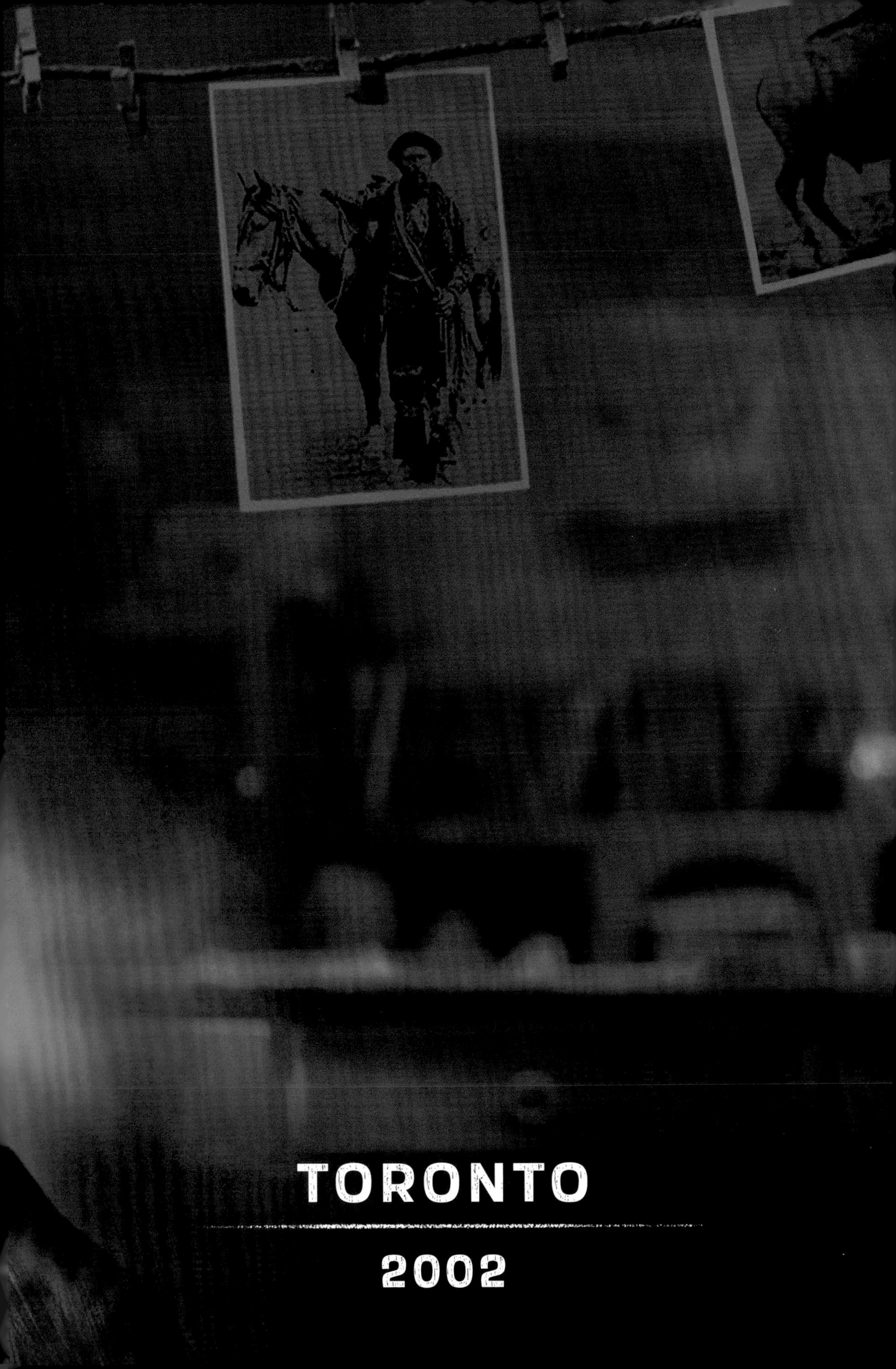

TORONTO

2002

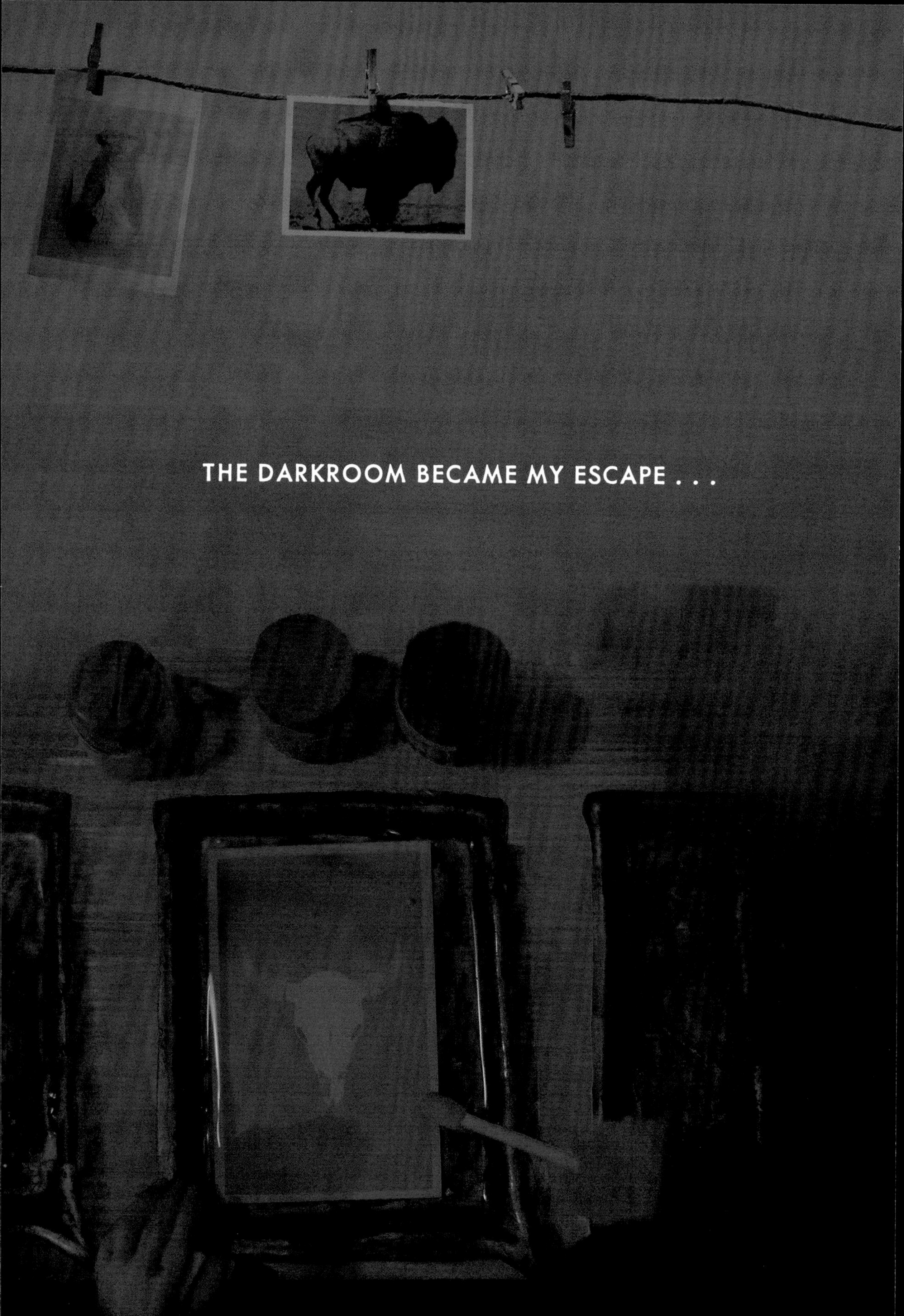

THE DARKROOM BECAME MY ESCAPE . . .

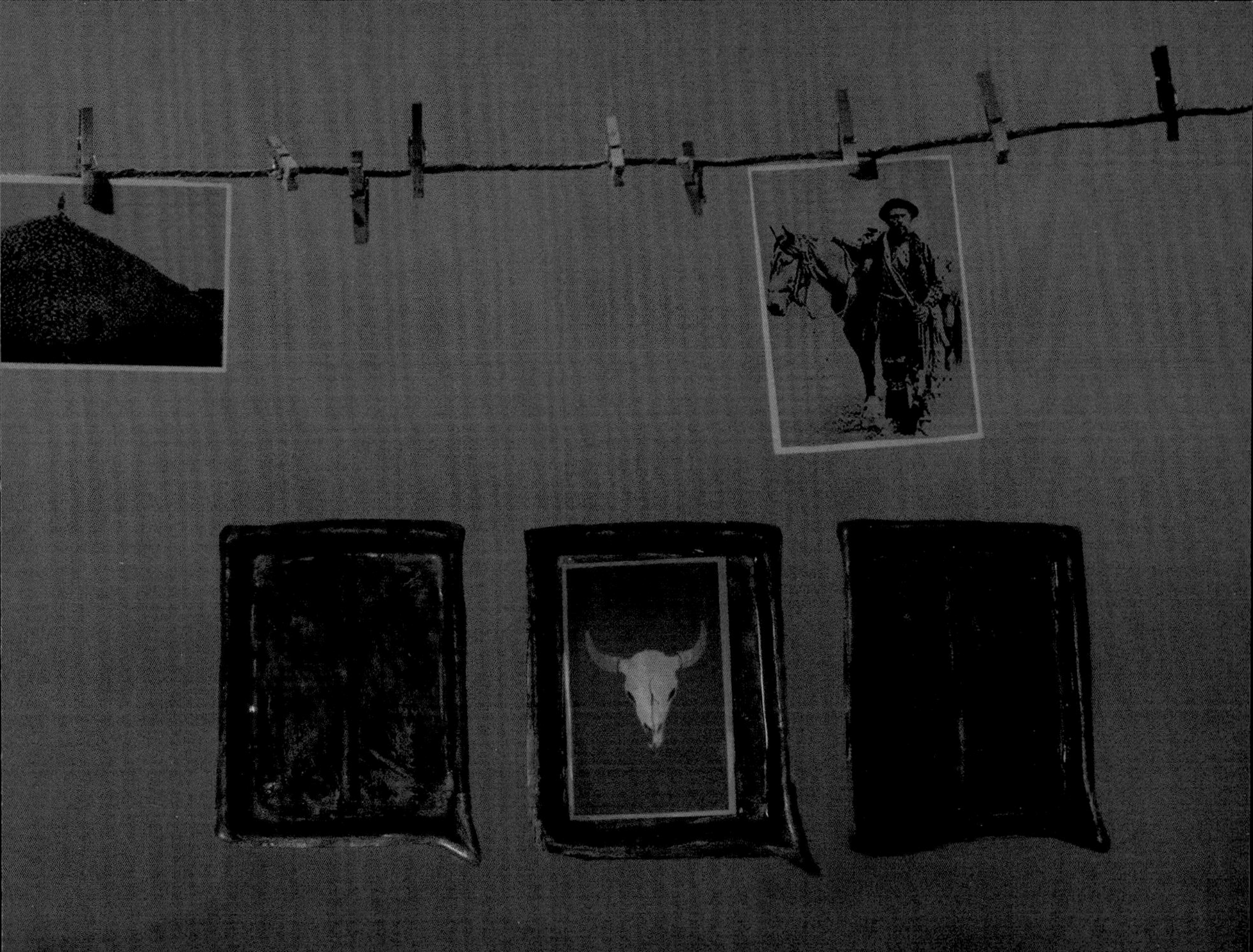

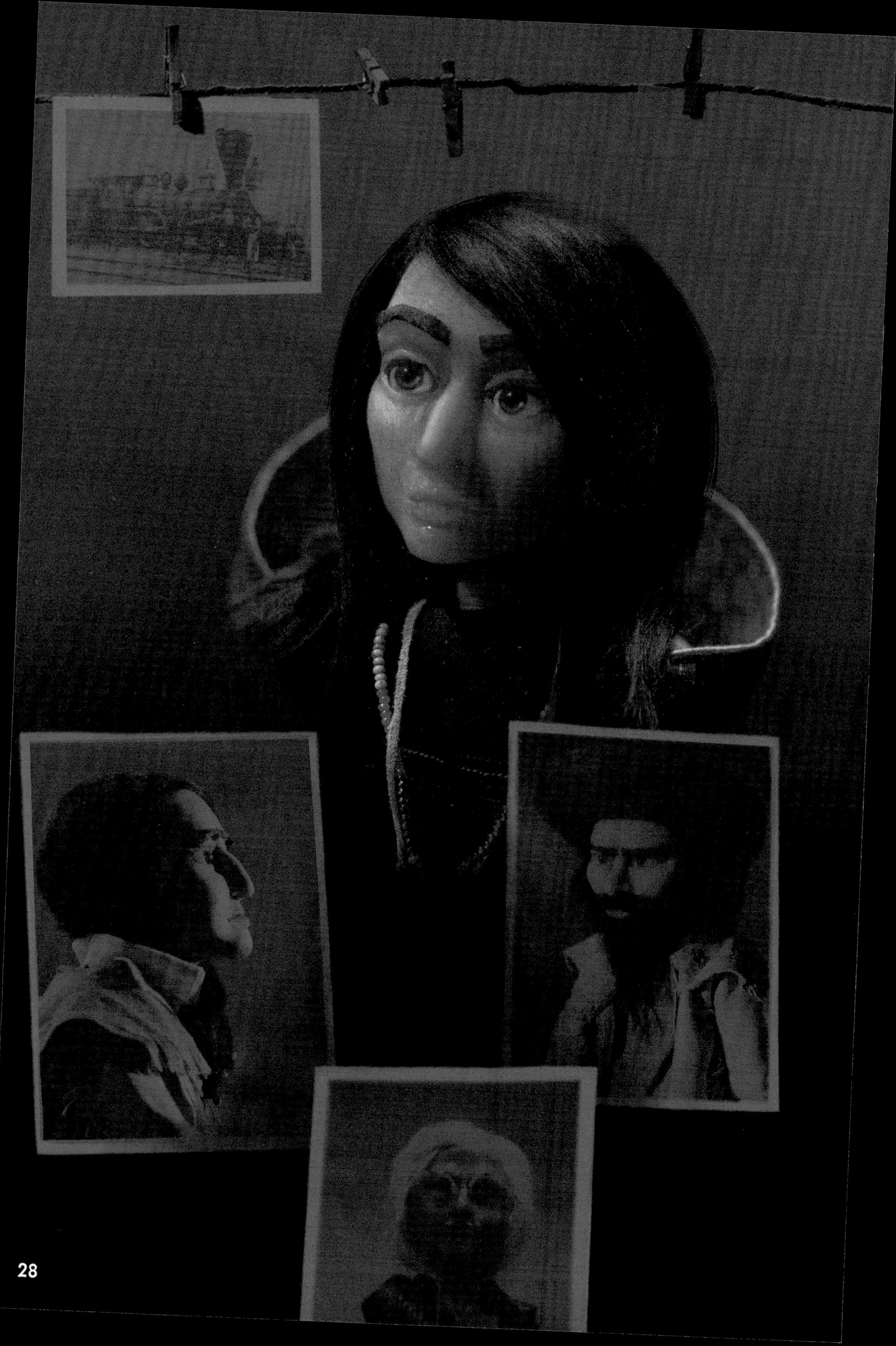

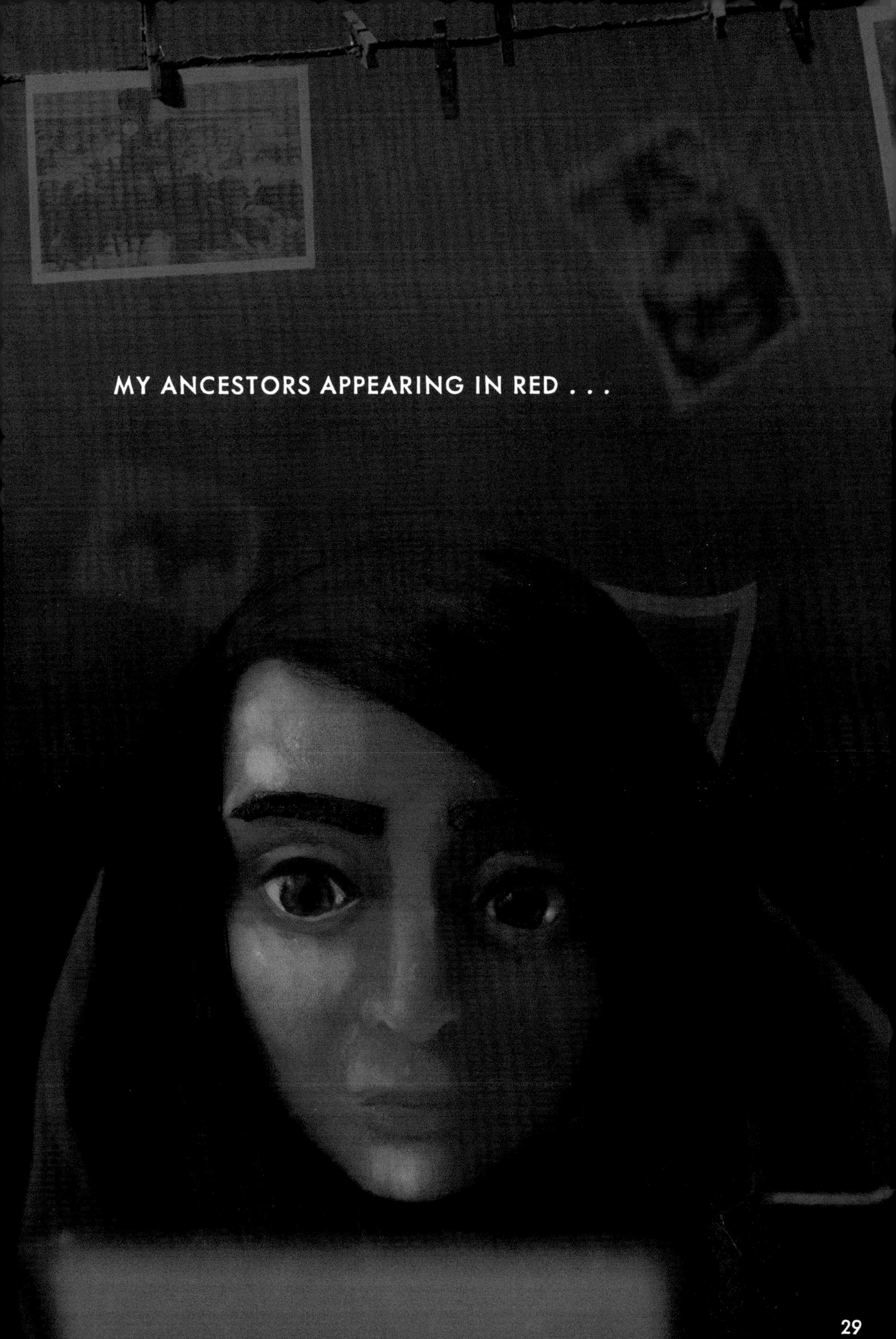
MY ANCESTORS APPEARING IN RED . . .

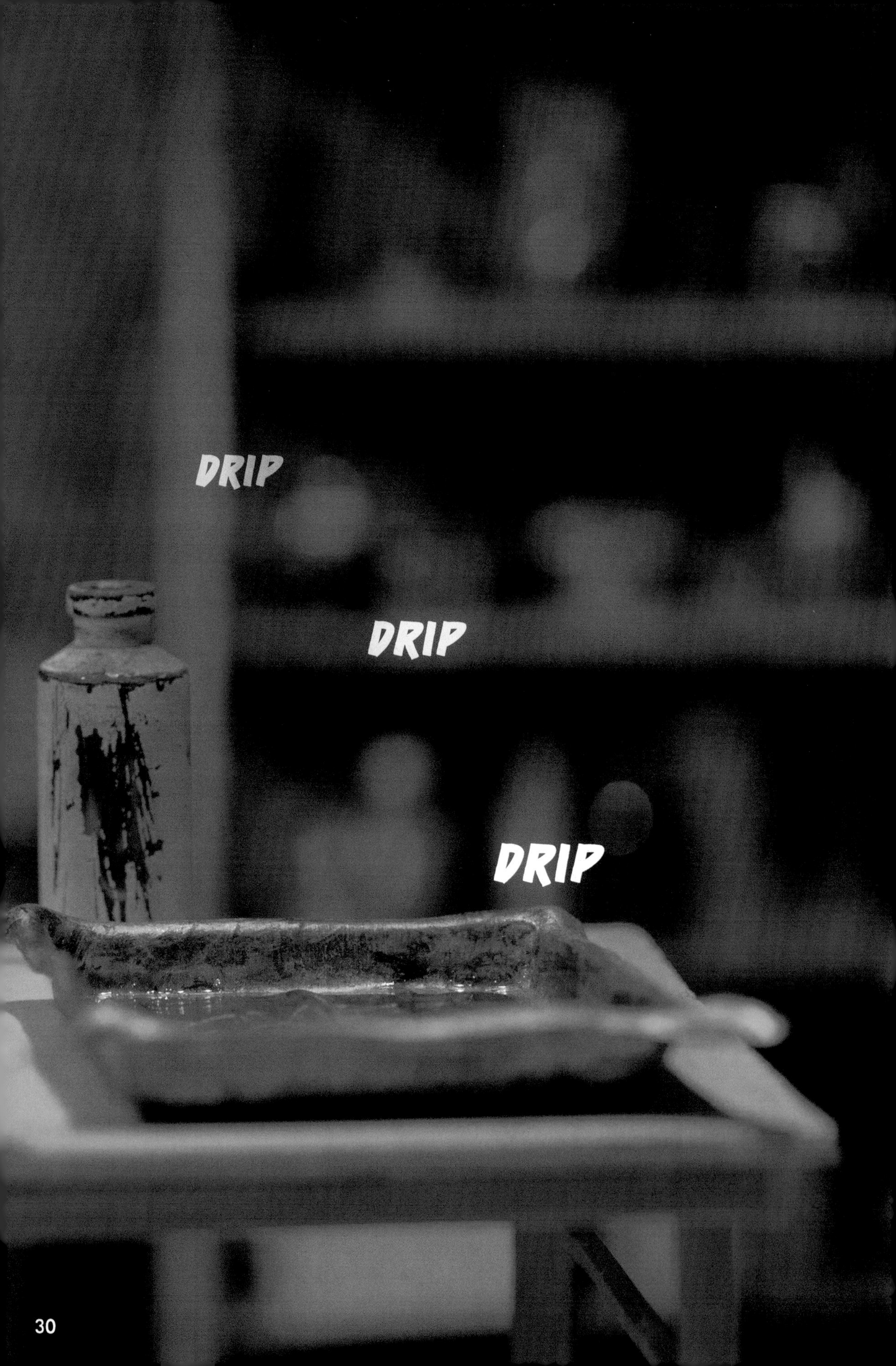
DRIP
DRIP
DRIP

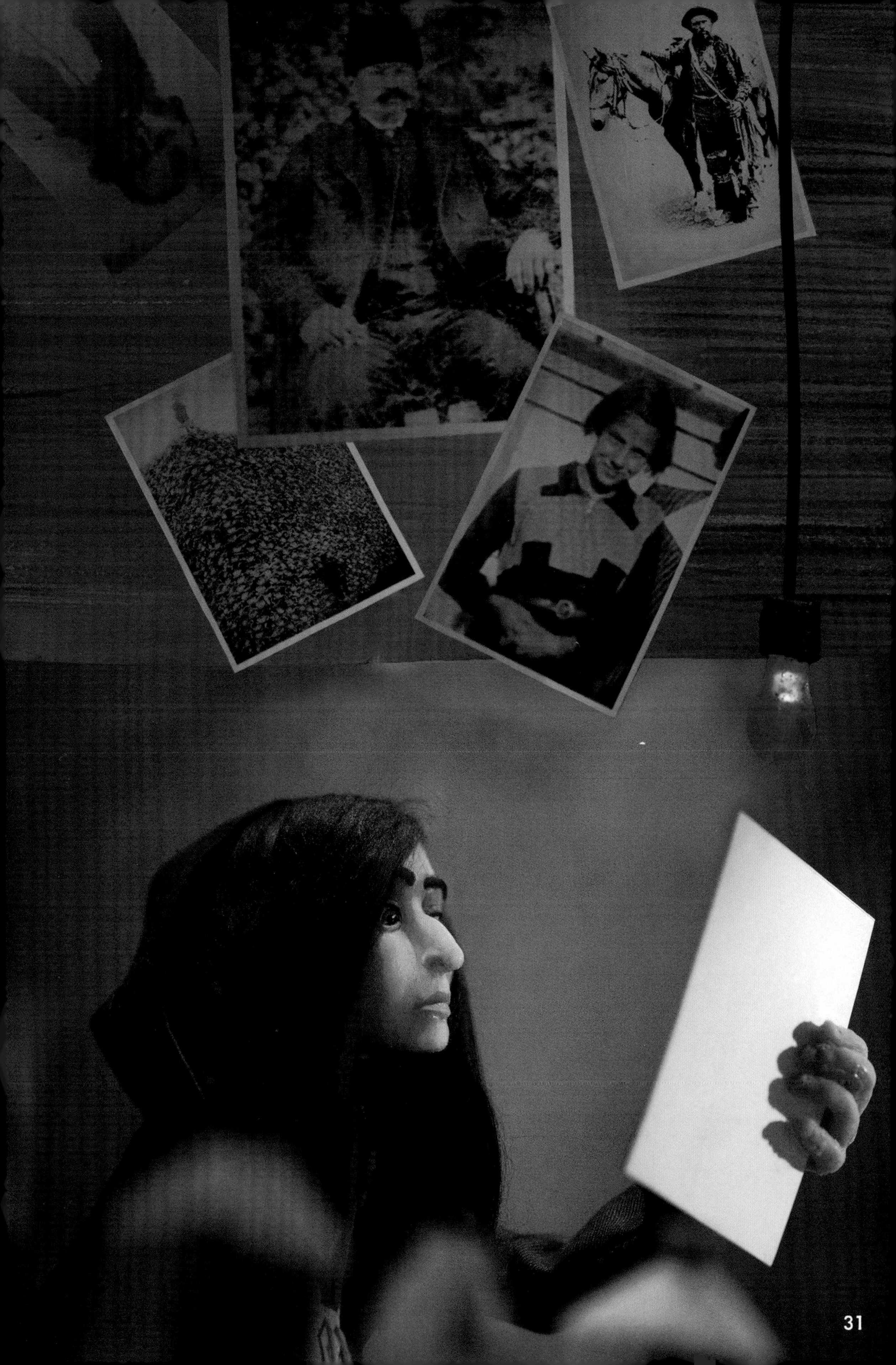

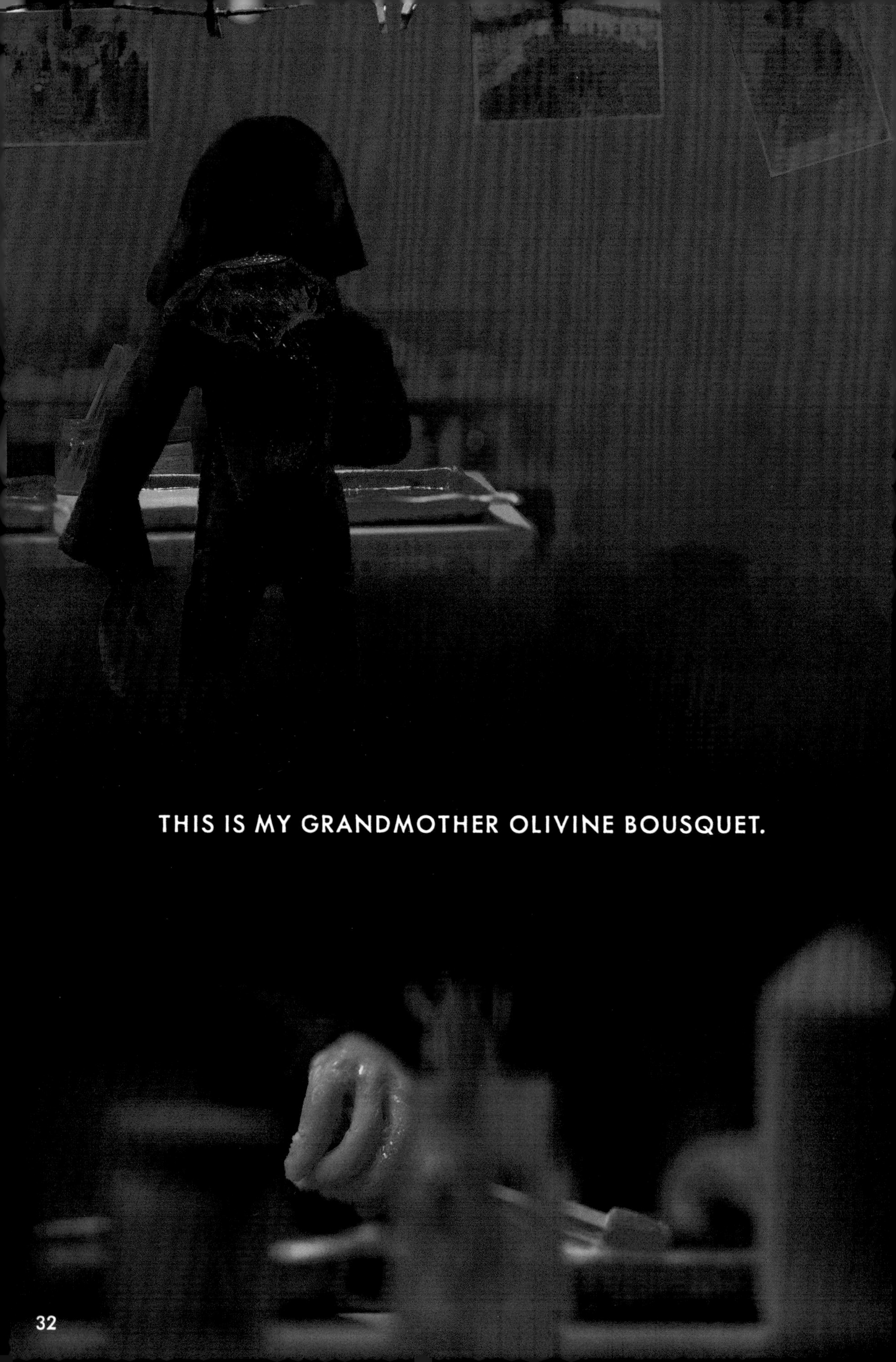
THIS IS MY GRANDMOTHER OLIVINE BOUSQUET.

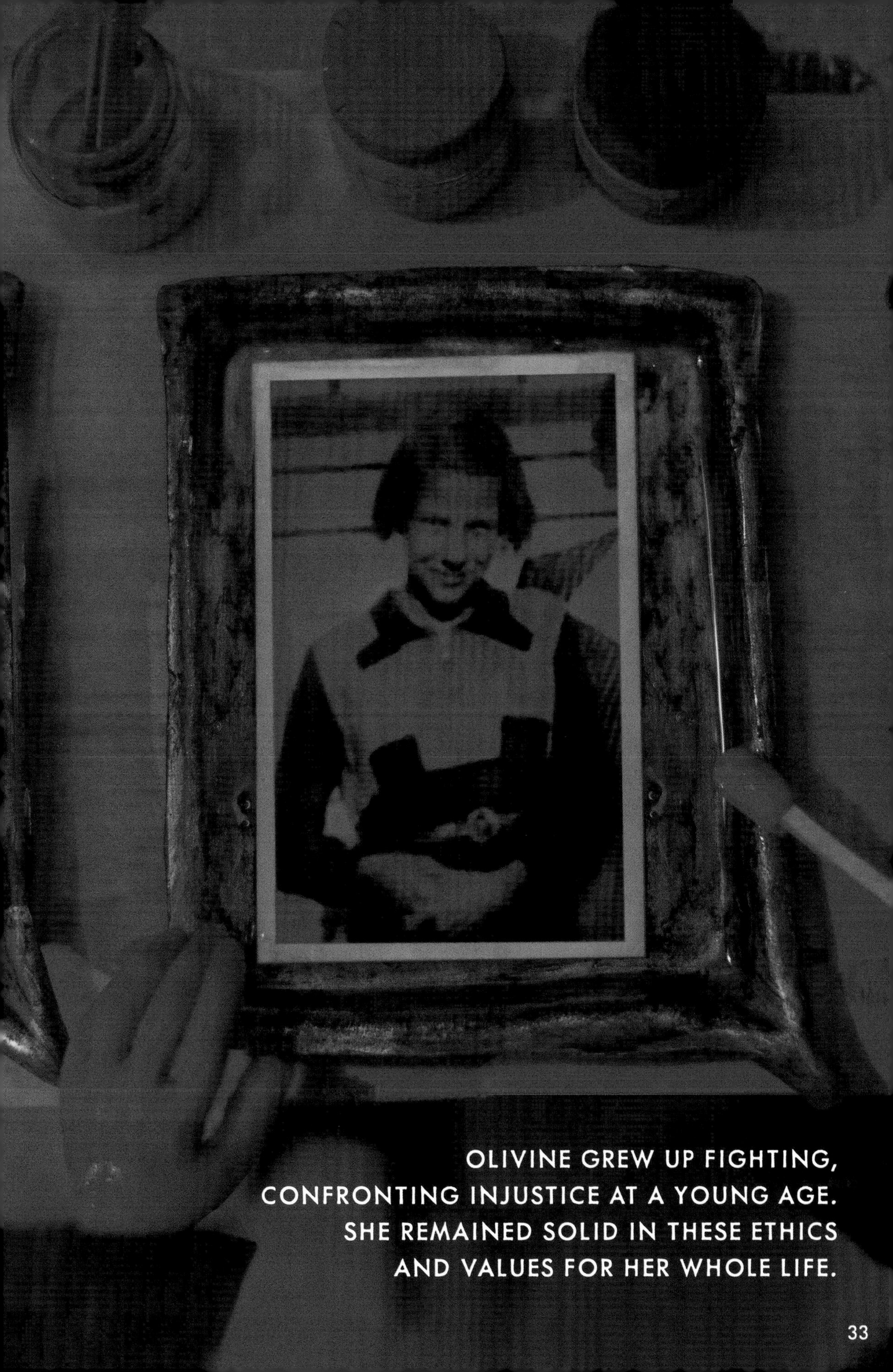

OLIVINE GREW UP FIGHTING, CONFRONTING INJUSTICE AT A YOUNG AGE. SHE REMAINED SOLID IN THESE ETHICS AND VALUES FOR HER WHOLE LIFE.

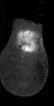

I AM ON A WALK
WITH MY ANCESTORS . . .

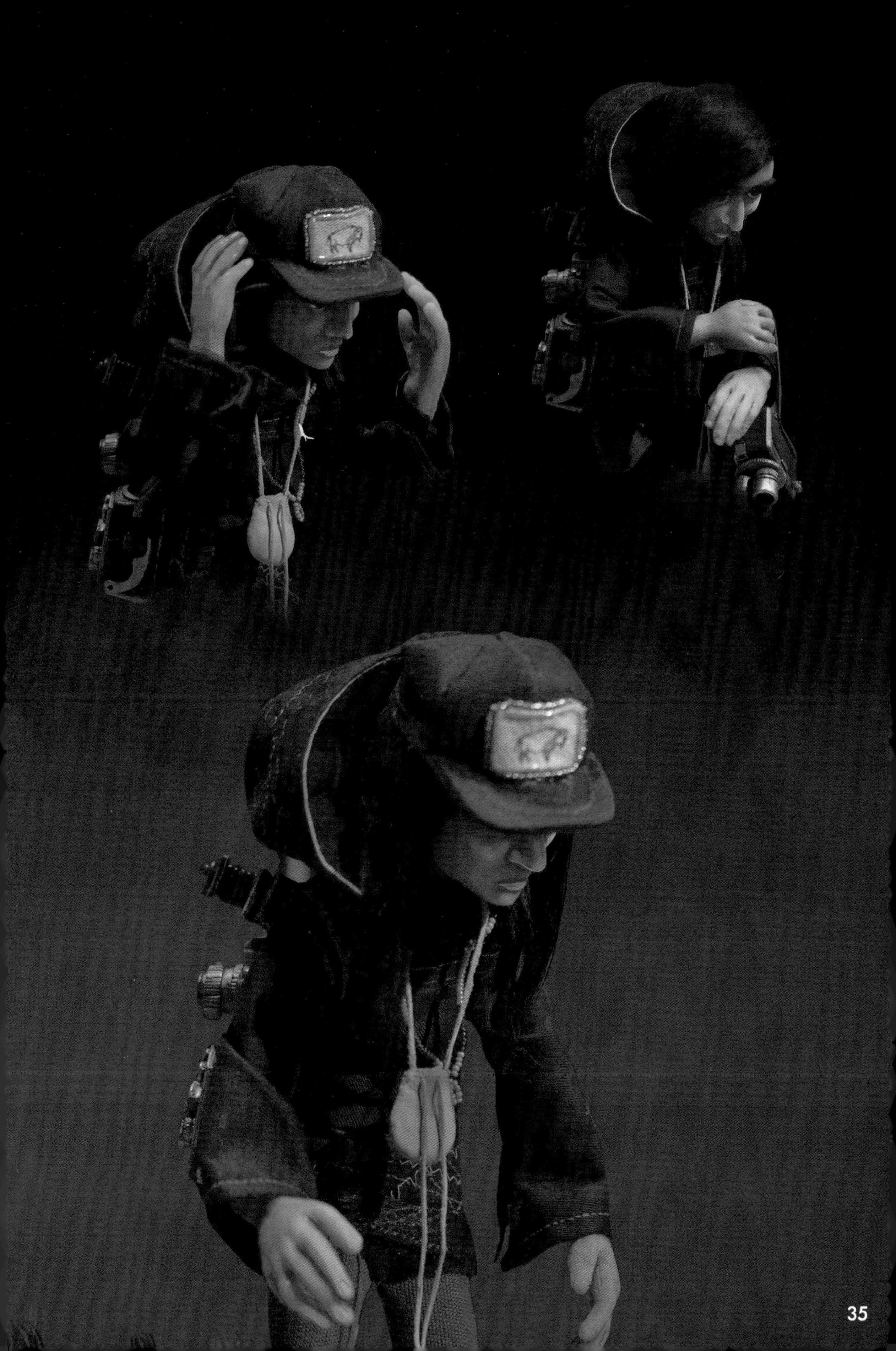

ST. BONIFACE

1938

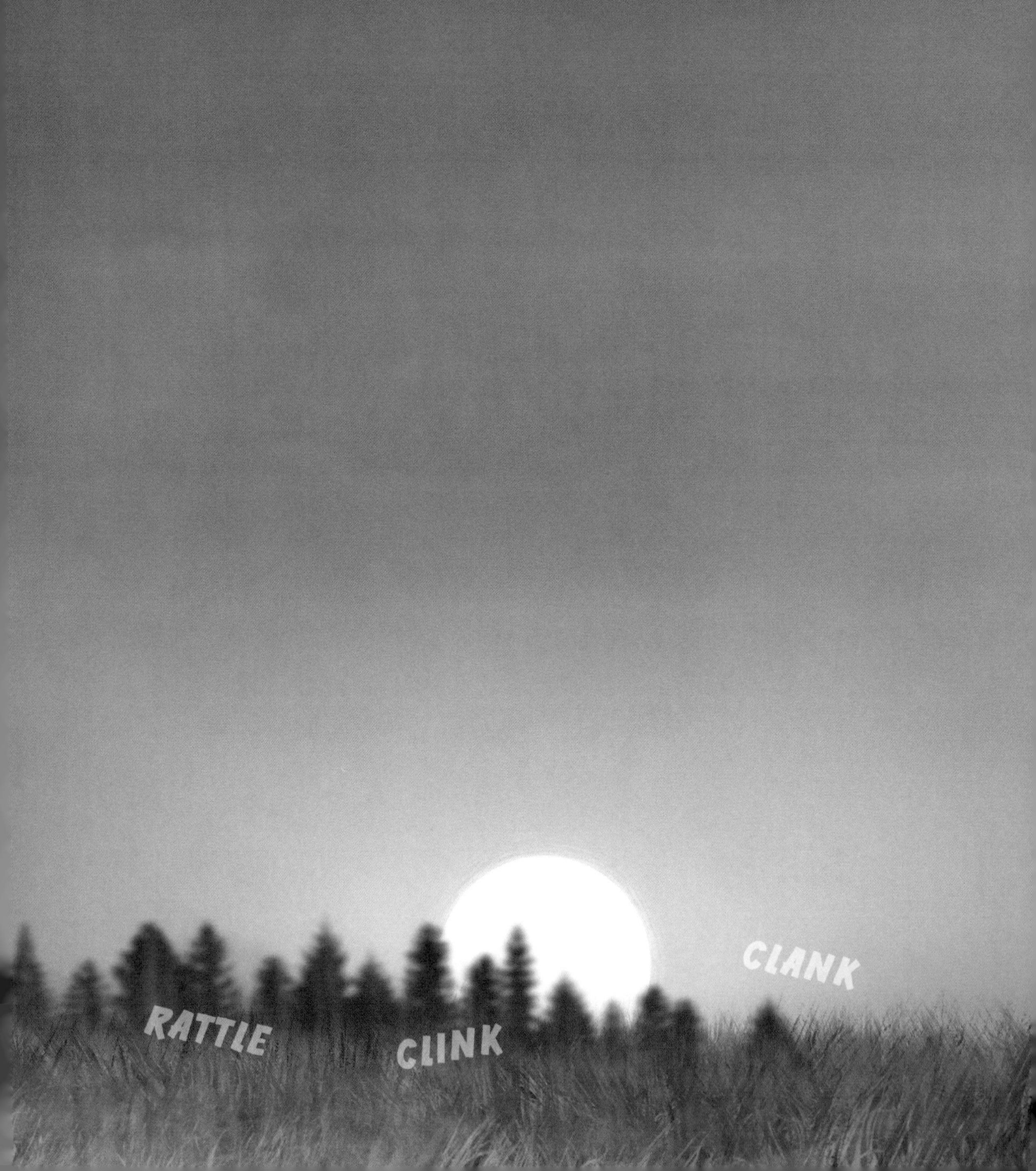
RATTLE
CLINK
CLANK

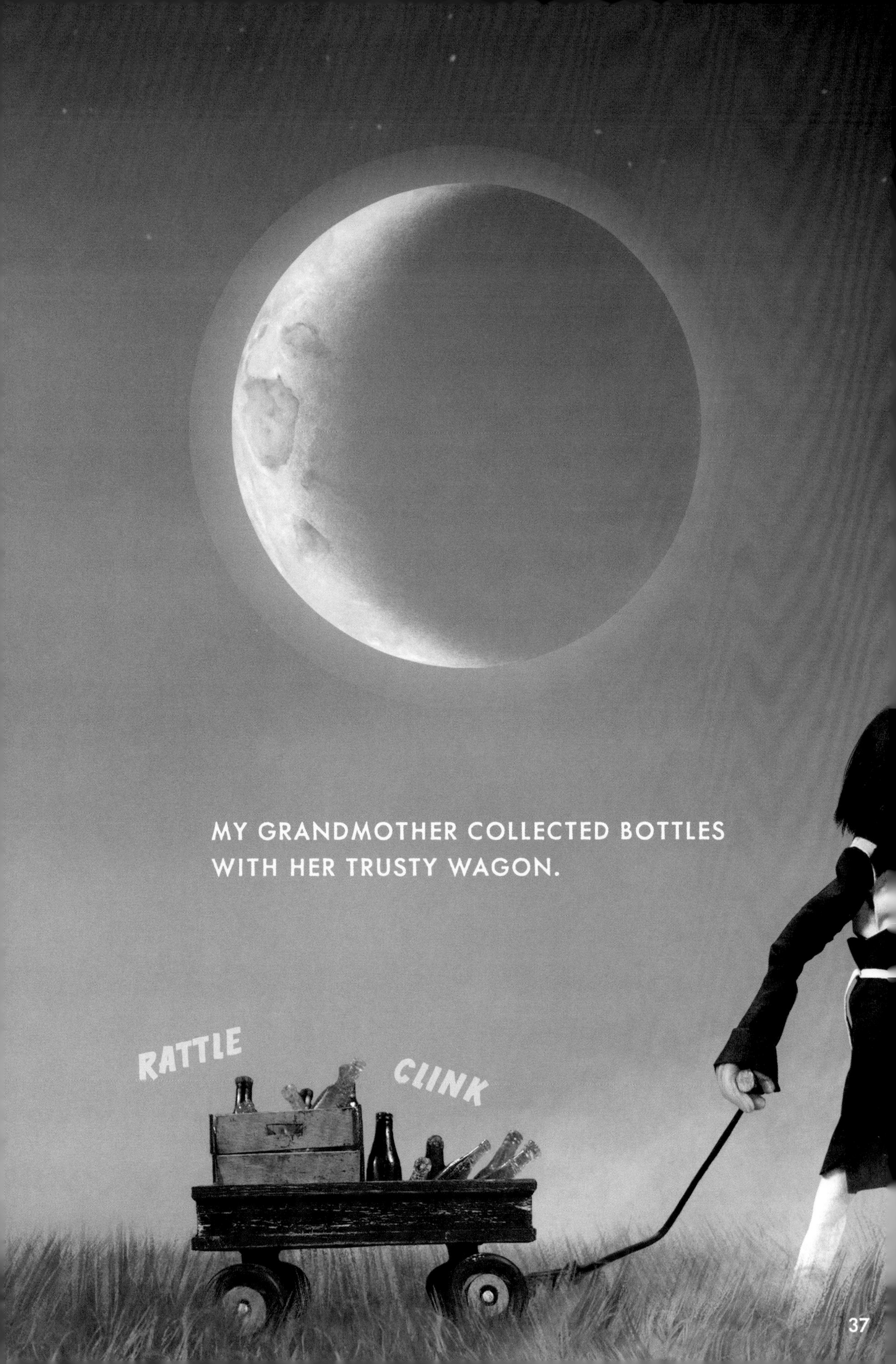
RATTLE
CLINK

MY GRANDMOTHER COLLECTED BOTTLES
WITH HER TRUSTY WAGON.

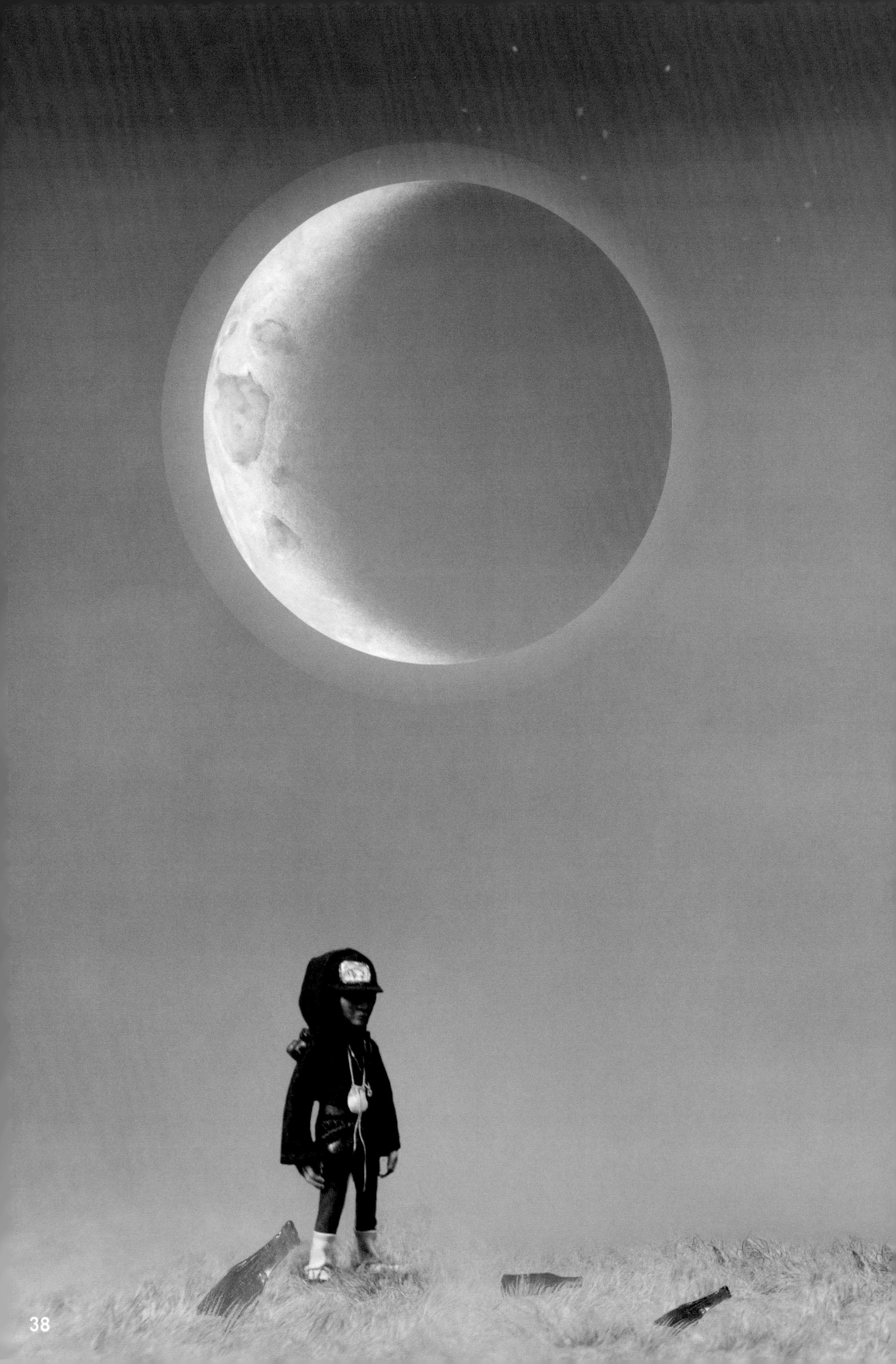

SHE SKIPPED SUNDAY SCHOOL
TO GATHER THE GLASS OFFERINGS
AND USED THE MONEY SHE MADE
TO HELP HER FAMILY.

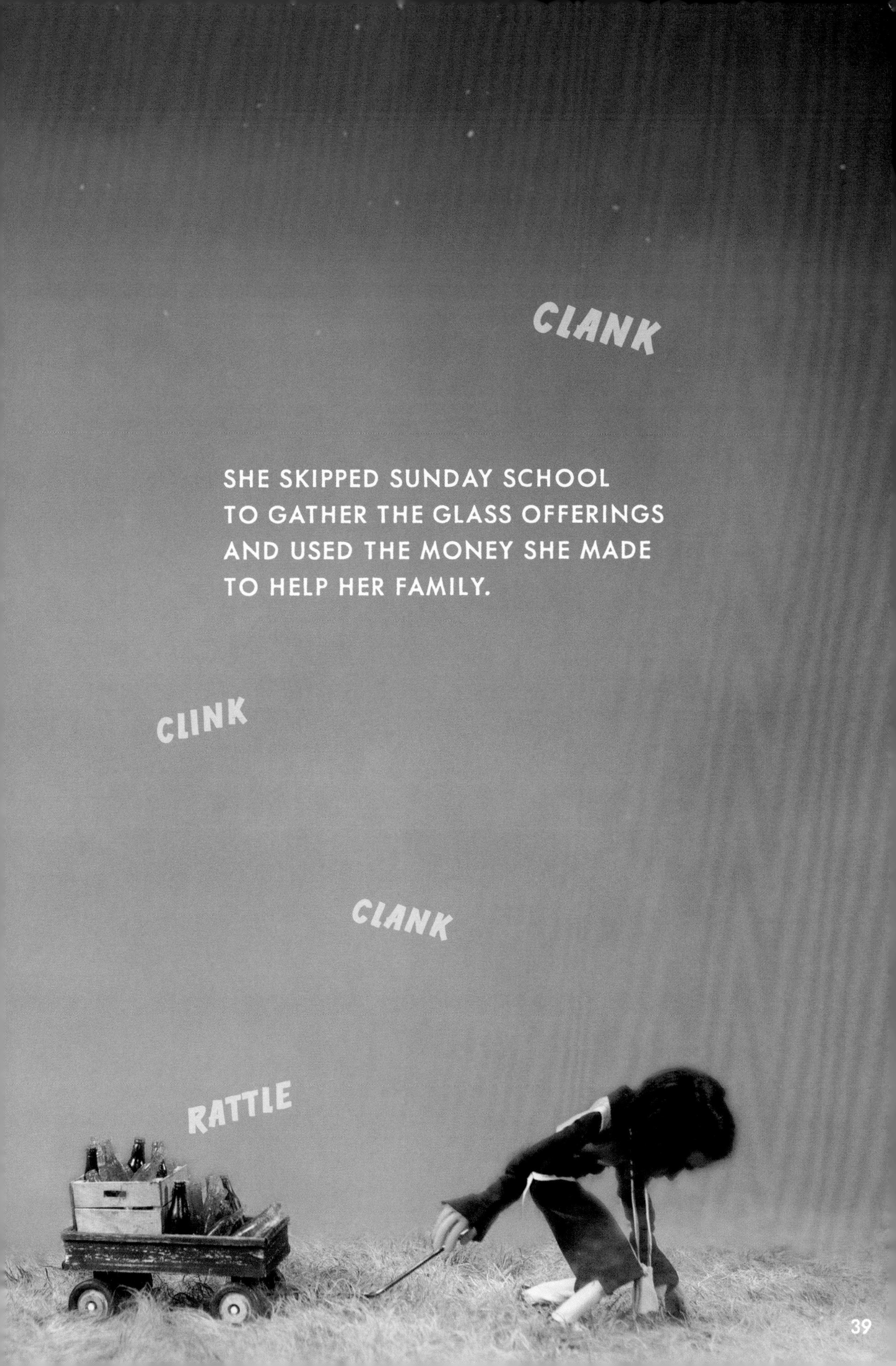
CLANK
CLINK
CLANK
RATTLE

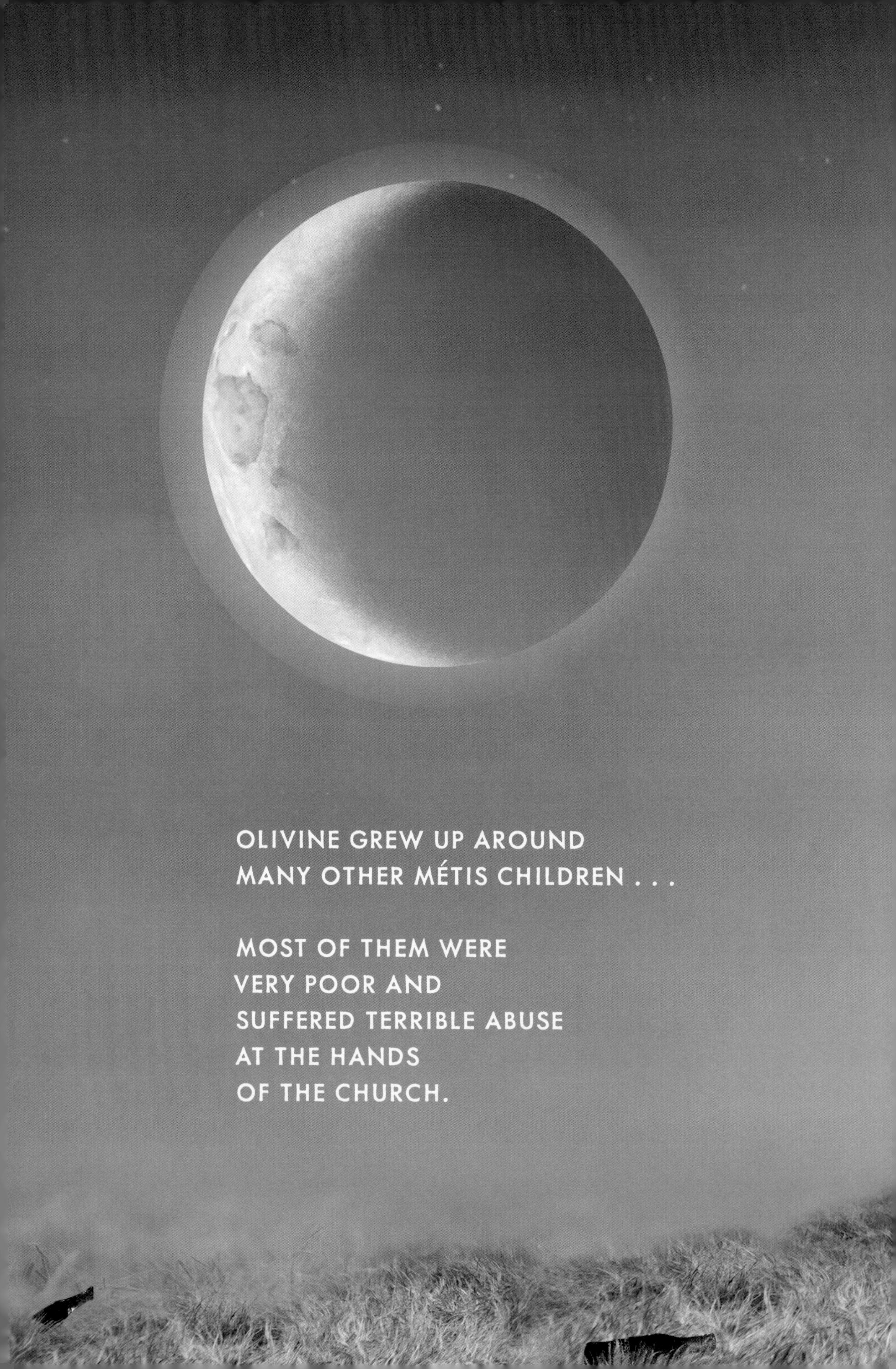

OLIVINE GREW UP AROUND
MANY OTHER MÉTIS CHILDREN . . .

MOST OF THEM WERE
VERY POOR AND
SUFFERED TERRIBLE ABUSE
AT THE HANDS
OF THE CHURCH.

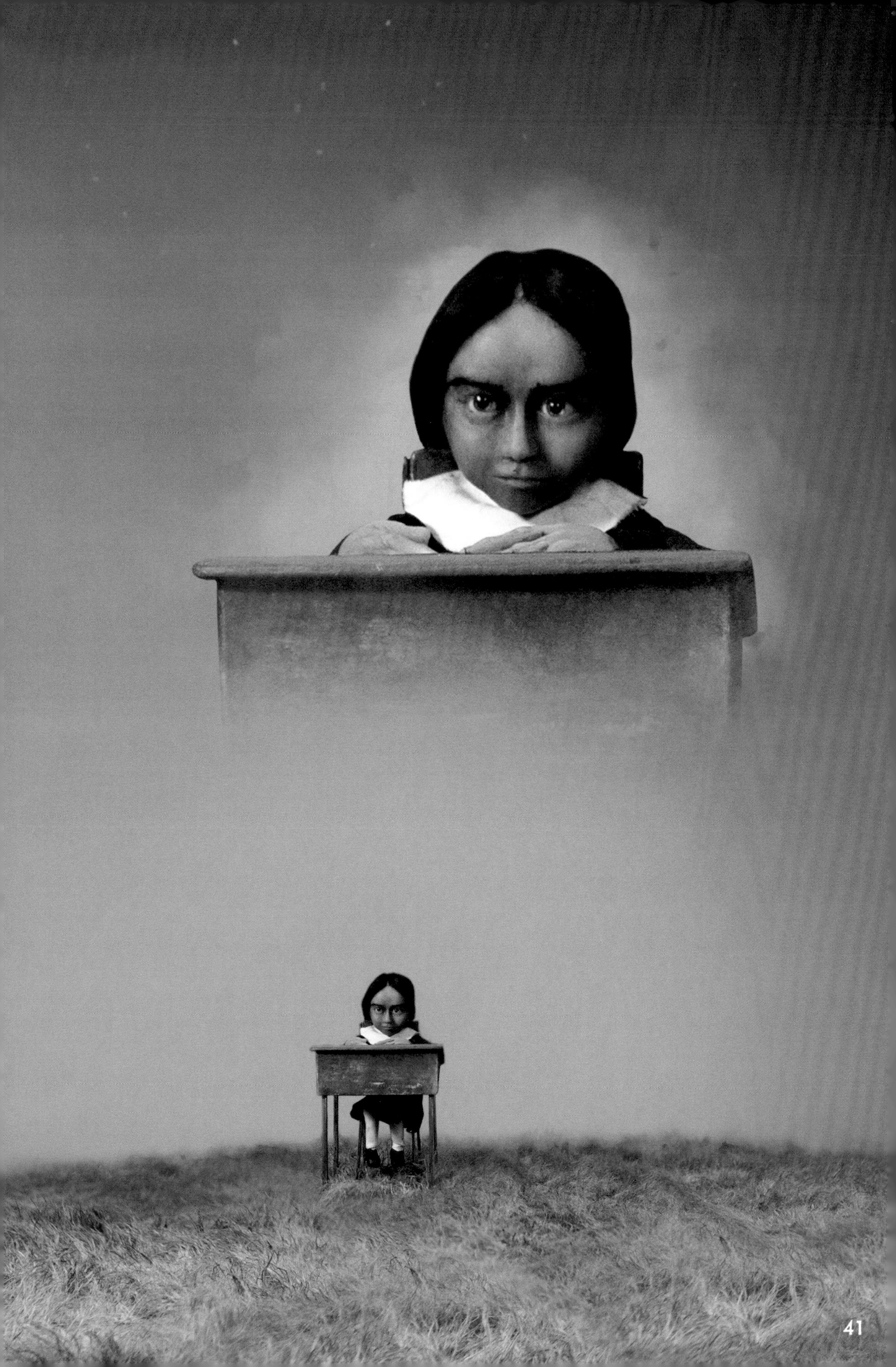

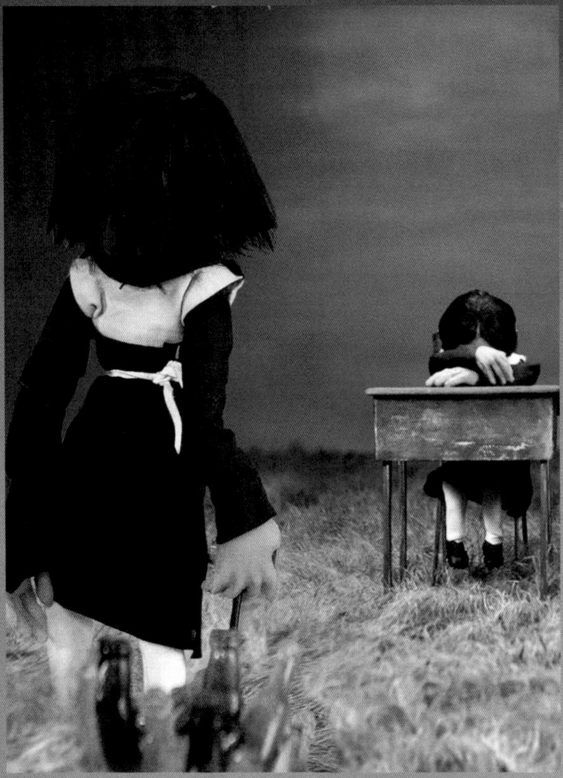
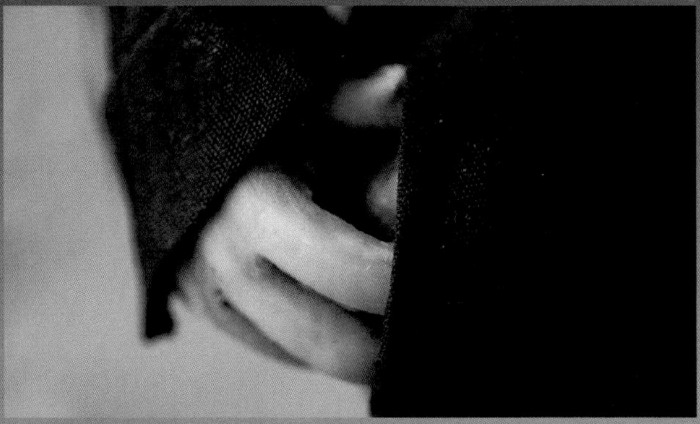
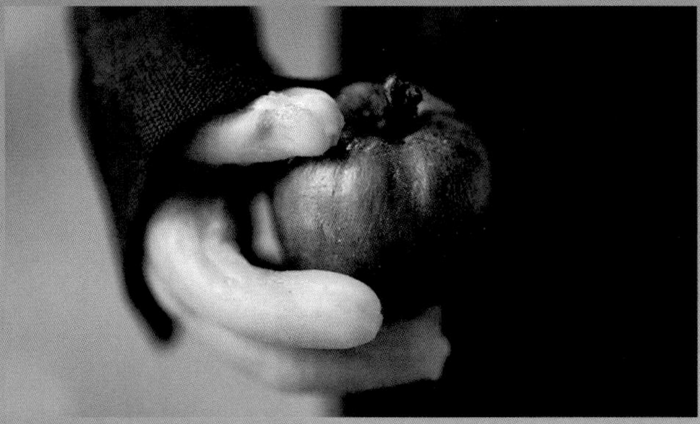
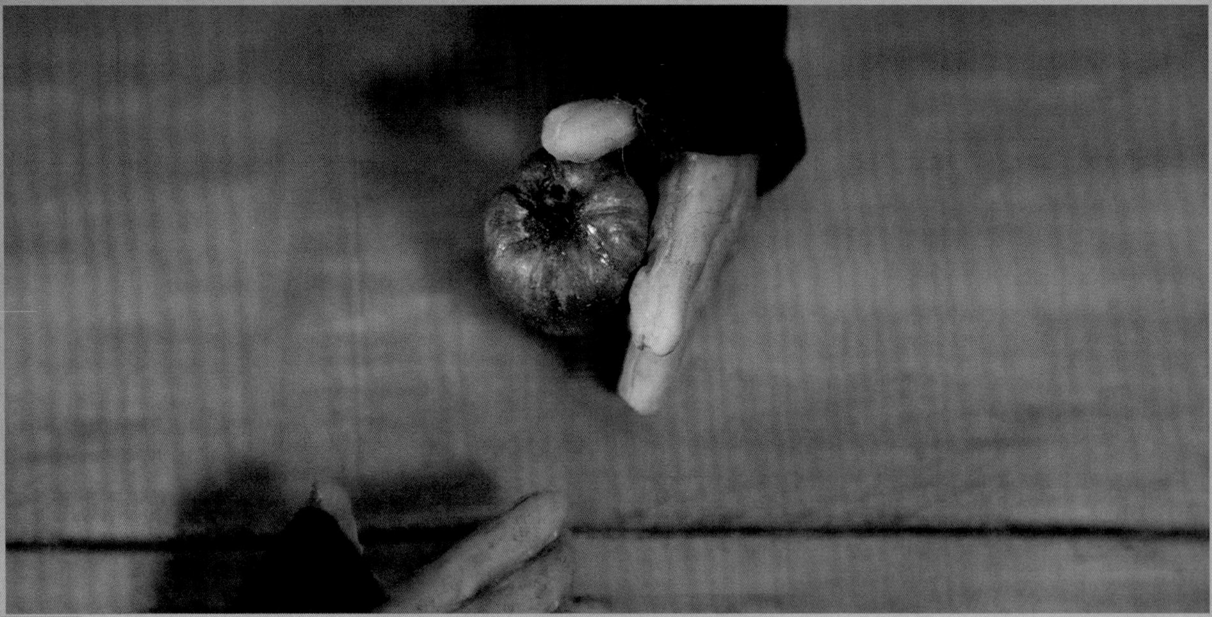
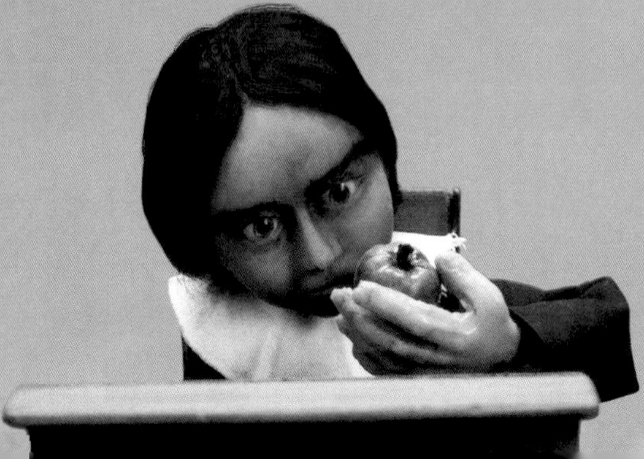

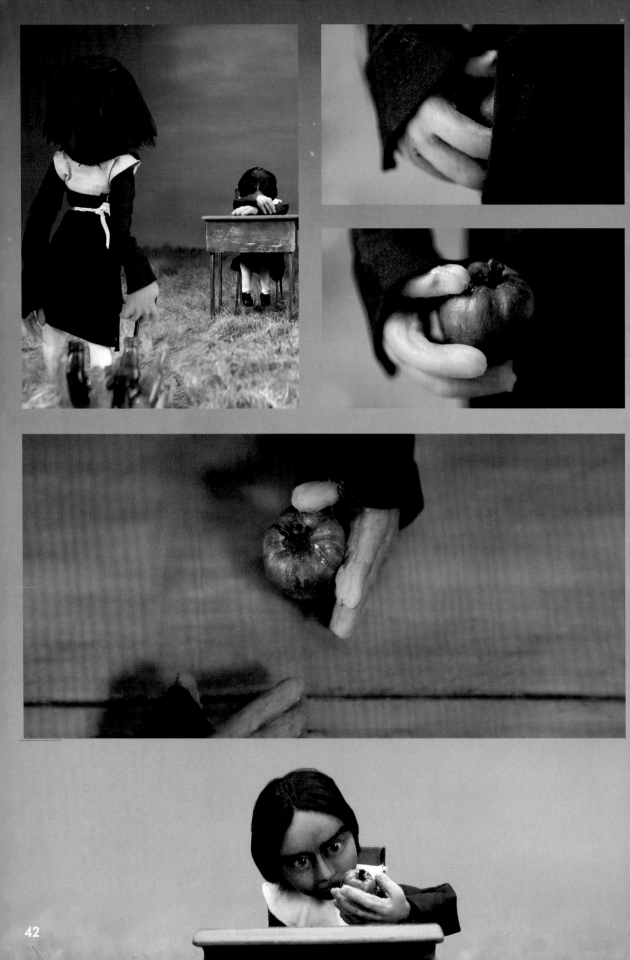

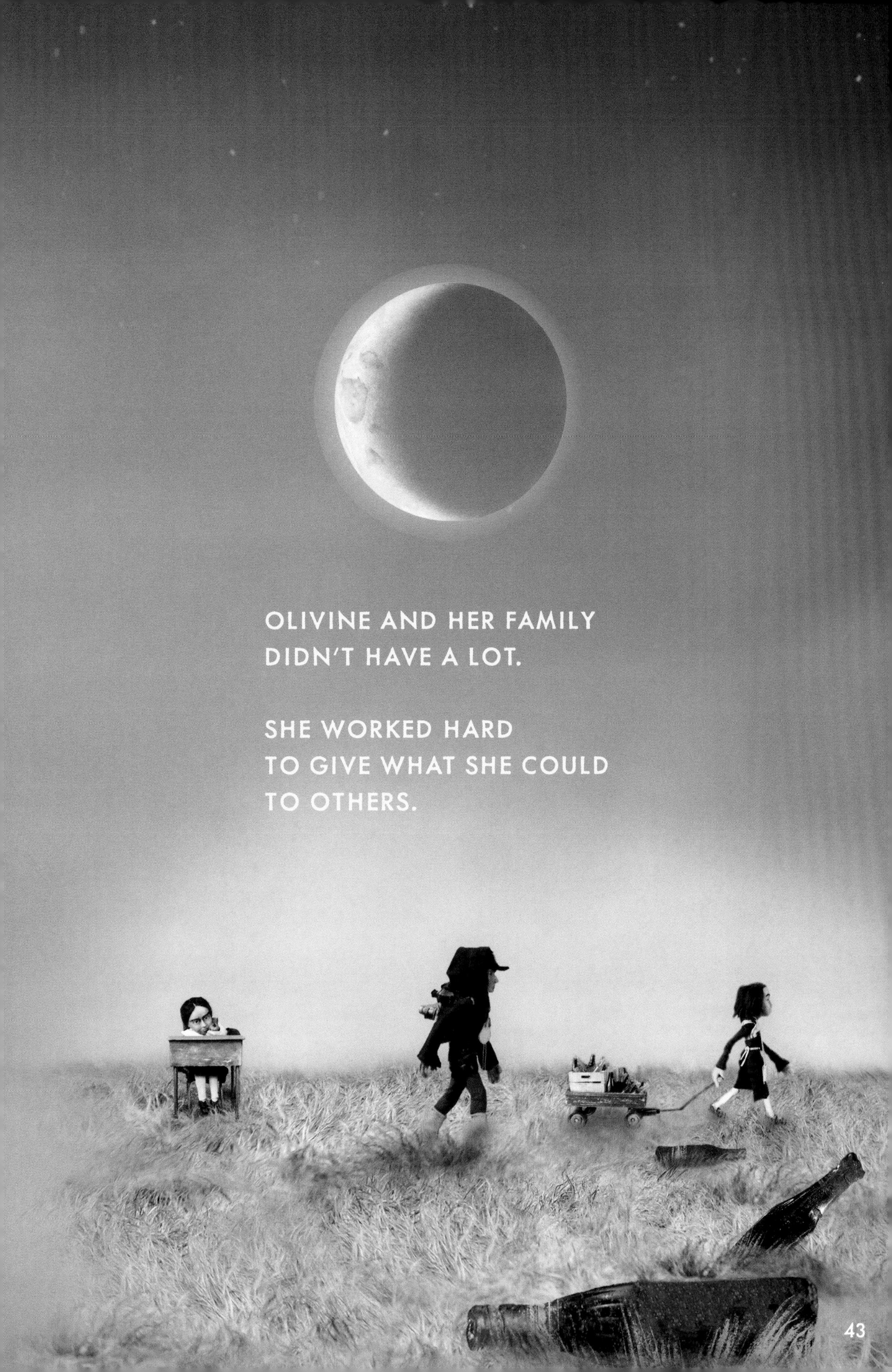

OLIVINE AND HER FAMILY
DIDN'T HAVE A LOT.

SHE WORKED HARD
TO GIVE WHAT SHE COULD
TO OTHERS.

OLIVINE REBELLED AGAINST THE ENFORCED TEACHINGS FROM THE NUNS AND PRIESTS AT CATHOLIC SCHOOL.

SHE CHALLENGED THEM EVERY DAY.

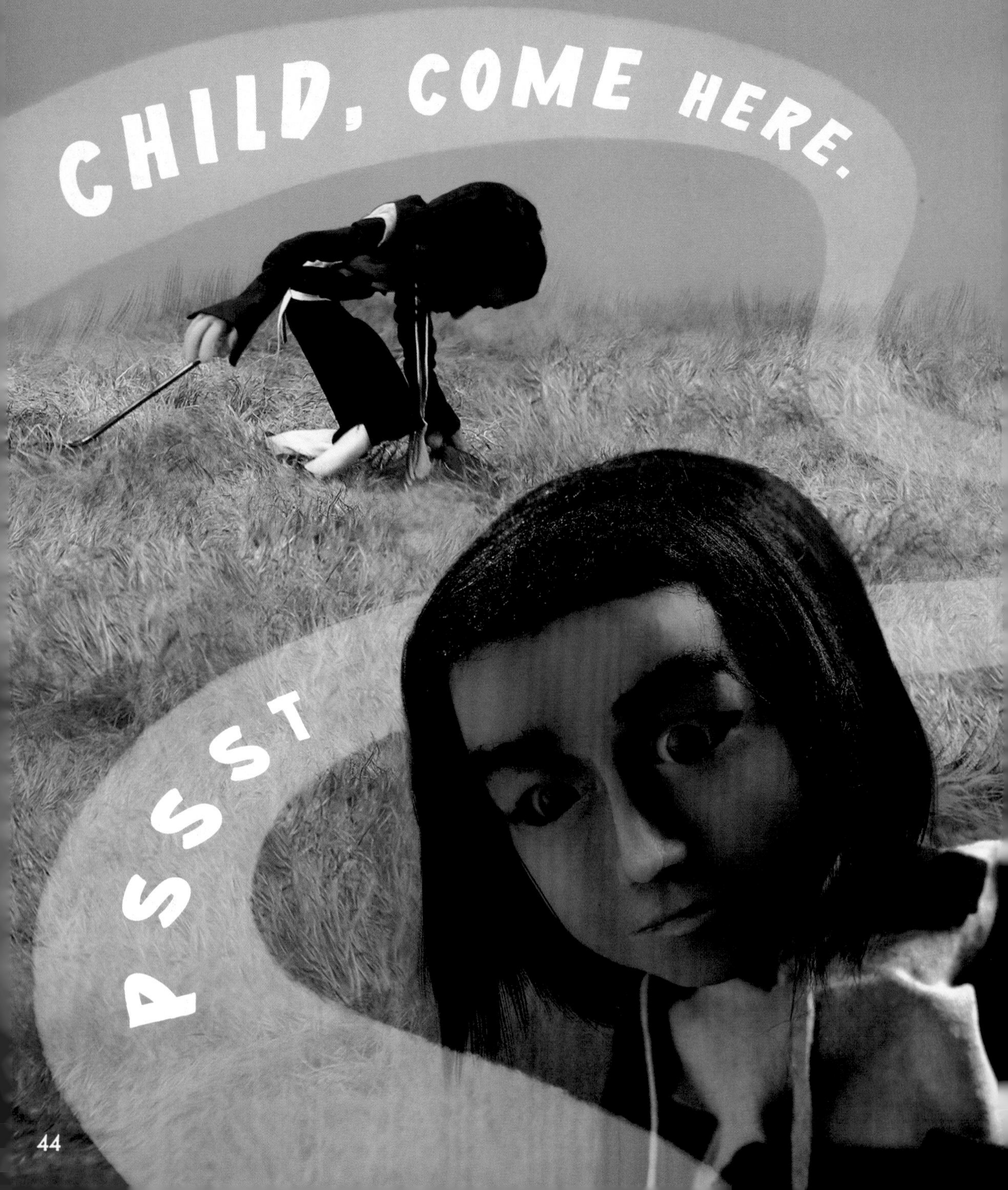
CHILD, COME HERE.
PSSST

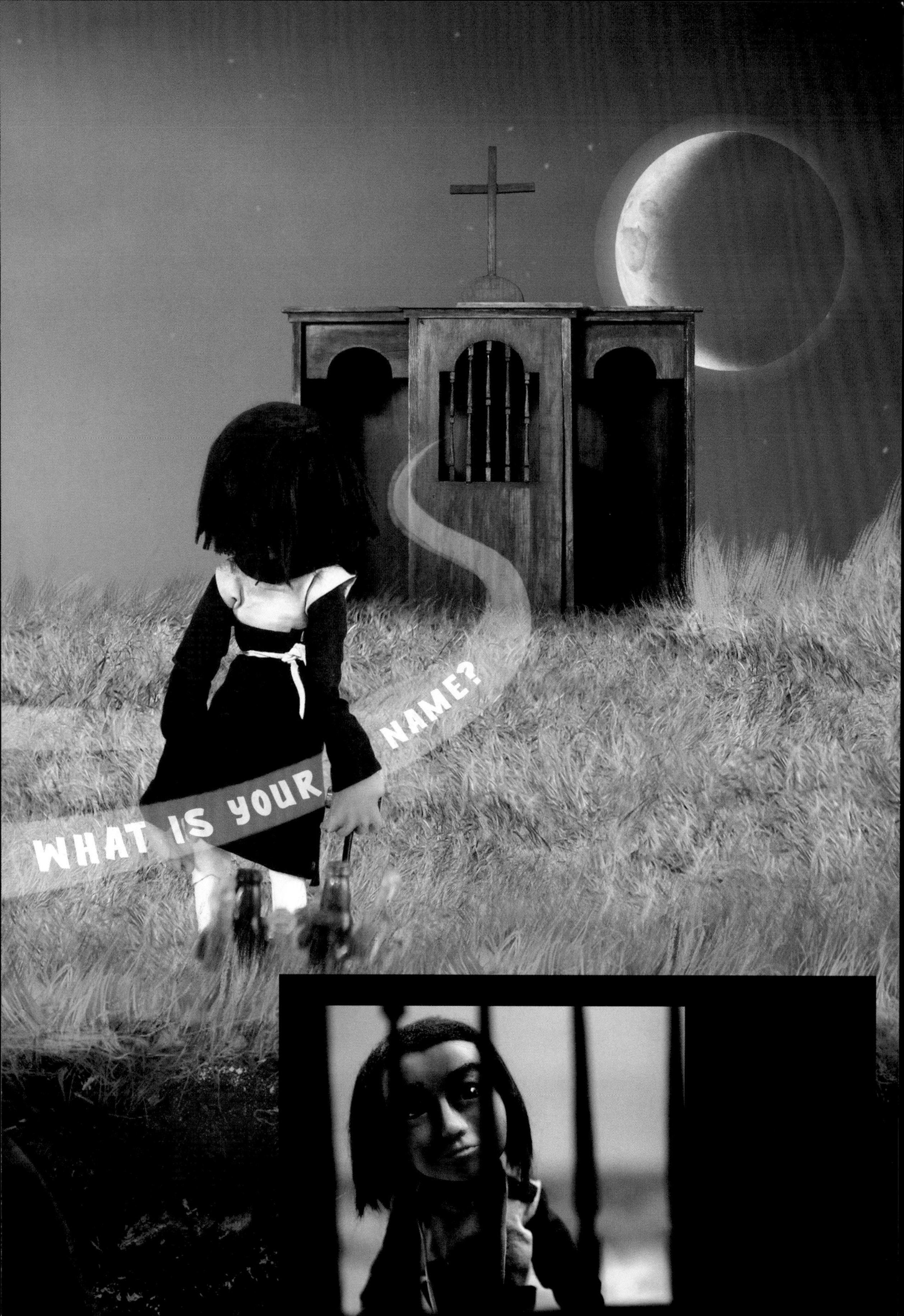
WHAT IS YOUR NAME?

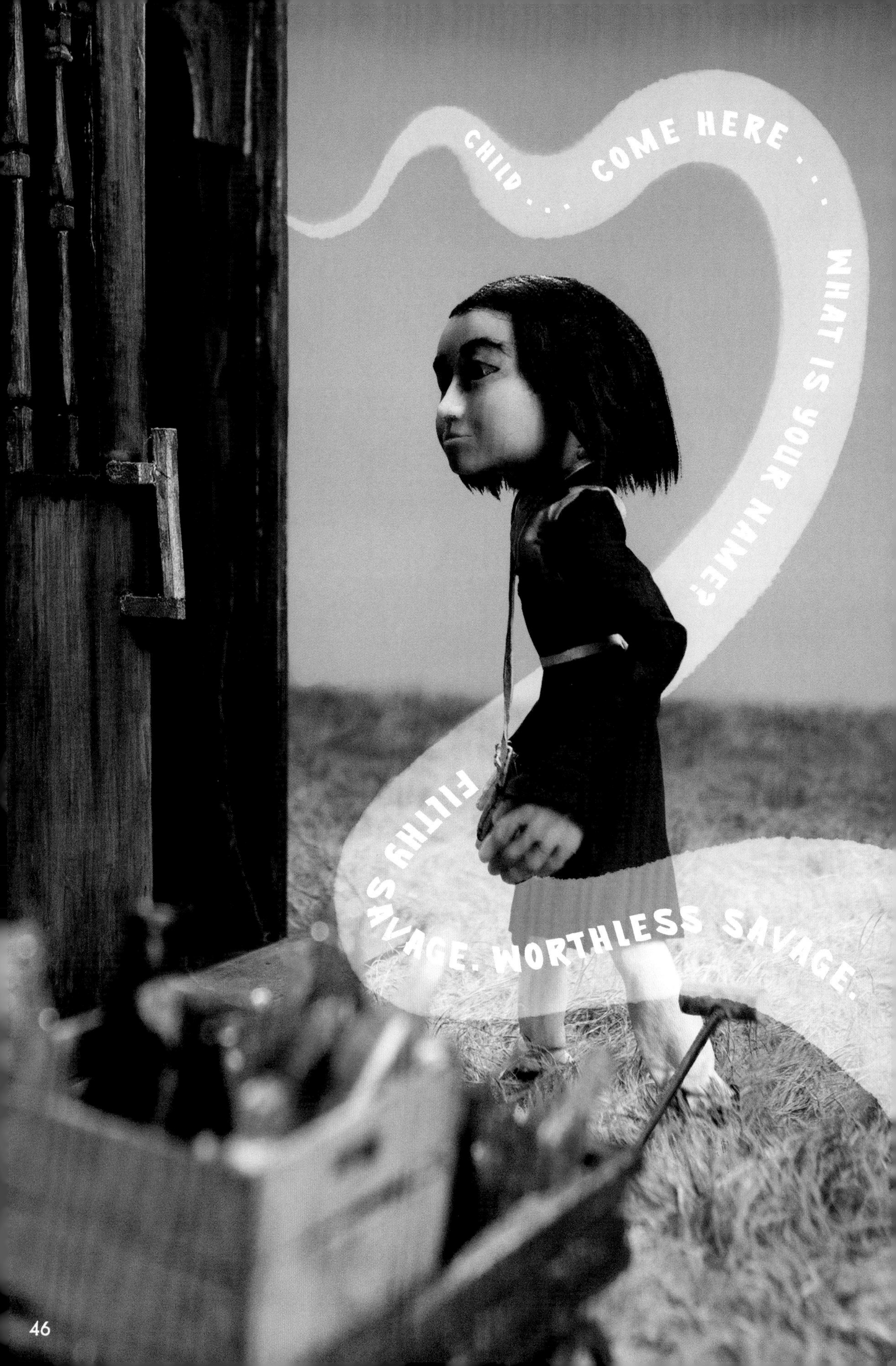
CHILD . . . COME HERE . . .
WHAT IS YOUR NAME?
FILTHY SAVAGE. WORTHLESS SAVAGE.

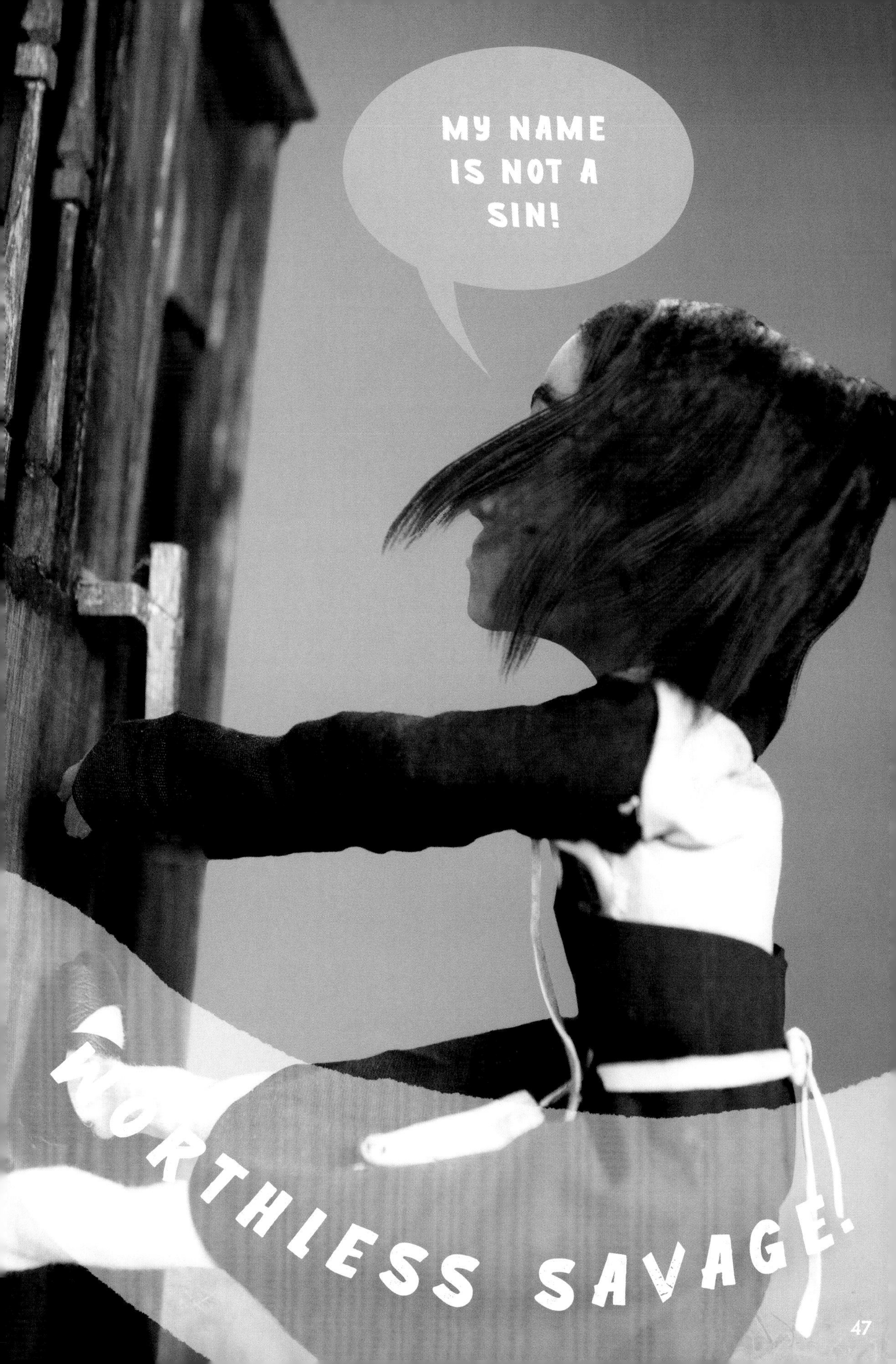
MY NAME IS NOT A SIN!
WORTHLESS SAVAGE!

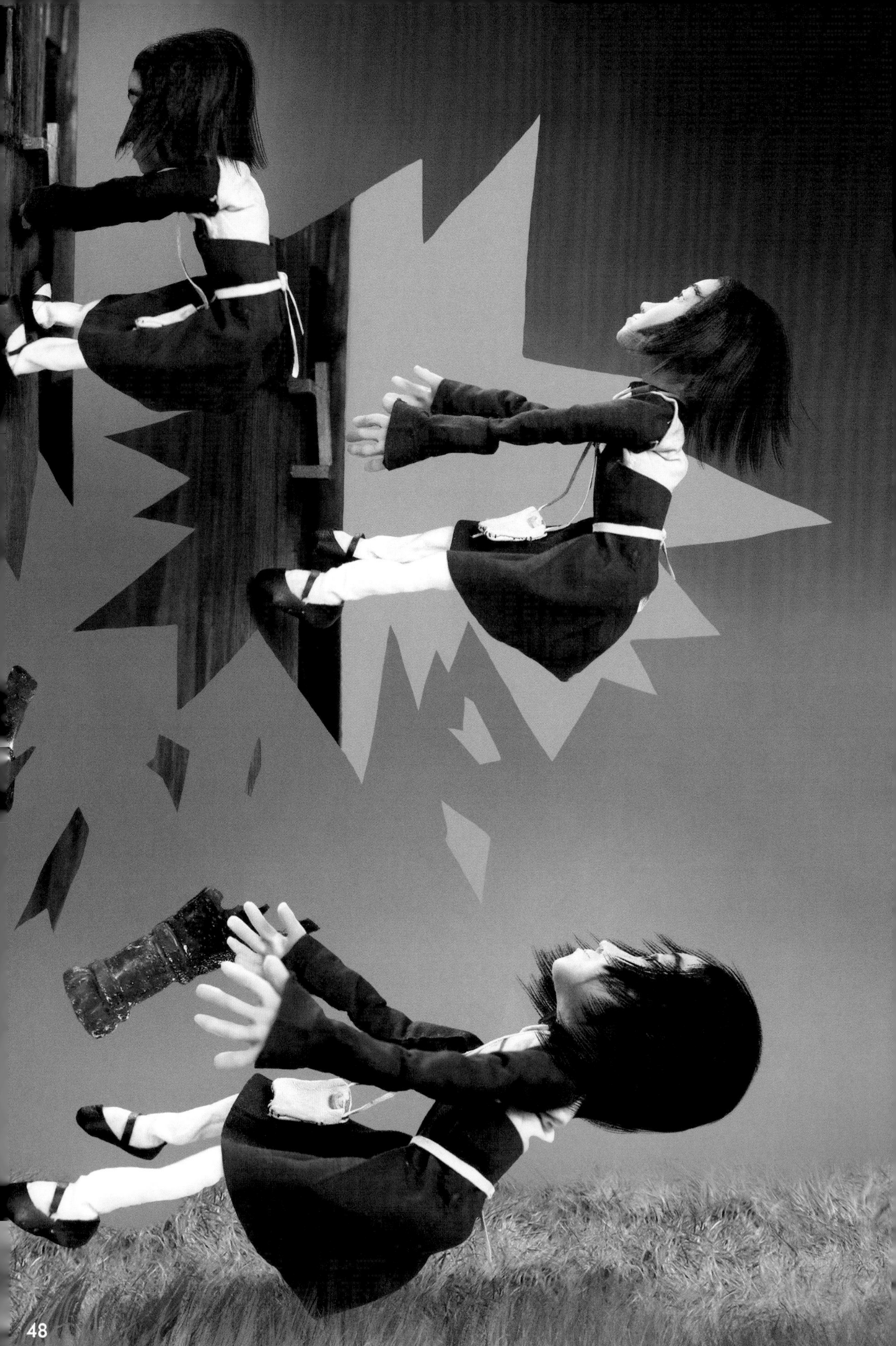

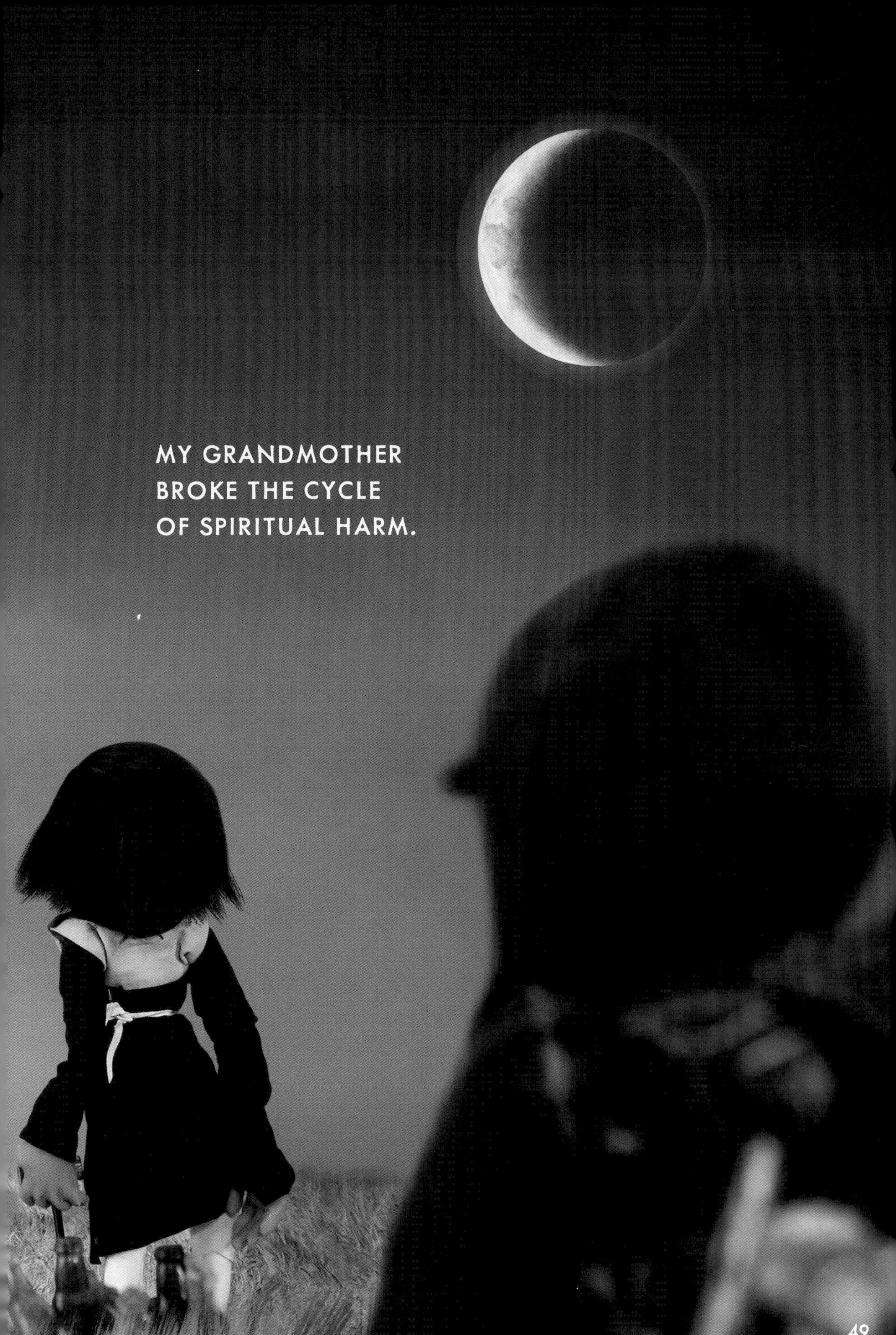
MY GRANDMOTHER
BROKE THE CYCLE
OF SPIRITUAL HARM.

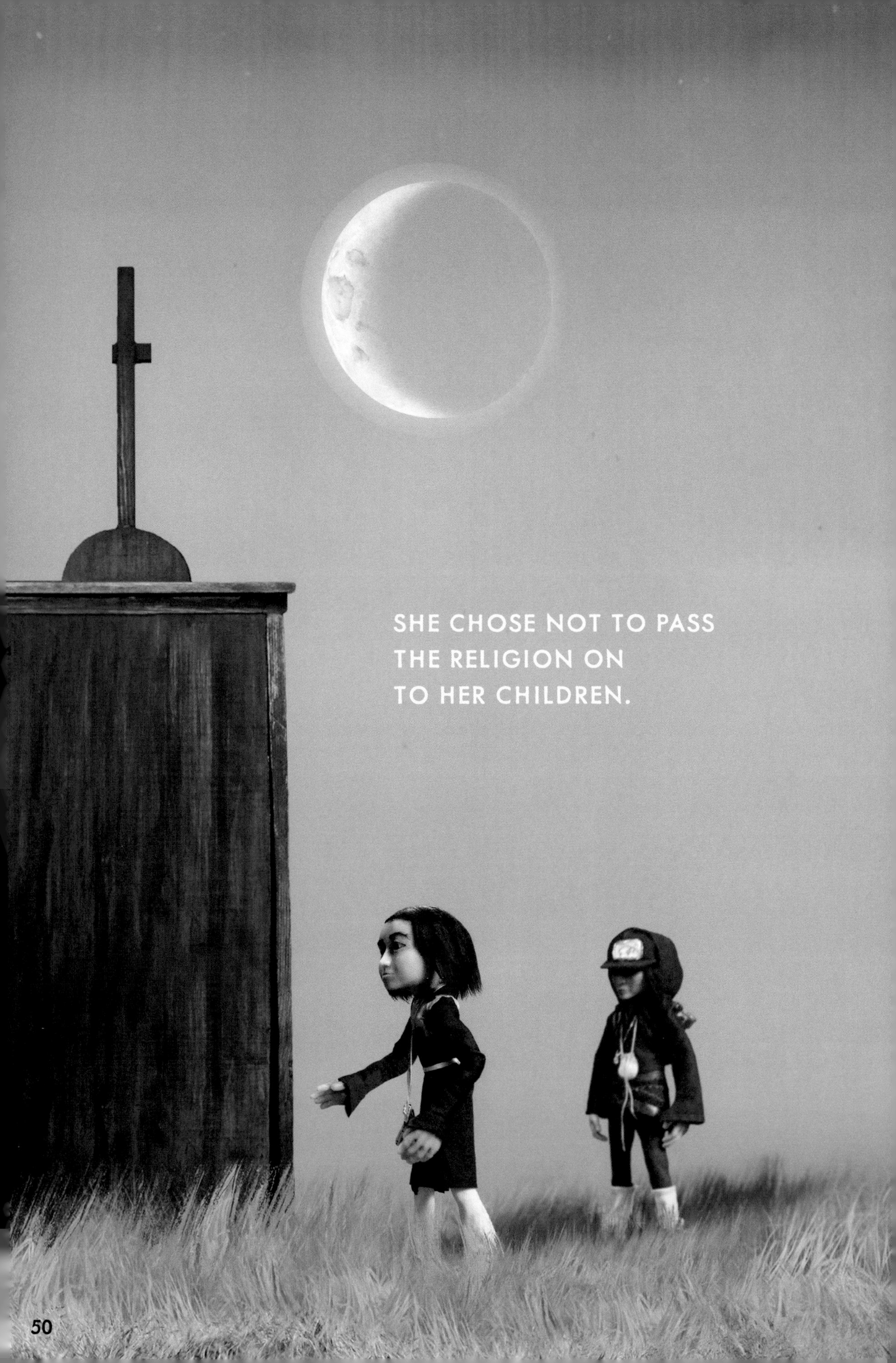

SHE CHOSE NOT TO PASS
THE RELIGION ON
TO HER CHILDREN.

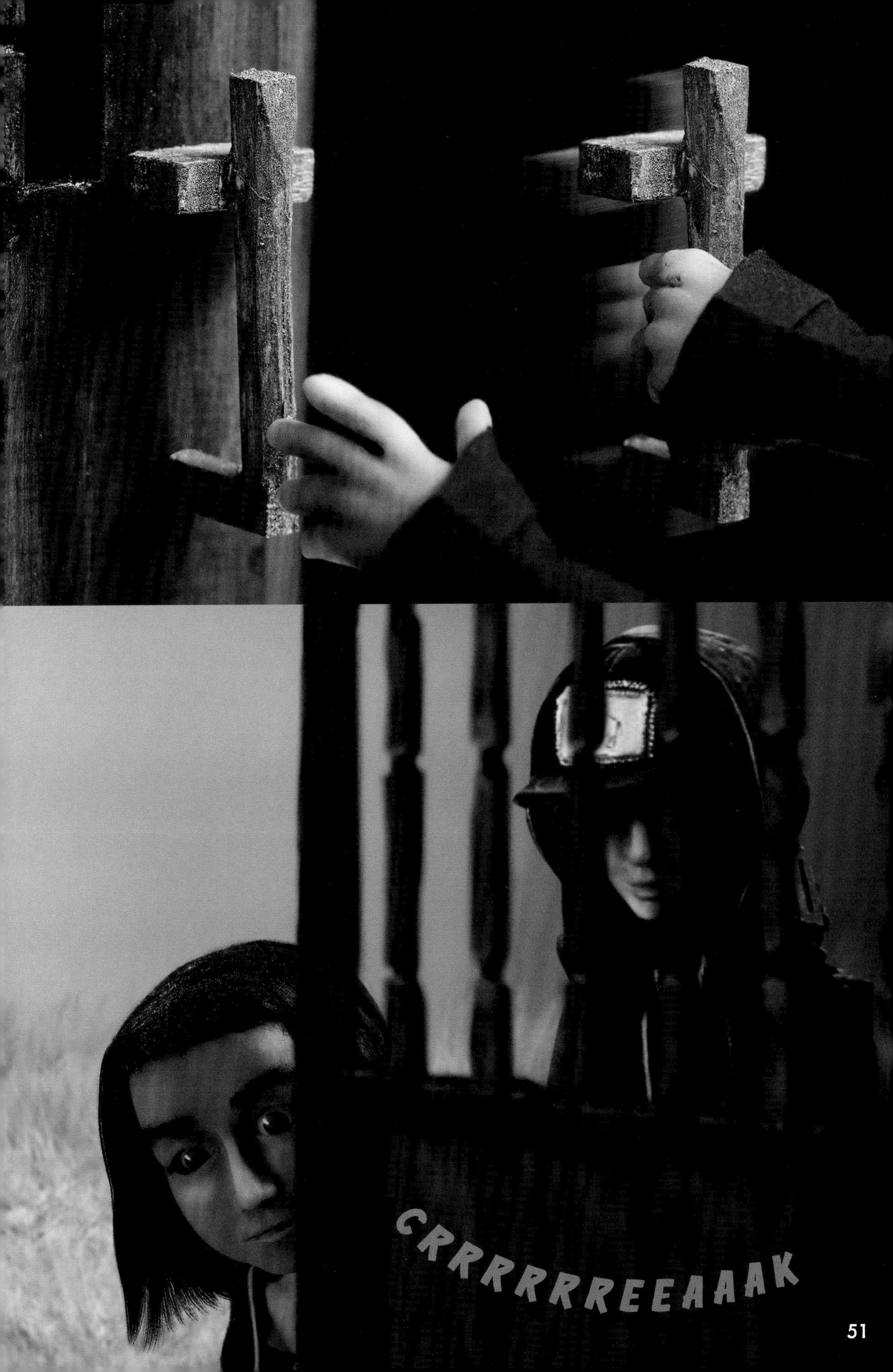
CRRRRRREEAAAK

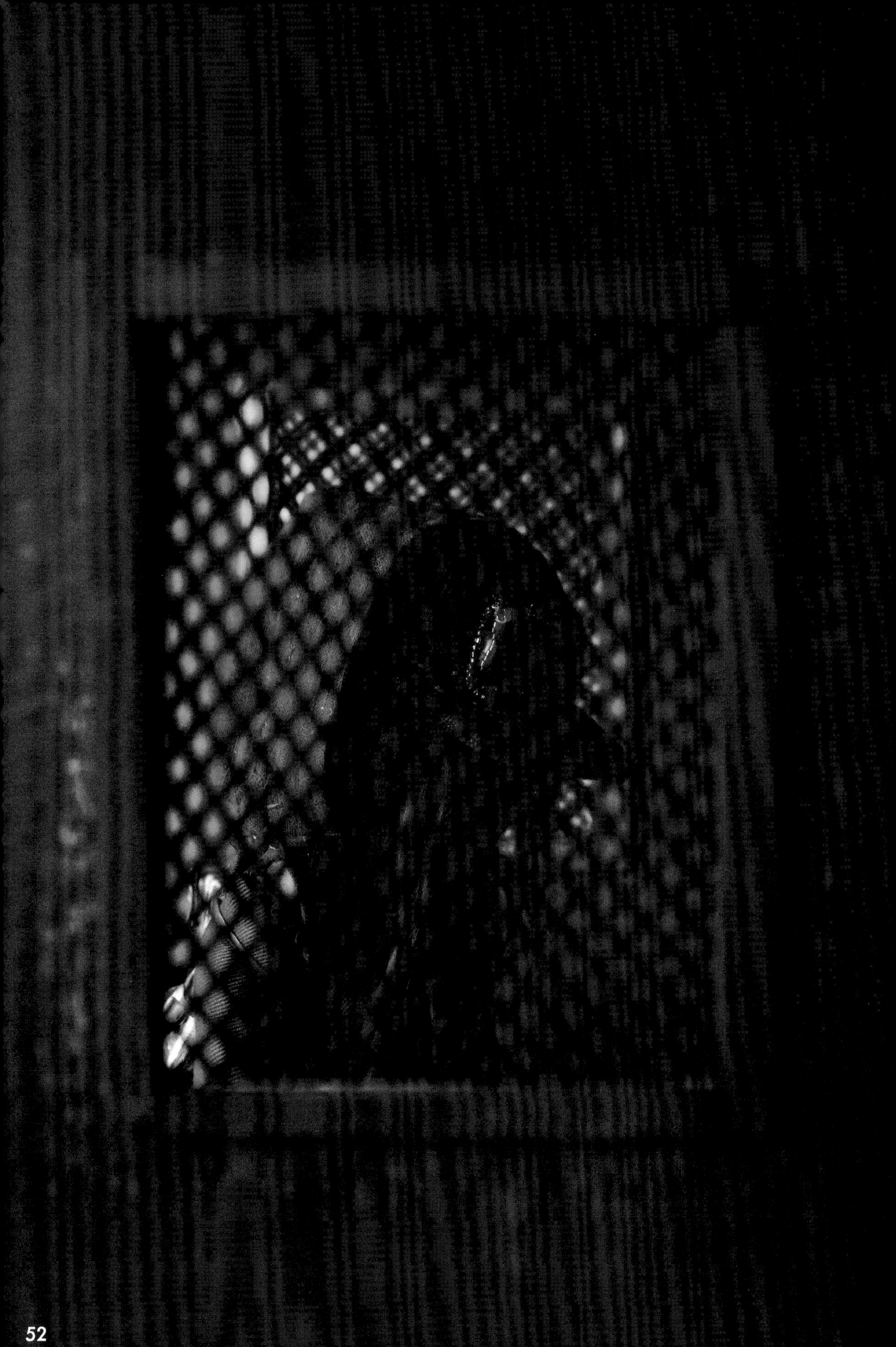

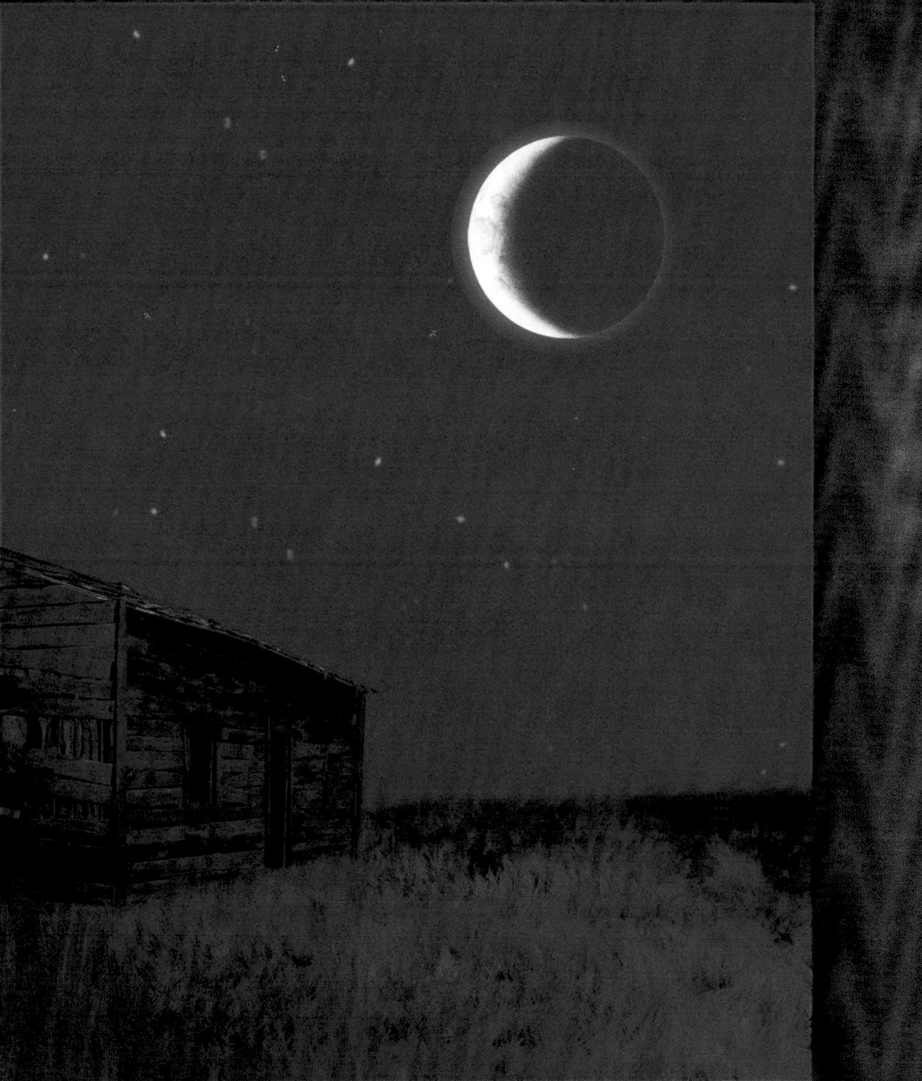

CHAPTER TWO
HALF MOON

WE PLANT WITH THE MOON
IN GROUND THAT ONCE SHOOK
WITH THUNDER.
AIMING, PIERCING, MOVING,
WE WORK WITH THE CHANGES.
WE WORK LIKE ARROWS
TO RISE AGAIN.

KEYAKUM KISTIKANANAW, TAPISKOCH OSKIPESIM
OTA ASKI, MISIWEH KAKI PETAKUSICIK PEHASEWAK
ITTUHIKEWAK, SAPOOSTAWAOWAK,
WAWAPEHSEWSTUN
EHATOSKATAMAK, TAHTO KIKWAY KAKWESKIMAKAK
EHATOSKATAMAK, TAPISKOOCH UK'USKWUK
KASIPWEHACIK ASSAY MINA.

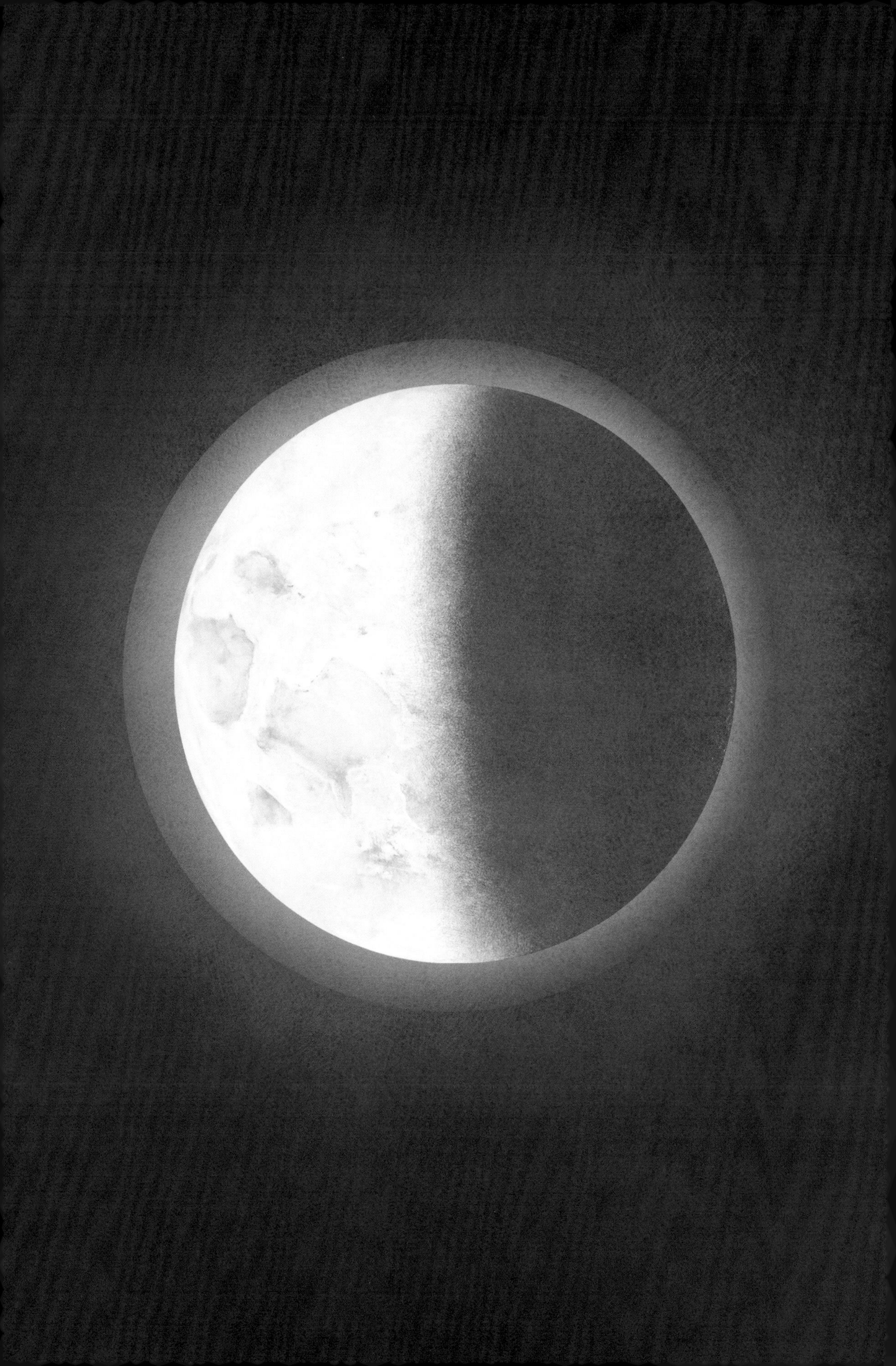

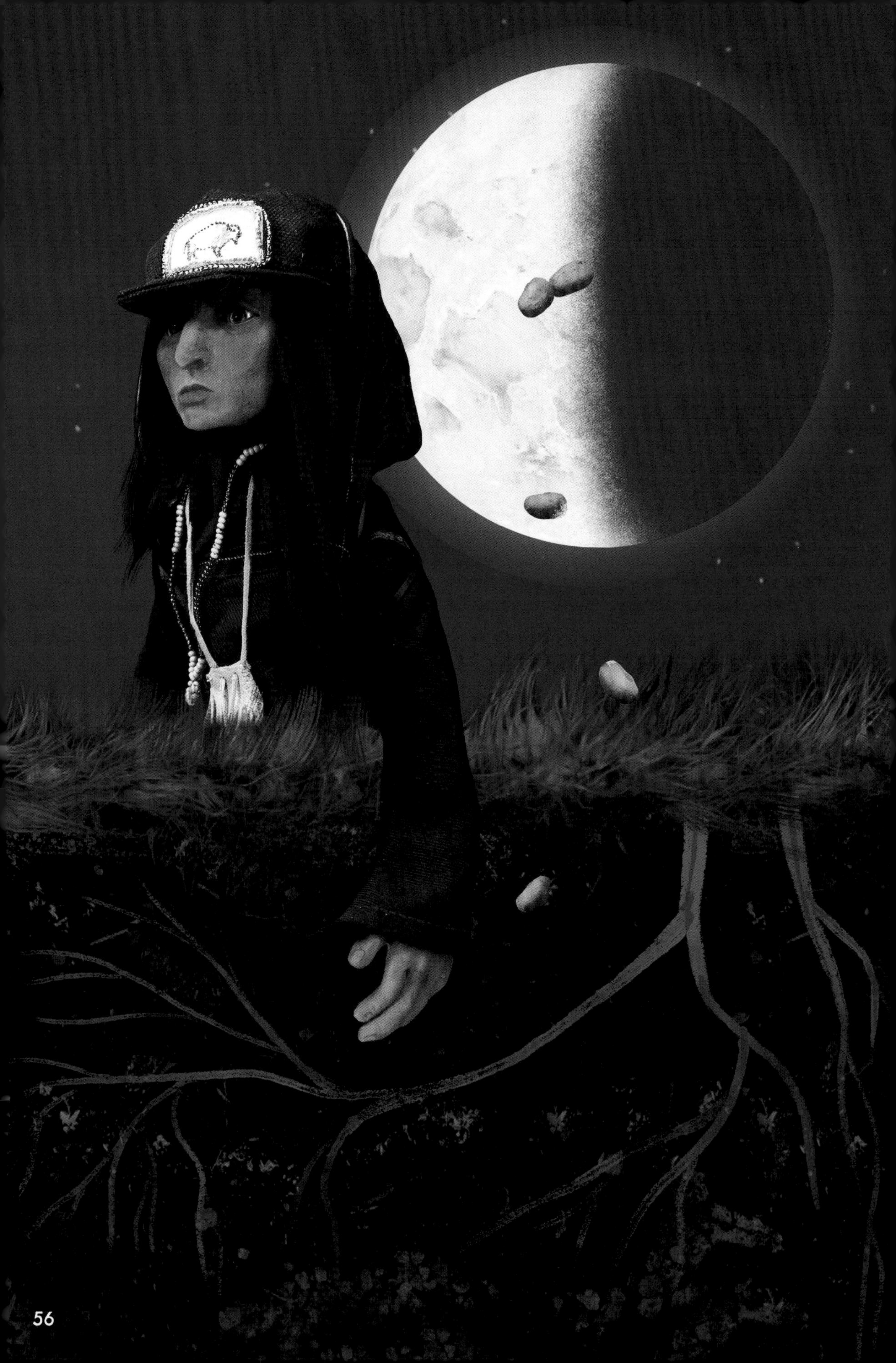

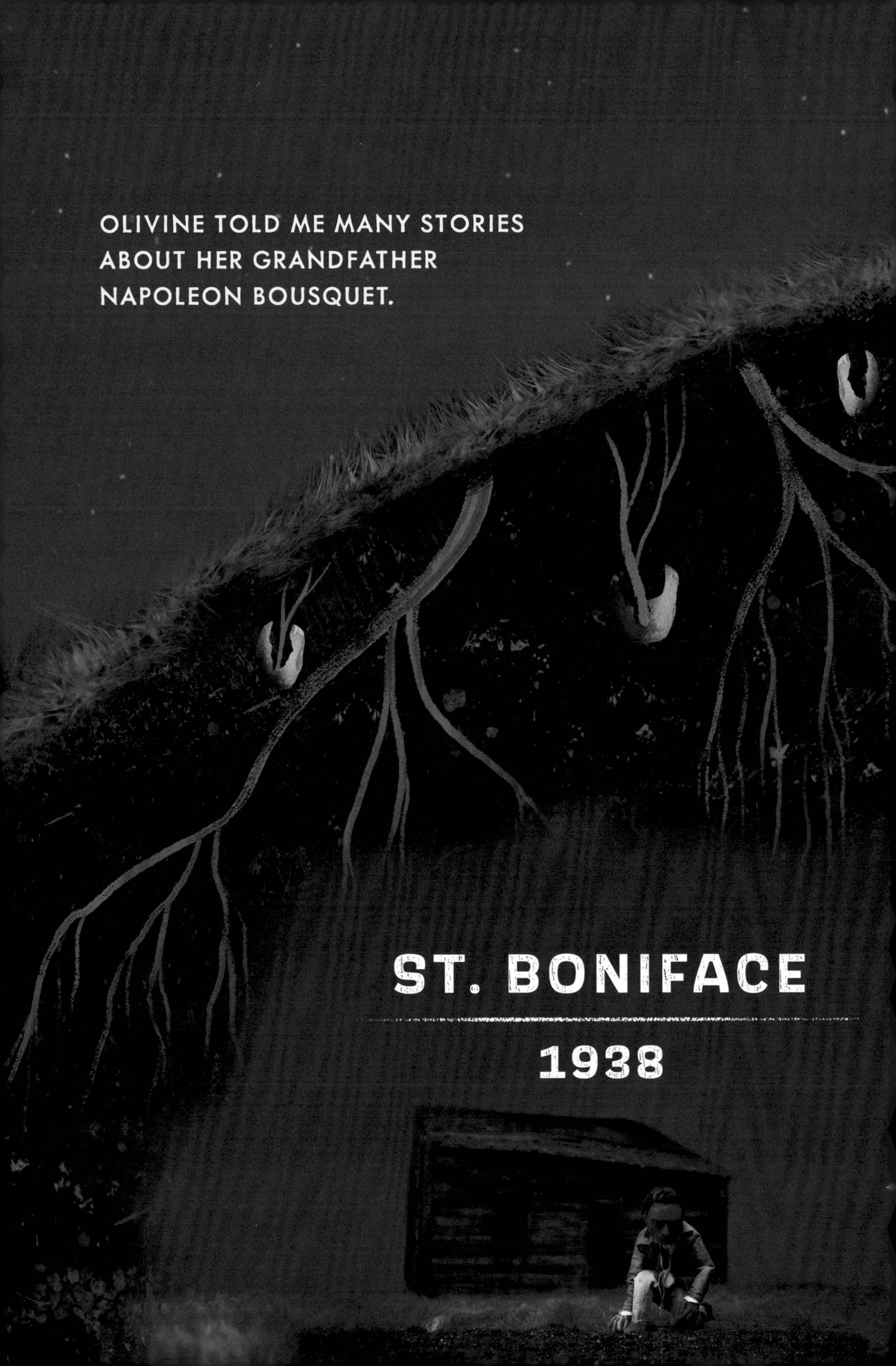
OLIVINE TOLD ME MANY STORIES ABOUT HER GRANDFATHER NAPOLEON BOUSQUET.
ST. BONIFACE
1938

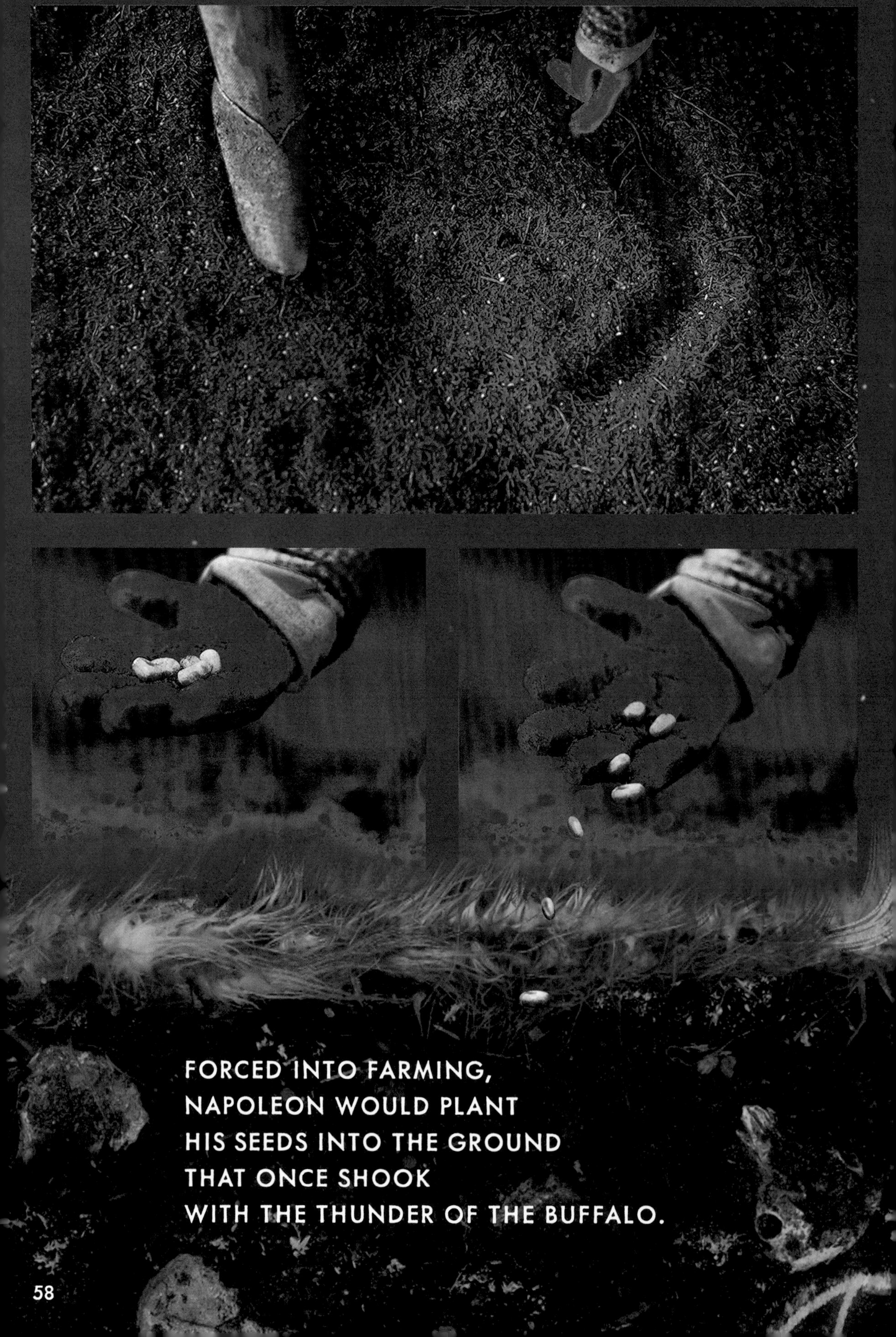
FORCED INTO FARMING,
NAPOLEON WOULD PLANT
HIS SEEDS INTO THE GROUND
THAT ONCE SHOOK
WITH THE THUNDER OF THE BUFFALO.

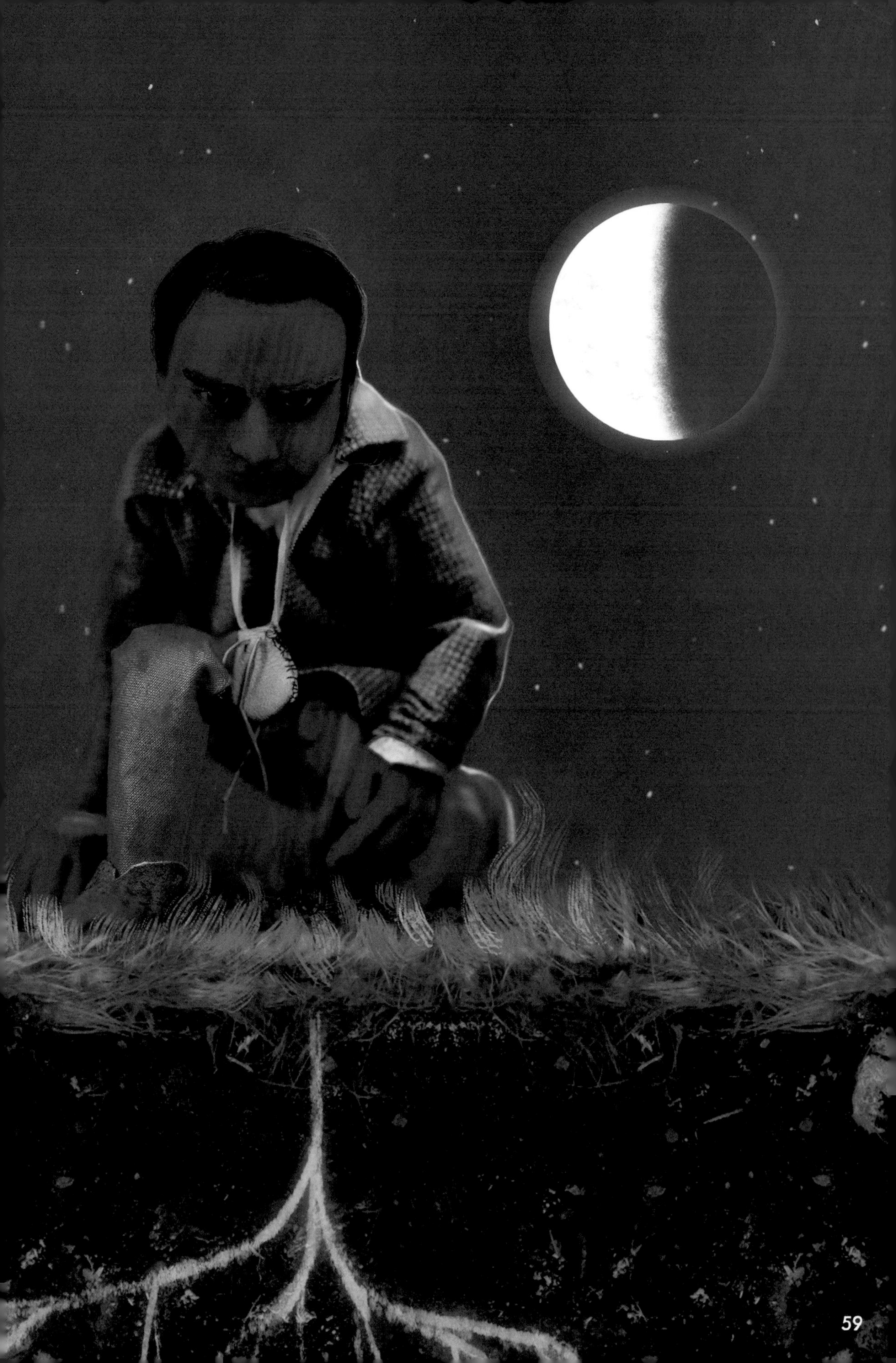

OUR FAMILY WAS GIVEN SCRIPS
BY THE GOVERNMENT
GUARANTEEING HIM LAND
IN NORTH DAKOTA AND MANITOBA.

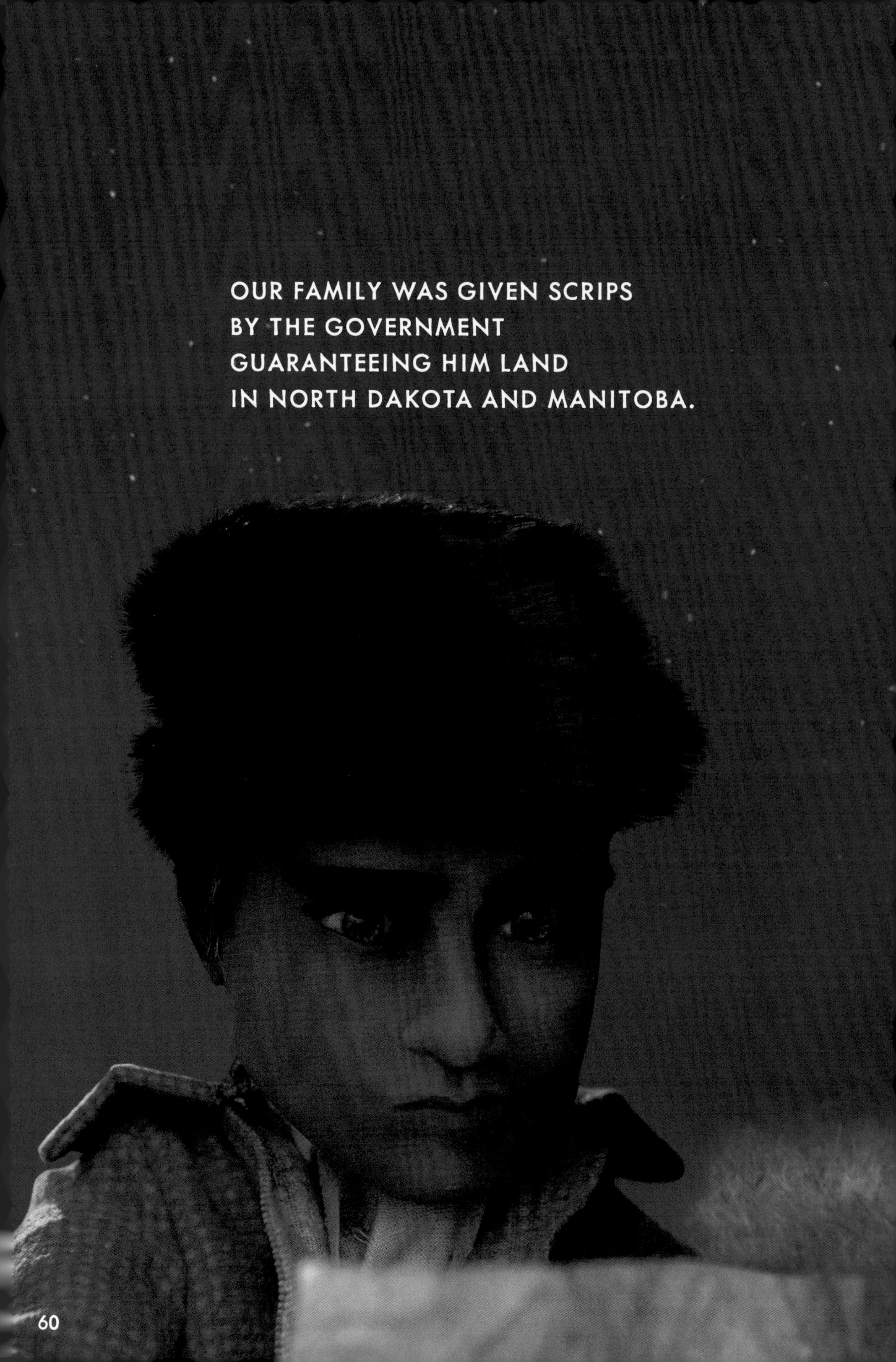

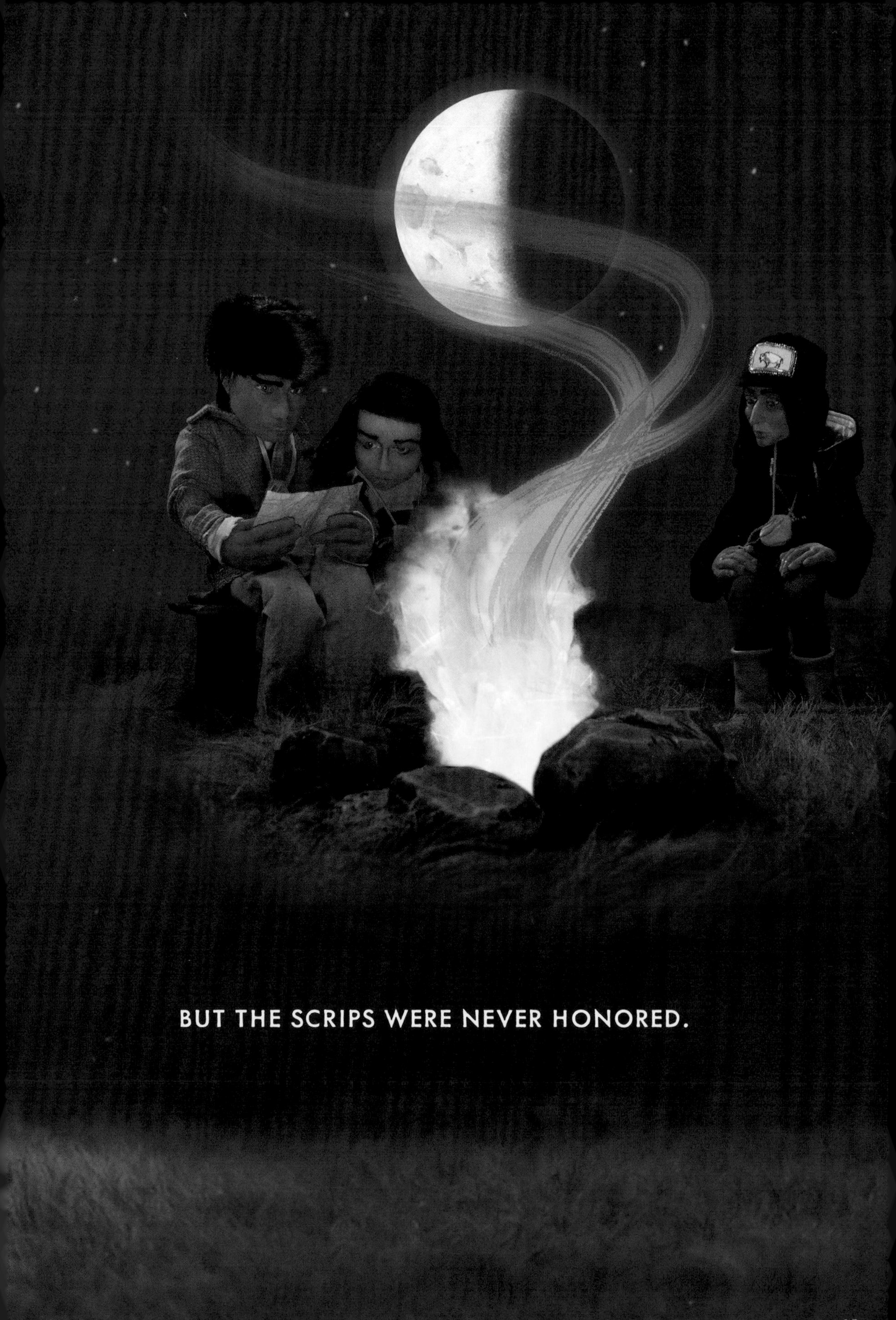
BUT THE SCRIPS WERE NEVER HONORED.

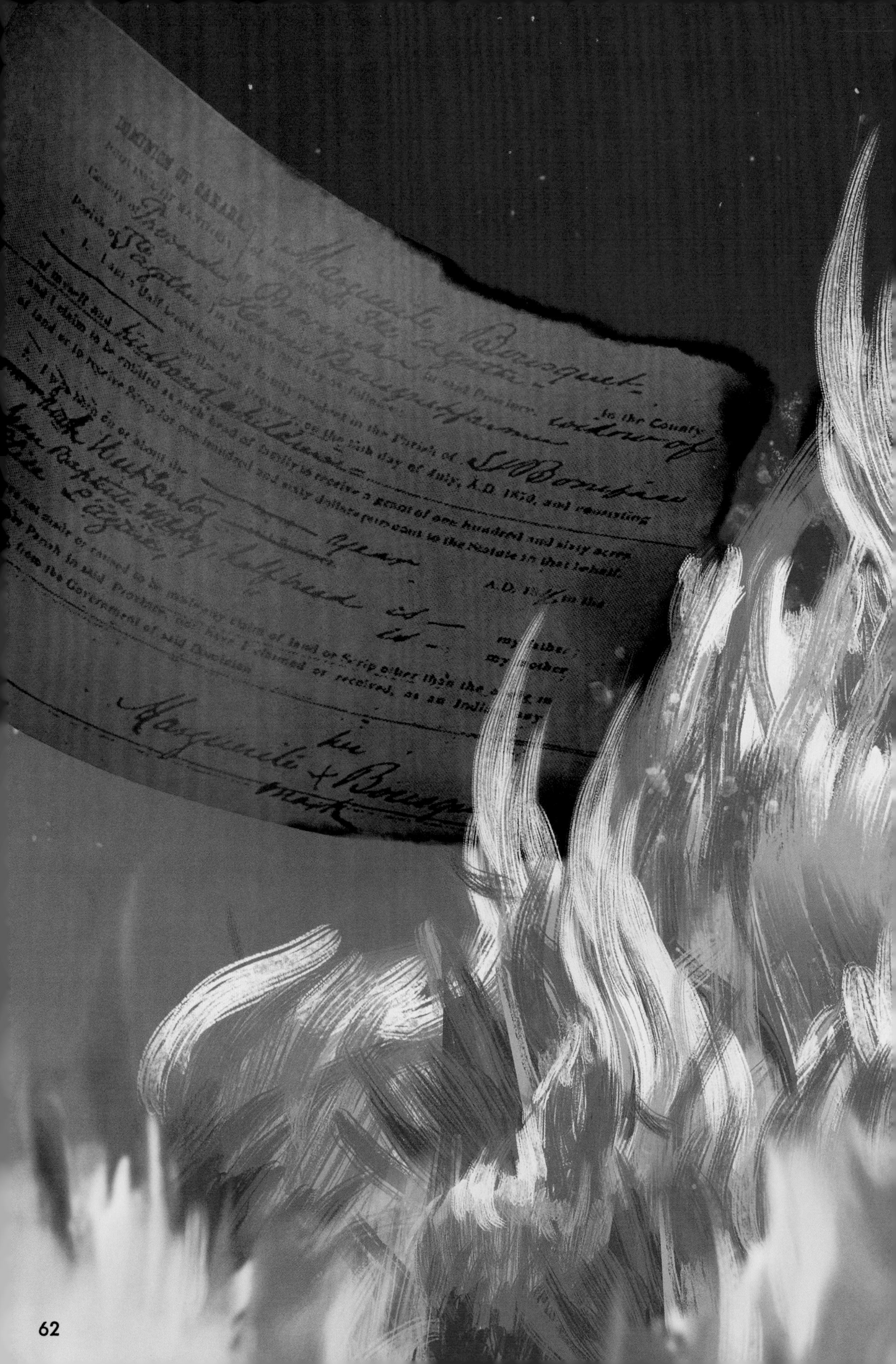
in the County
the Parish of
day of July, A.D. 1870, and remaining
a grant of one hundred and sixty acres
pursuant to the Statute in that behalf.
my father
my mother
as an Indian
Marguerite + Bourque
her mark

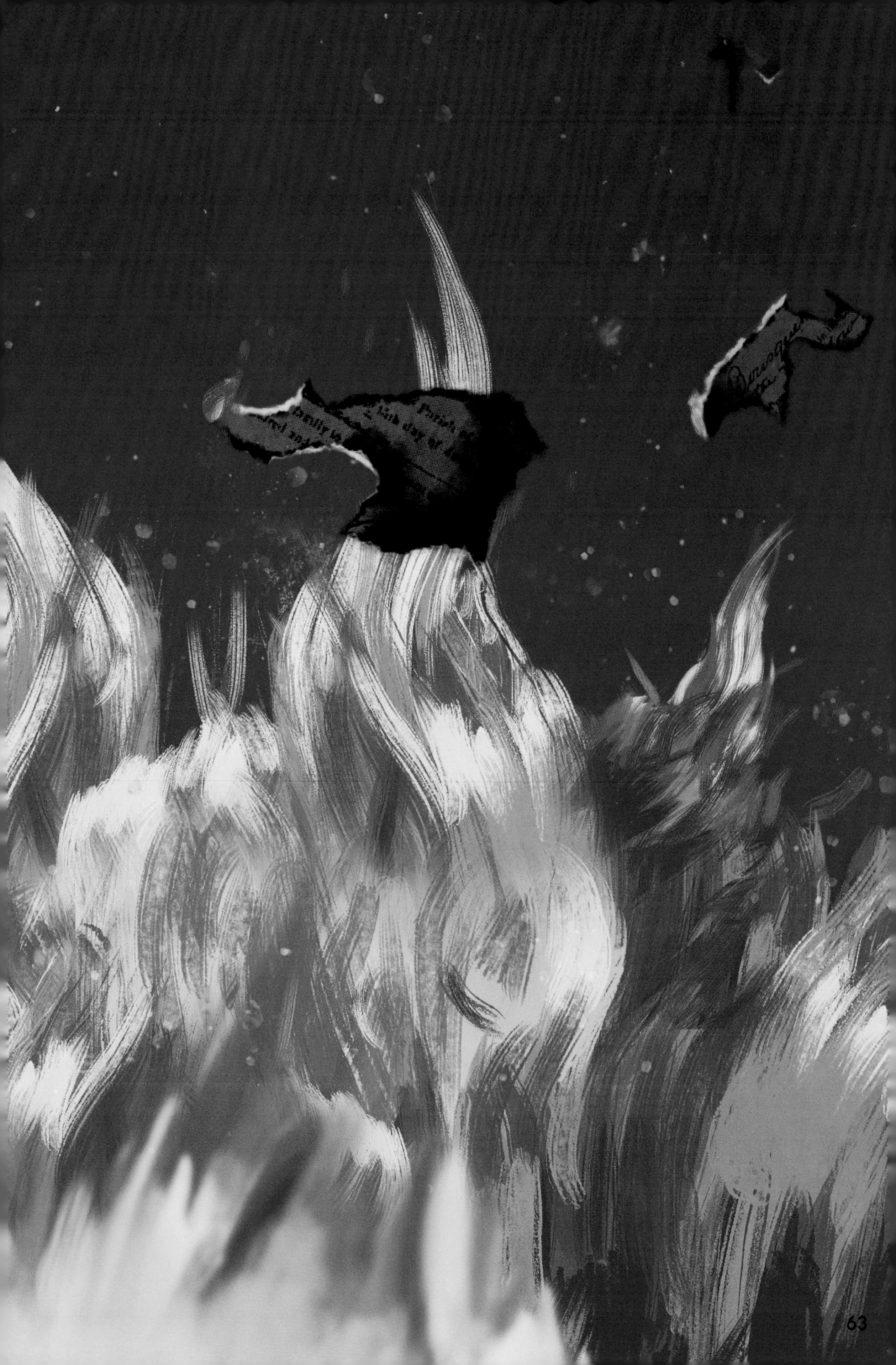

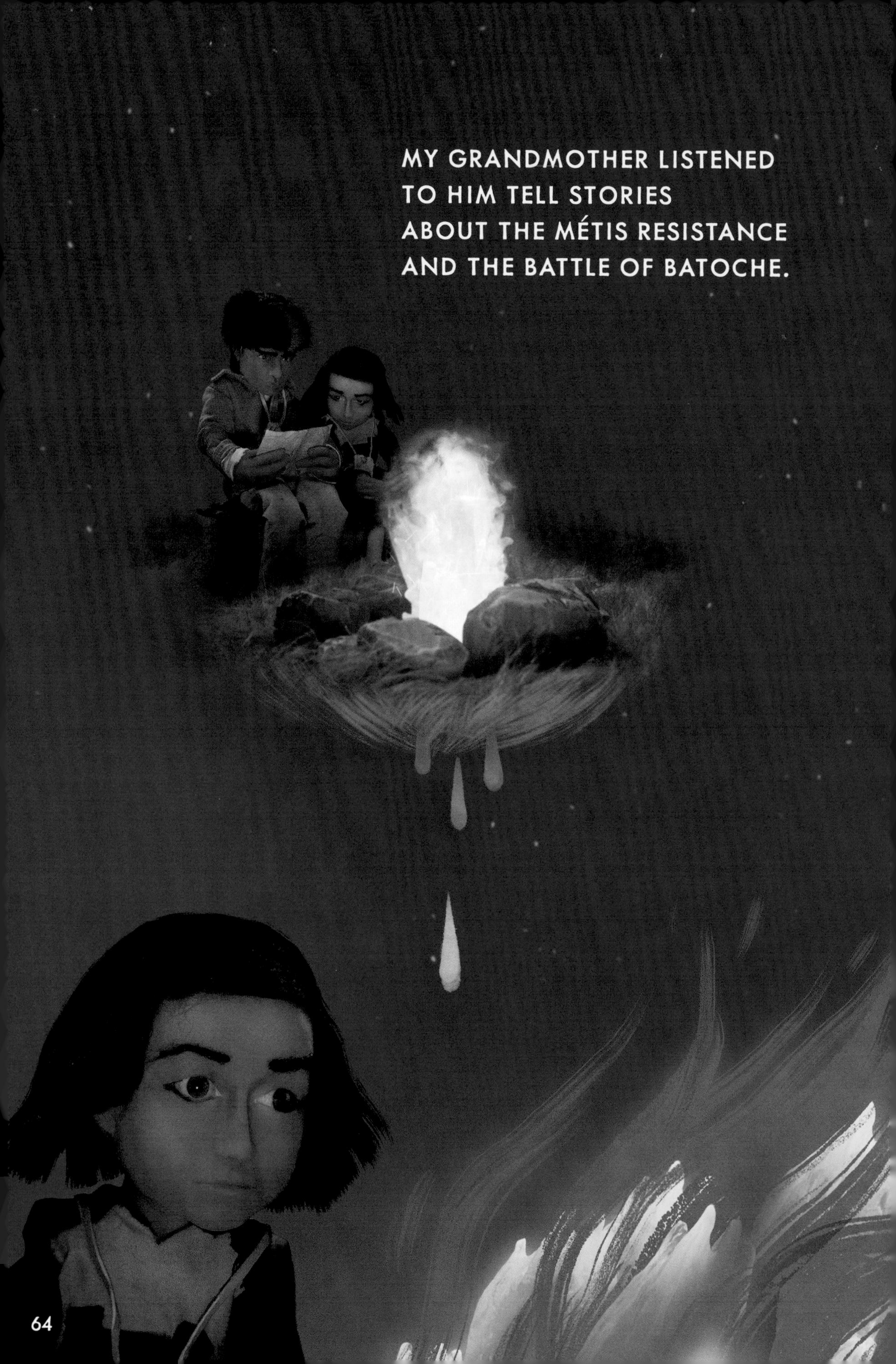
MY GRANDMOTHER LISTENED
TO HIM TELL STORIES
ABOUT THE MÉTIS RESISTANCE
AND THE BATTLE OF BATOCHE.

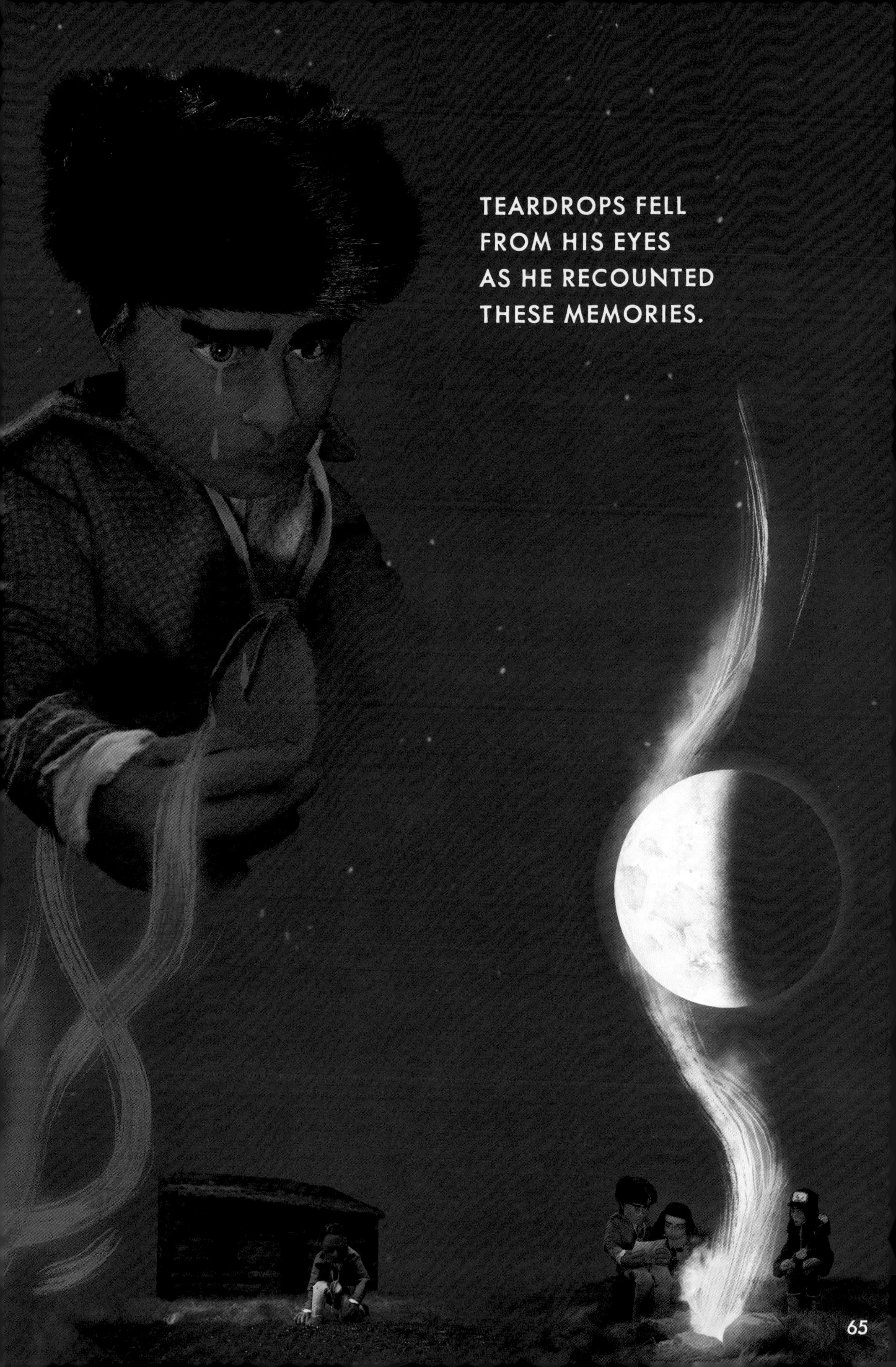
TEARDROPS FELL
FROM HIS EYES
AS HE RECOUNTED
THESE MEMORIES.

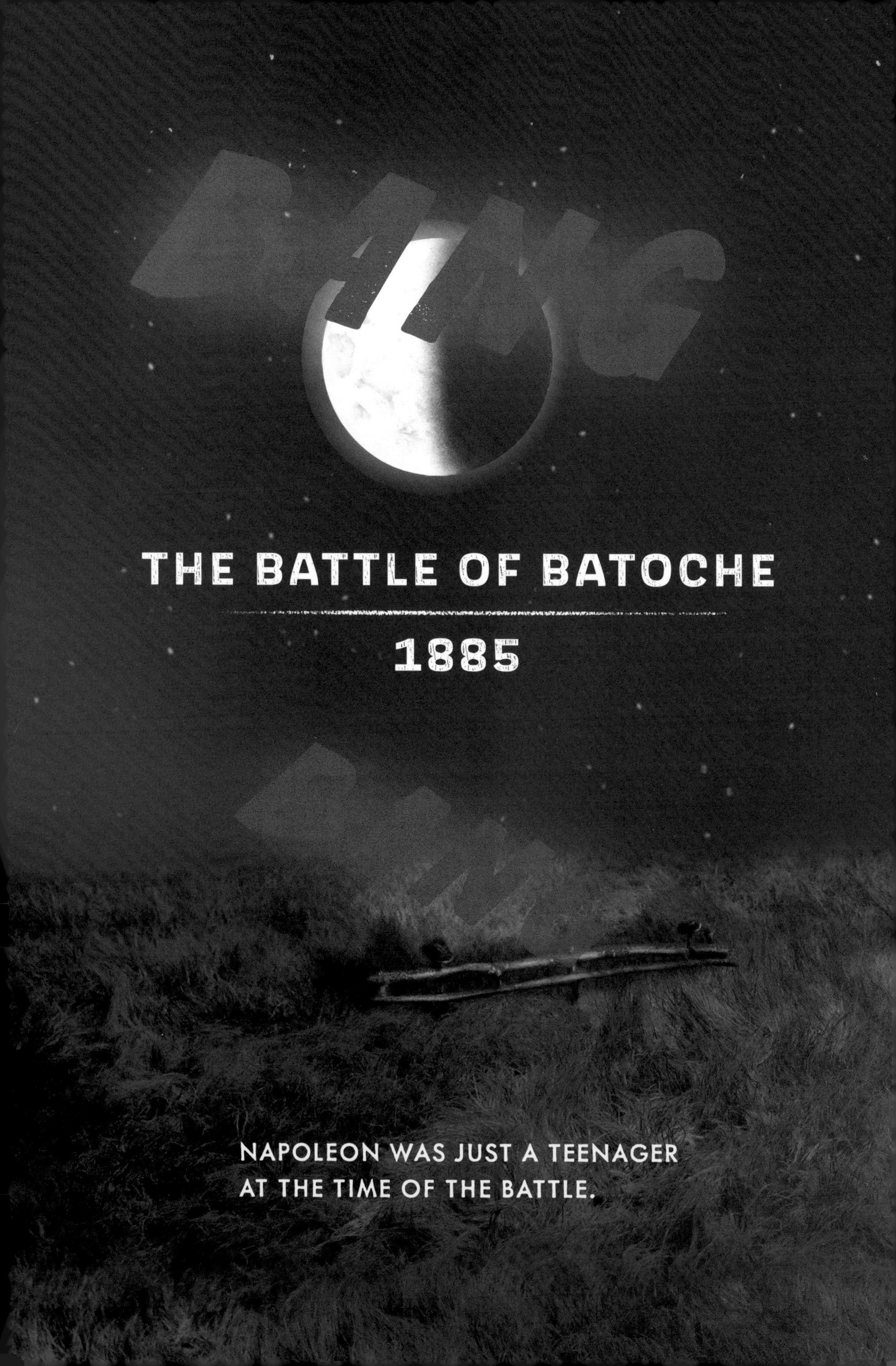

THE BATTLE OF BATOCHE

1885

NAPOLEON WAS JUST A TEENAGER
AT THE TIME OF THE BATTLE.

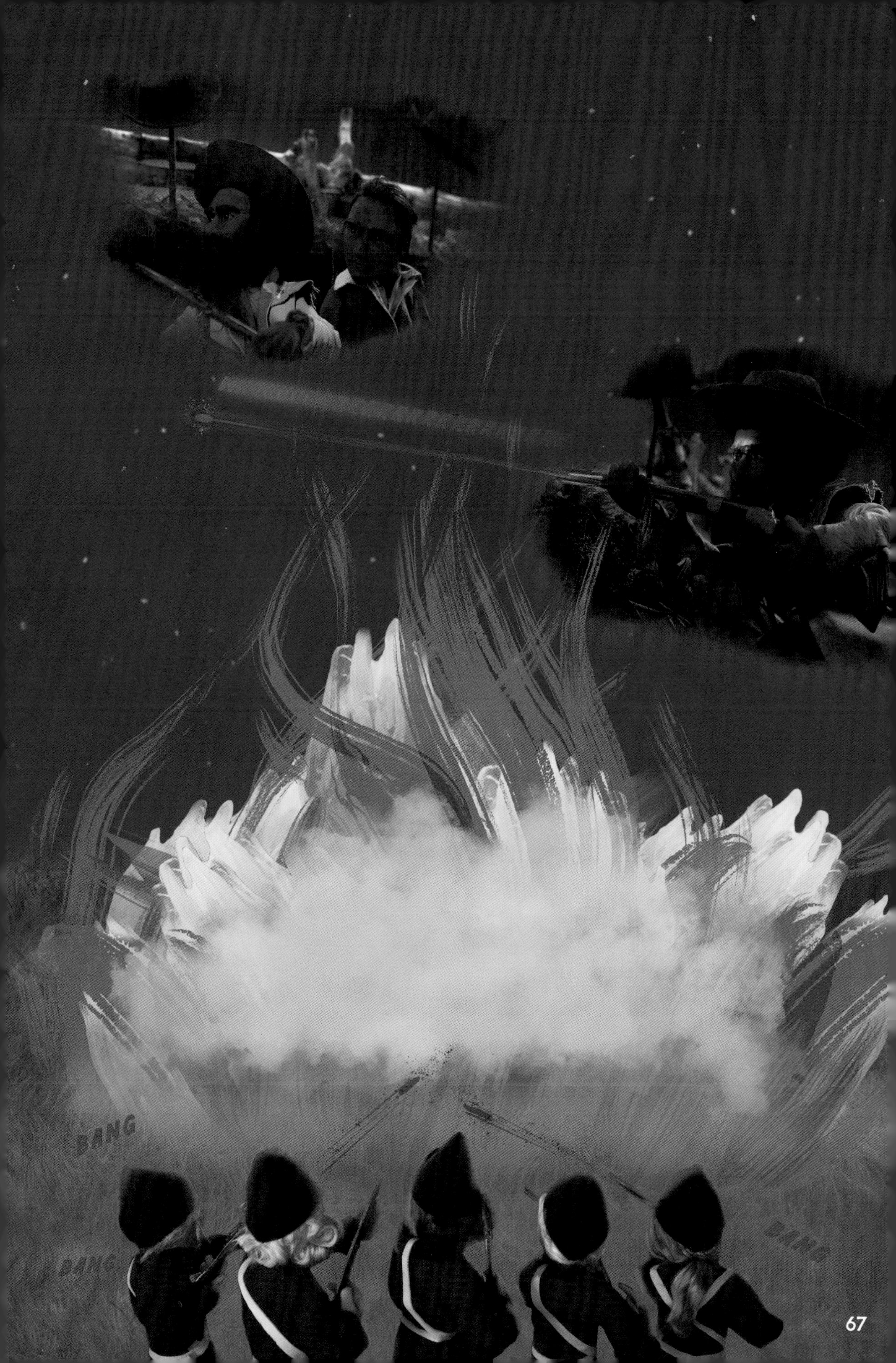
BANG
BANG
BANG

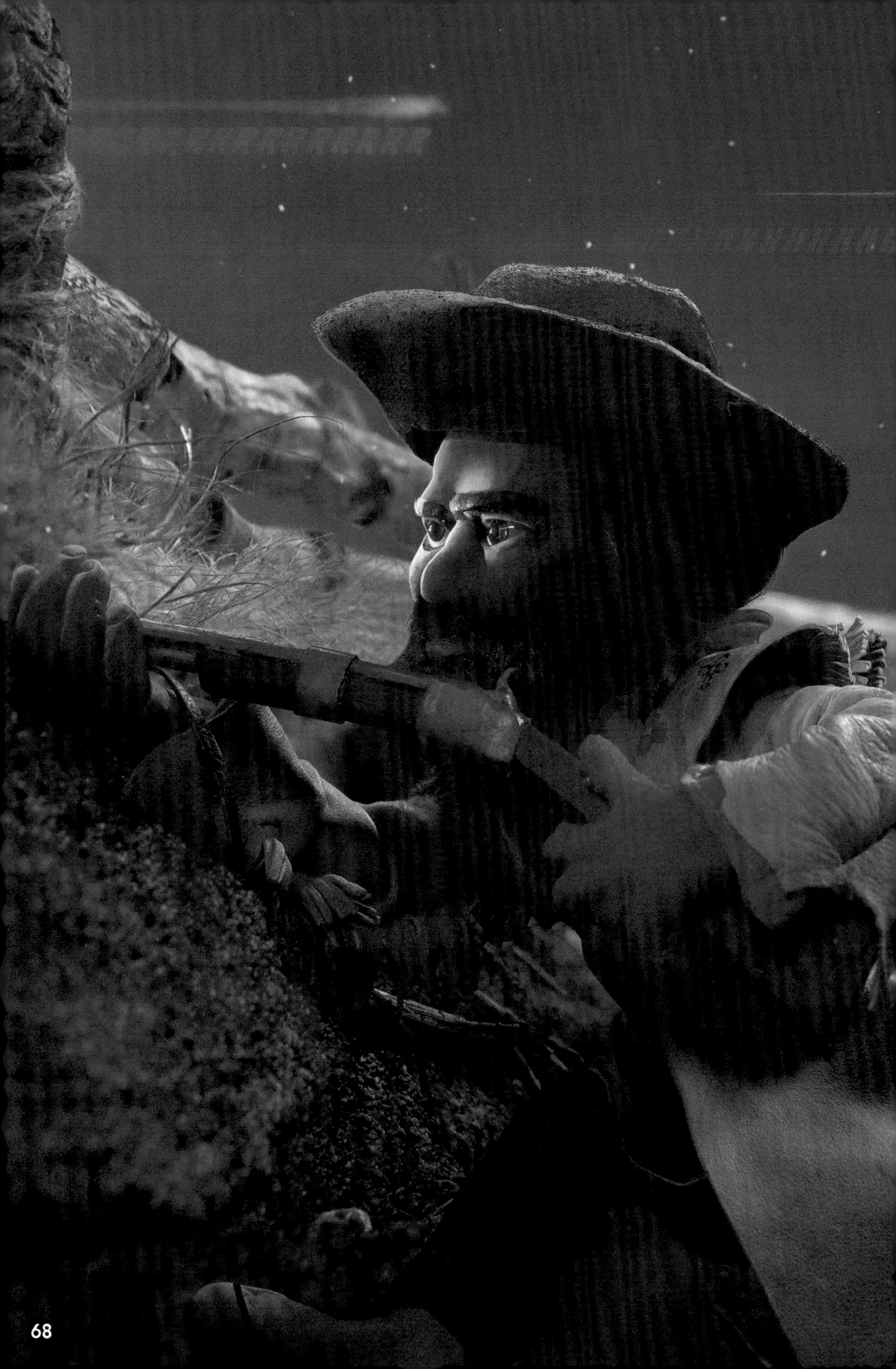

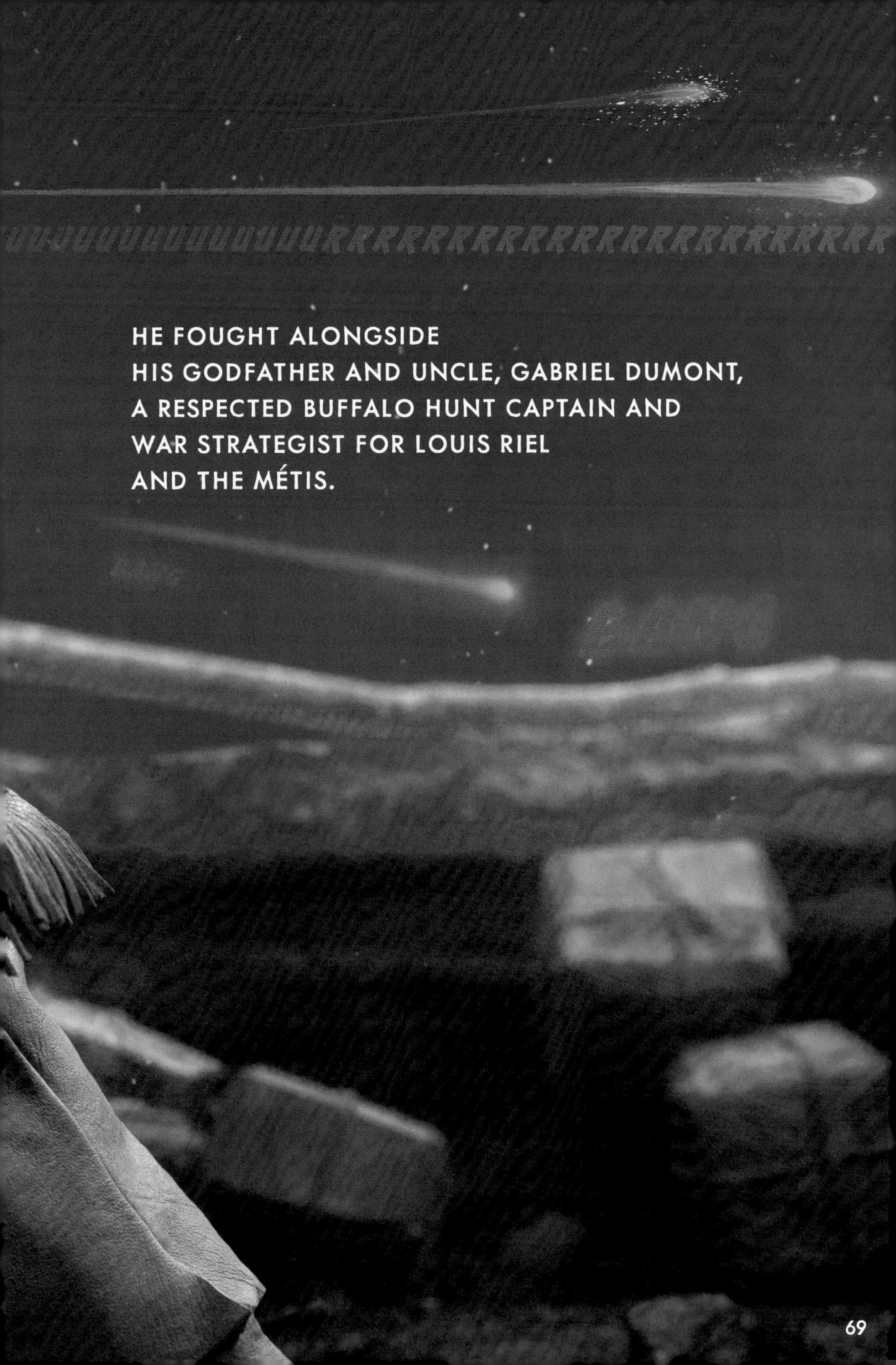
UUUUUUUUUUUUUURRRRRRRRRRRRRRRRRRRRRRR
HE FOUGHT ALONGSIDE
HIS GODFATHER AND UNCLE, GABRIEL DUMONT,
A RESPECTED BUFFALO HUNT CAPTAIN AND
WAR STRATEGIST FOR LOUIS RIEL
AND THE MÉTIS.

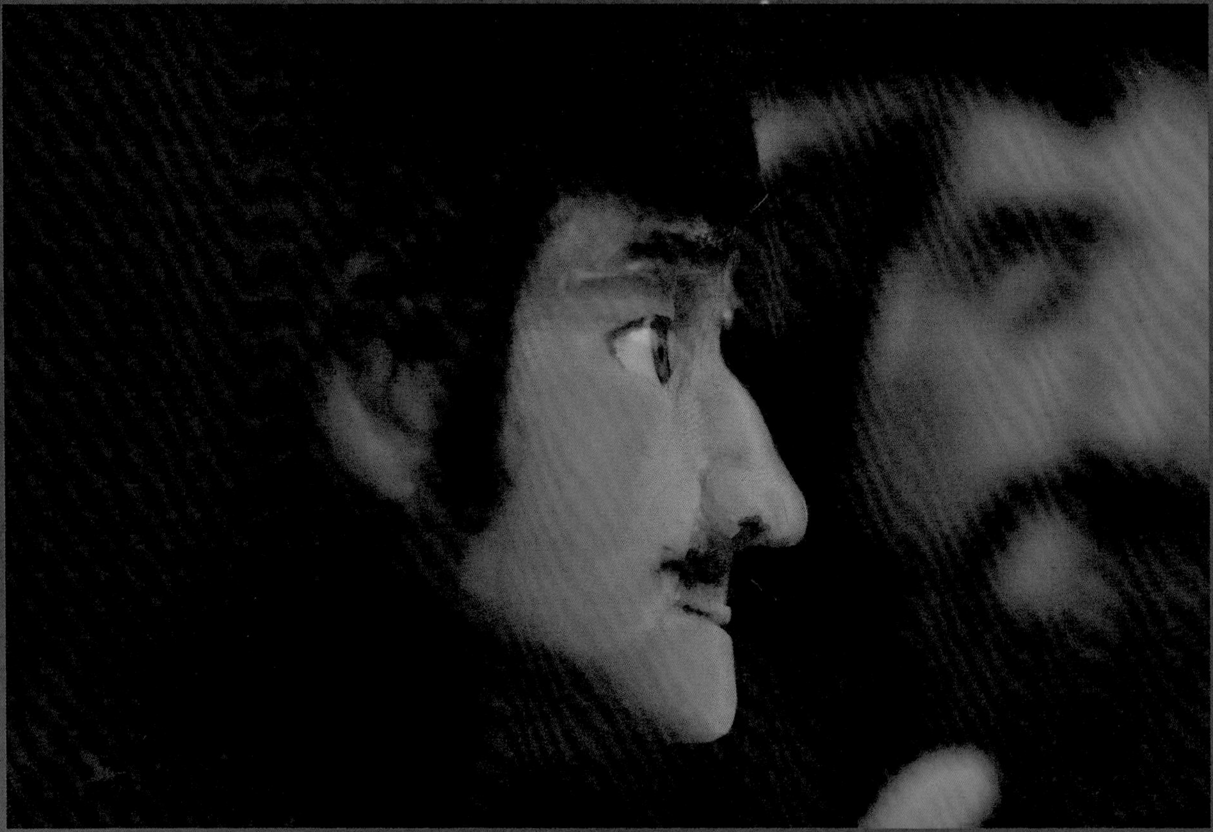

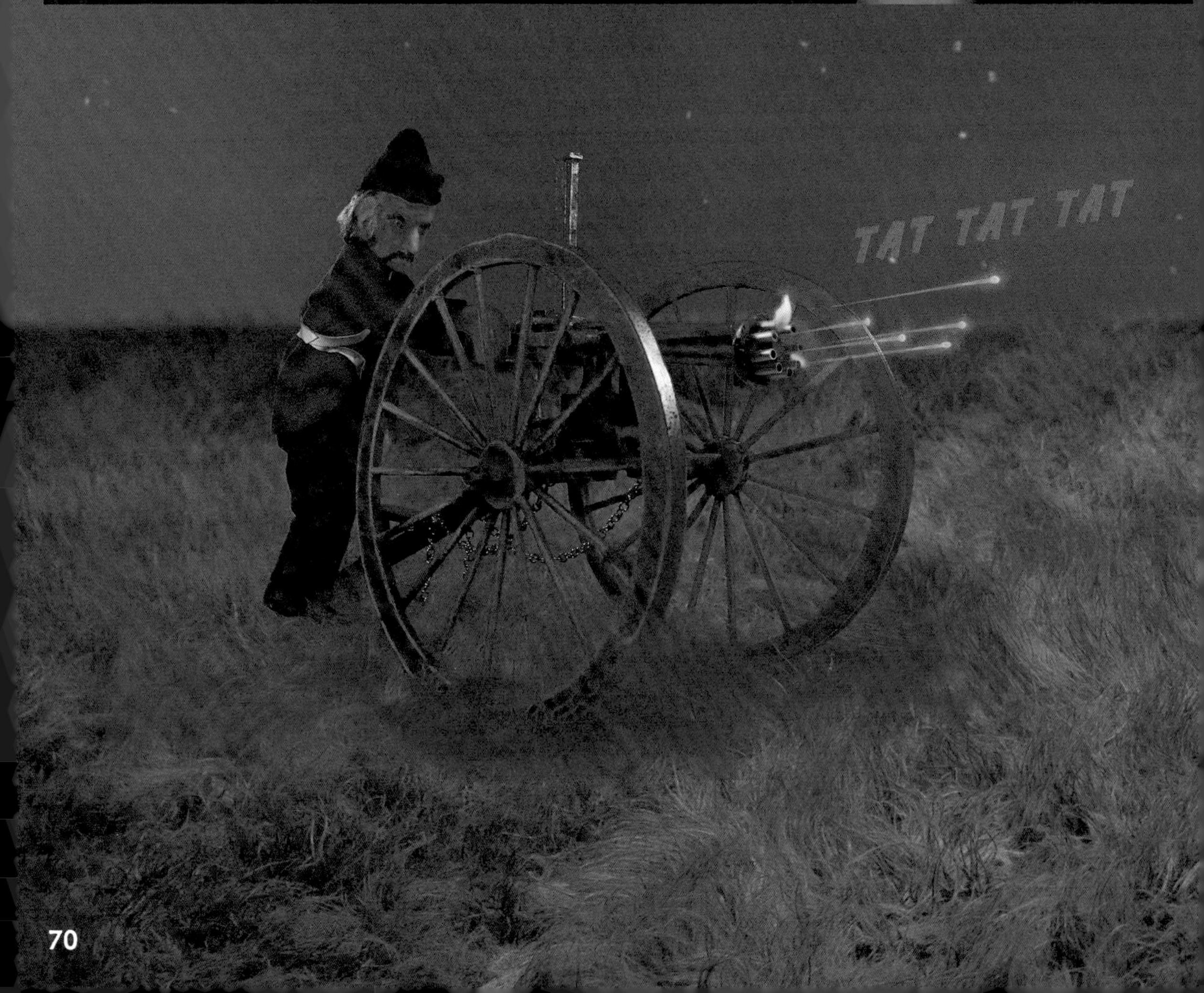
TAT TAT TAT

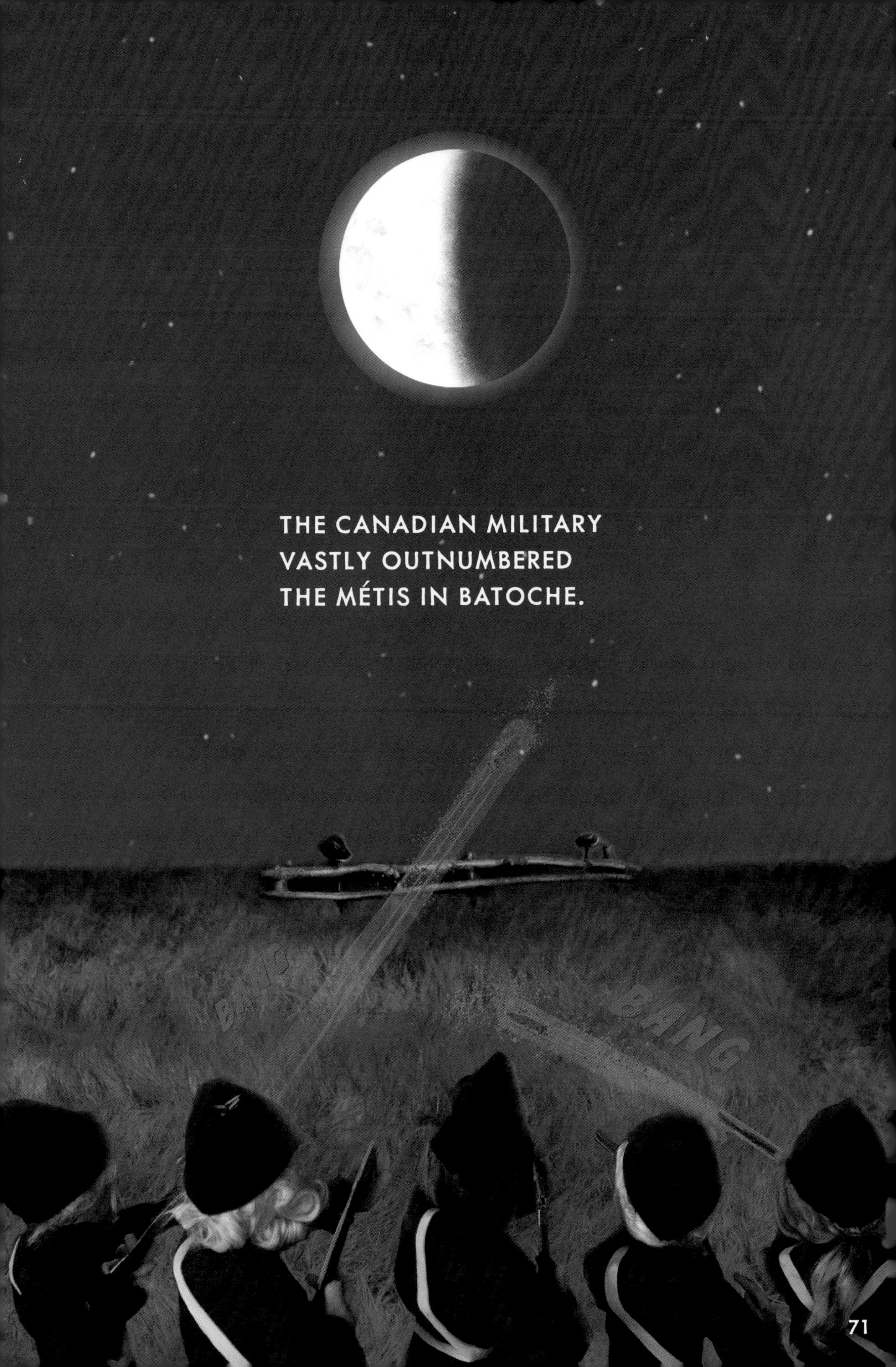
THE CANADIAN MILITARY
VASTLY OUTNUMBERED
THE MÉTIS IN BATOCHE.
BANG
BANG

THE SOLDIERS SHELLED THEIR HOMES
WITH THE RAPID-FIRE GATLING GUN.

WOMEN AND CHILDREN
JOINED THE FIGHT
TO PROTECT THEIR LANDS.

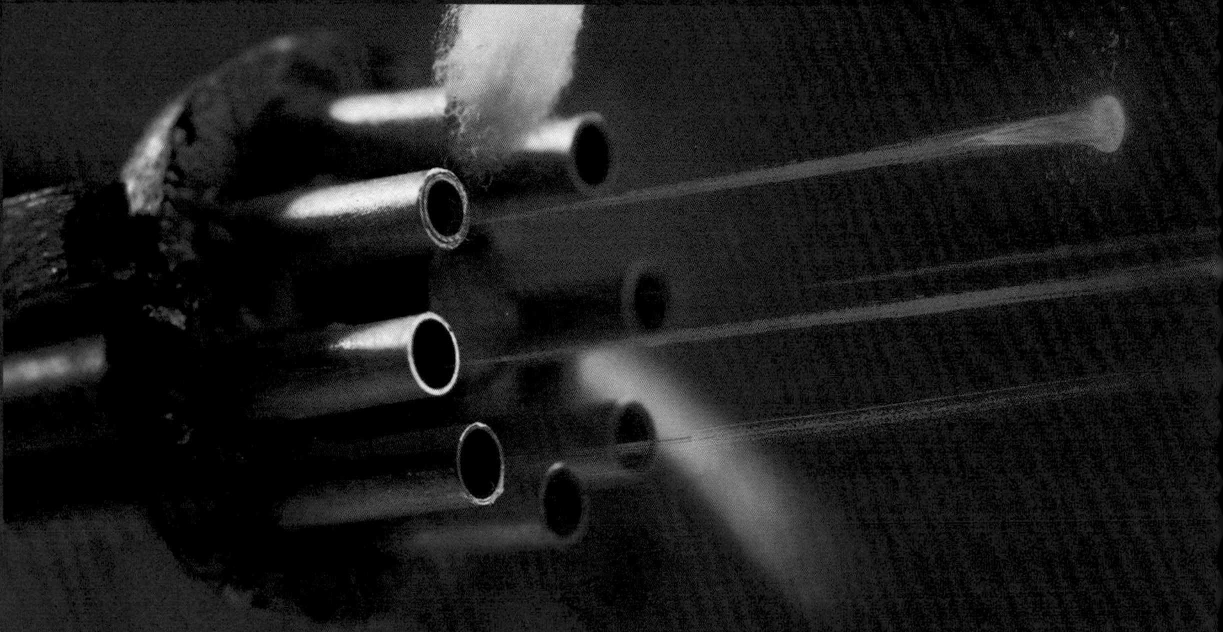

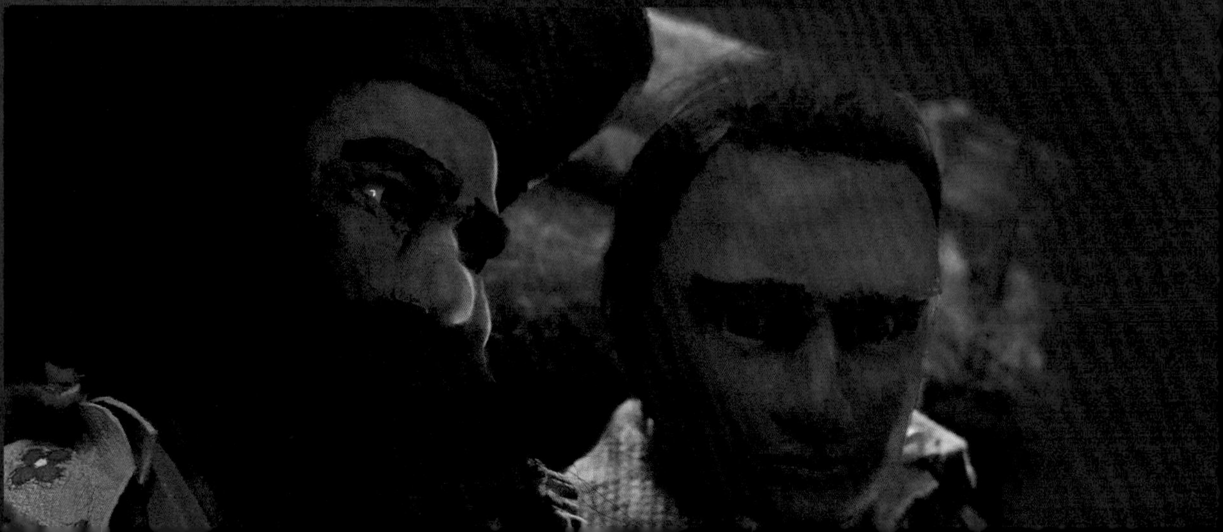

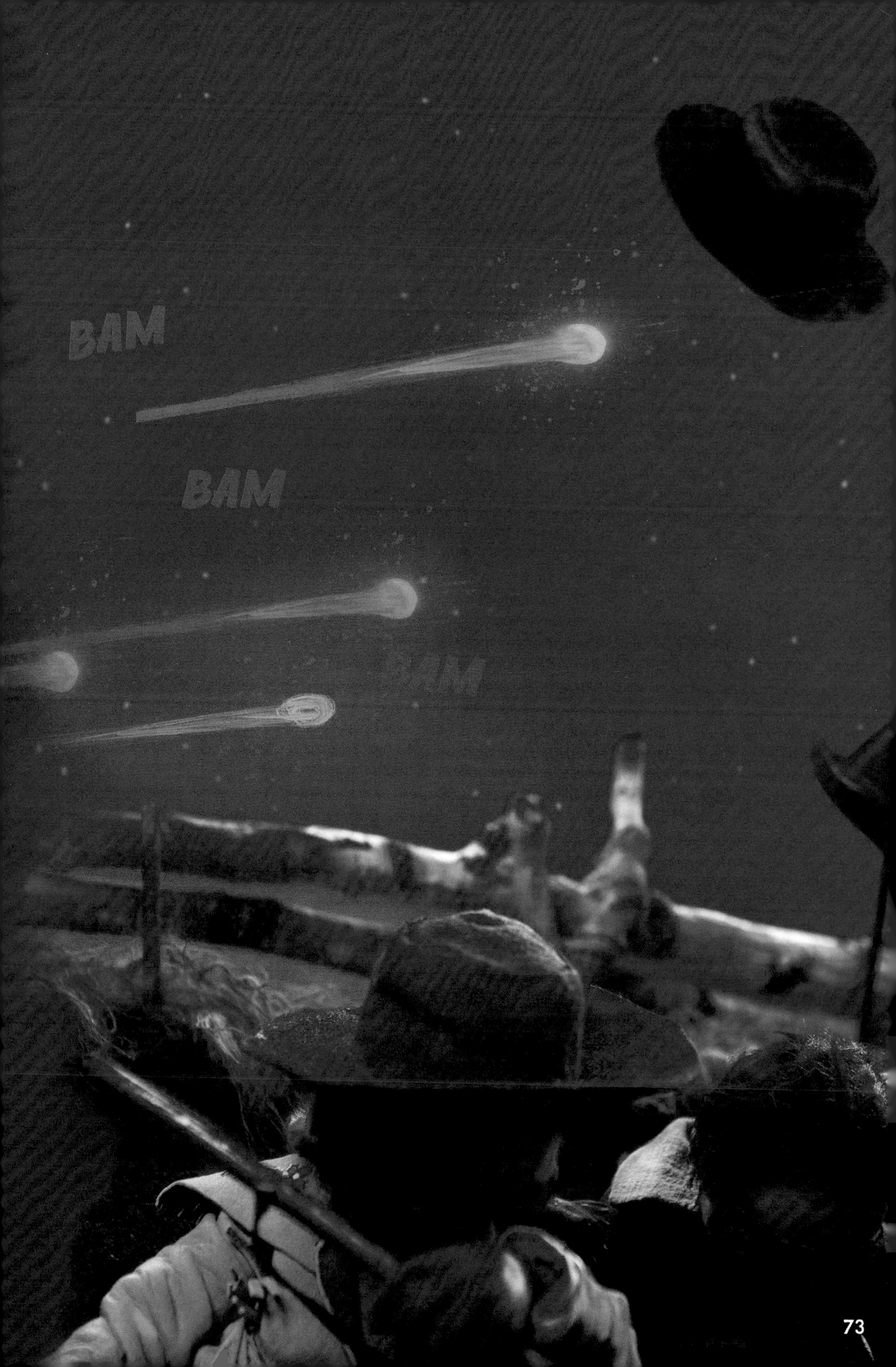
BAM
BAM
BAM

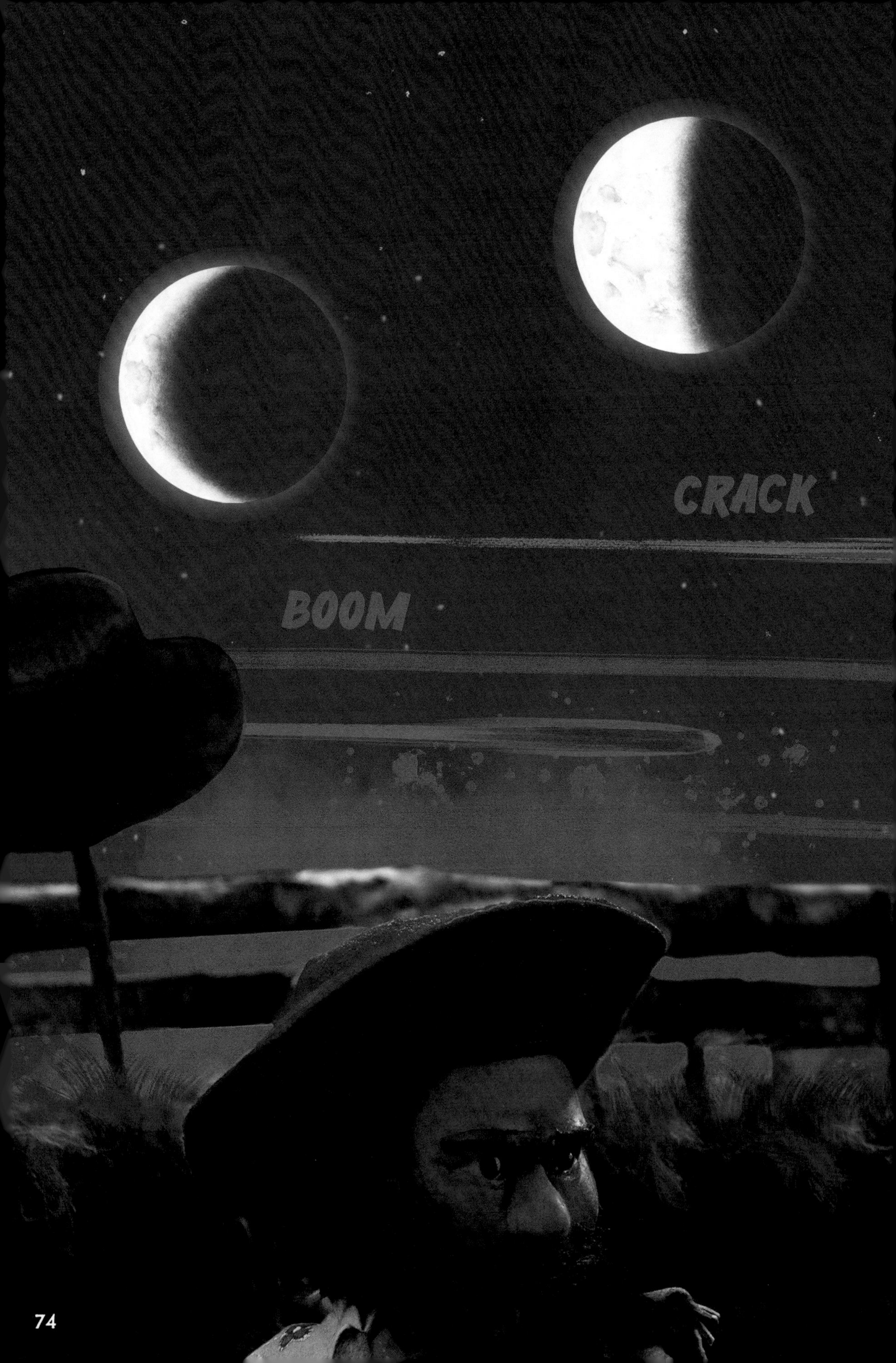
CRACK
BOOM

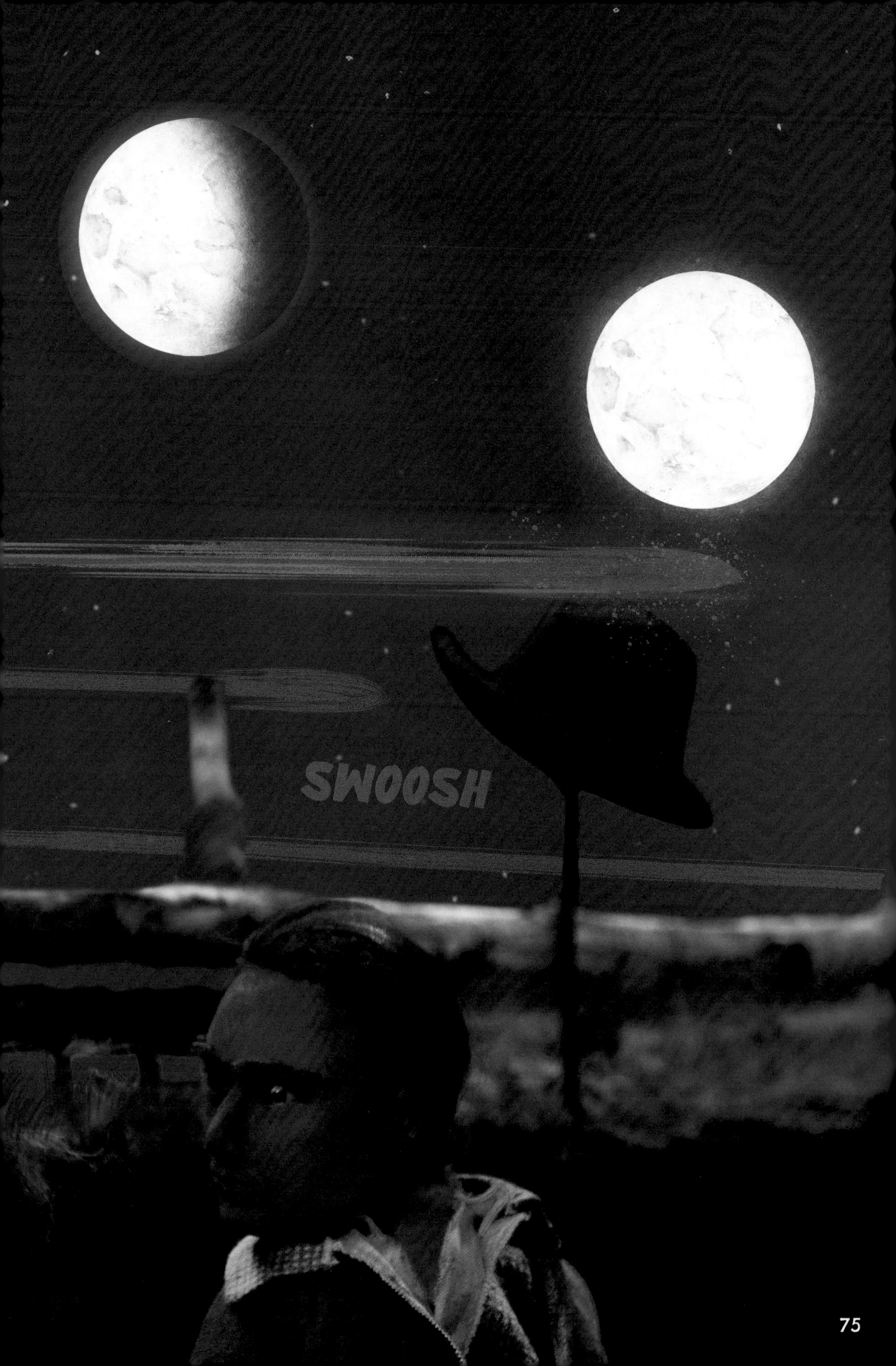
SWOOSH

FOR THREE DAYS,
THEY HUNKERED DOWN
IN THE RIFLE PIT.

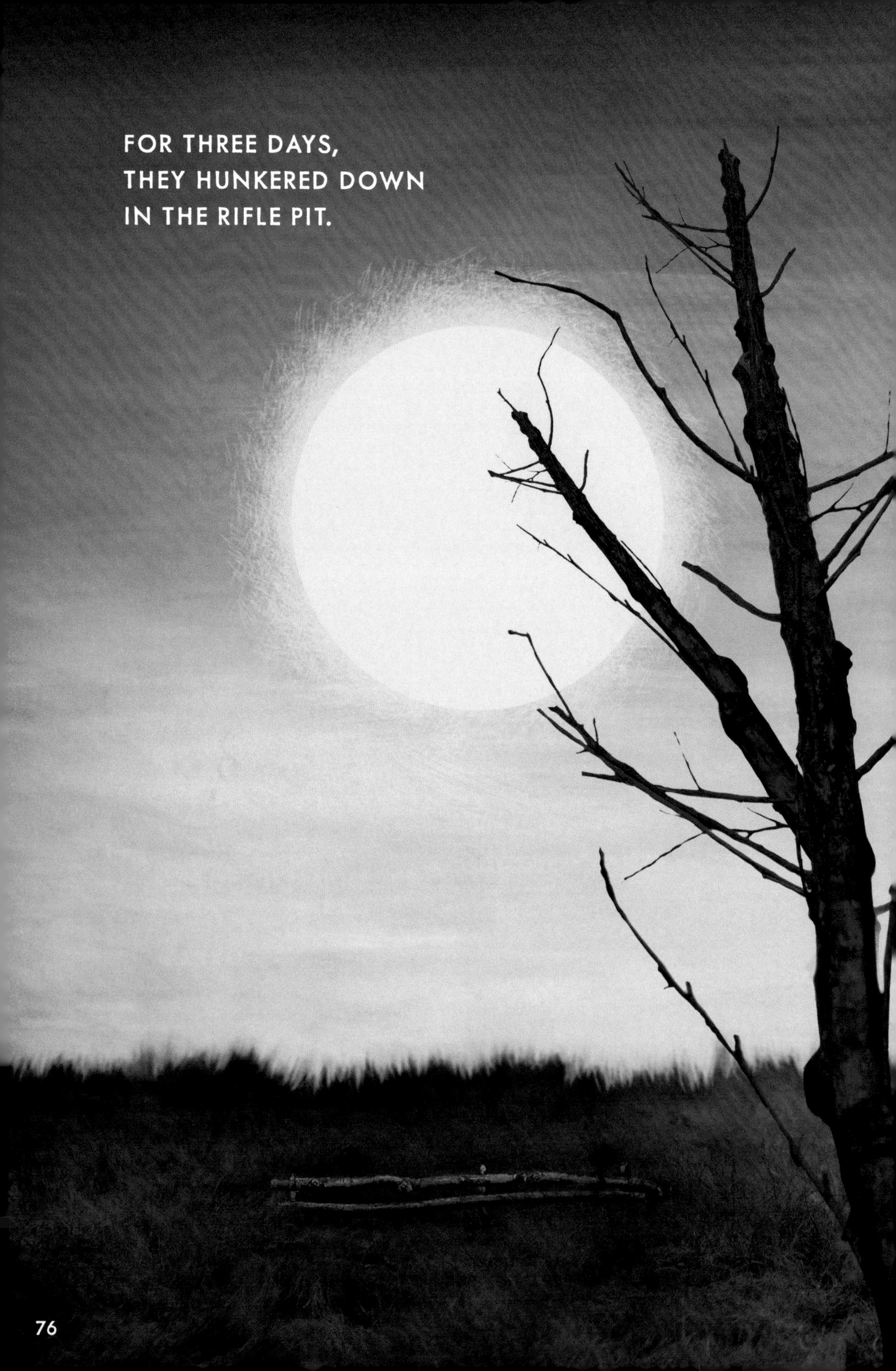

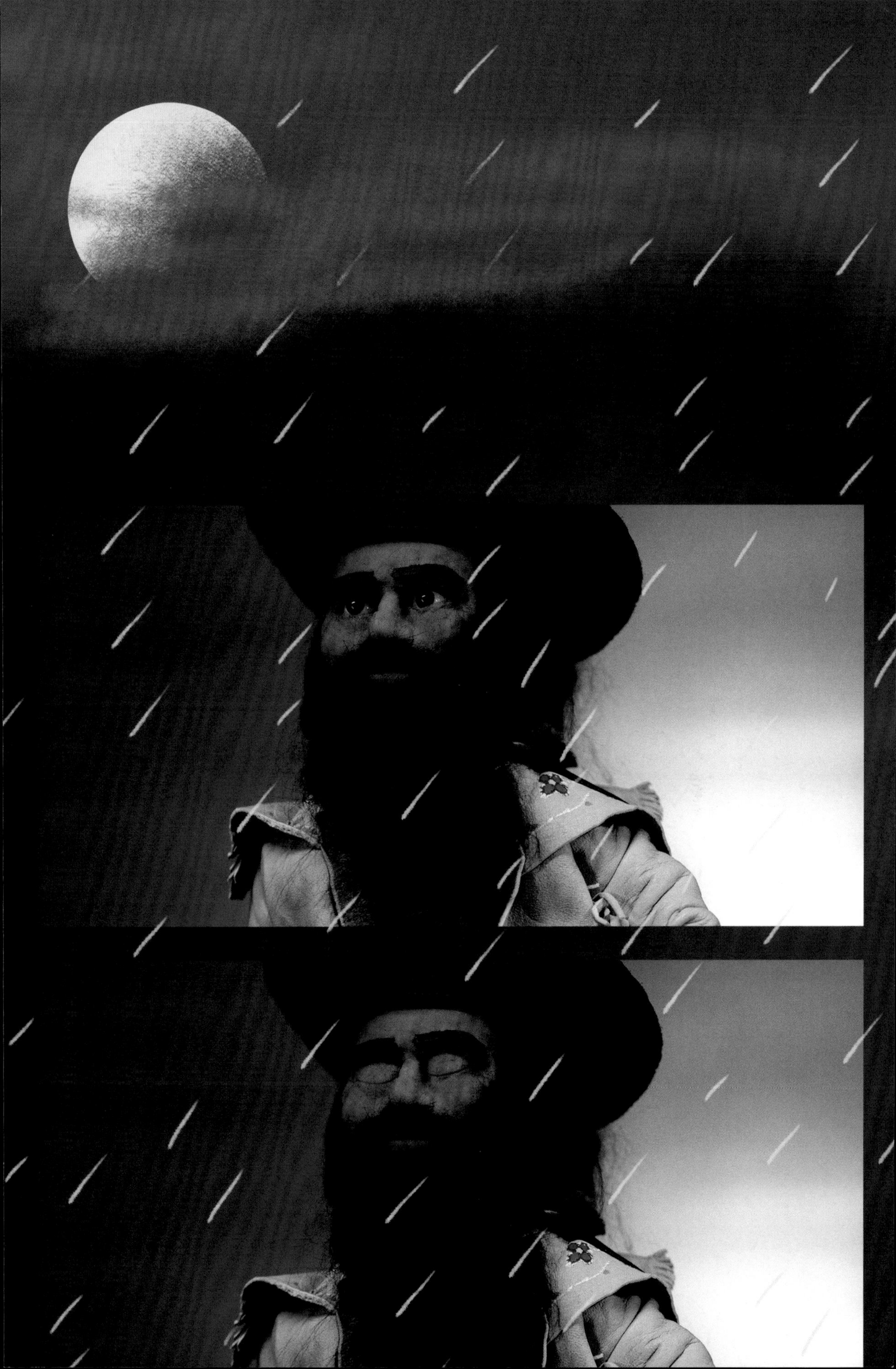

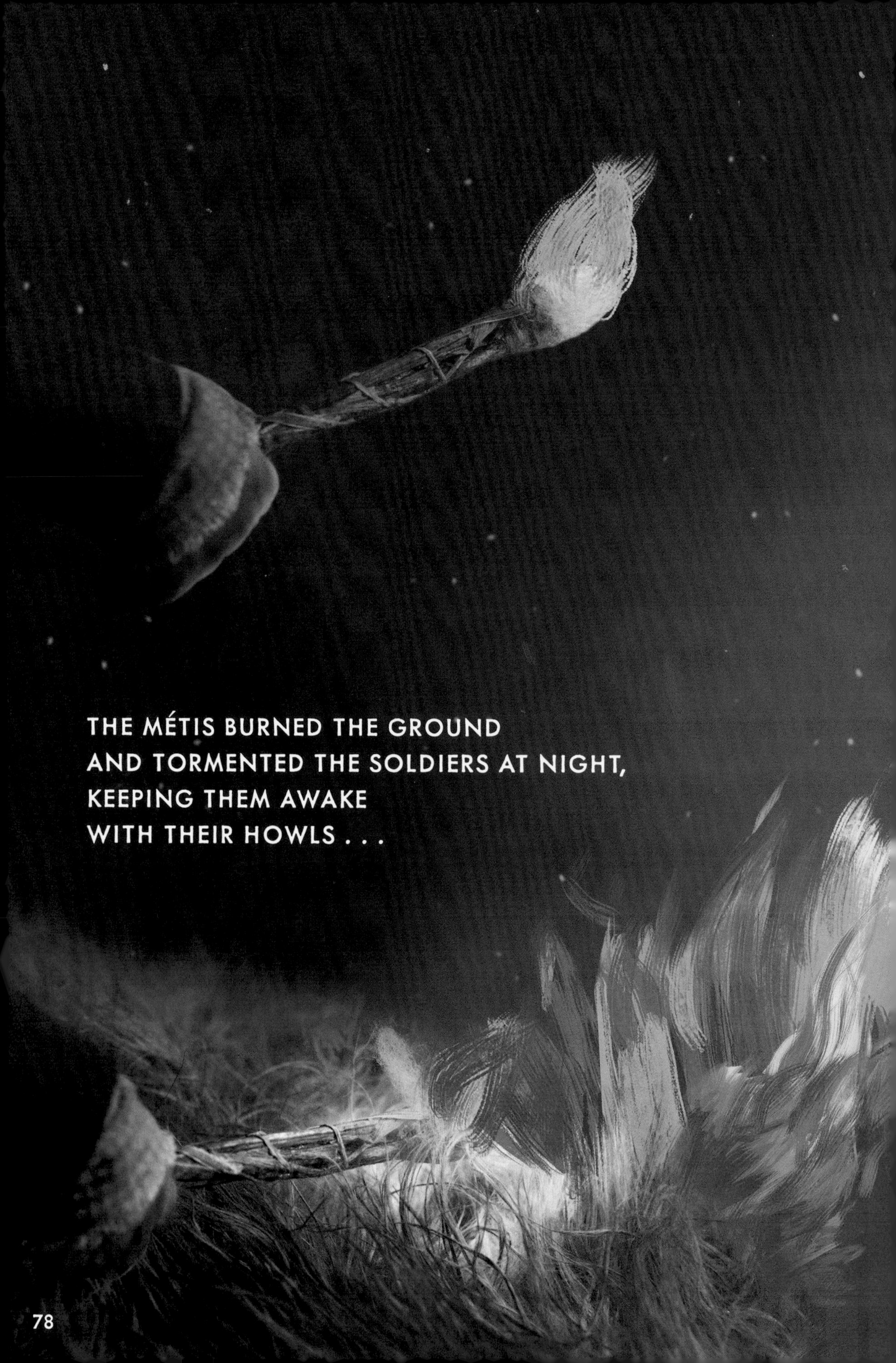

THE MÉTIS BURNED THE GROUND
AND TORMENTED THE SOLDIERS AT NIGHT,
KEEPING THEM AWAKE
WITH THEIR HOWLS . . .

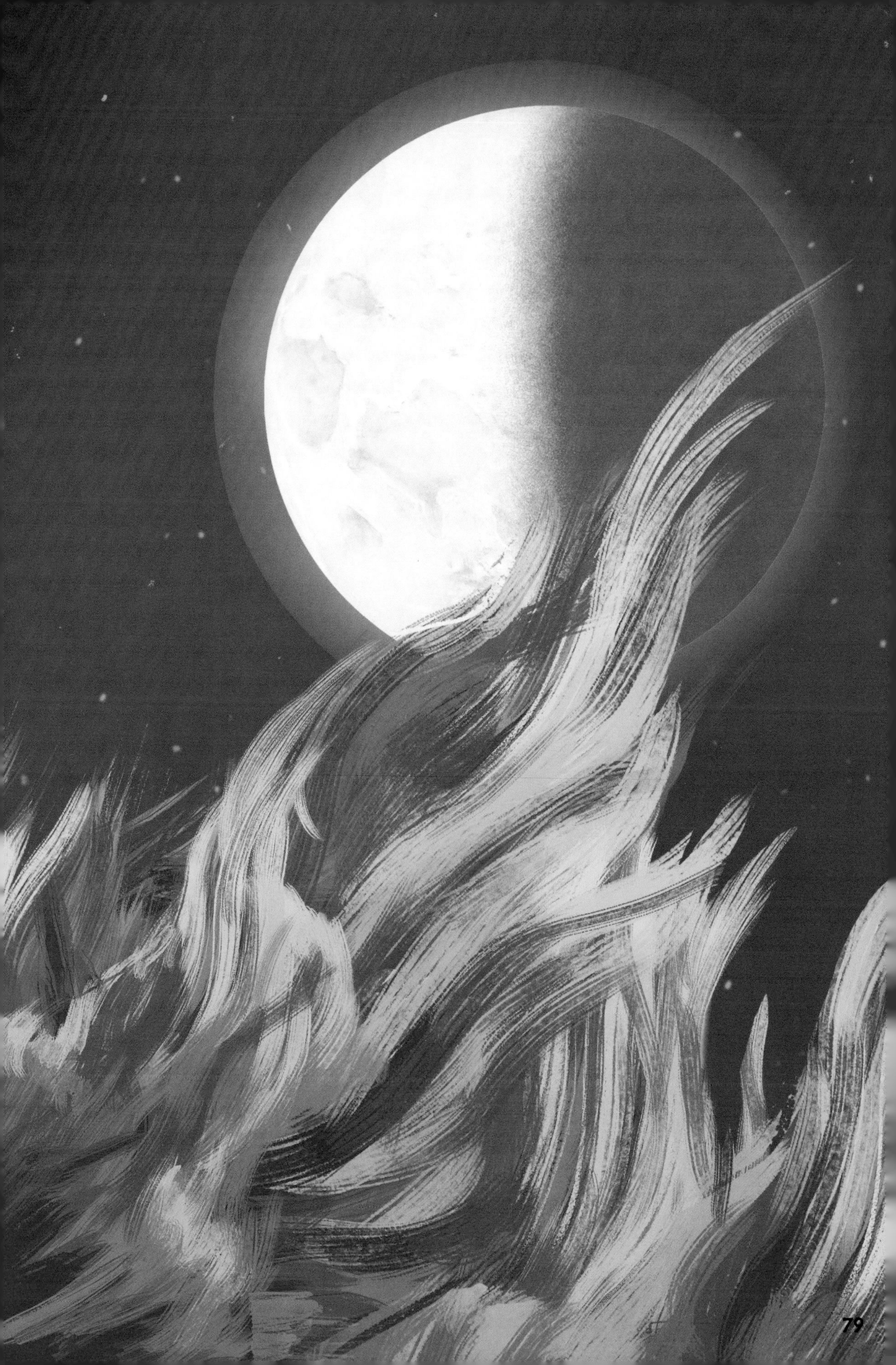

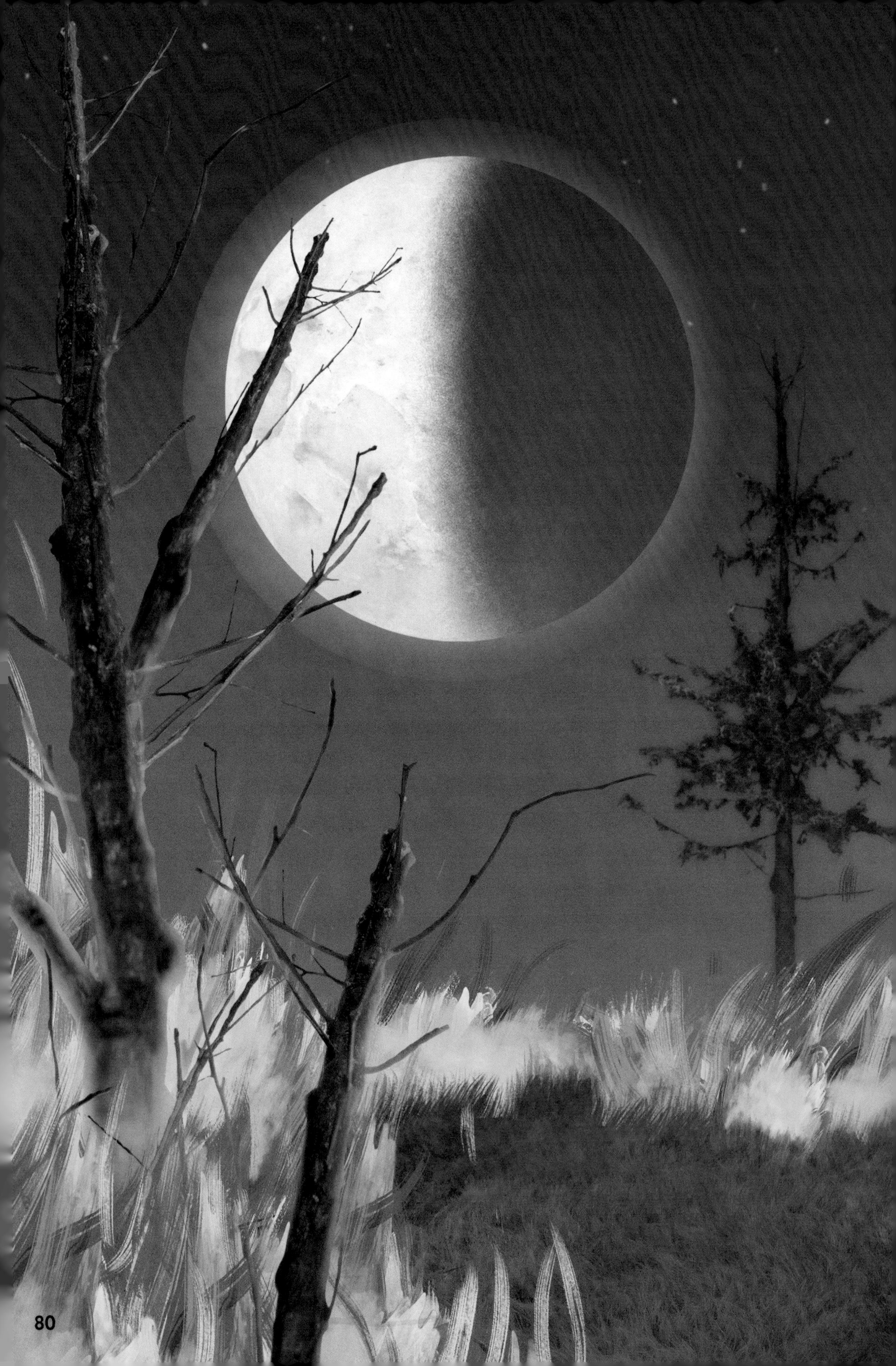

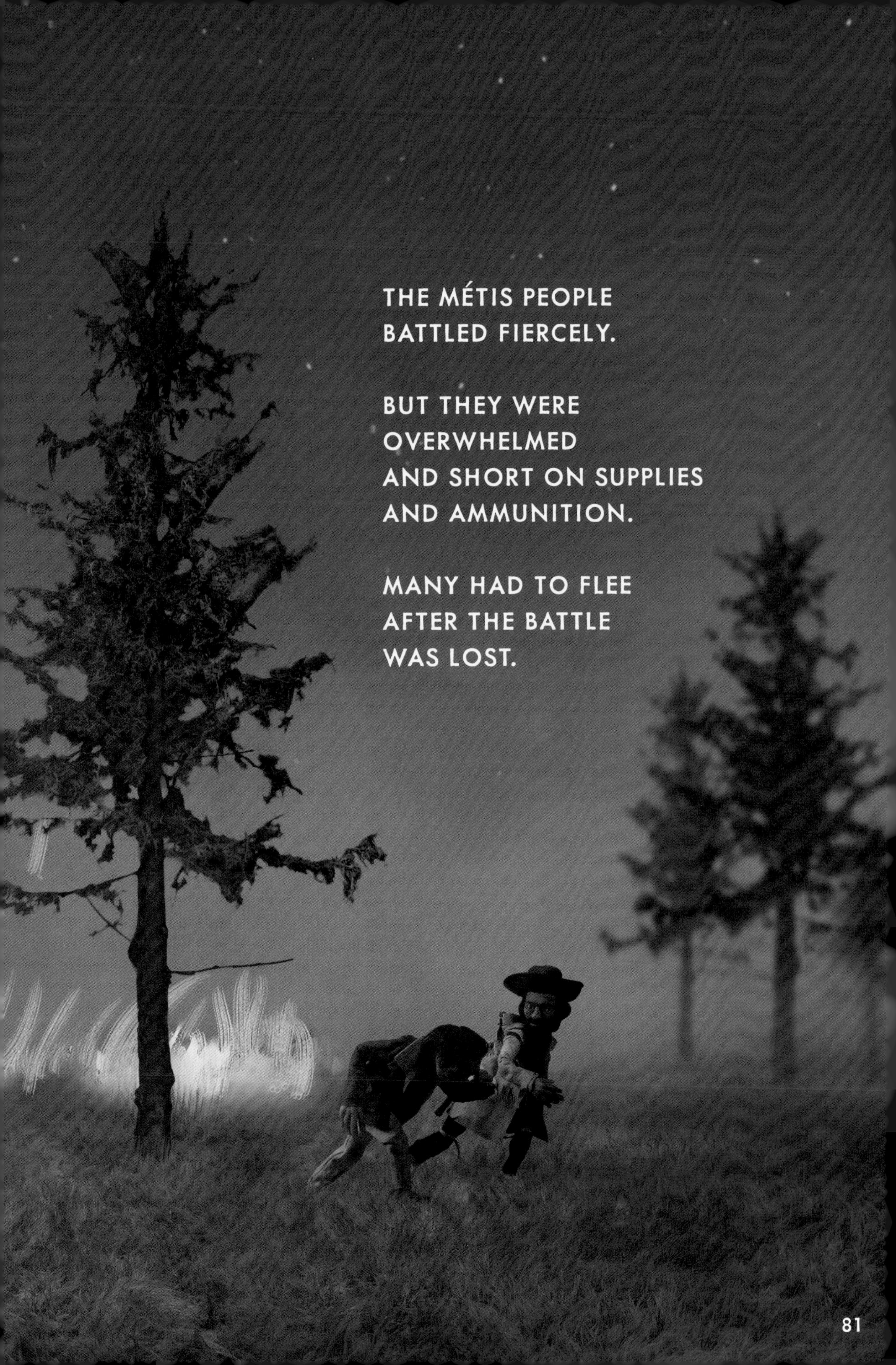

THE MÉTIS PEOPLE
BATTLED FIERCELY.

BUT THEY WERE
OVERWHELMED
AND SHORT ON SUPPLIES
AND AMMUNITION.

MANY HAD TO FLEE
AFTER THE BATTLE
WAS LOST.

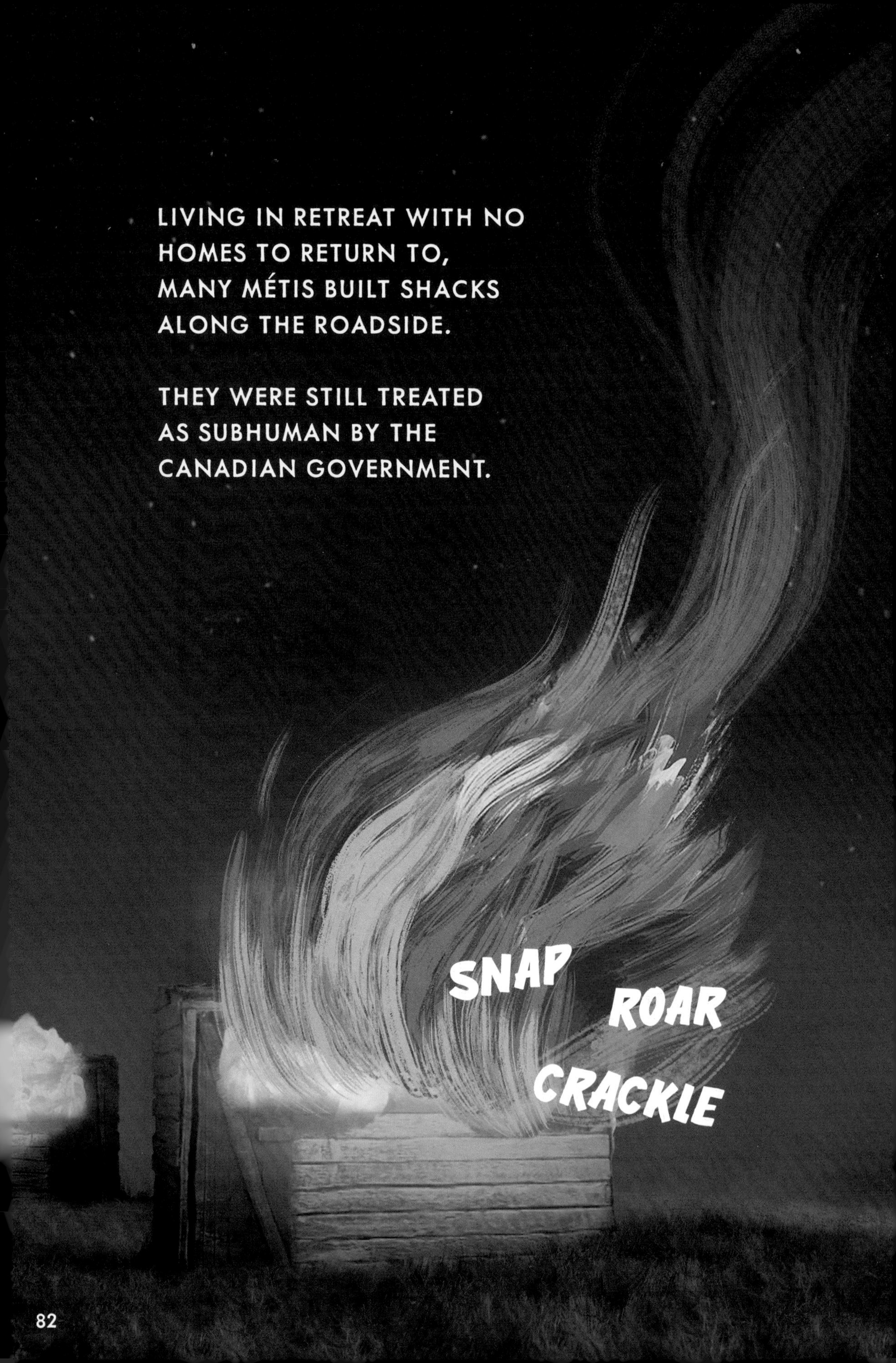
LIVING IN RETREAT WITH NO HOMES TO RETURN TO, MANY MÉTIS BUILT SHACKS ALONG THE ROADSIDE.
THEY WERE STILL TREATED AS SUBHUMAN BY THE CANADIAN GOVERNMENT.
SNAP
ROAR
CRACKLE

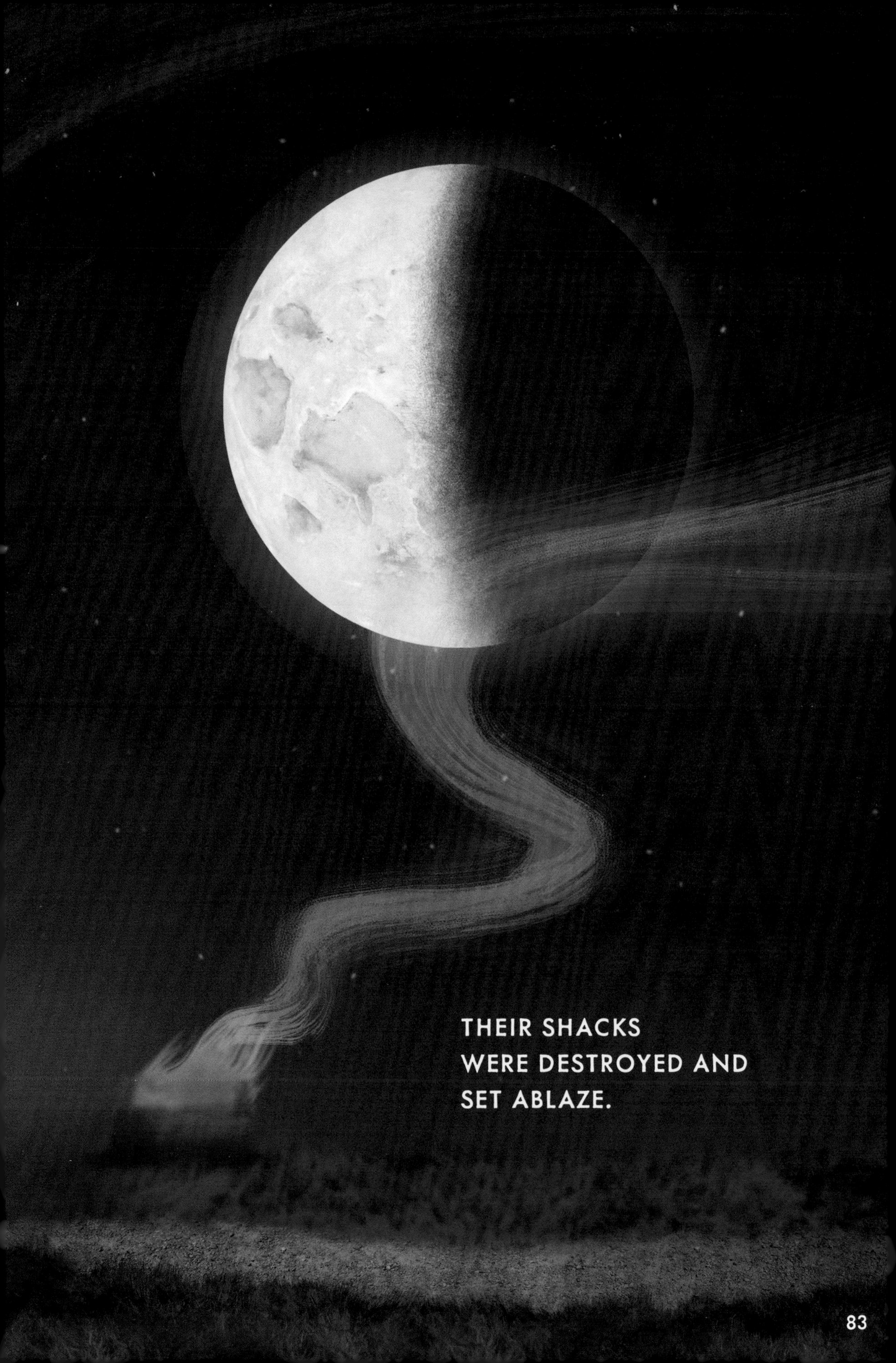

THEIR SHACKS
WERE DESTROYED AND
SET ABLAZE.

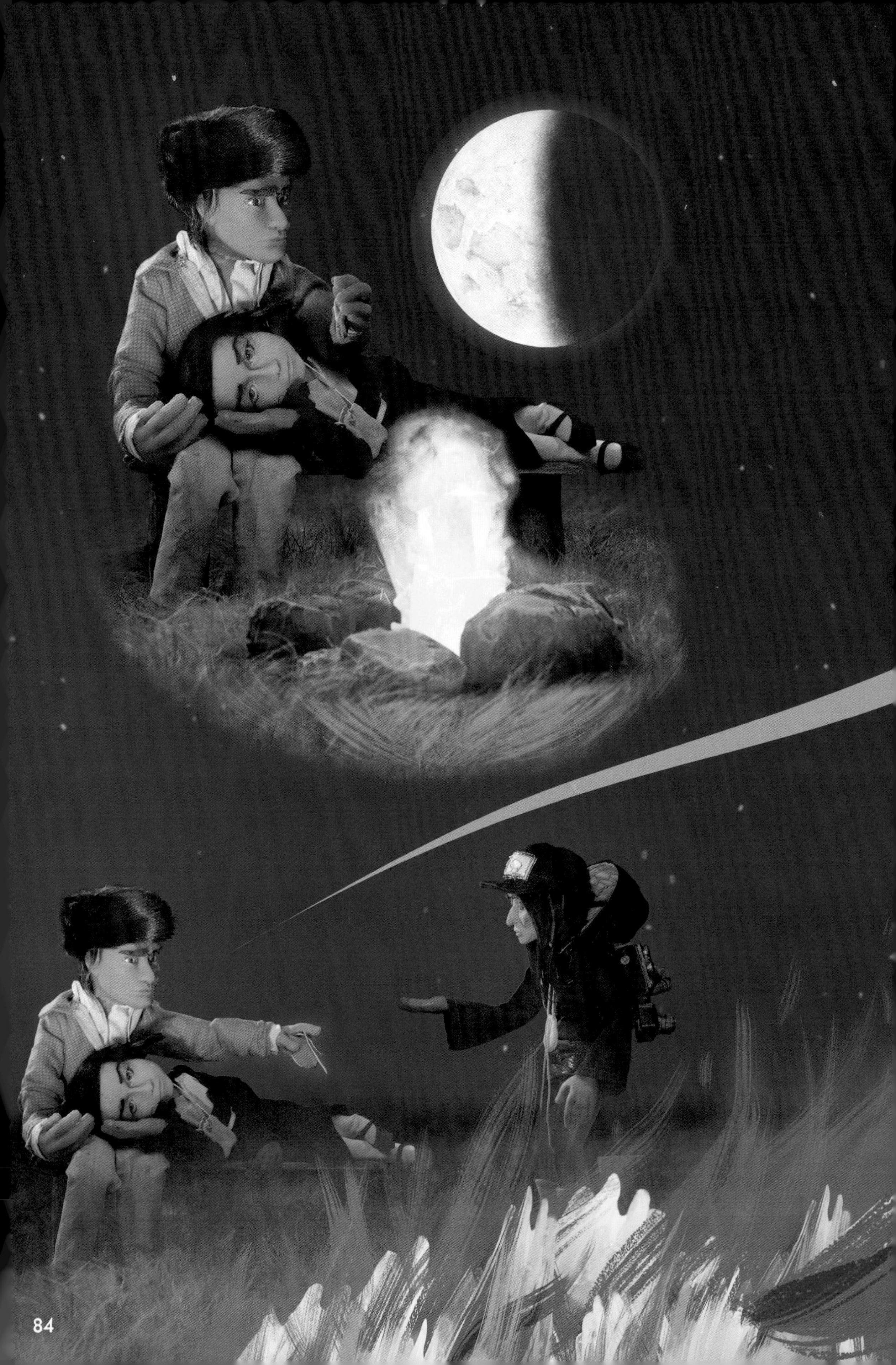

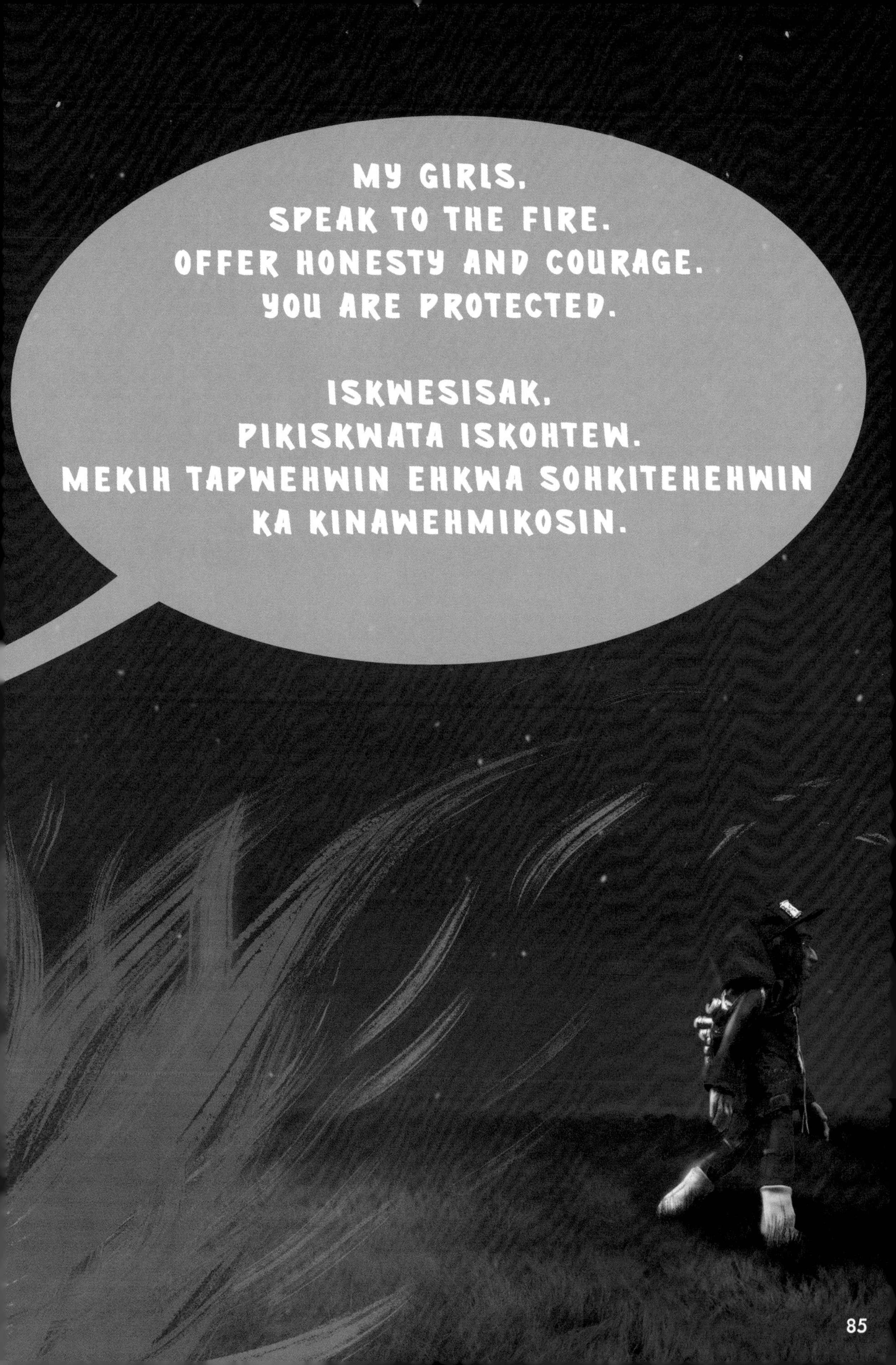
MY GIRLS.
SPEAK TO THE FIRE.
OFFER HONESTY AND COURAGE.
YOU ARE PROTECTED.
ISKWESISAK.
PIKISKWATA ISKOHTEW.
MEKIH TAPWEHWIN EHKWA SOHKITEHEHWIN
KA KINAWEHMIKOSIN.

CHAPTER THREE
THREE-QUARTER MOON

VICTORY WAS LEFT
UNSATISFIED, UNSAVORY.
THEY WOULD NOT STOP
UNTIL EVERYTHING BECAME
UNRECOGNIZABLE, UNBALANCED.
ENEMY CRUSHED,
FLEEING INTO THE COSTUME OF SURVIVAL.

Ó'OHIYE
WACĮ'IYÓGIPIBIŠĮ, IYÓGIŠIJA
ĮNÁŽĮBIŠĮ
ŽEHÁGEH OWÁ
IYÉGIYEPIJAŠĮ, OŠÍJAGA
TÓGA WĮCÁGASÓDABI
WÓKOYAGE NÍBI STÉH ONÁPABI

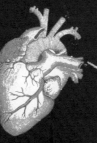

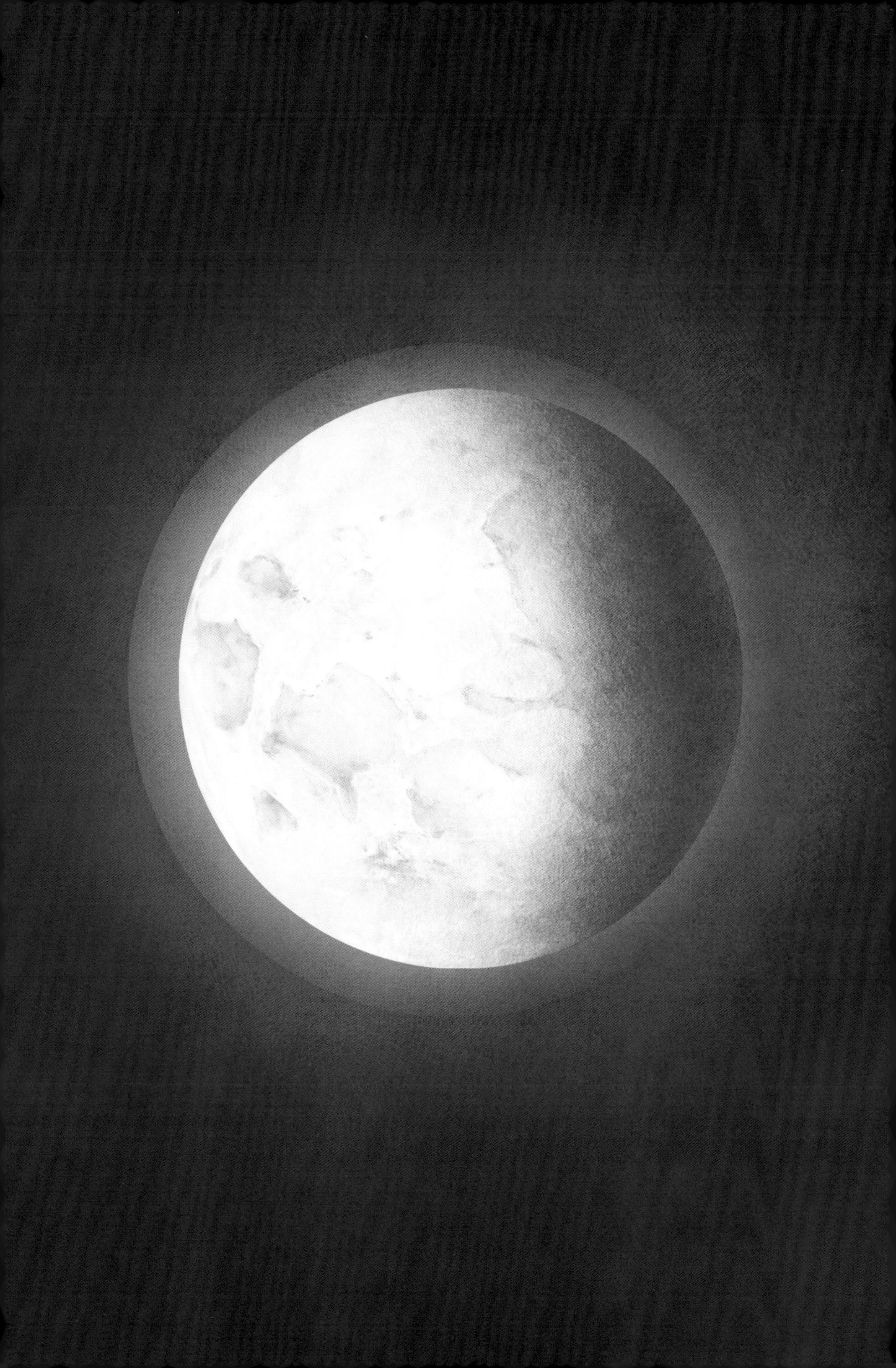

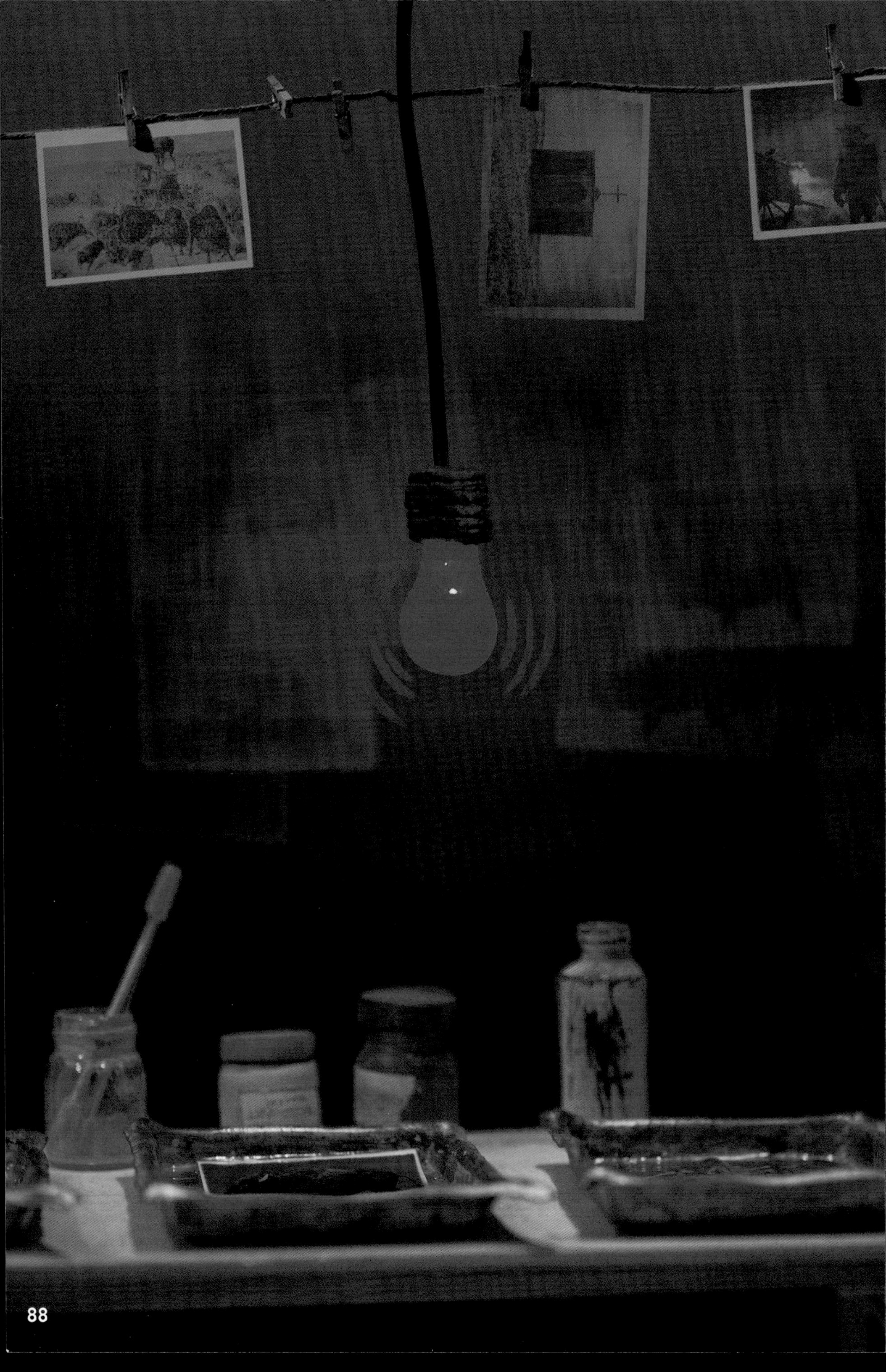

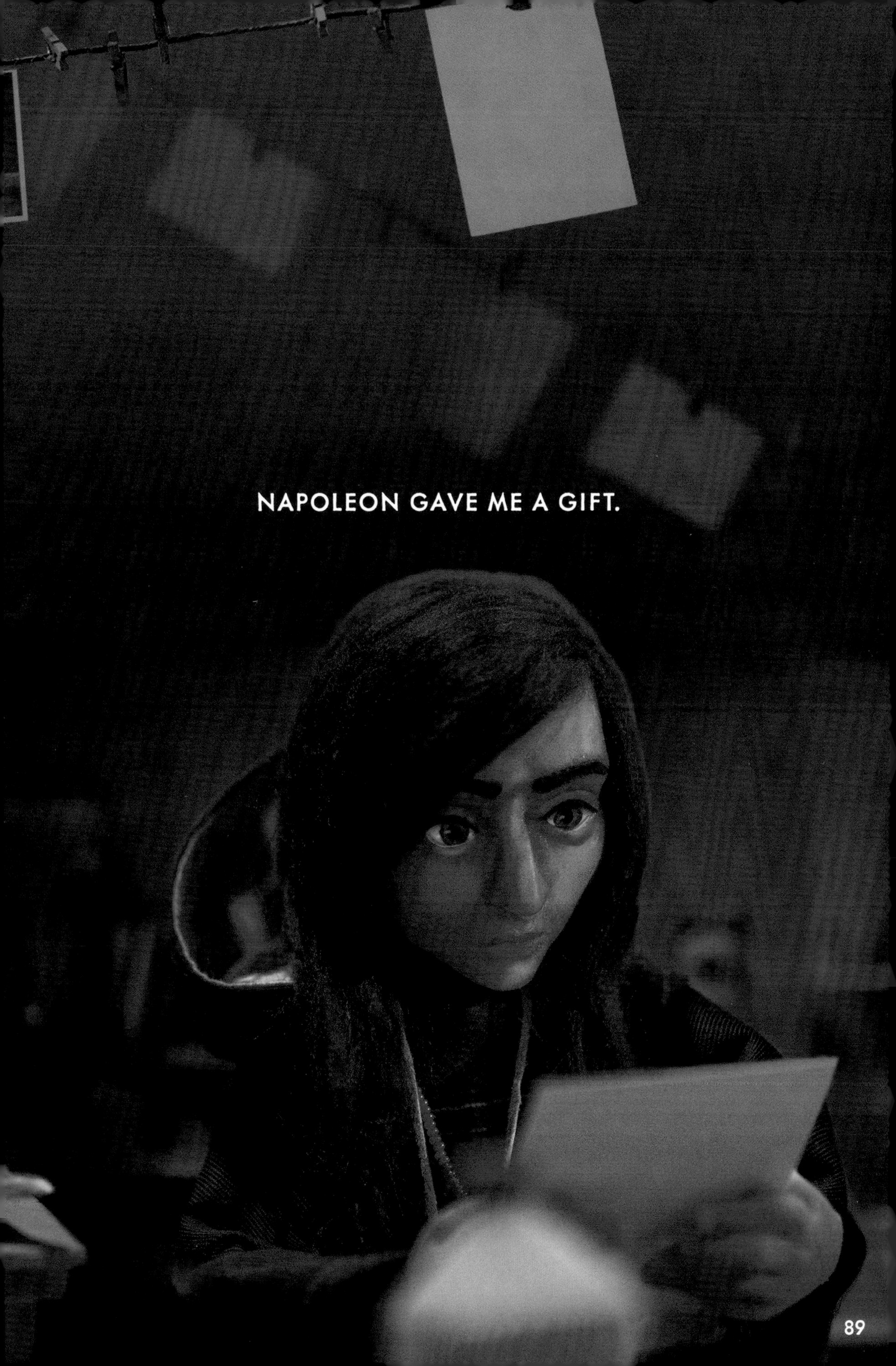
NAPOLEON GAVE ME A GIFT.

HE IS MY PROTECTOR AND TEACHER.

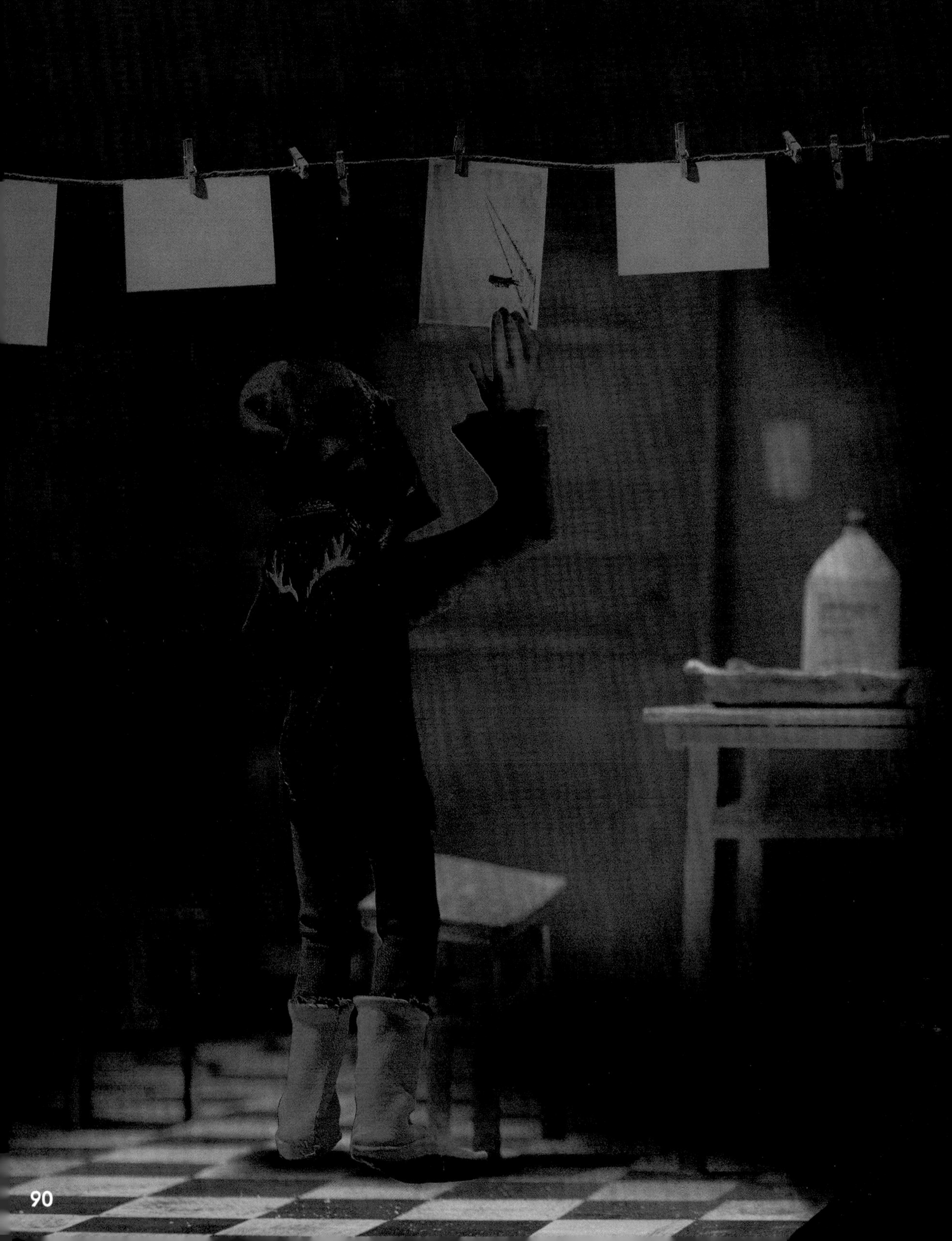

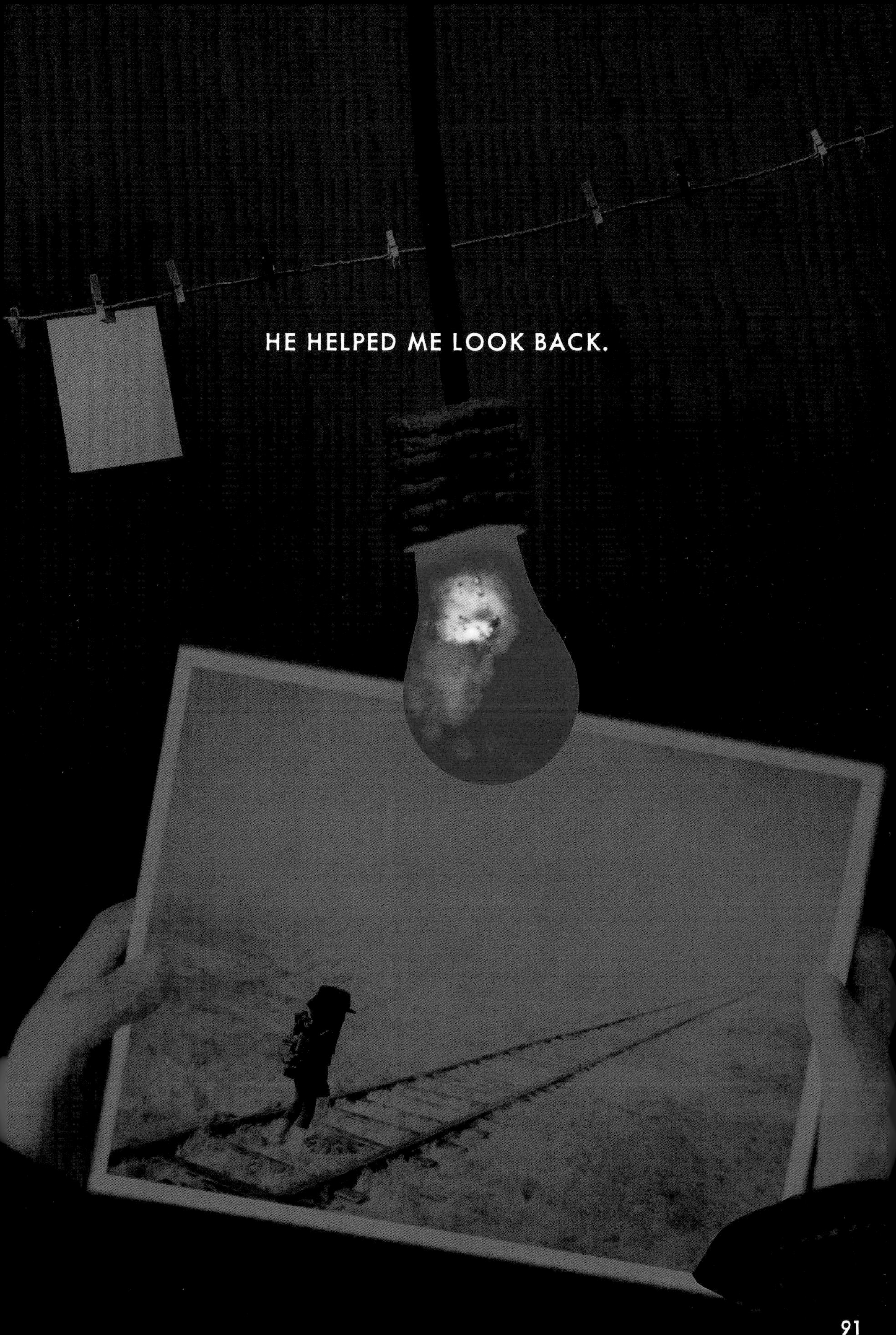
HE HELPED ME LOOK BACK.

SASKATCHEWAN

1880

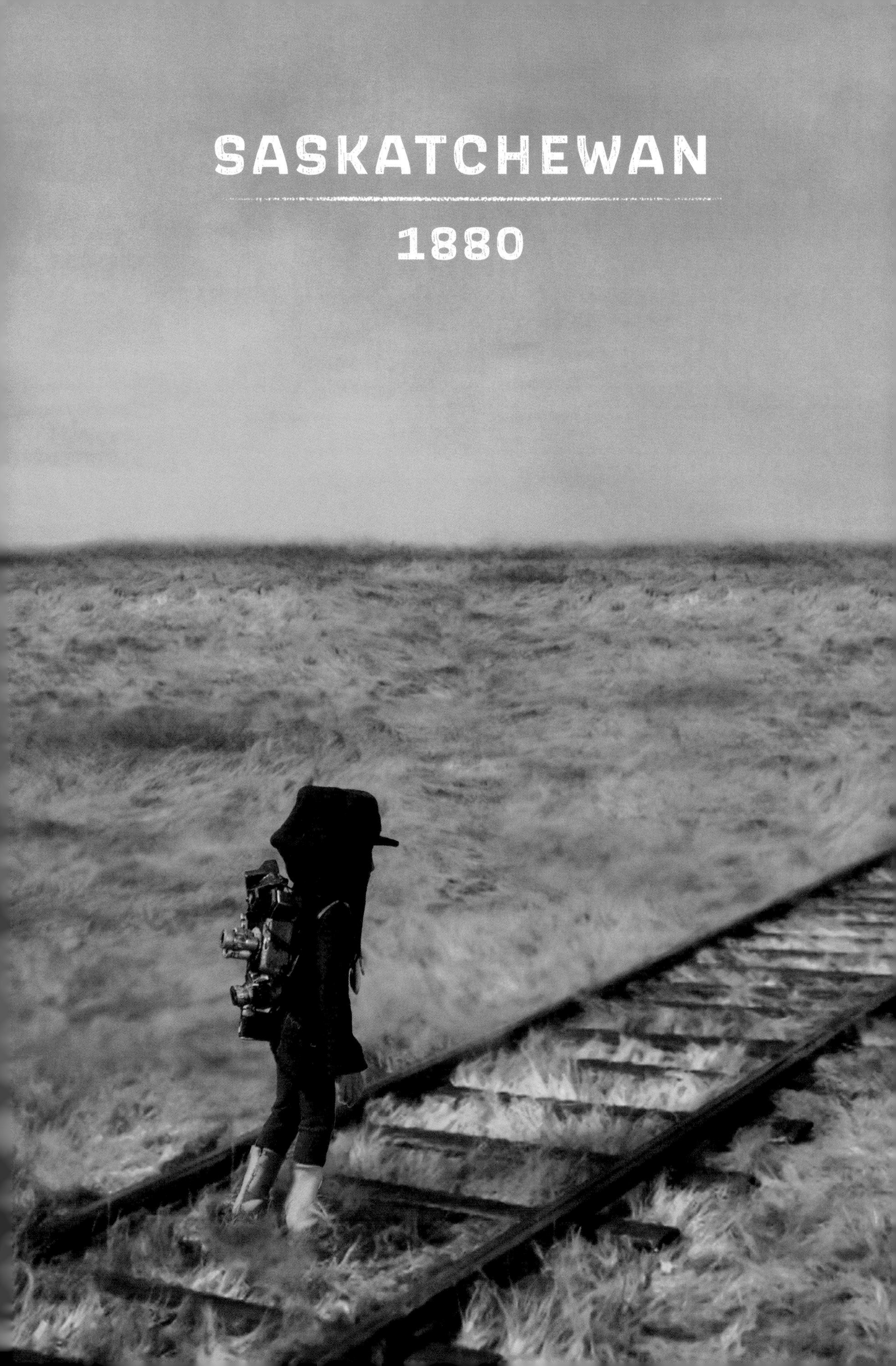

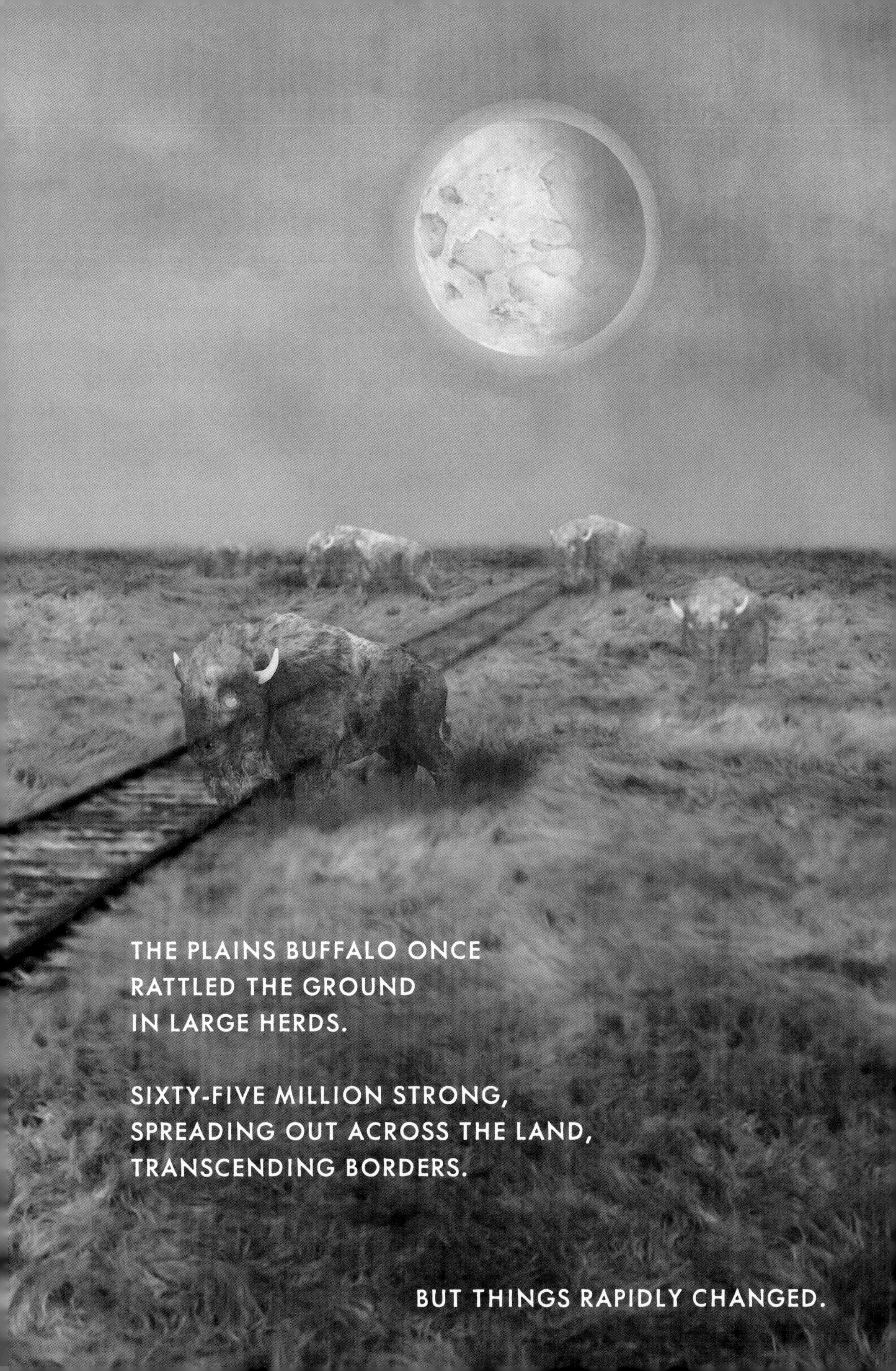

THE PLAINS BUFFALO ONCE
RATTLED THE GROUND
IN LARGE HERDS.

SIXTY-FIVE MILLION STRONG,
SPREADING OUT ACROSS THE LAND,
TRANSCENDING BORDERS.

BUT THINGS RAPIDLY CHANGED.

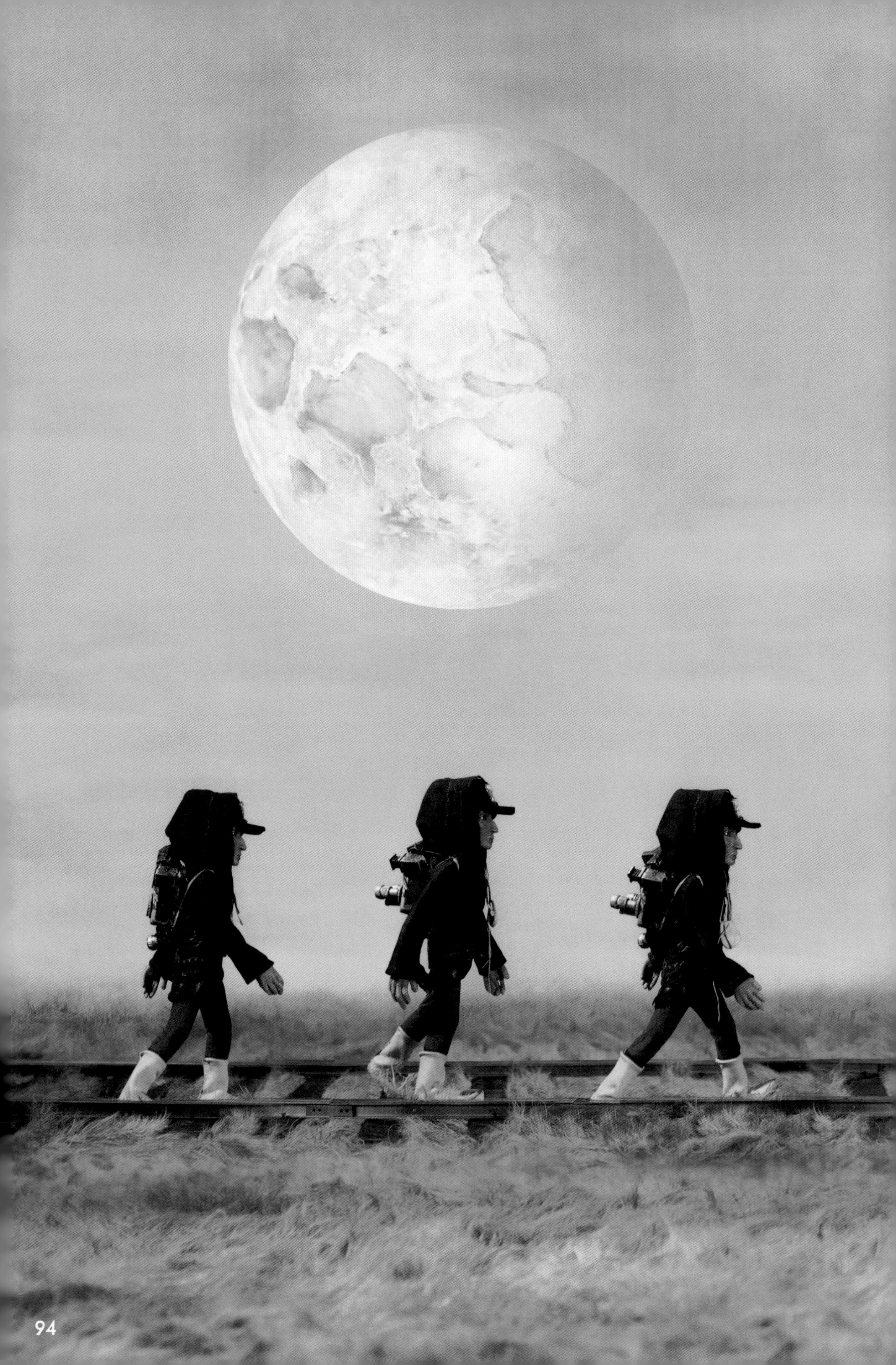

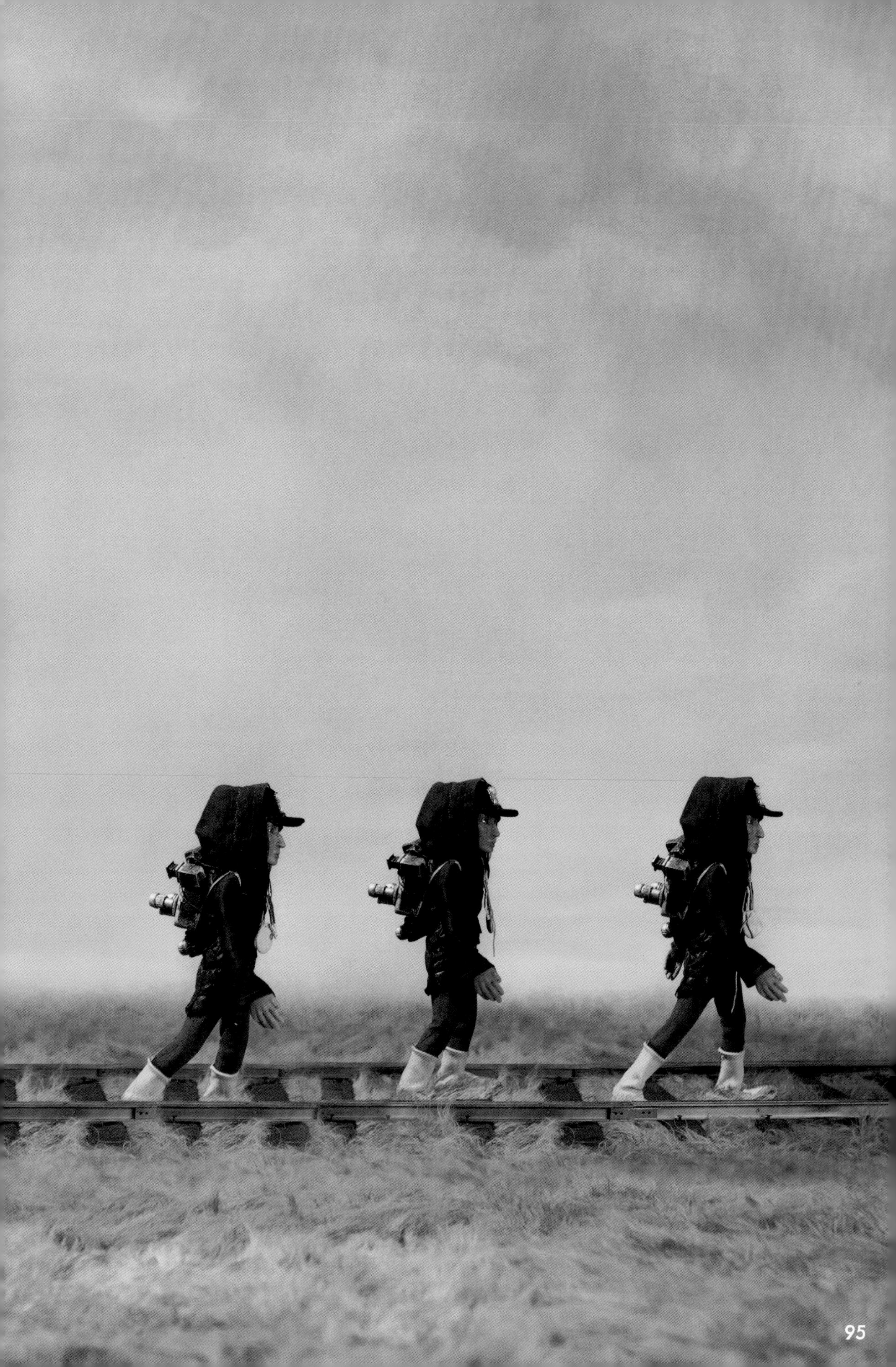

MÉTIS MEN WERE HIRED
TO CLEAN UP THE BONES
THAT COVERED THE PRAIRIES.

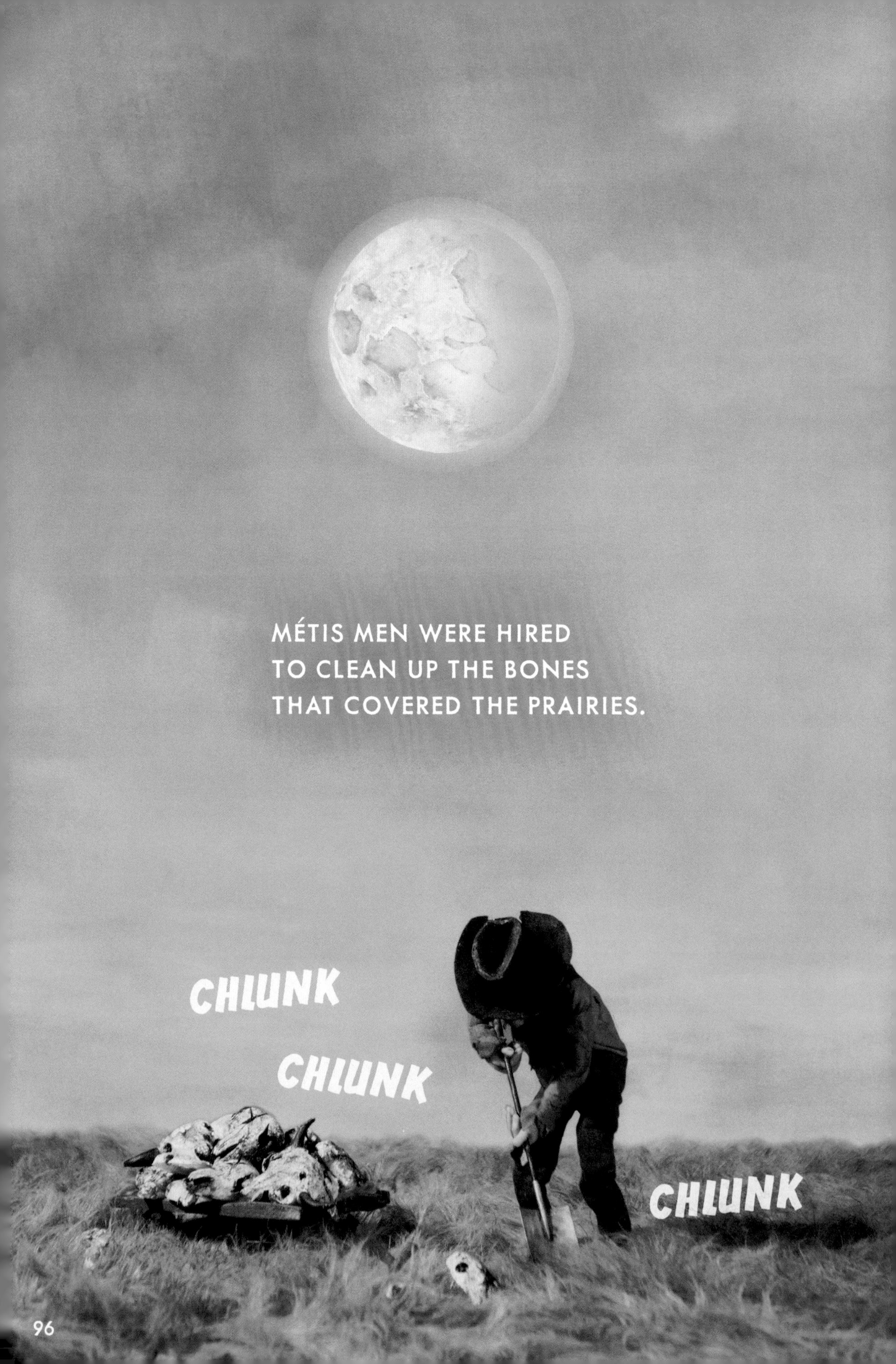
CHLUNK
CHLUNK
CHLUNK

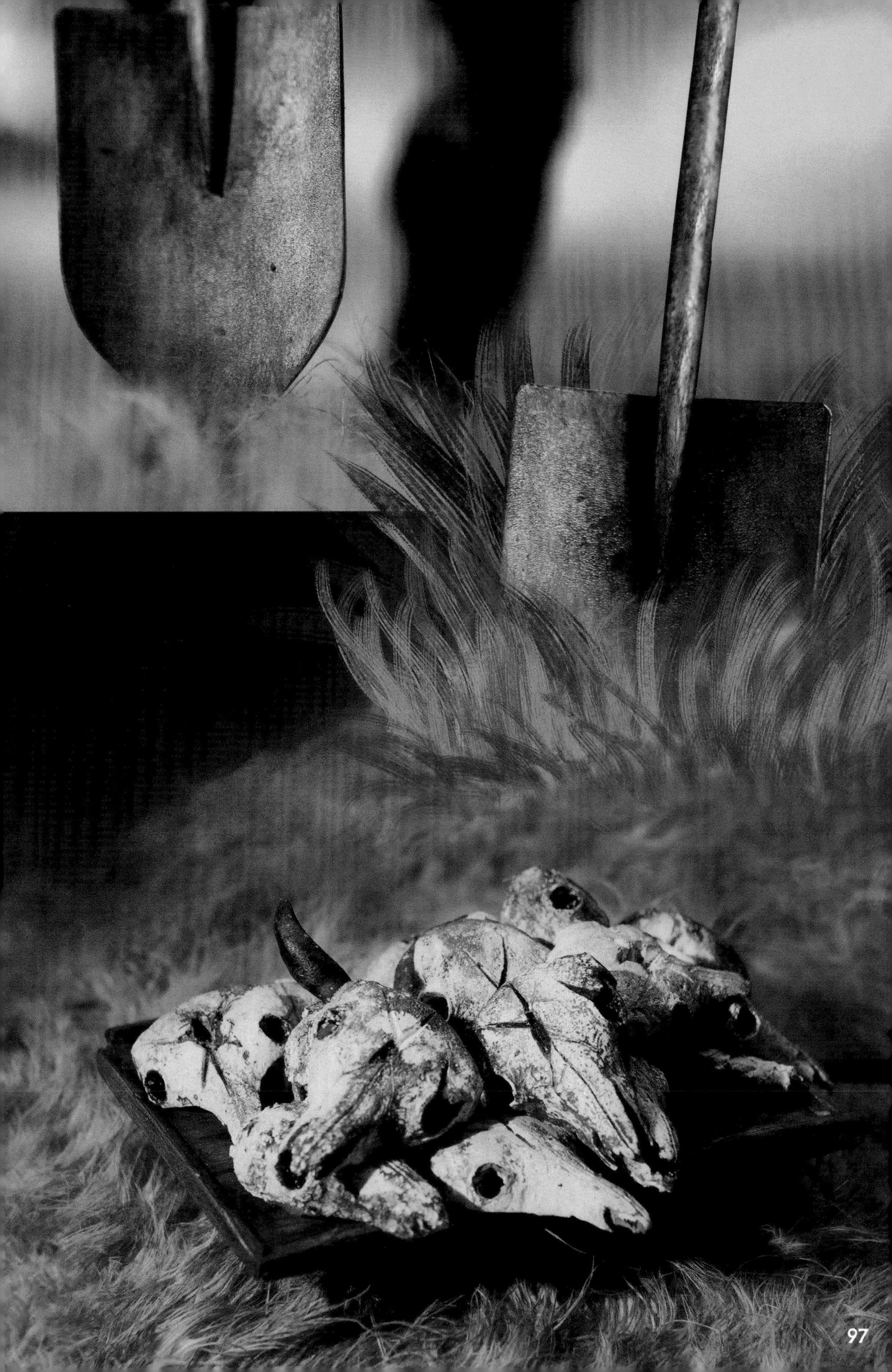

WHEN I AM OUT ON THE LAND,
I THINK ABOUT THE BUFFALO
STORMING ACROSS THE EARTH.
THEIR SPIRITS MOVING
IN RHYTHM ACROSS TIME.

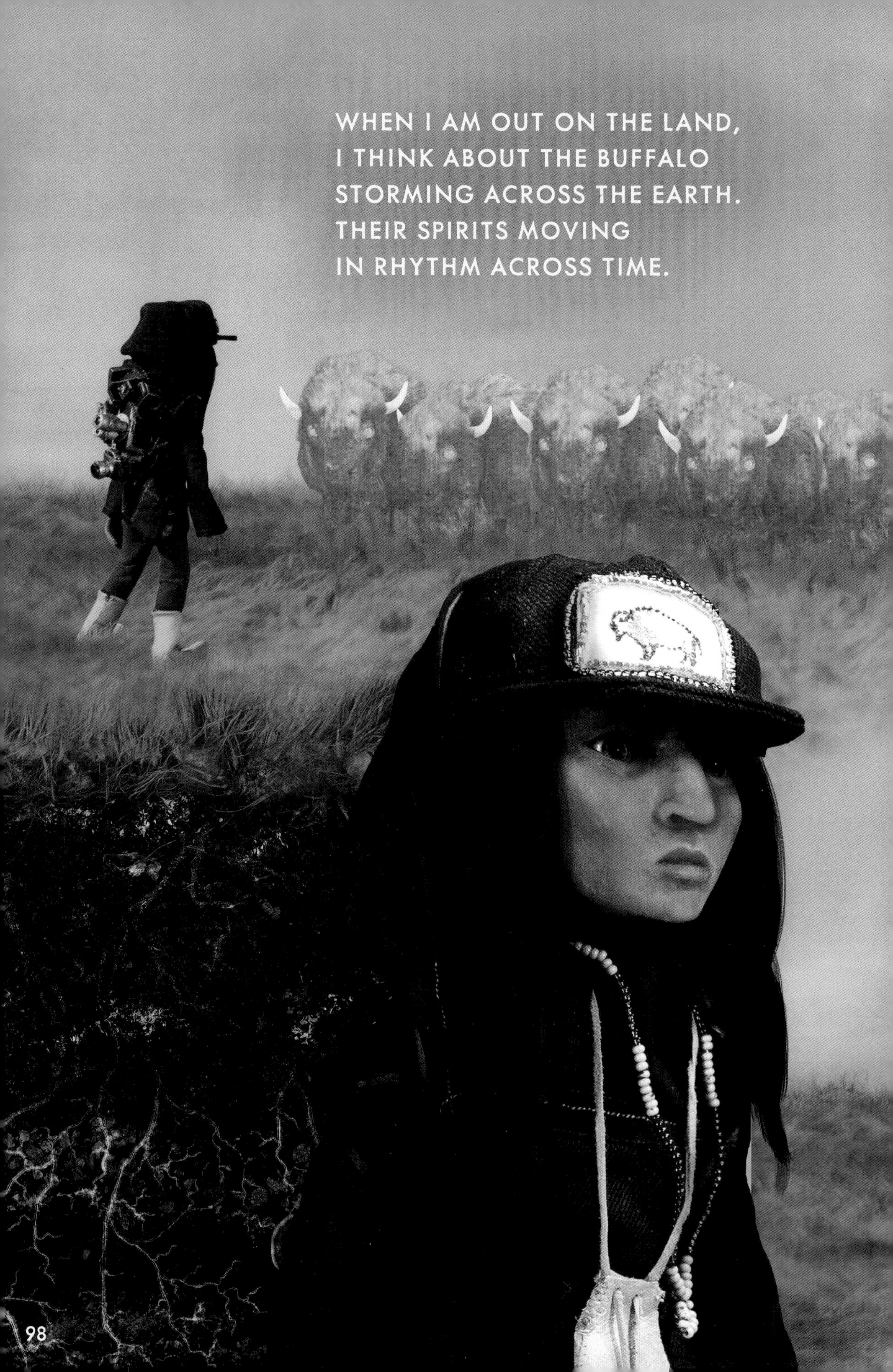

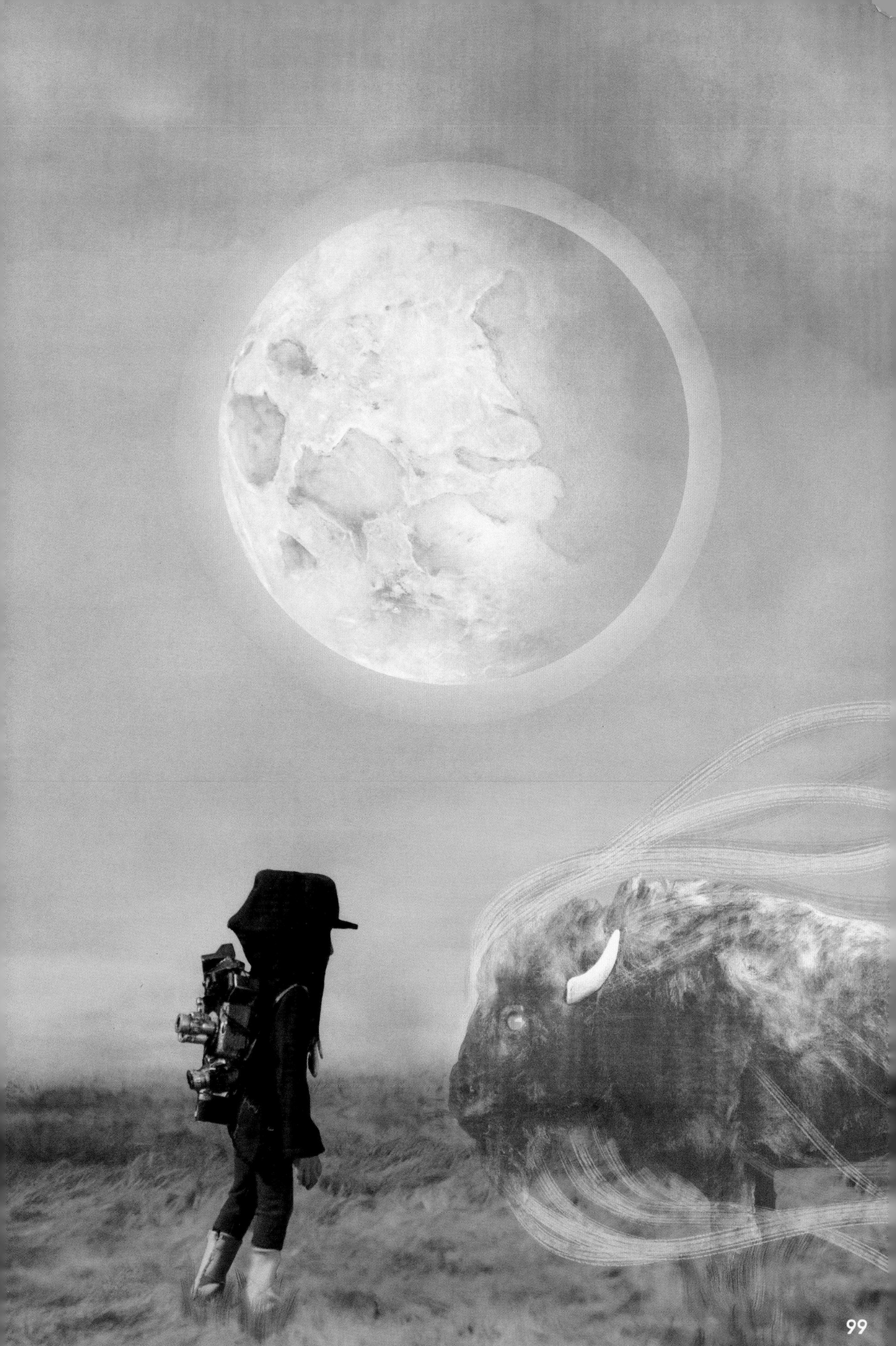

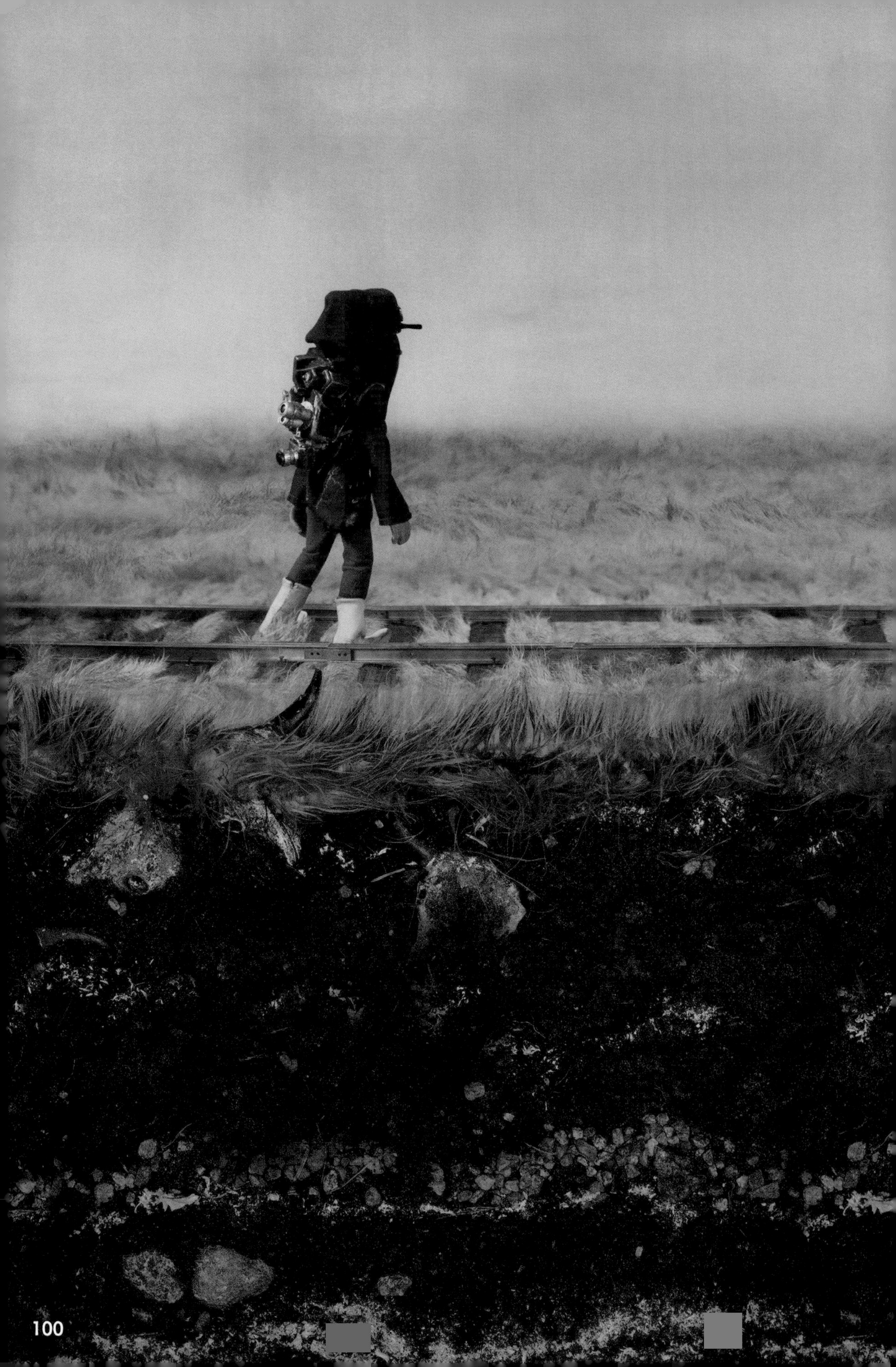

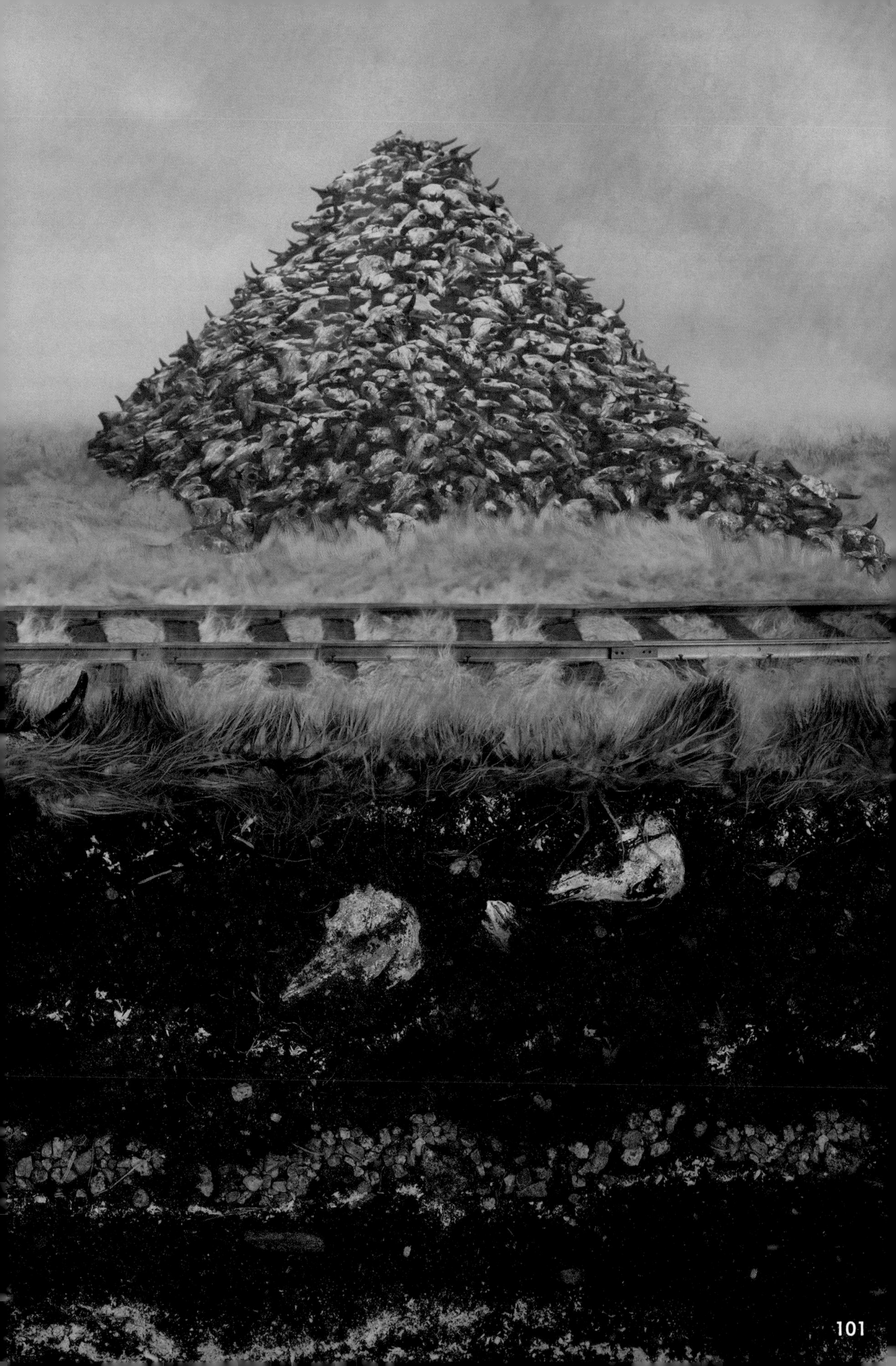

I OFFER THIS GIFT. THE LAND SPEAKS LIKE FAMILY, OFFERING DIRECTION.

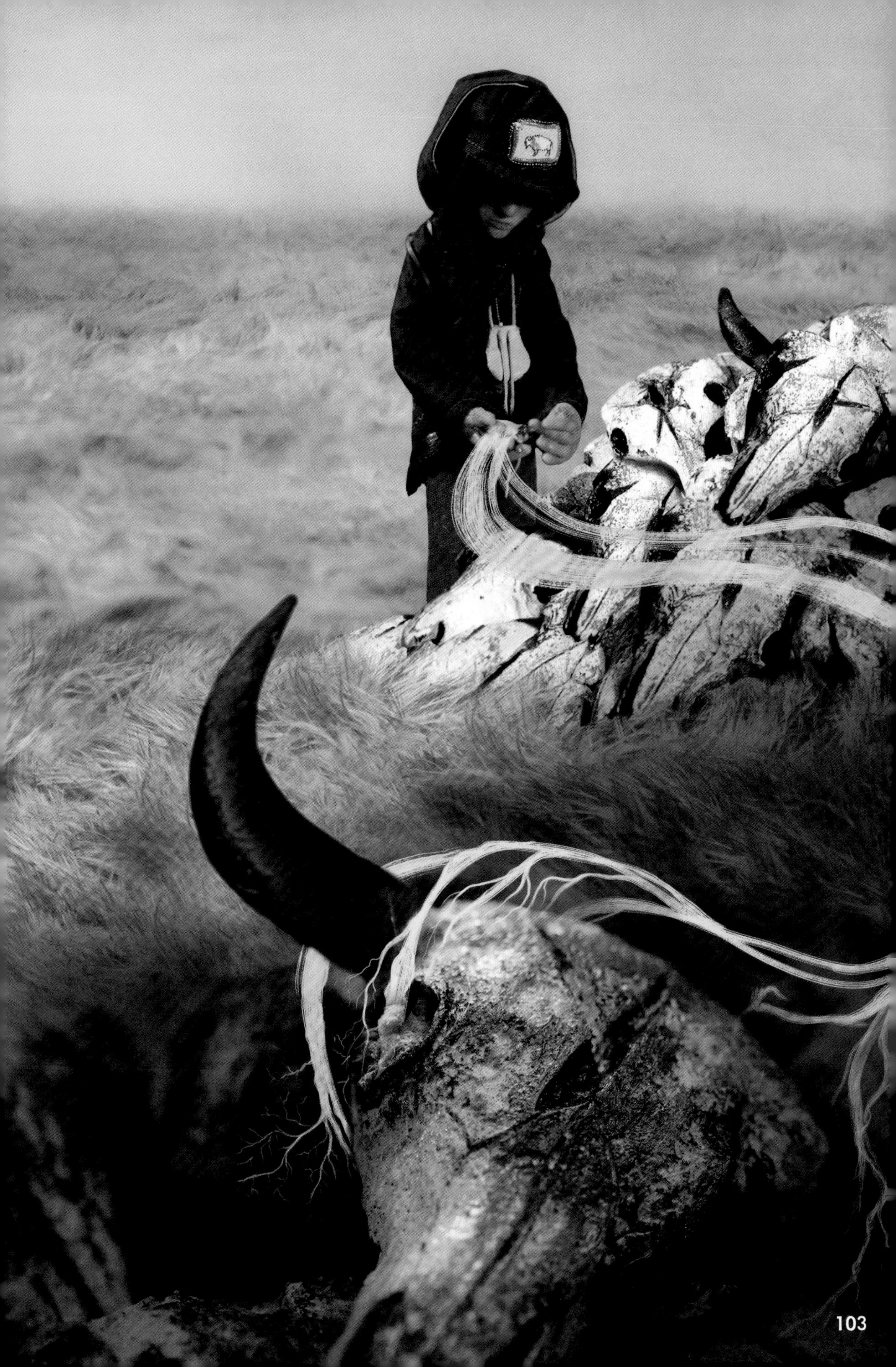

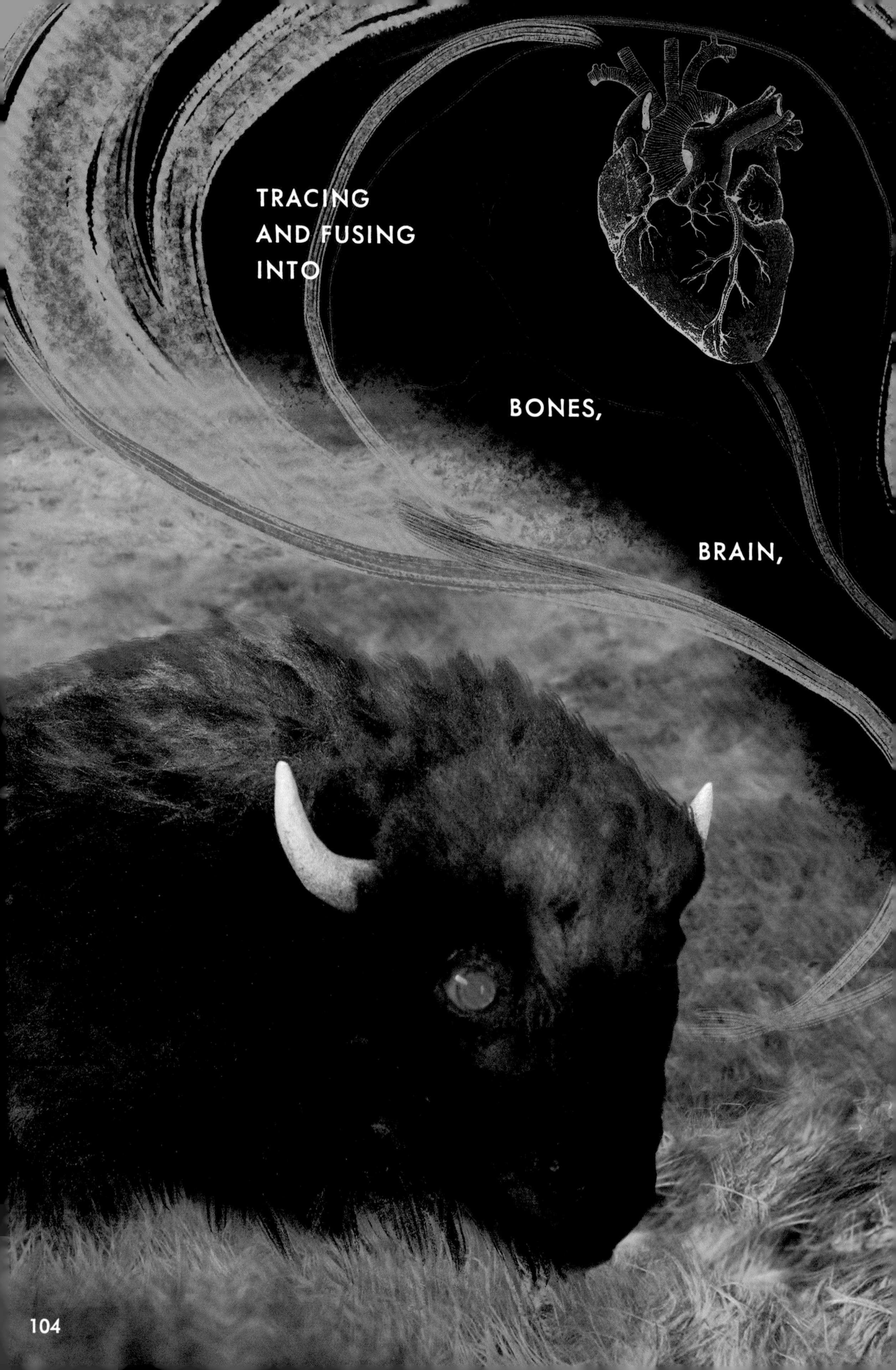

TRACING
AND FUSING
INTO

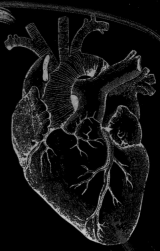

BONES,

BRAIN,

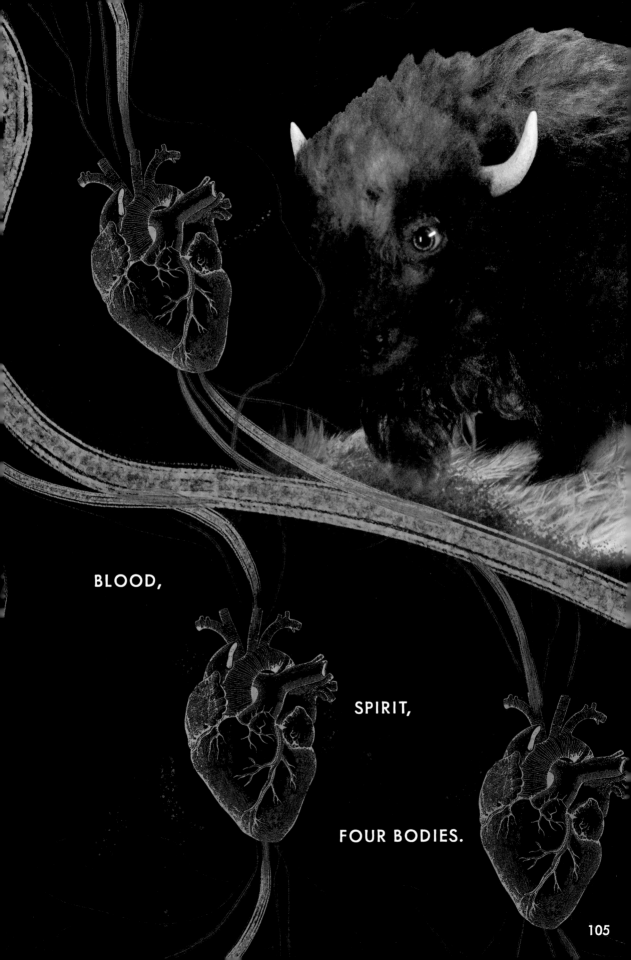

BLOOD,

SPIRIT,

FOUR BODIES.

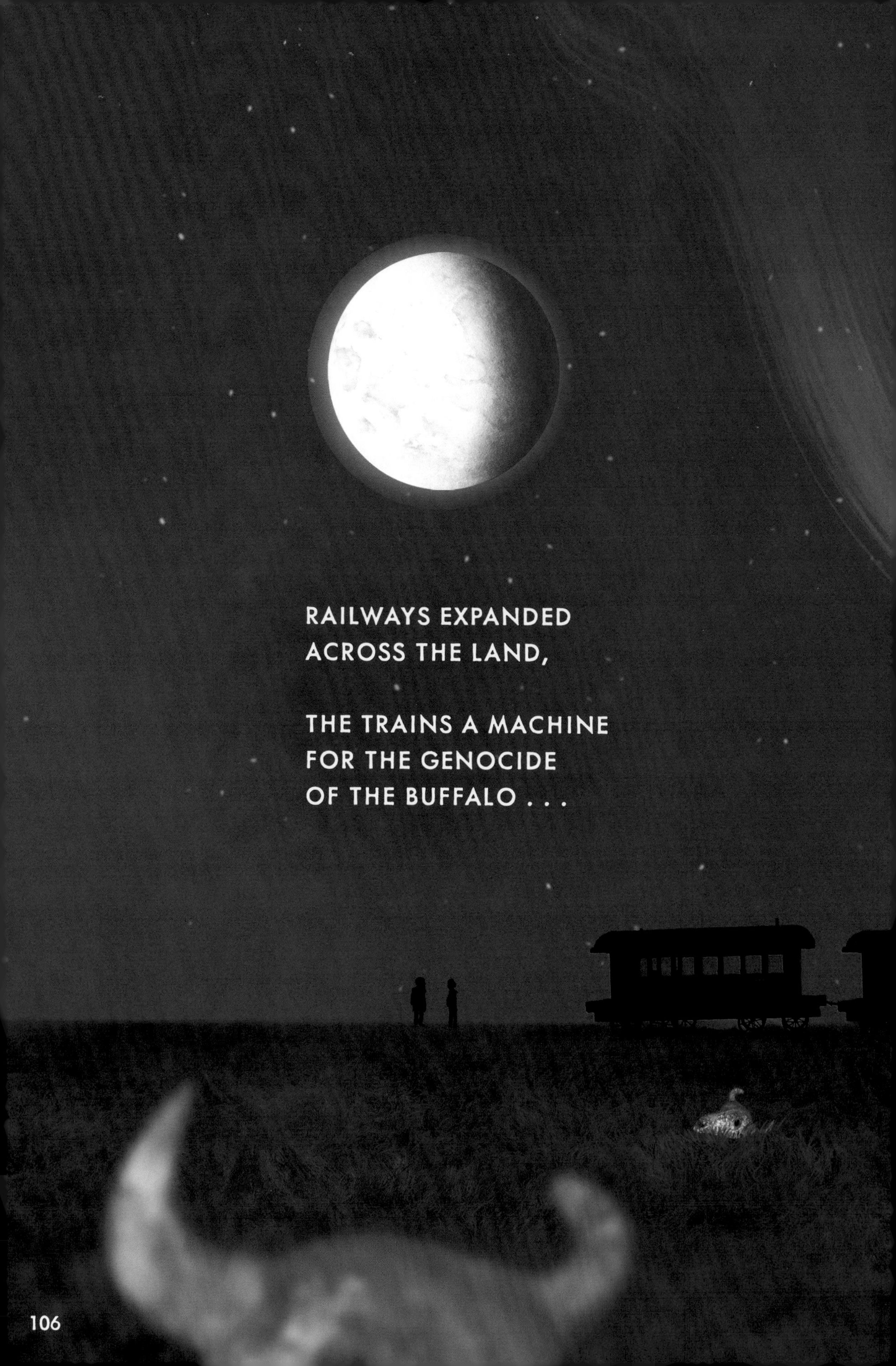
RAILWAYS EXPANDED
ACROSS THE LAND,
THE TRAINS A MACHINE
FOR THE GENOCIDE
OF THE BUFFALO . . .

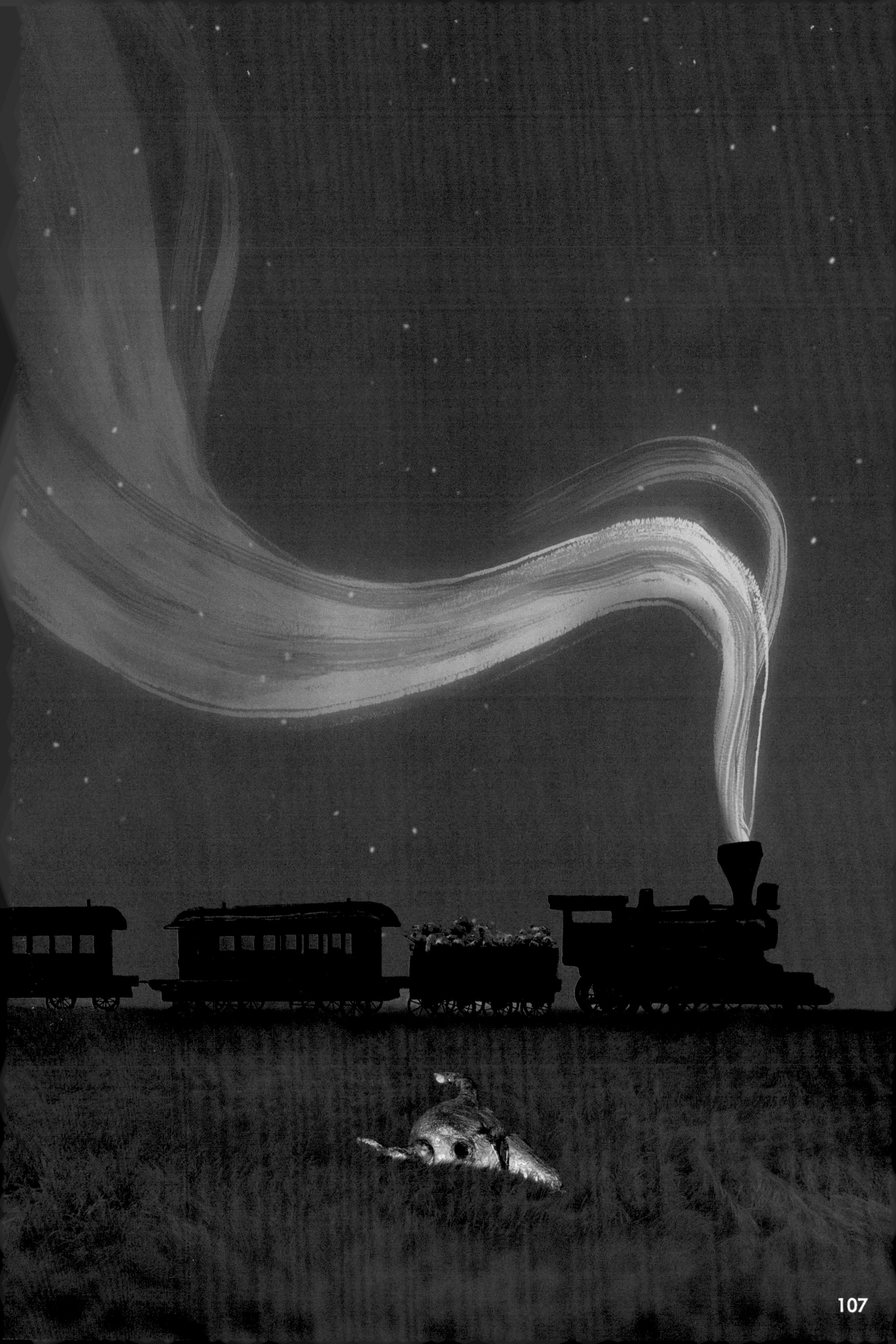

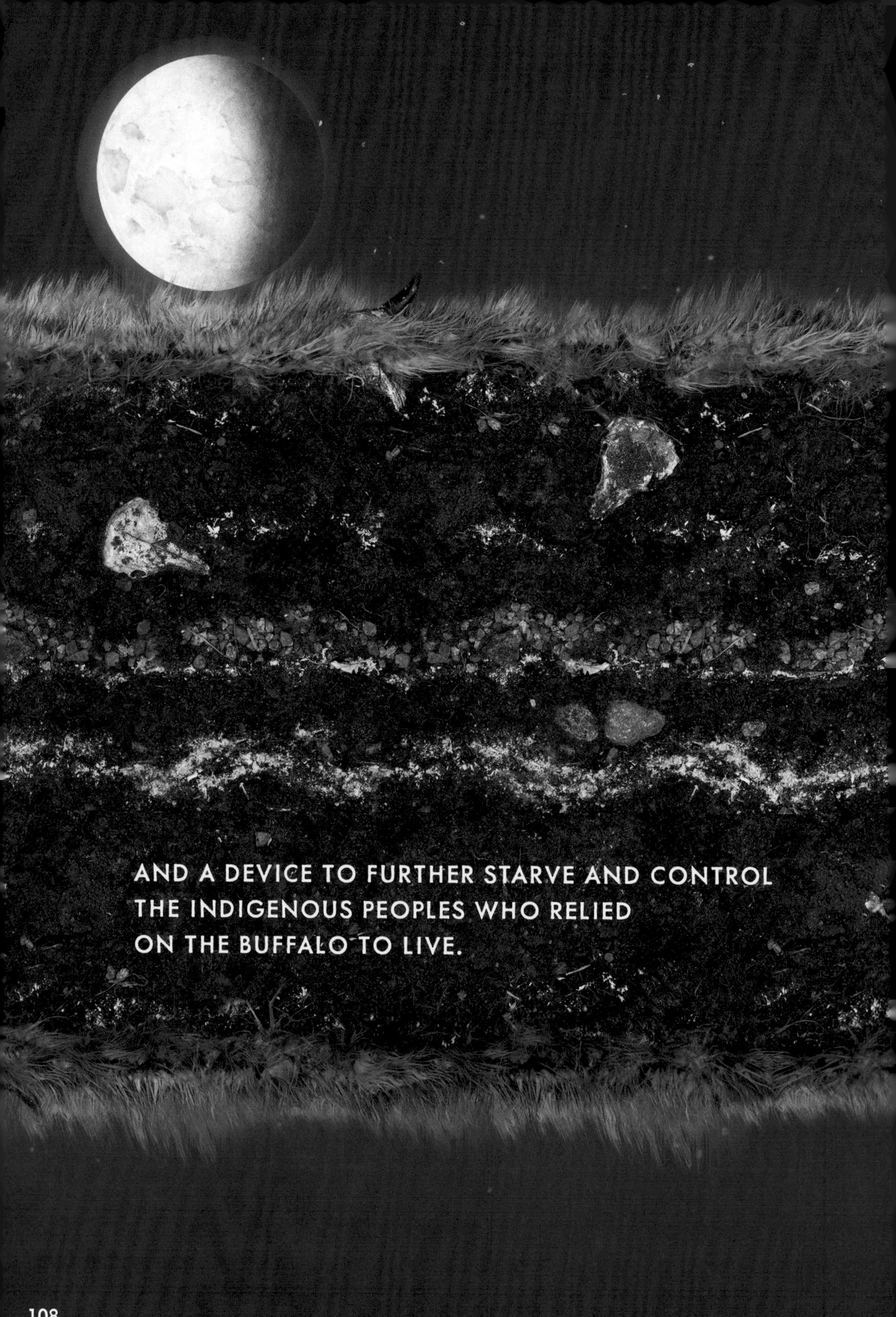

AND A DEVICE TO FURTHER STARVE AND CONTROL
THE INDIGENOUS PEOPLES WHO RELIED
ON THE BUFFALO TO LIVE.

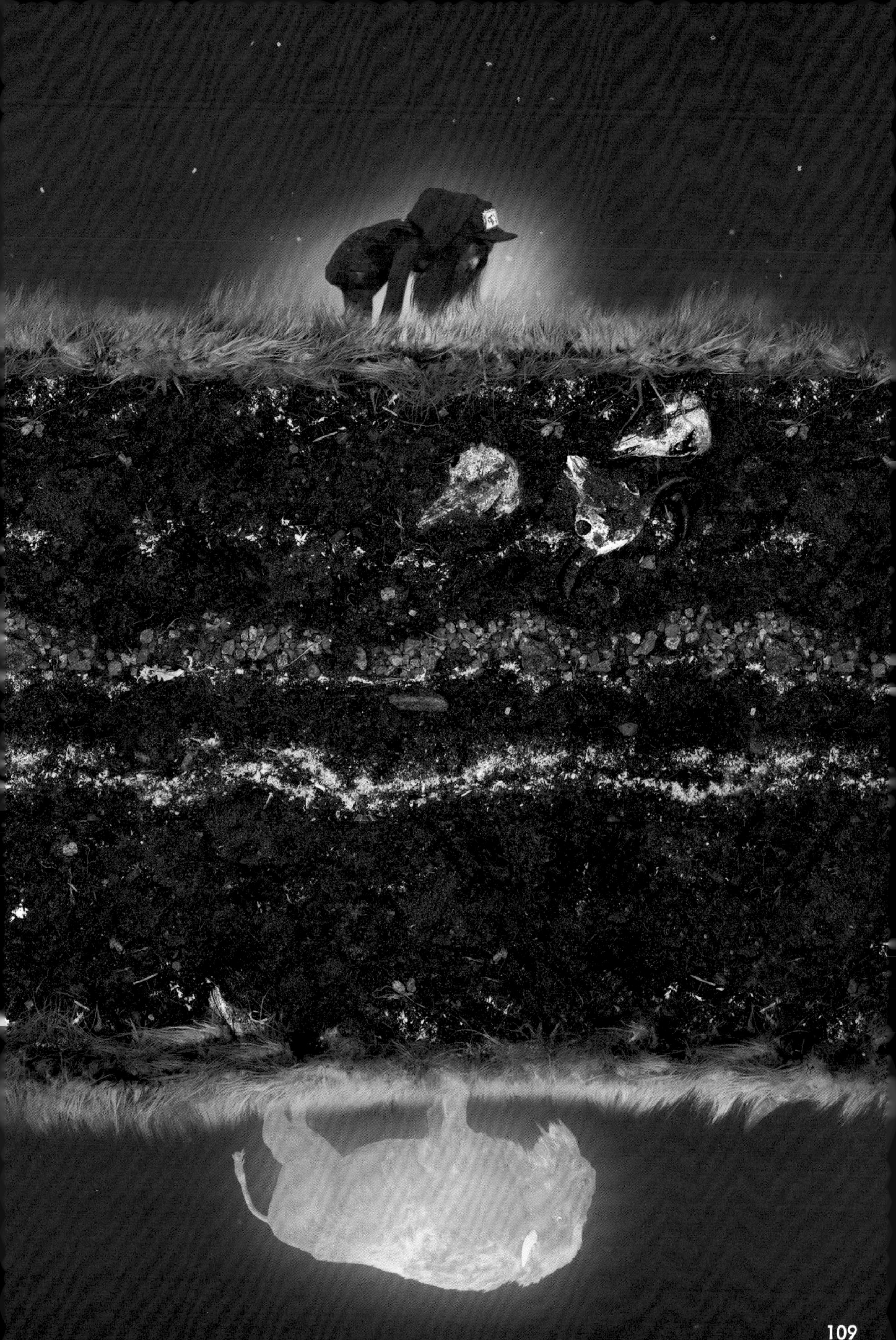

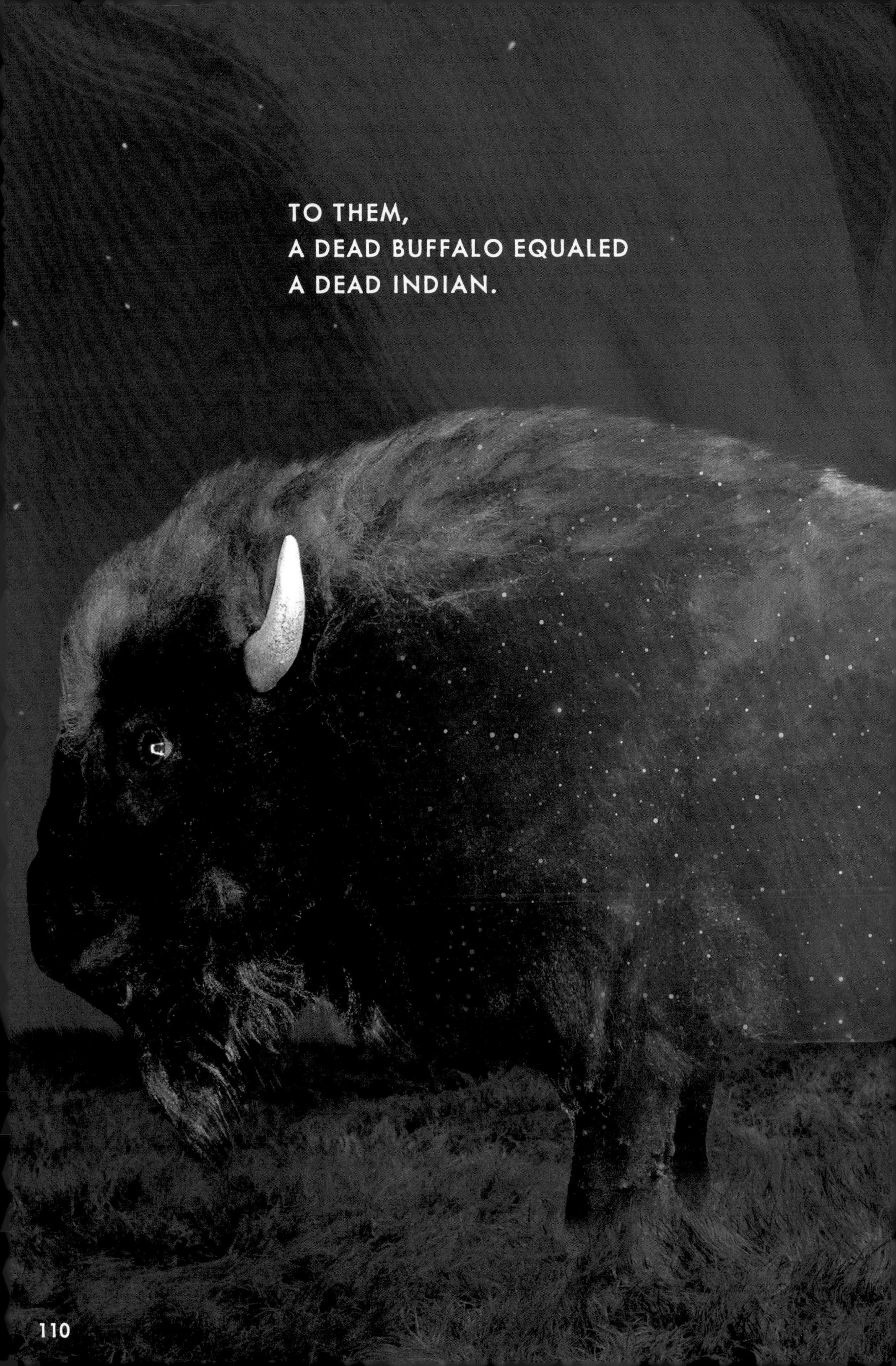

TO THEM,
A DEAD BUFFALO EQUALED
A DEAD INDIAN.

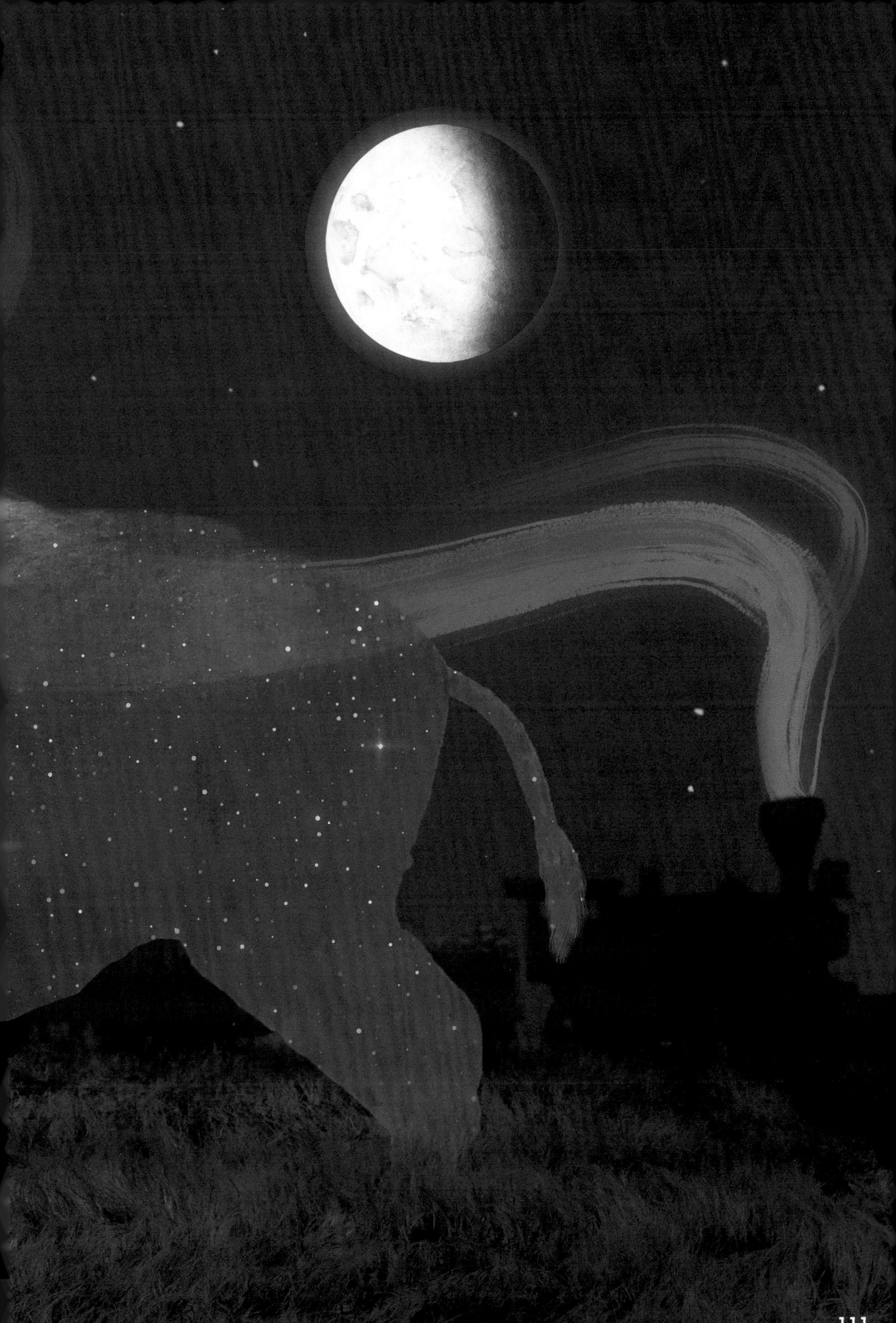

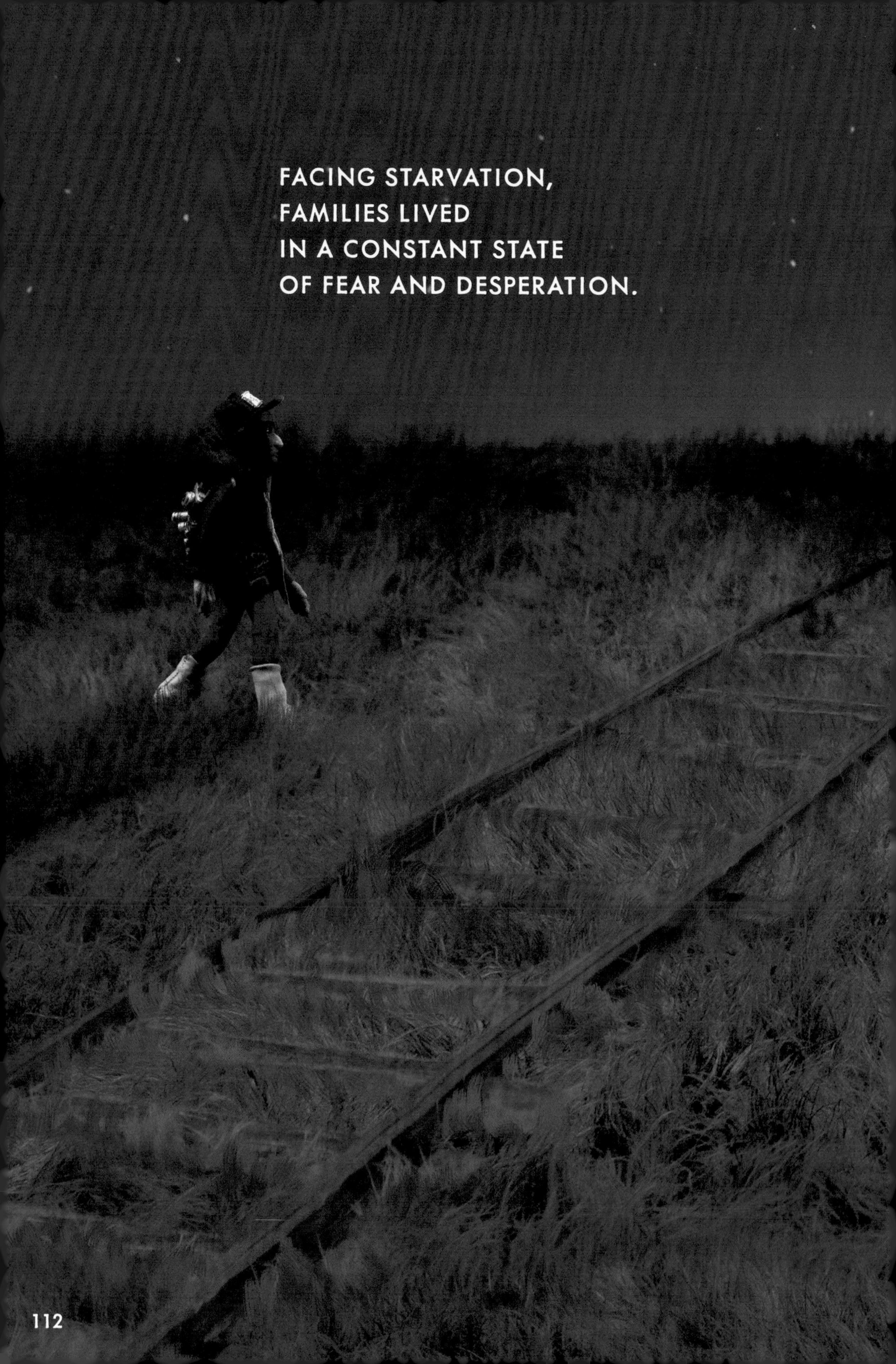

FACING STARVATION,
FAMILIES LIVED
IN A CONSTANT STATE
OF FEAR AND DESPERATION.

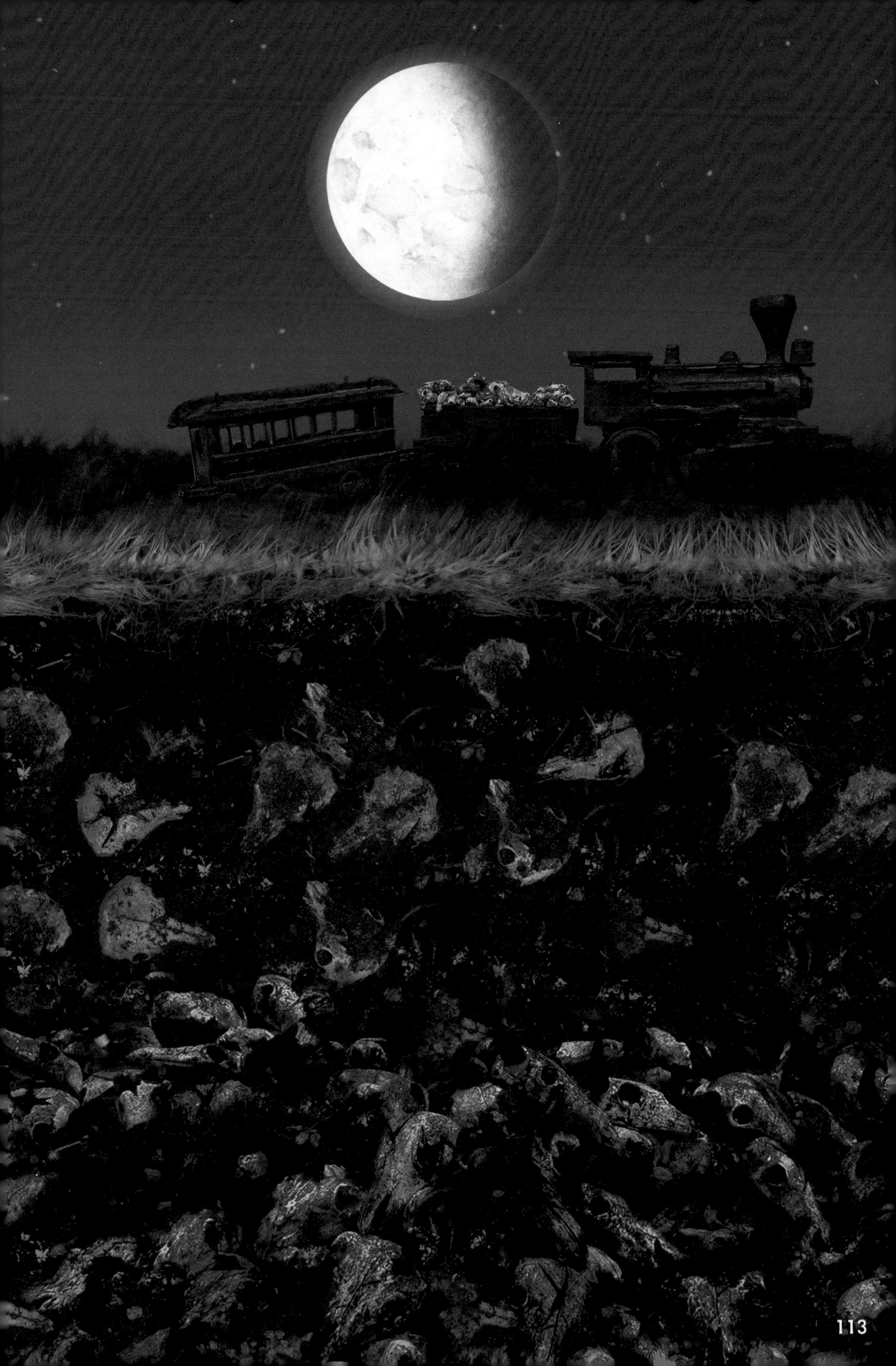

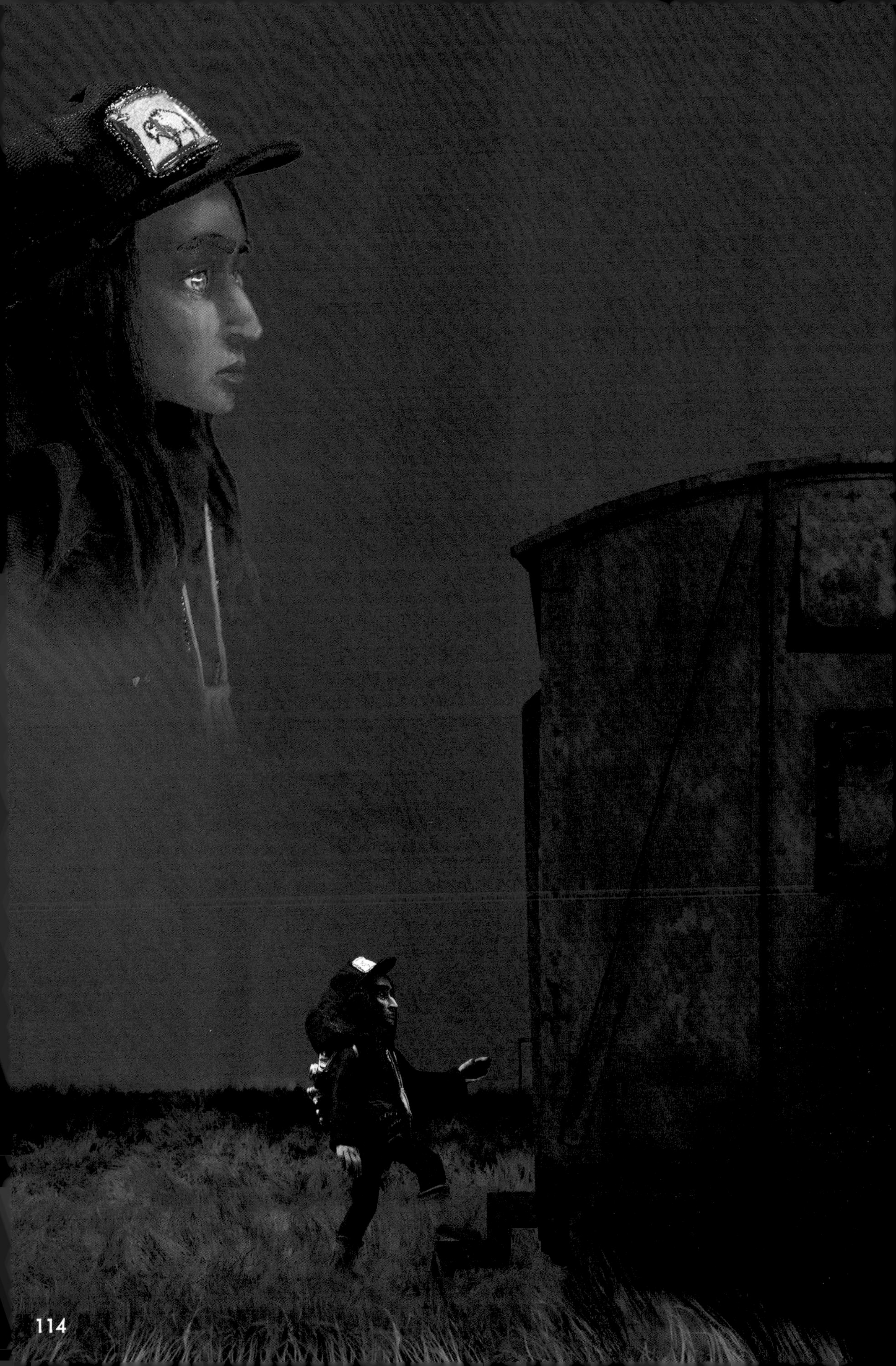

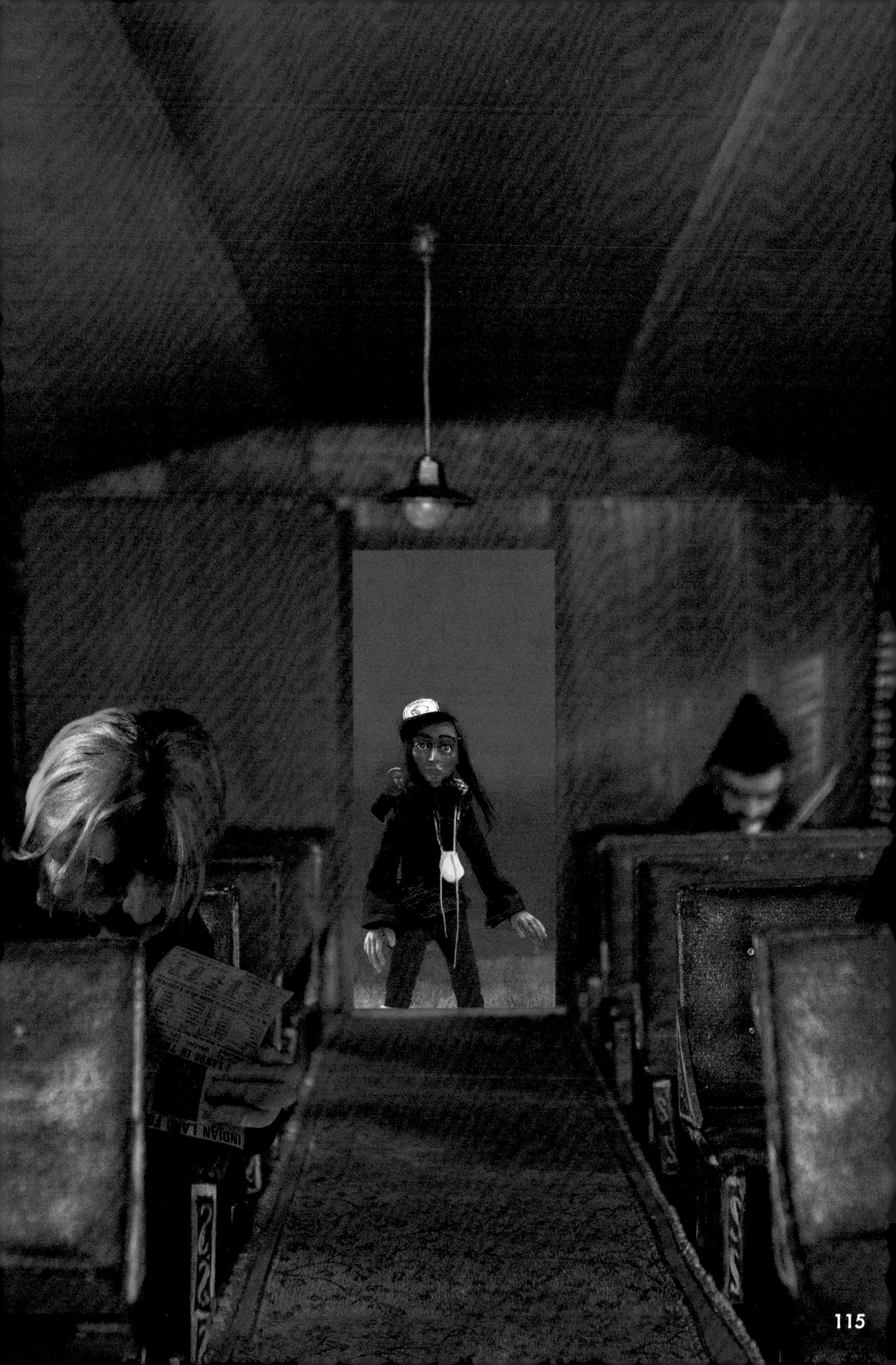
INDIAN LAND

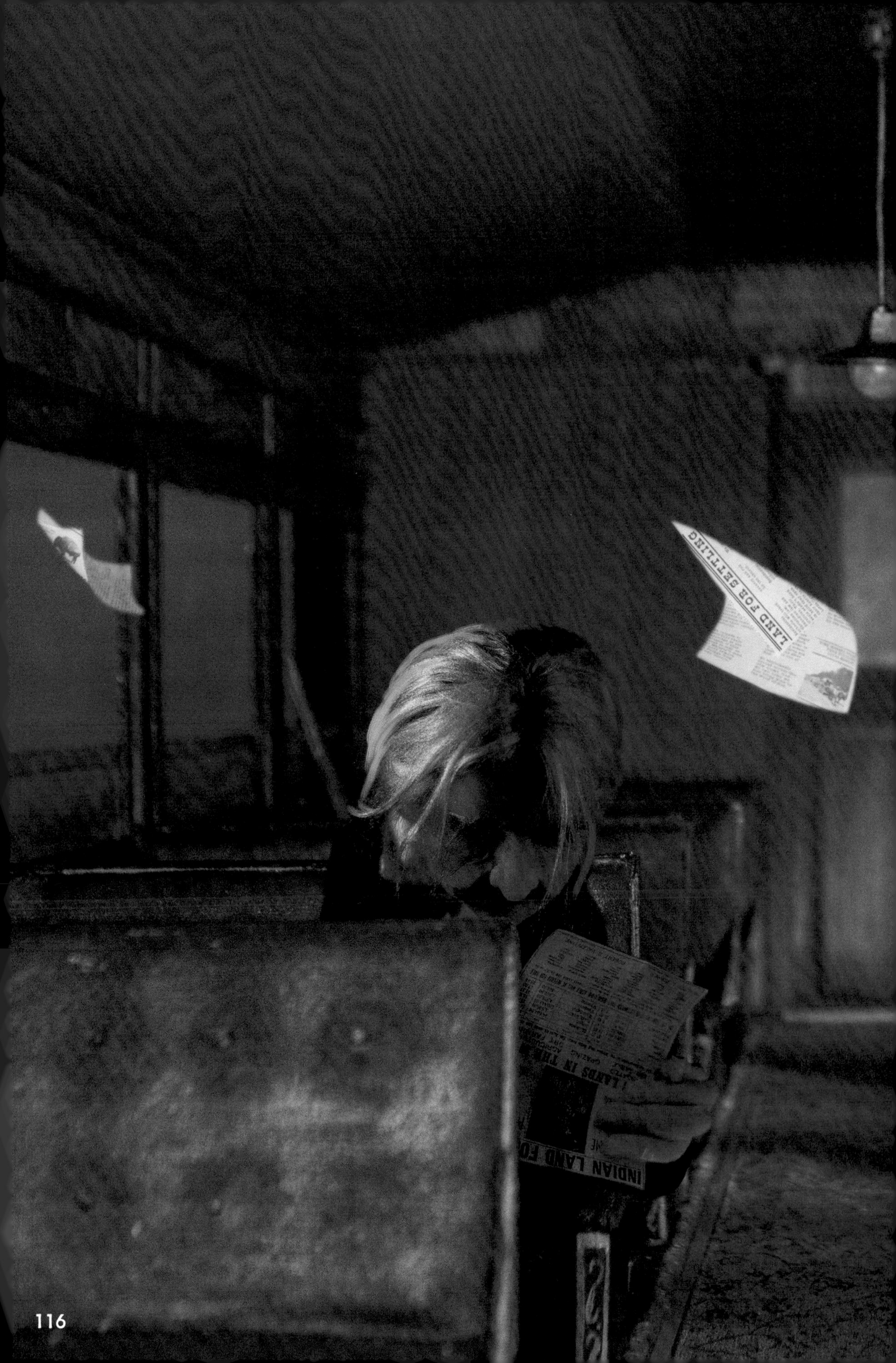
LAND FOR SETTLING
INDIAN LAND

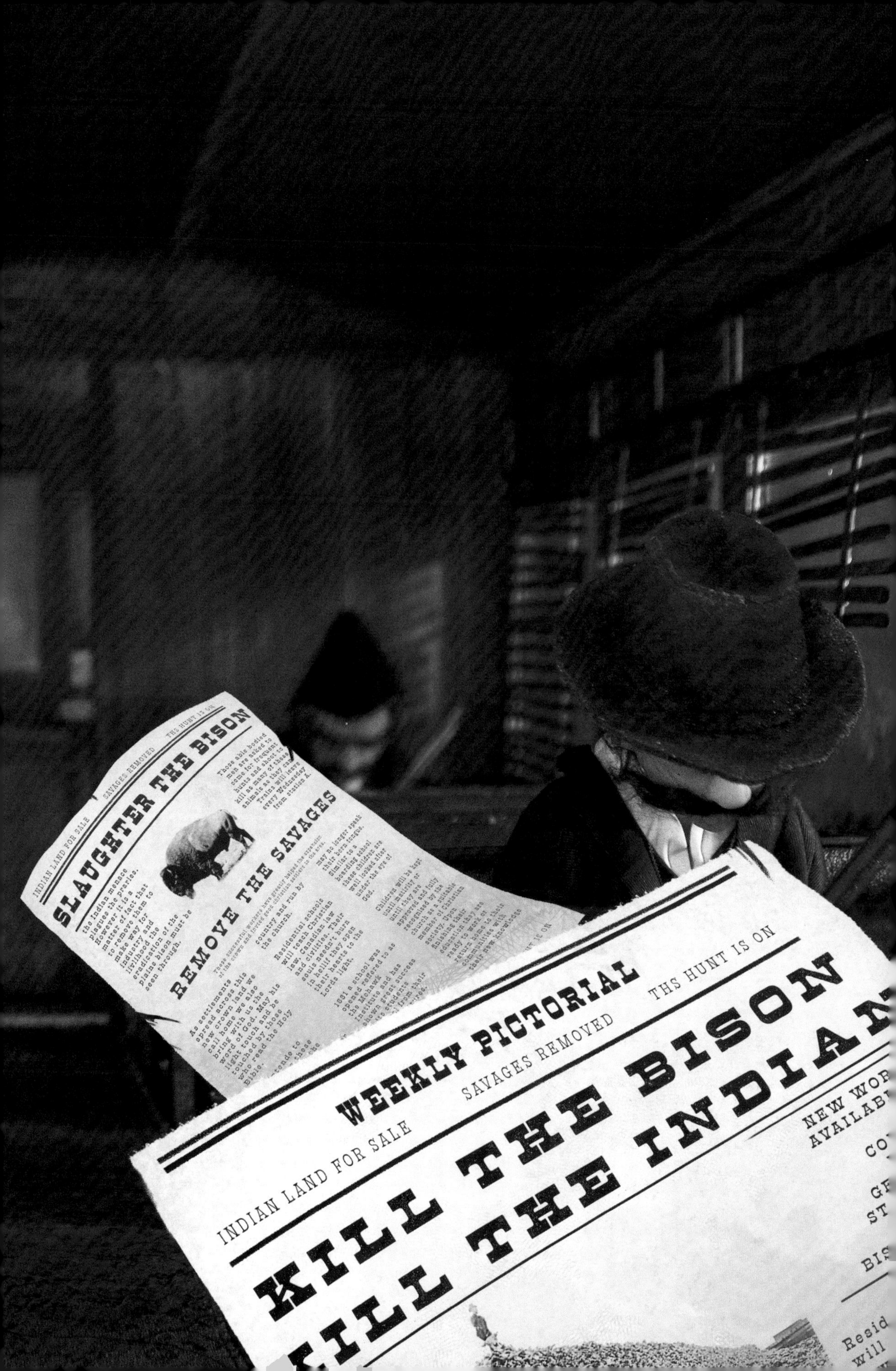

INDIAN LAND FOR SALE
SAVAGES REMOVED
THE HUNT IS ON
SLAUGHTER THE BISON
REMOVE THE SAVAGES
WEEKLY PICTORIAL
INDIAN LAND FOR SALE
SAVAGES REMOVED
THS HUNT IS ON
KILL THE BISON

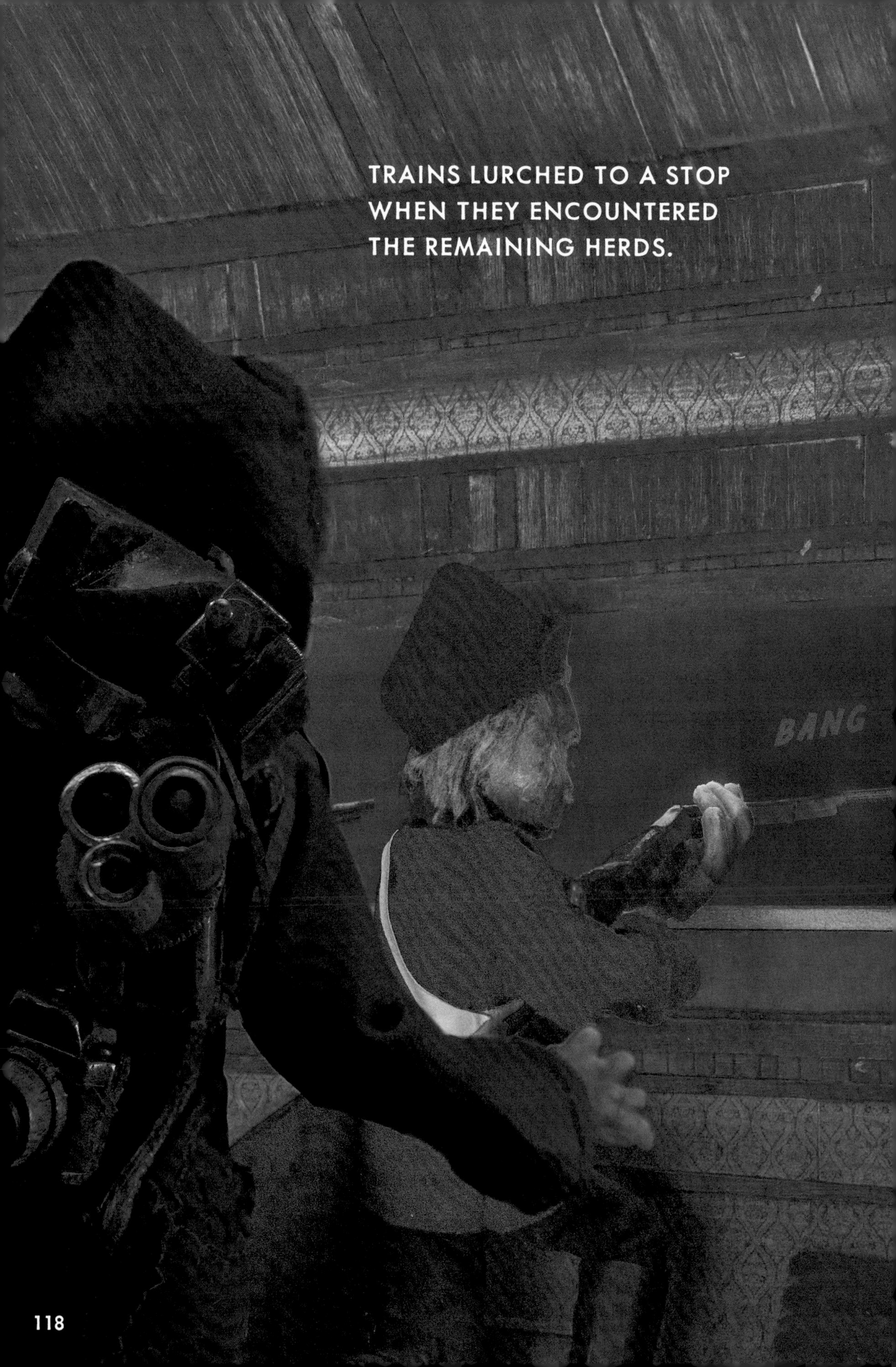
TRAINS LURCHED TO A STOP
WHEN THEY ENCOUNTERED
THE REMAINING HERDS.
BANG

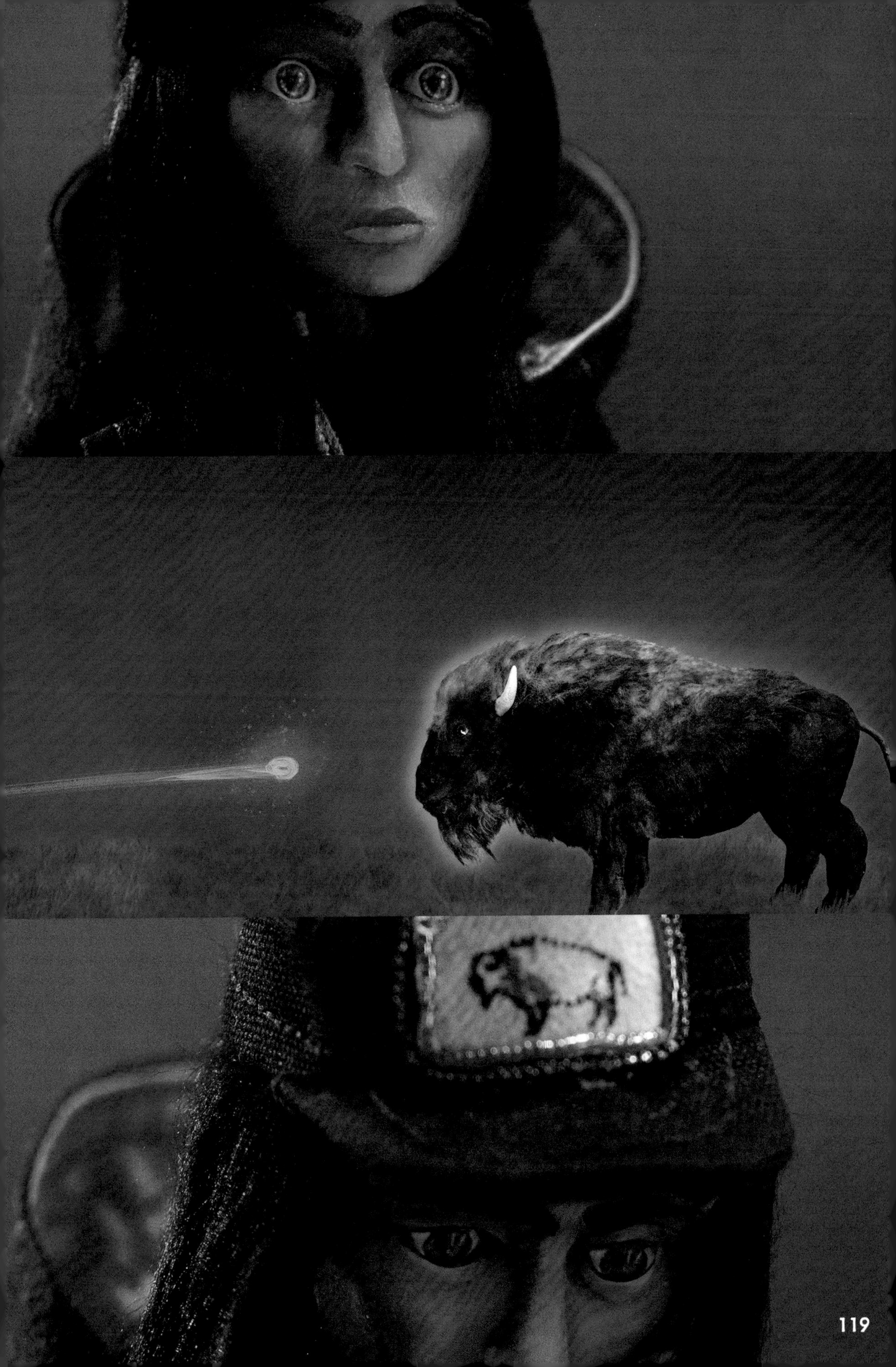

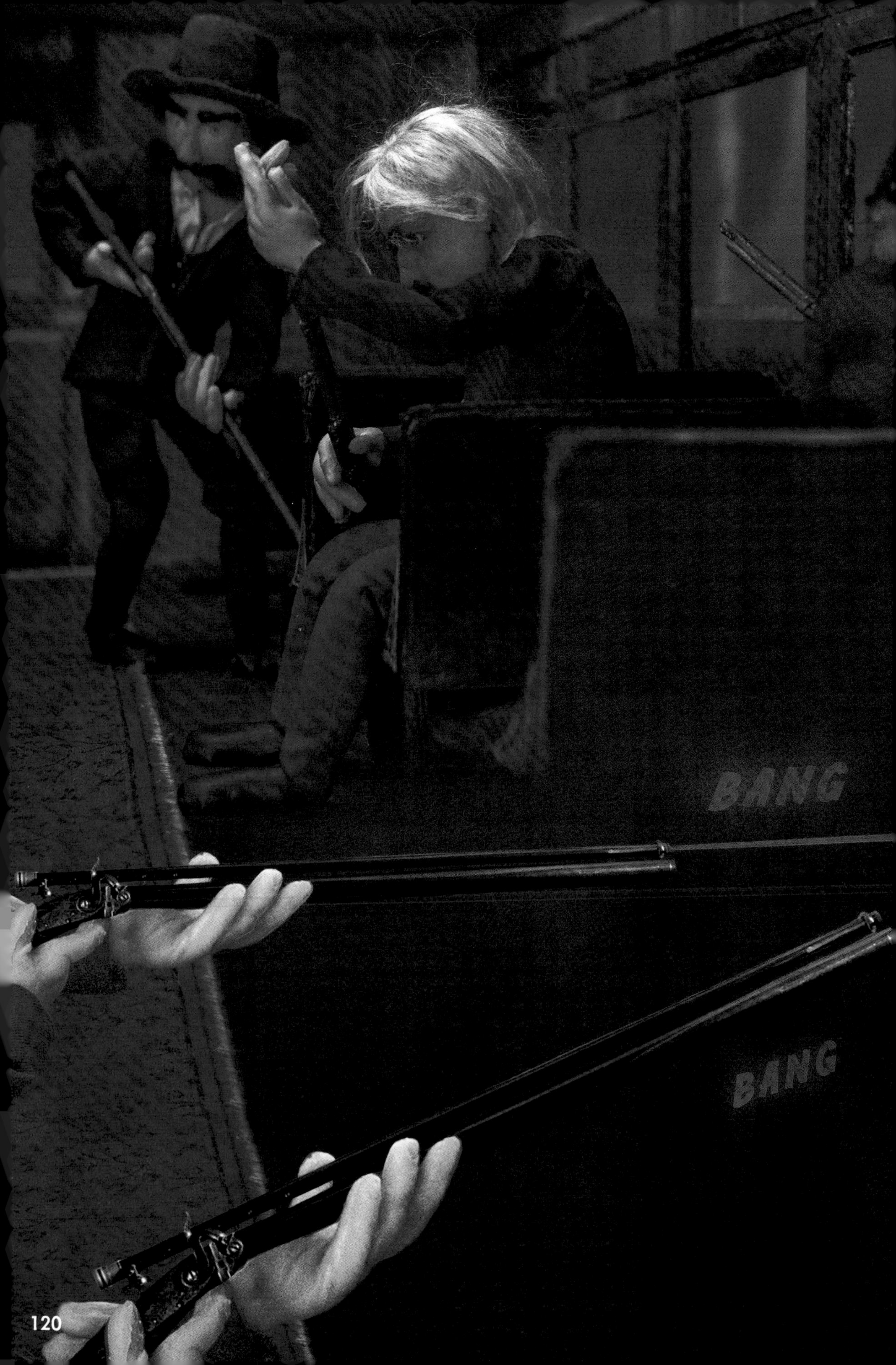
BANG
BANG

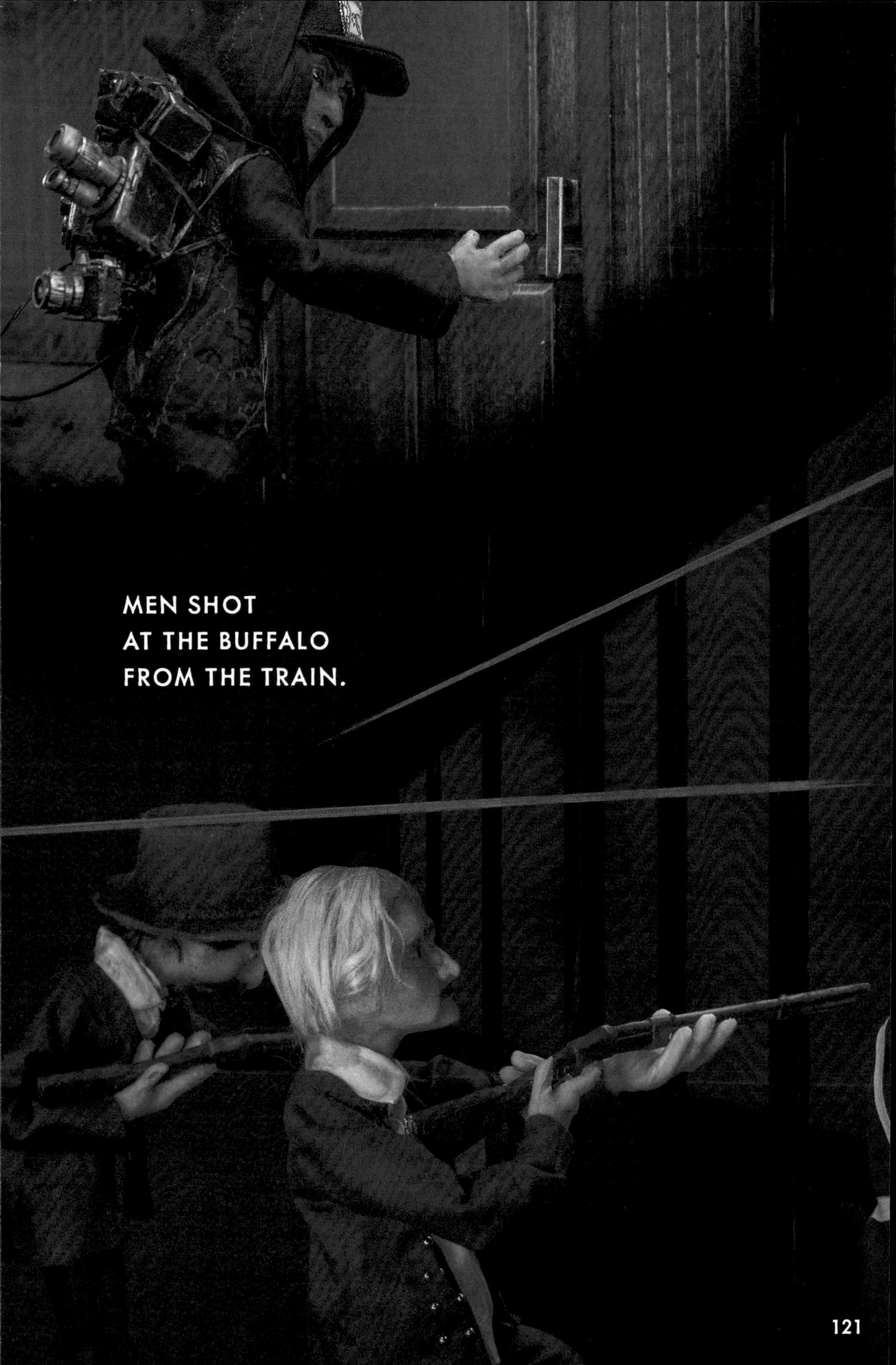

MEN SHOT
AT THE BUFFALO
FROM THE TRAIN.

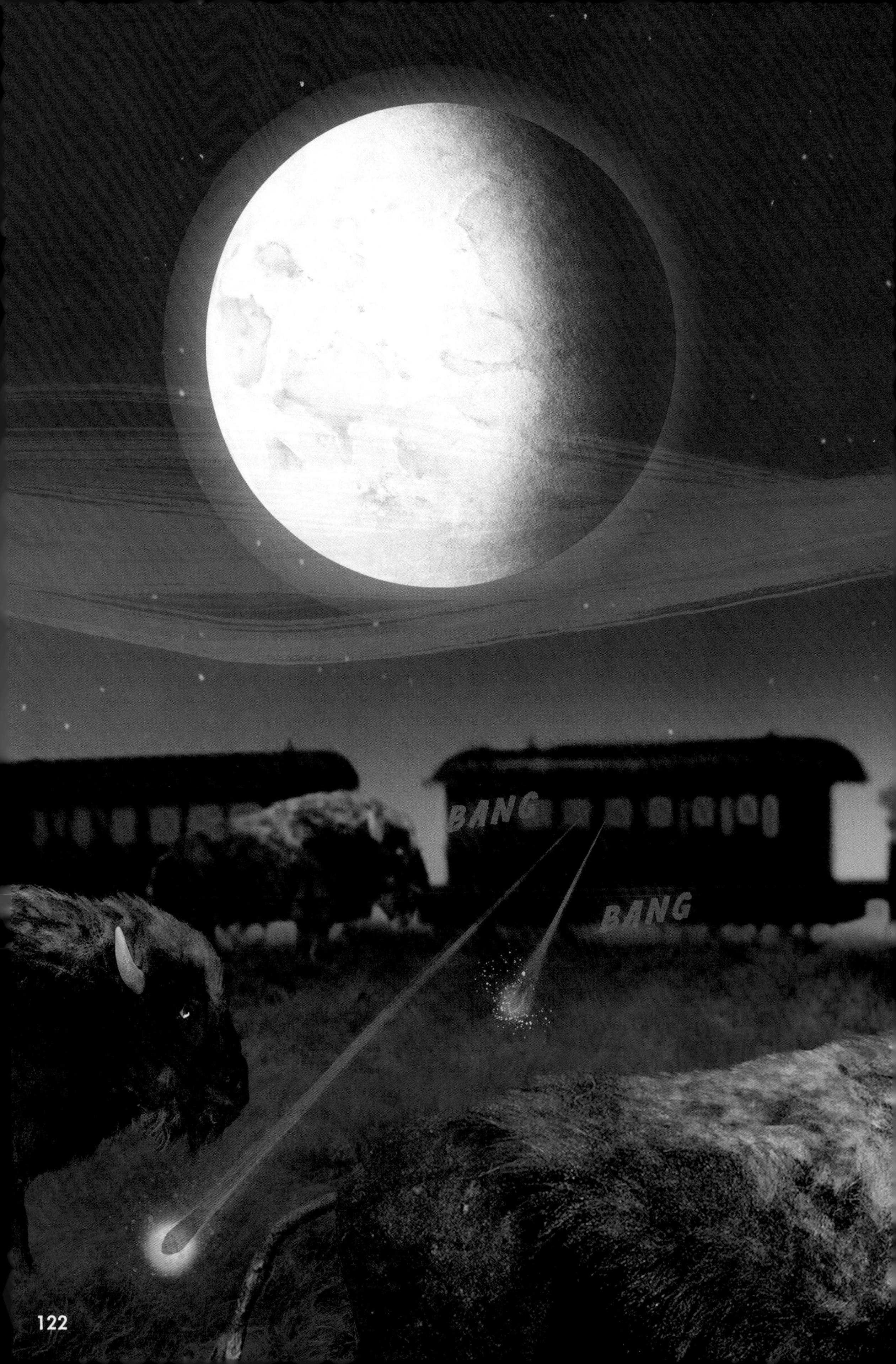
BANG
BANG

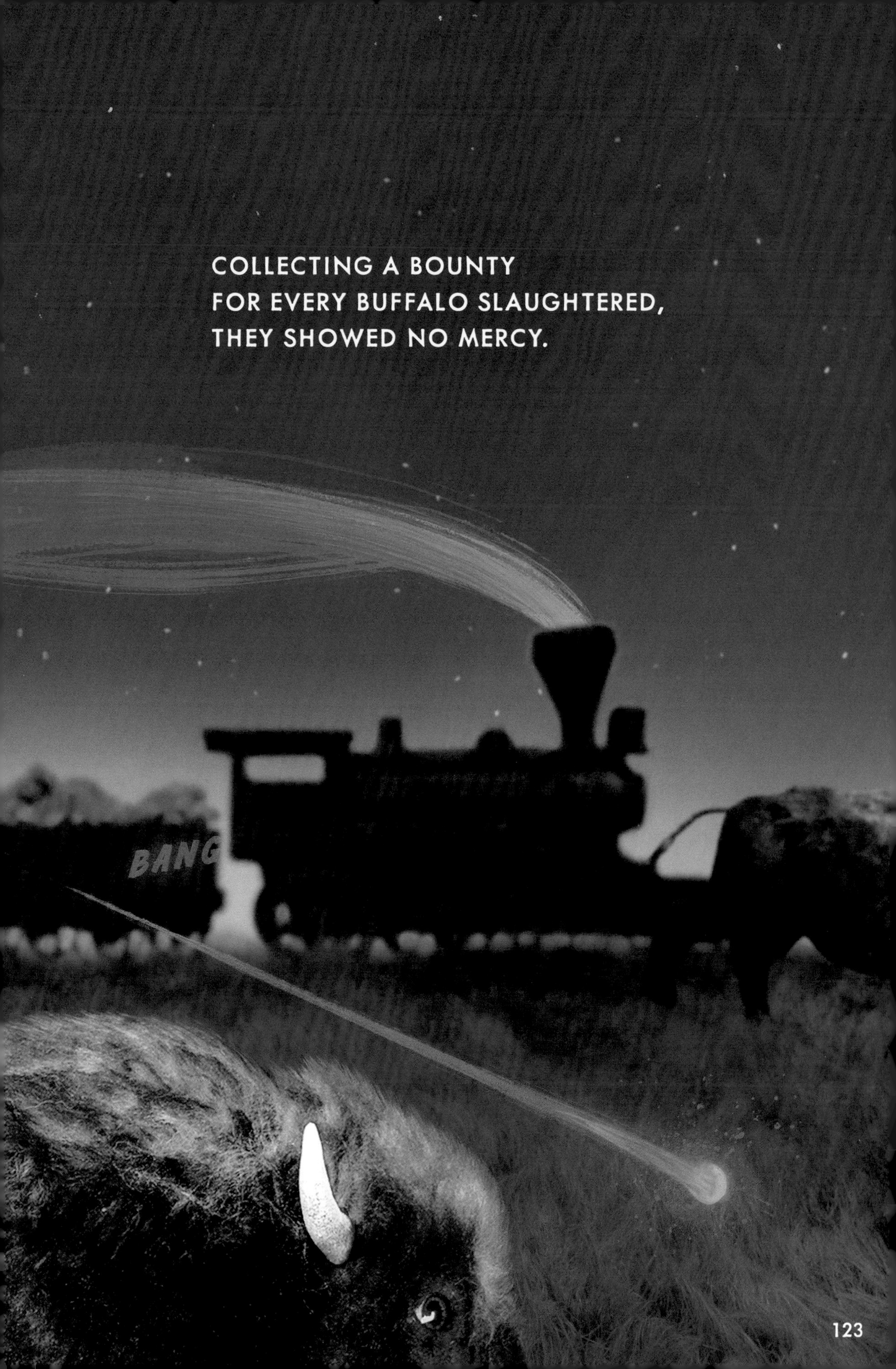
COLLECTING A BOUNTY
FOR EVERY BUFFALO SLAUGHTERED,
THEY SHOWED NO MERCY.
BANG

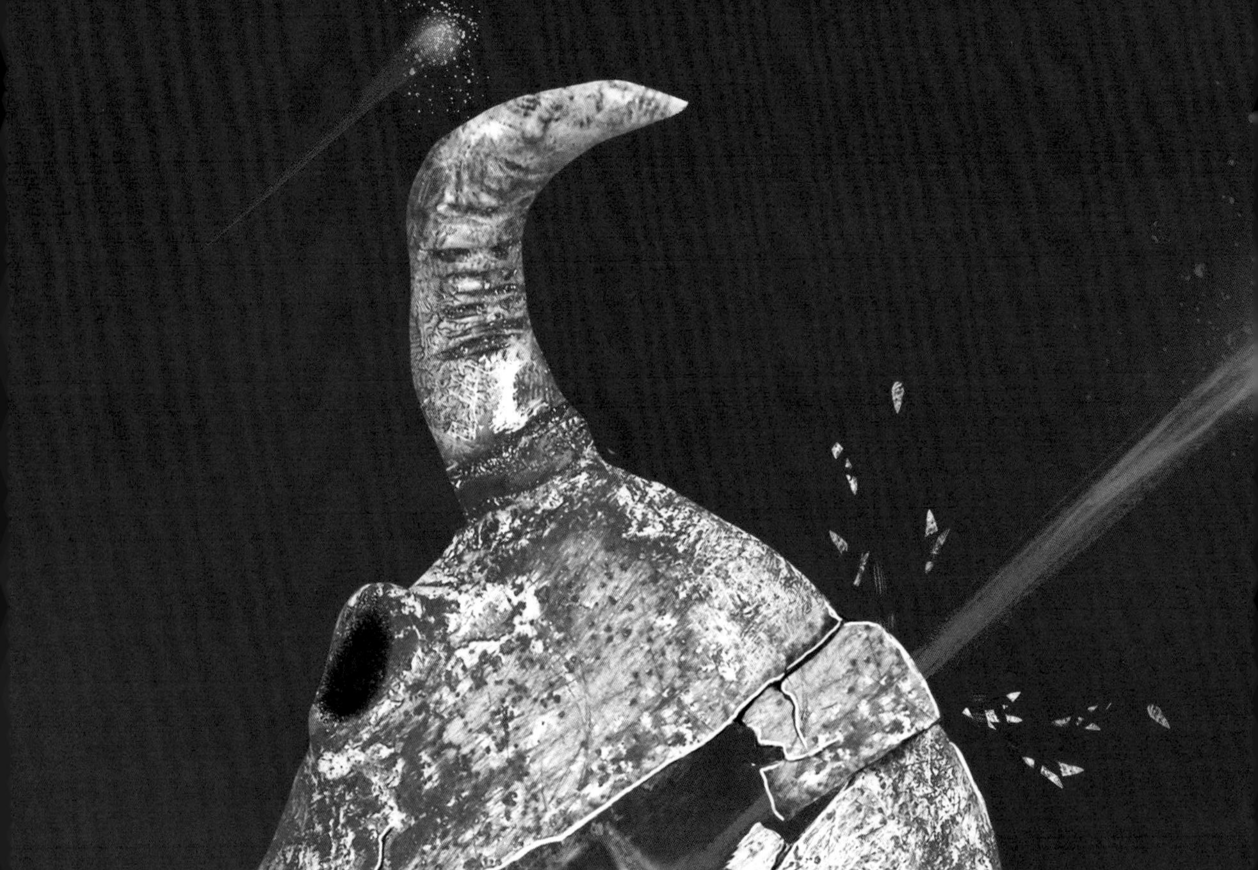

THEY WOULD NOT STOP
UNTIL EVERYTHING BECAME
UNRECOGNIZABLE.

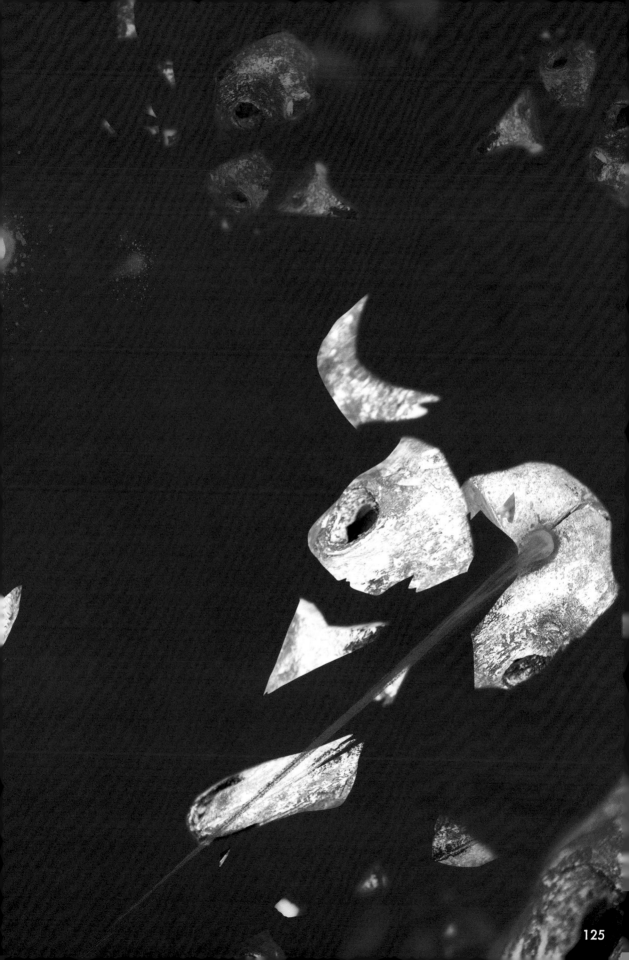

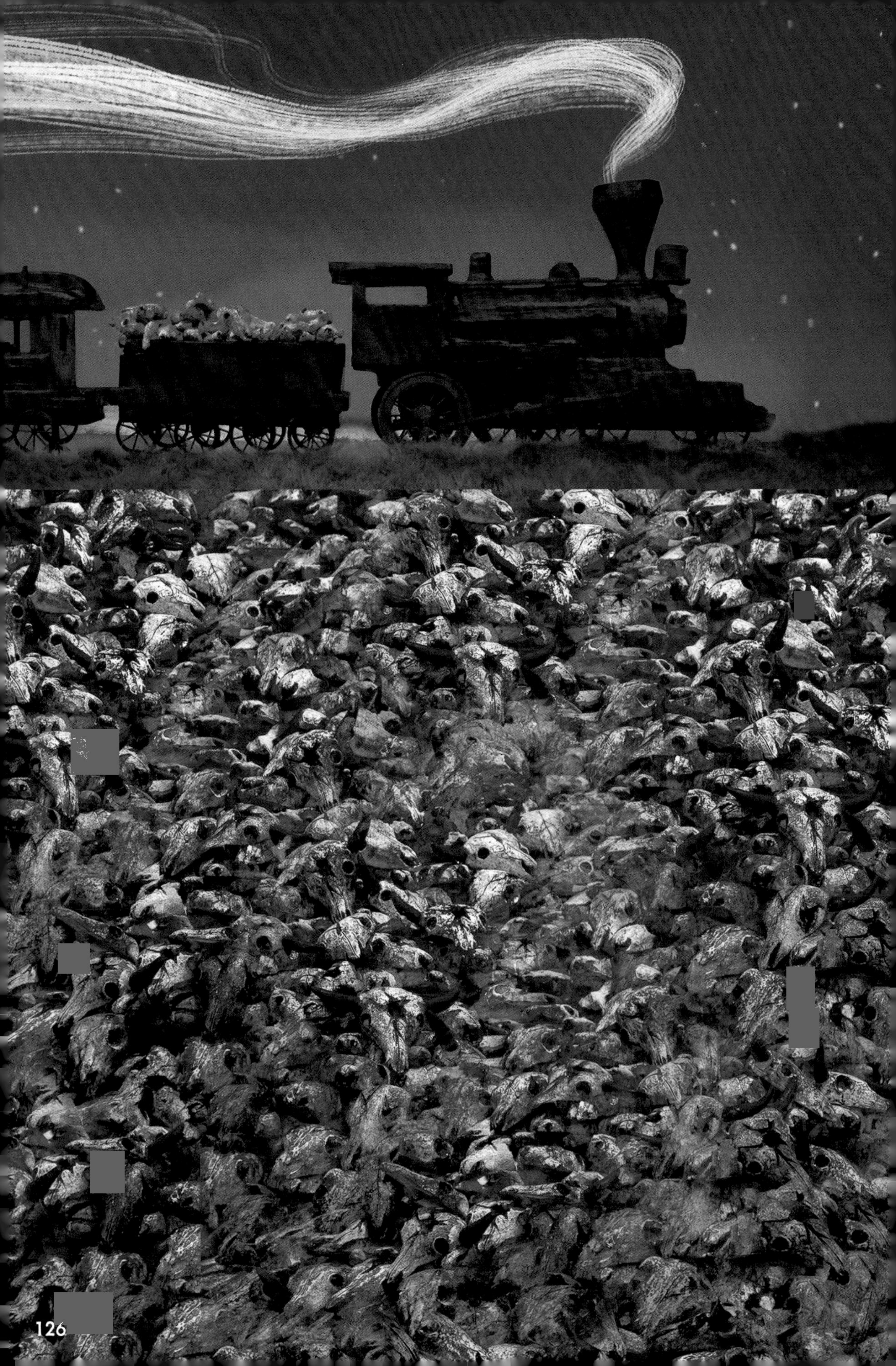

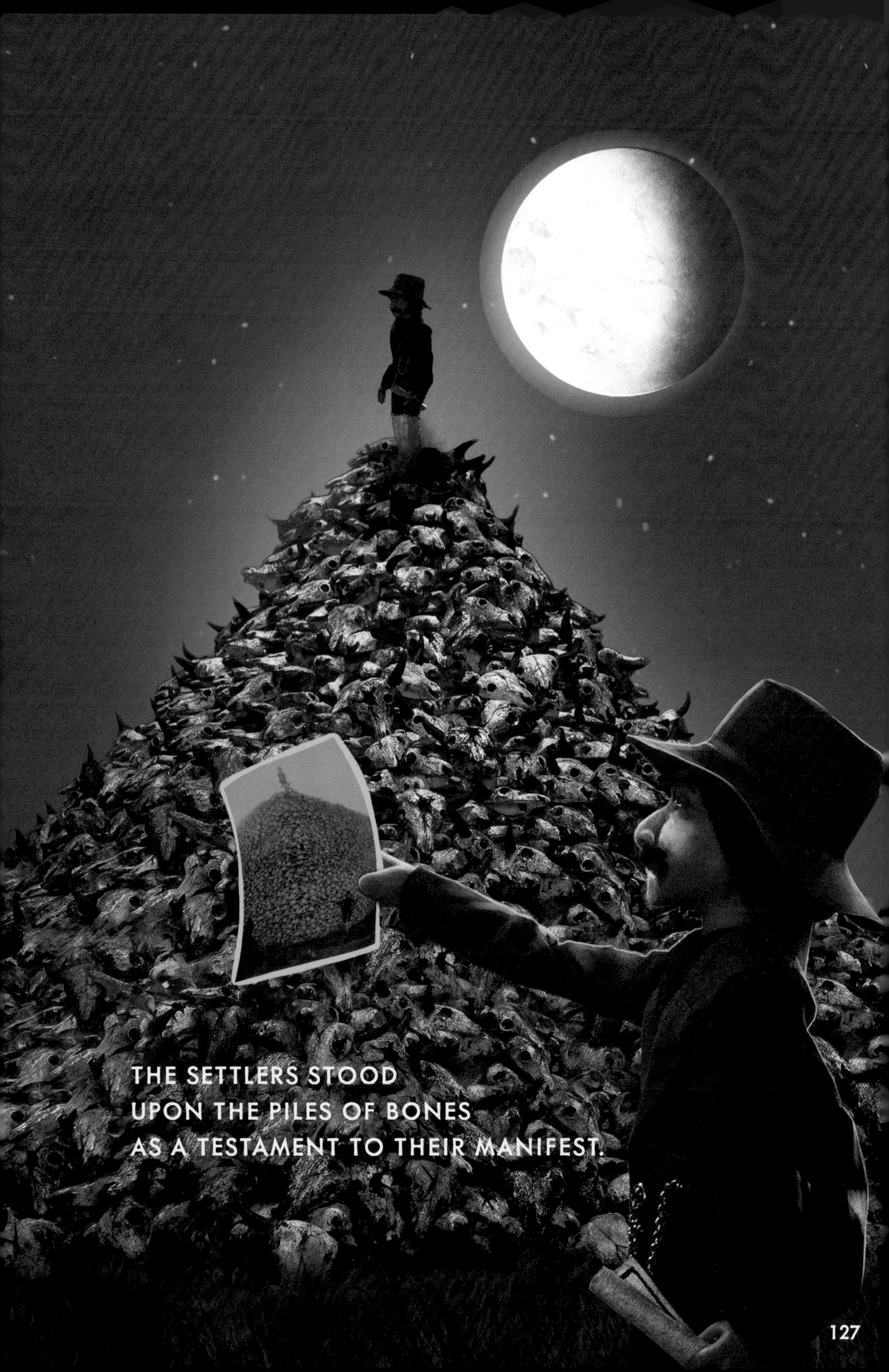
THE SETTLERS STOOD
UPON THE PILES OF BONES
AS A TESTAMENT TO THEIR MANIFEST.

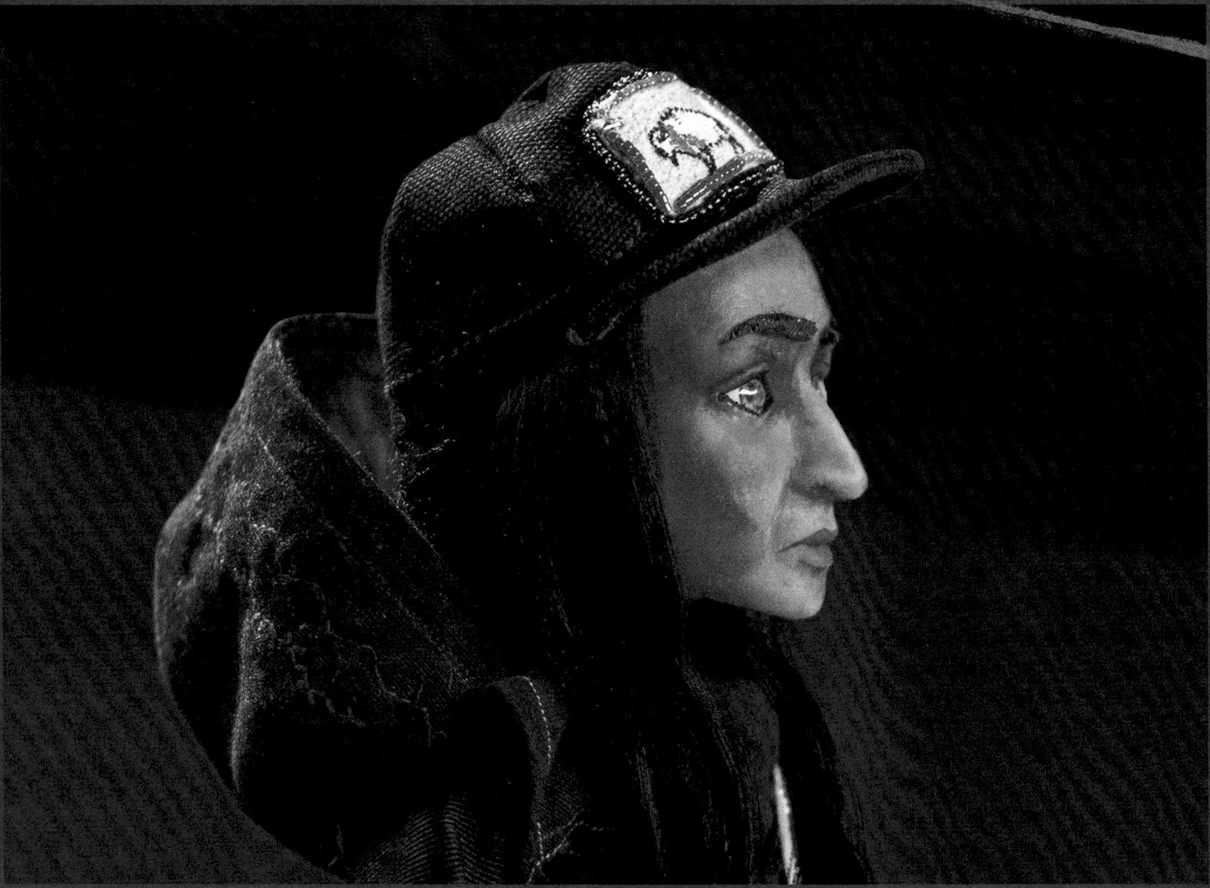

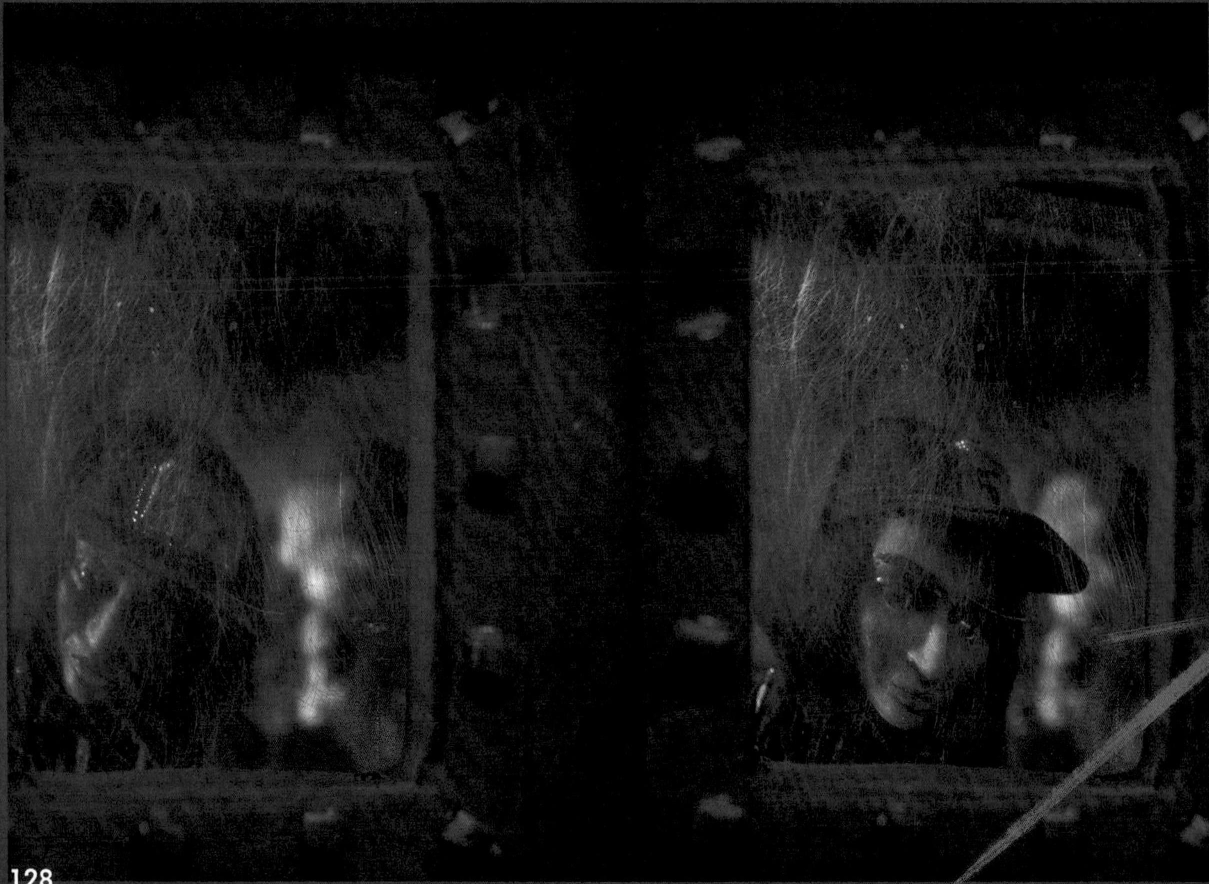

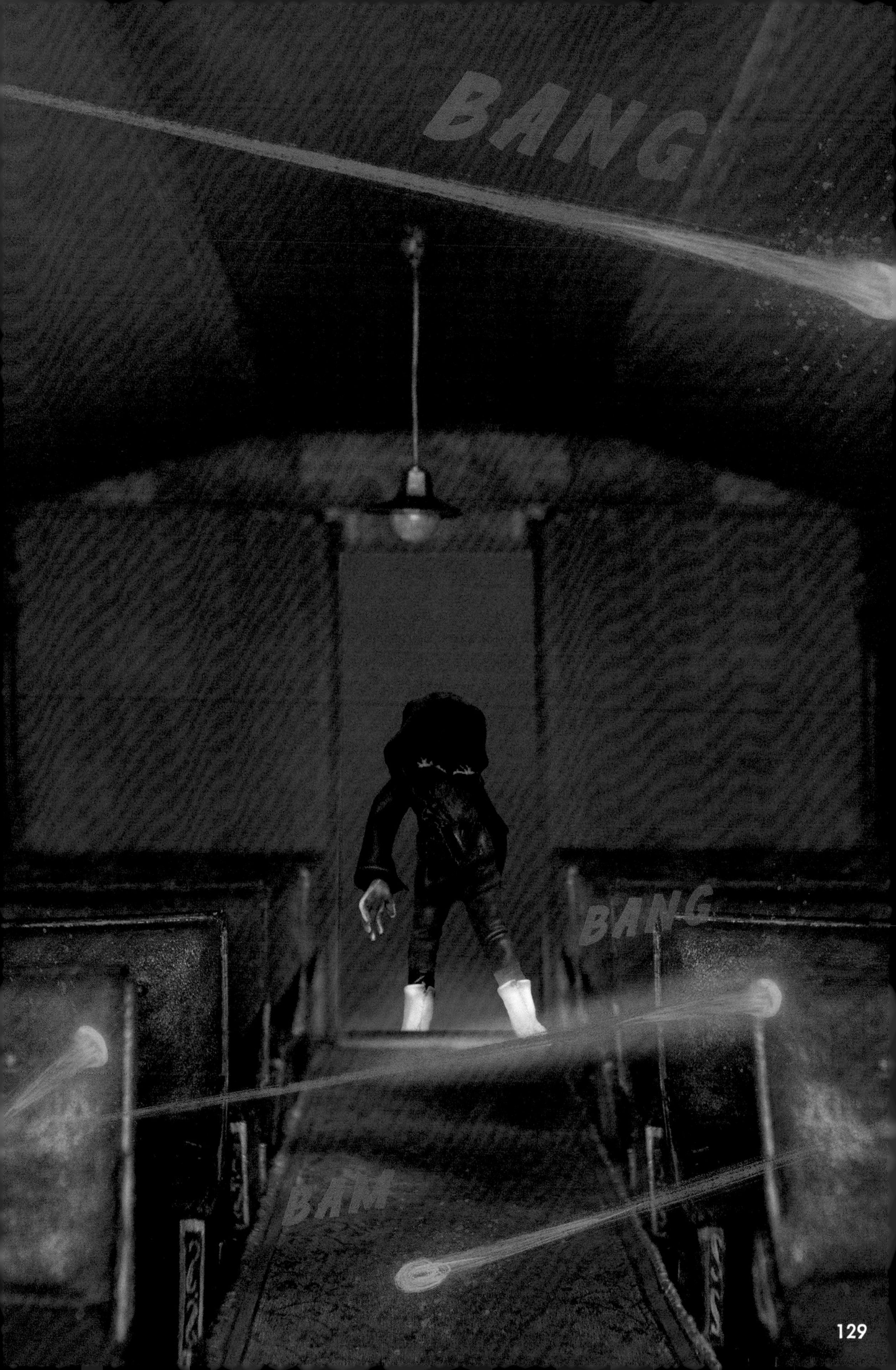
BANG
BANG
BAM

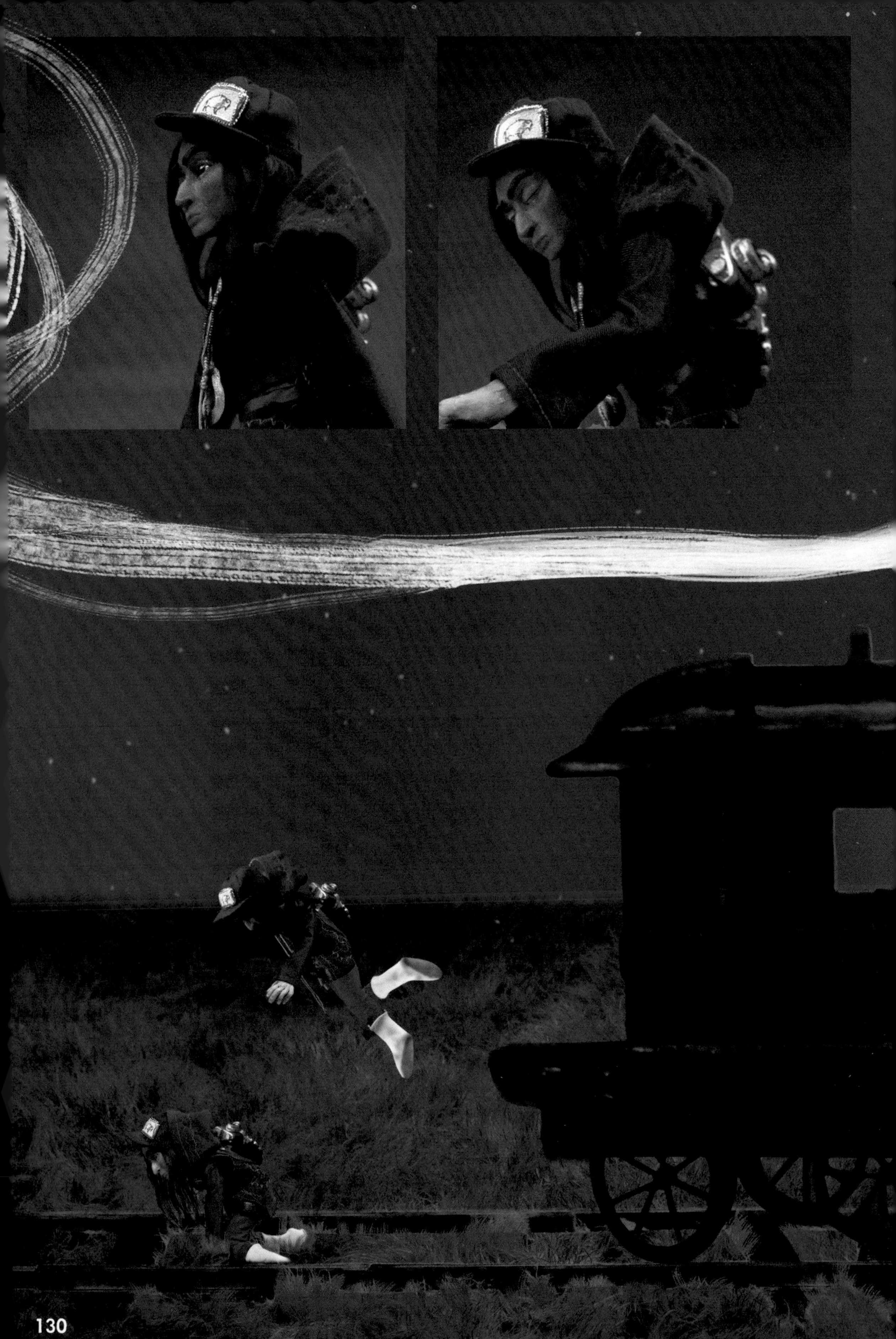

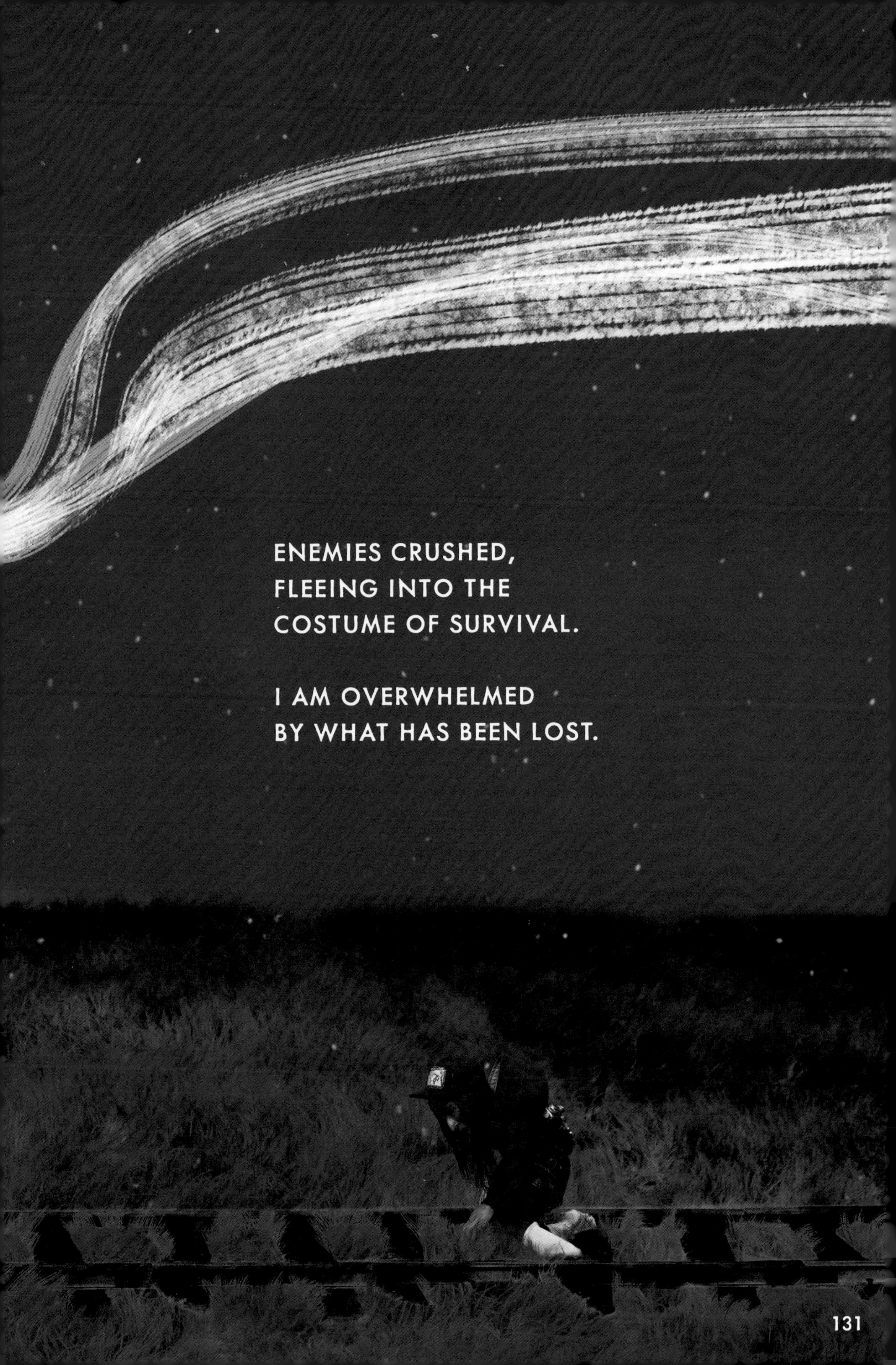

ENEMIES CRUSHED,
FLEEING INTO THE
COSTUME OF SURVIVAL.

I AM OVERWHELMED
BY WHAT HAS BEEN LOST.

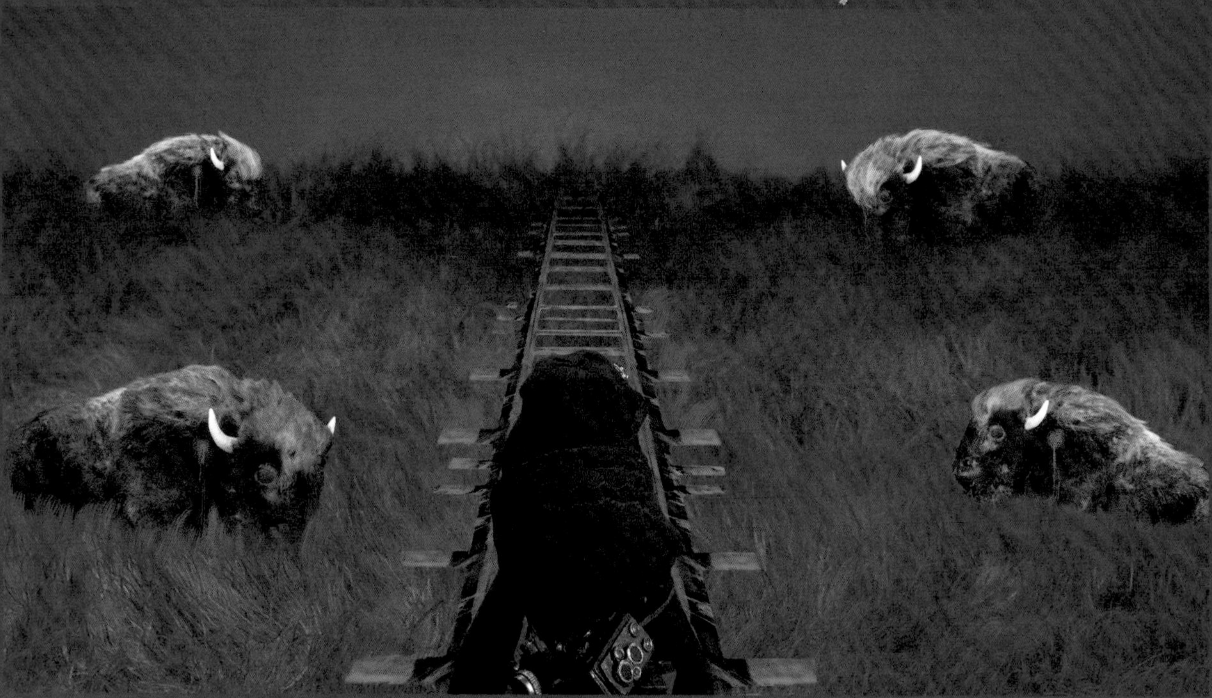

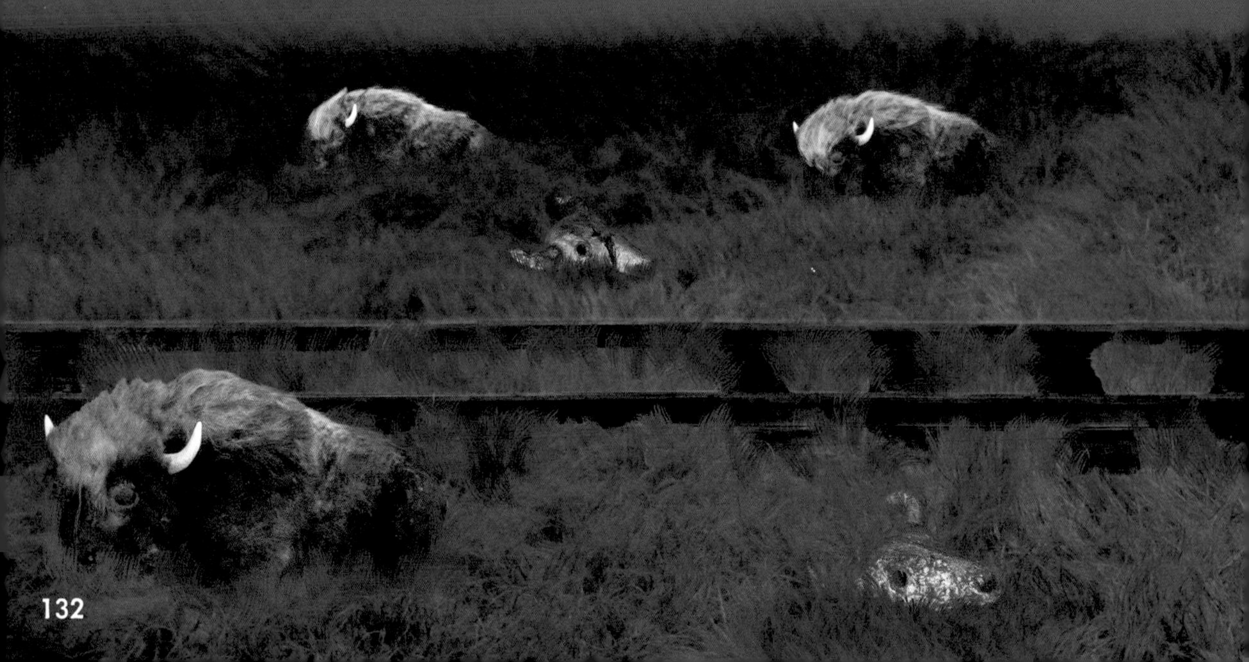

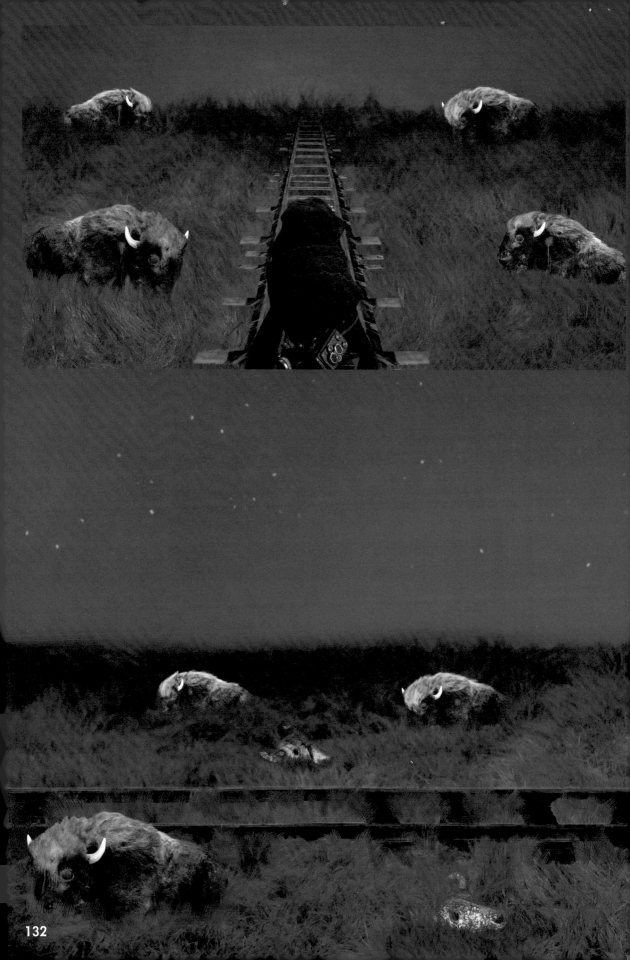

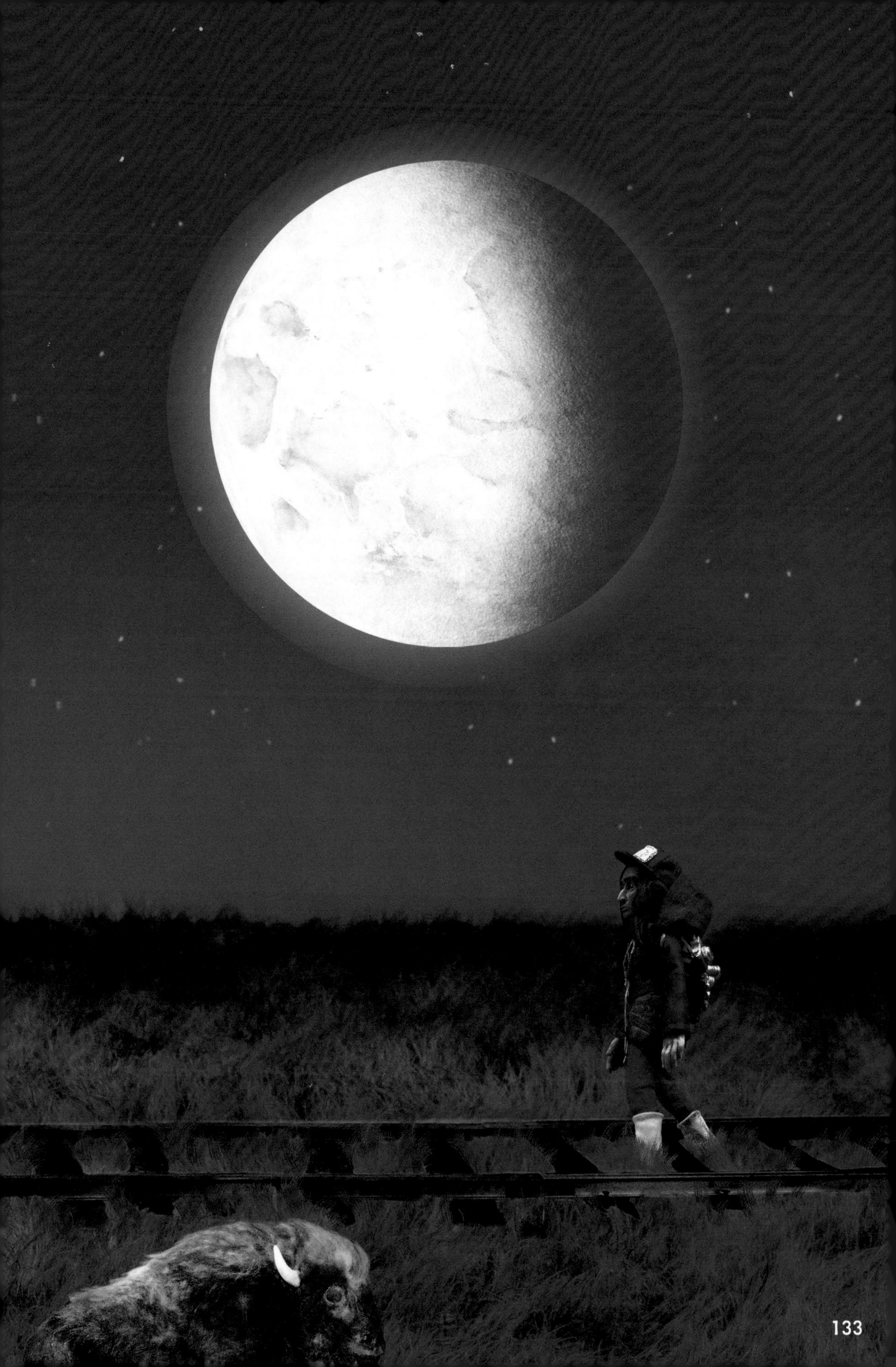

CHAPTER FOUR
FULL MOON

WE WALK TRAPPED IN THE MOON'S SHADOW.
TRACING TIME ON SKIN,
DIGGING UP THE MEDICINE
TO HEAL AND GROW STRONGER.

GII BIMOSEYANG, DASOOZO
BIINDE DBIK GIIZIS AGAWAATEY
AAZHAWEWESIJIGE ZHIGWA GIGISHKAW,
MOON'A-ASH-KIKIWE
AABAAKAWIZII MIINAWA IZHIGI MASHKAWIZI.

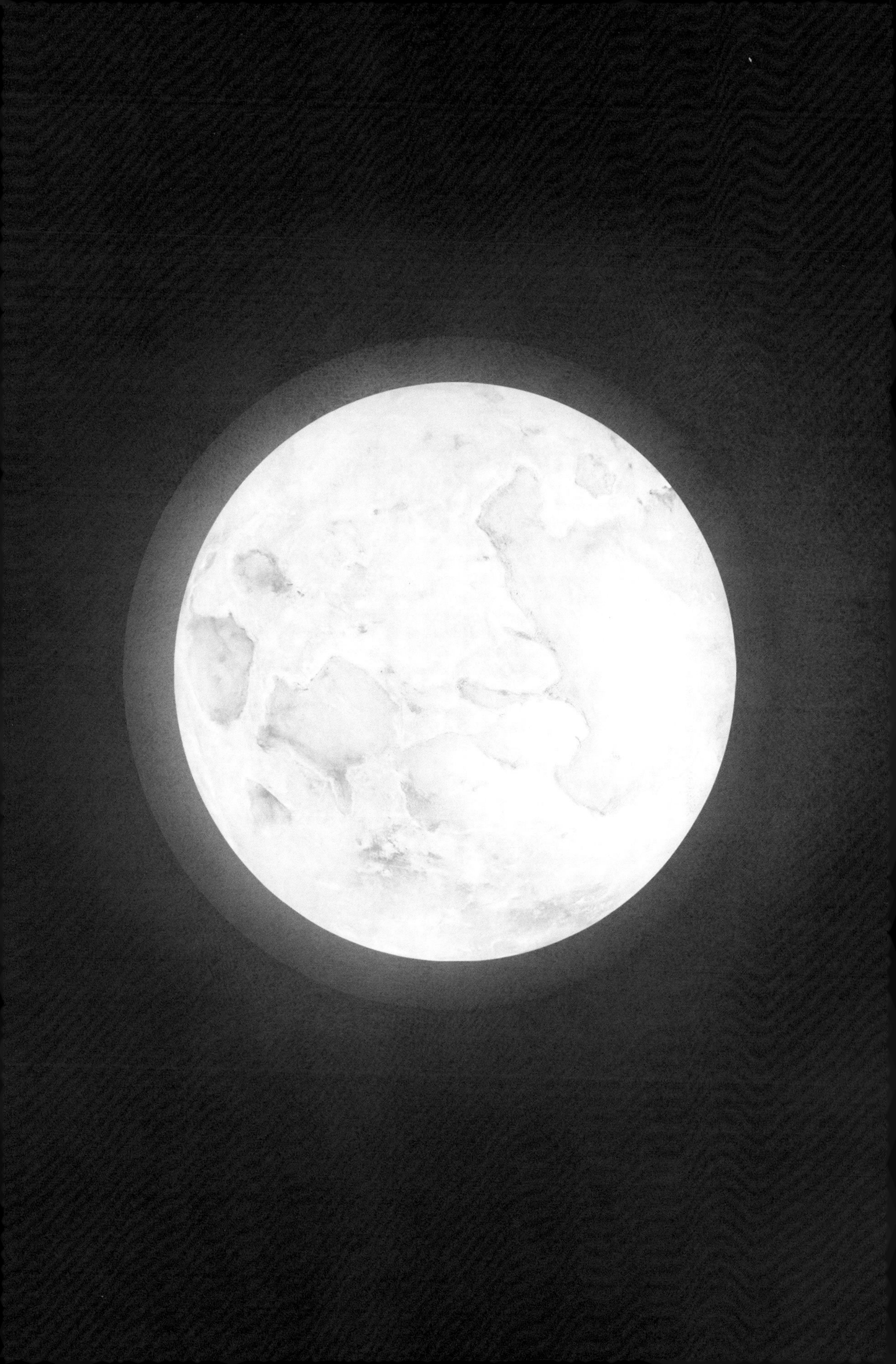

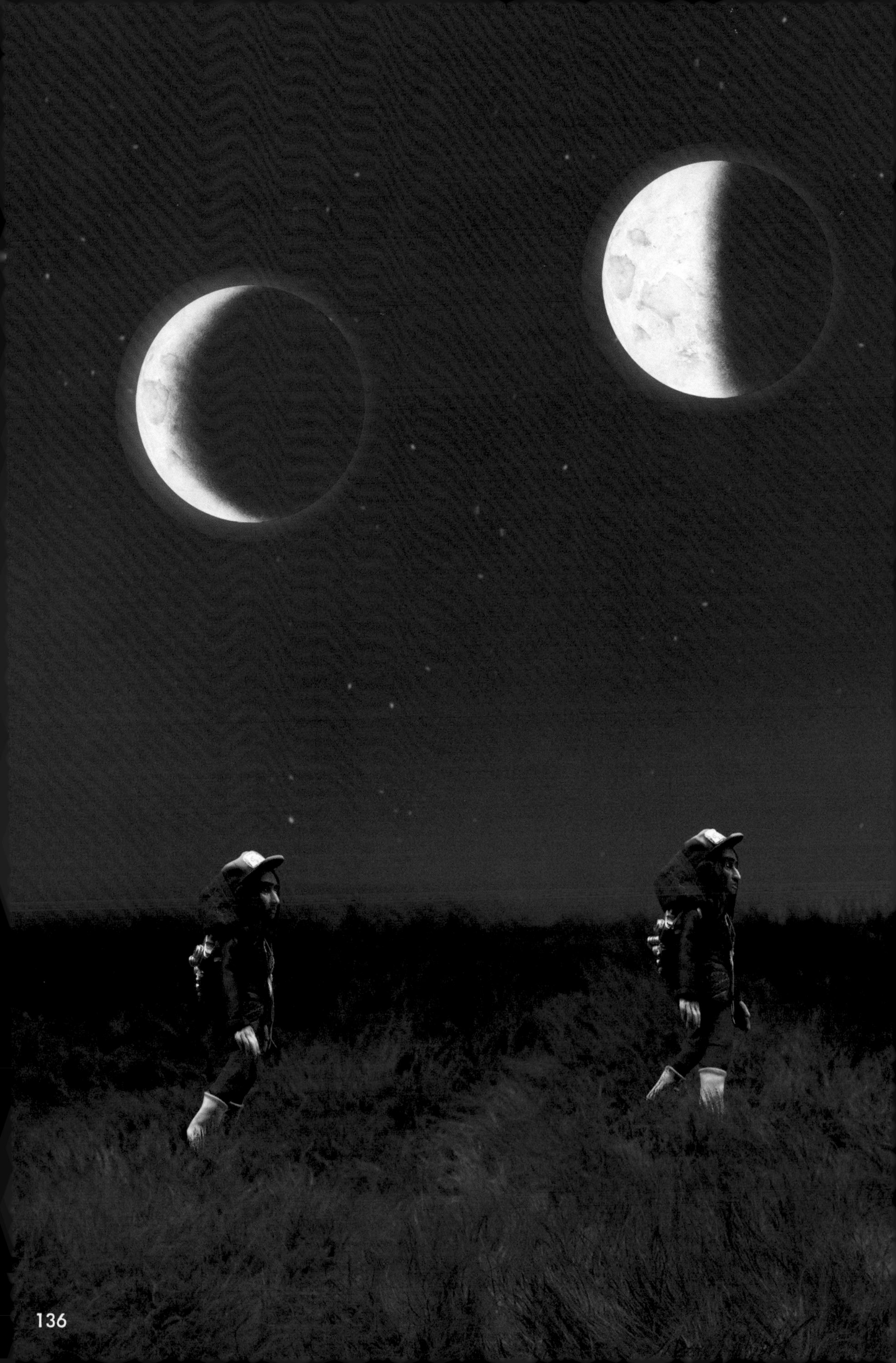

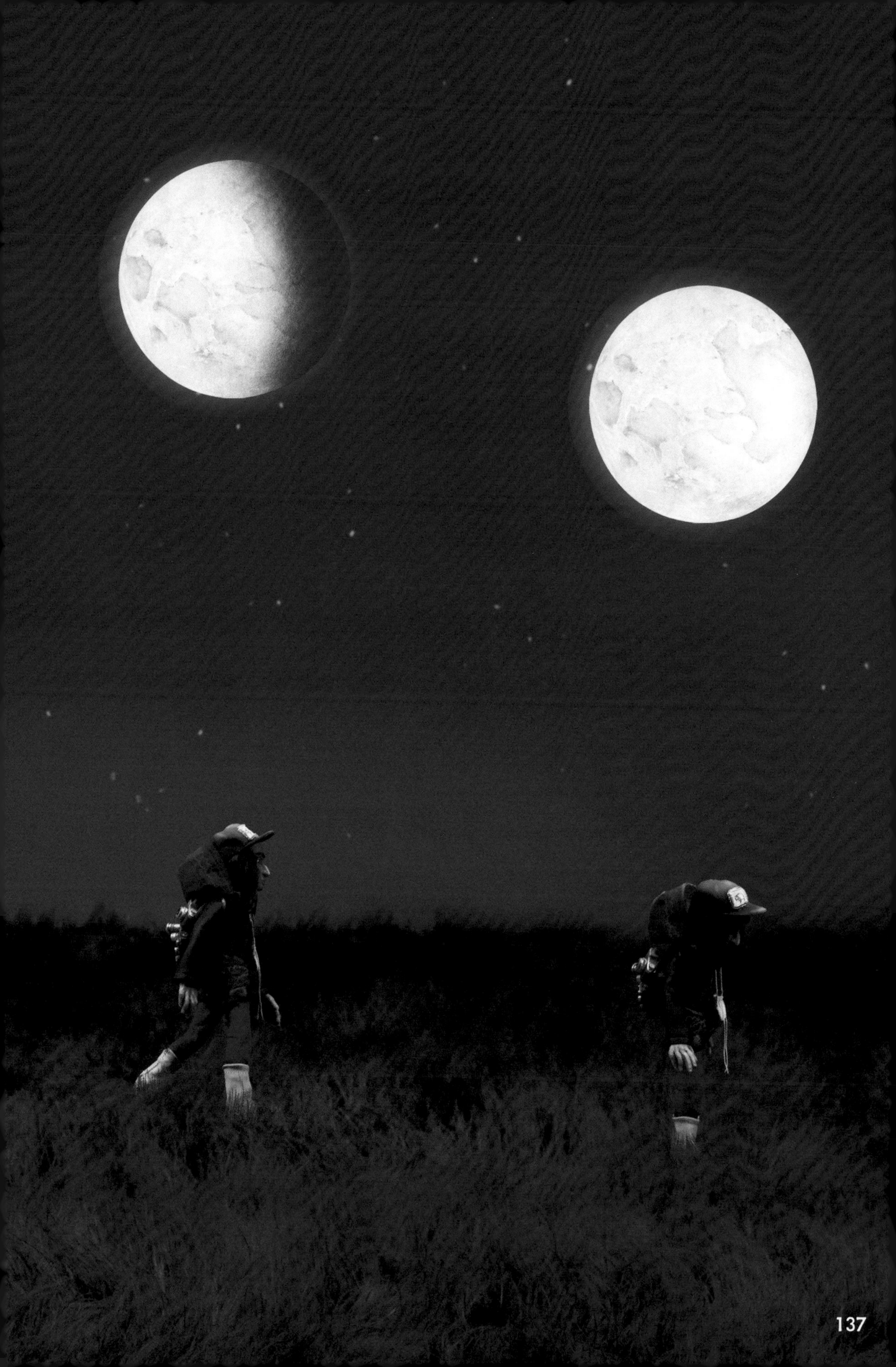

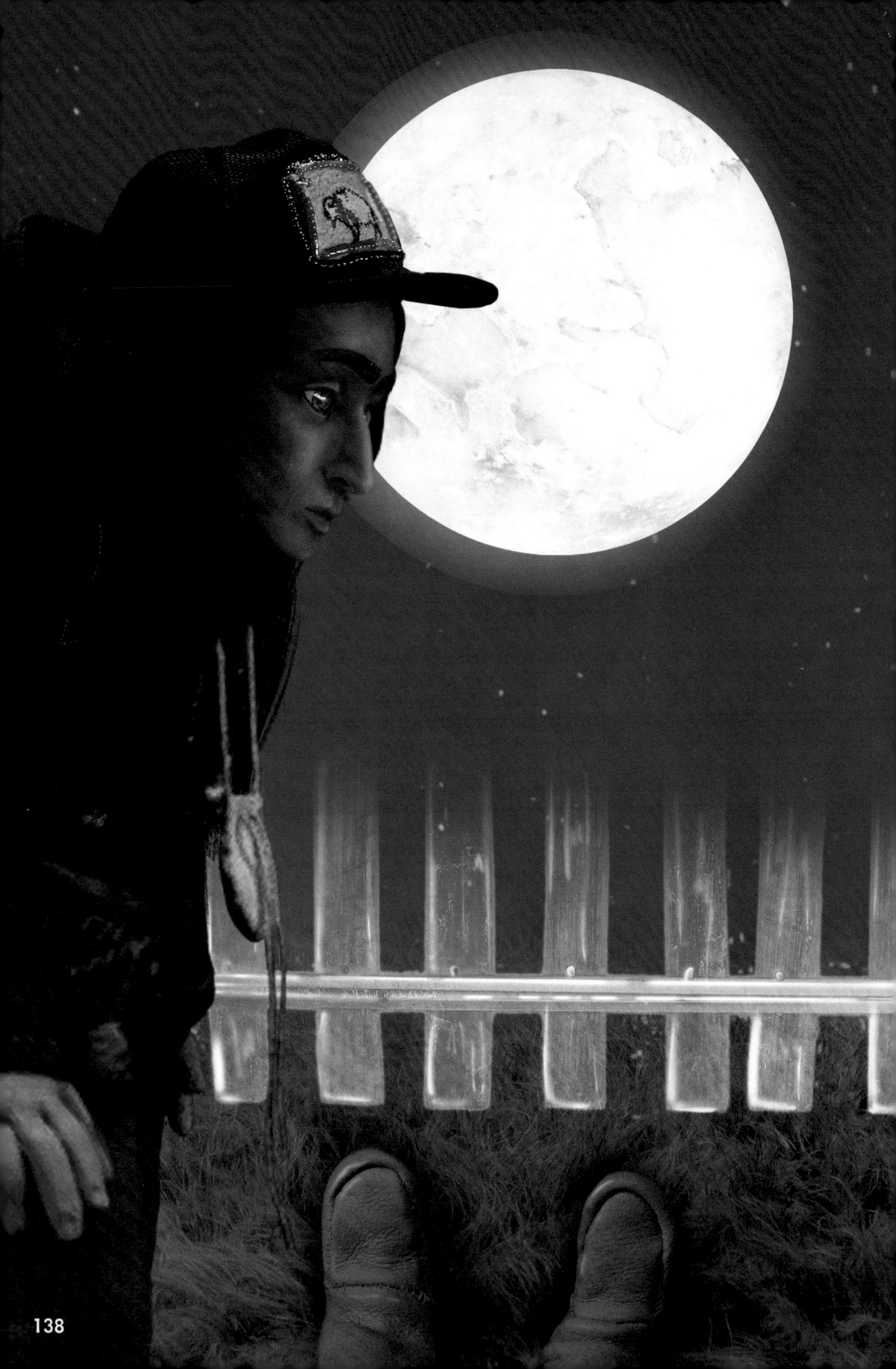

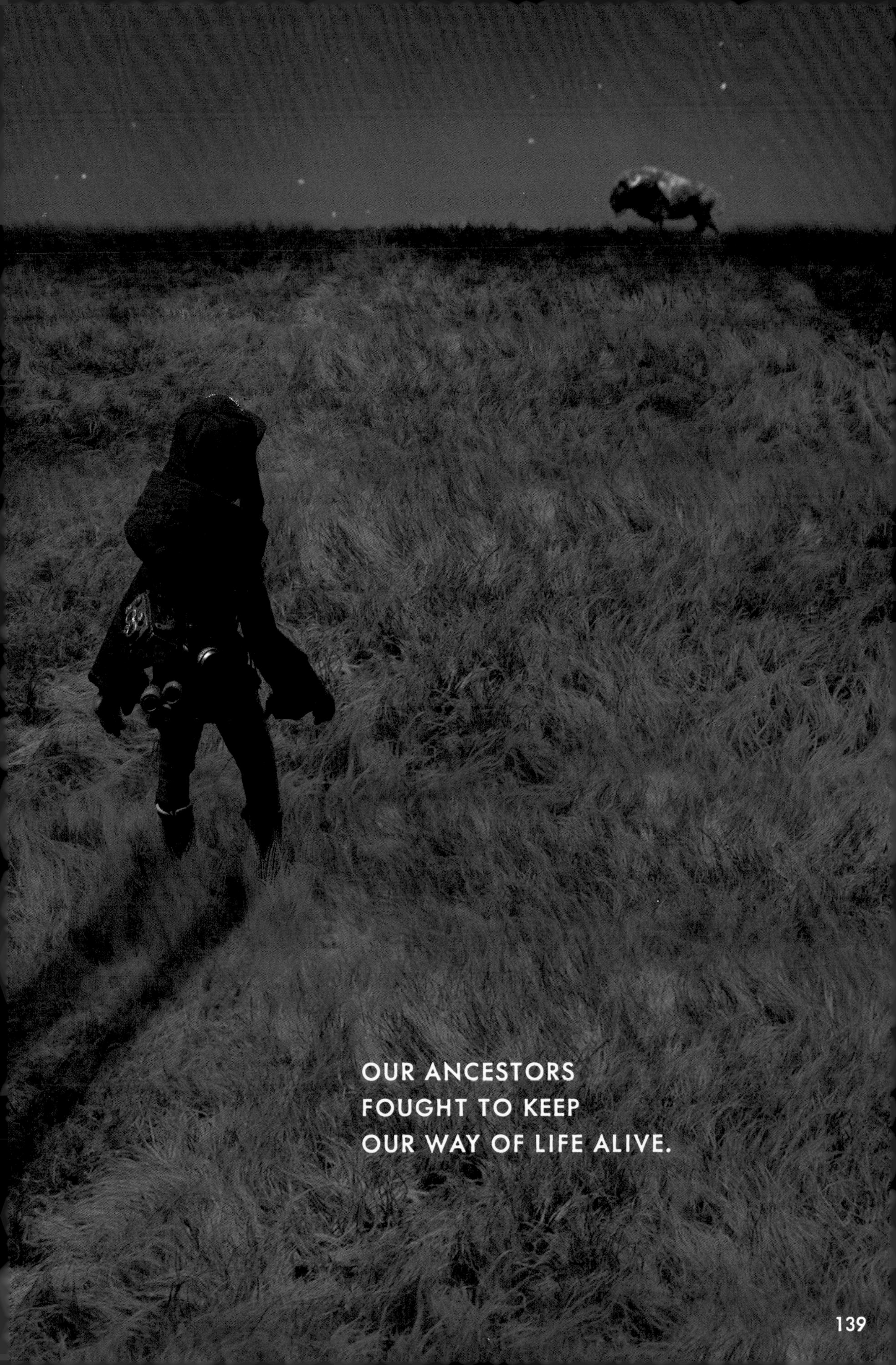
OUR ANCESTORS
FOUGHT TO KEEP
OUR WAY OF LIFE ALIVE.

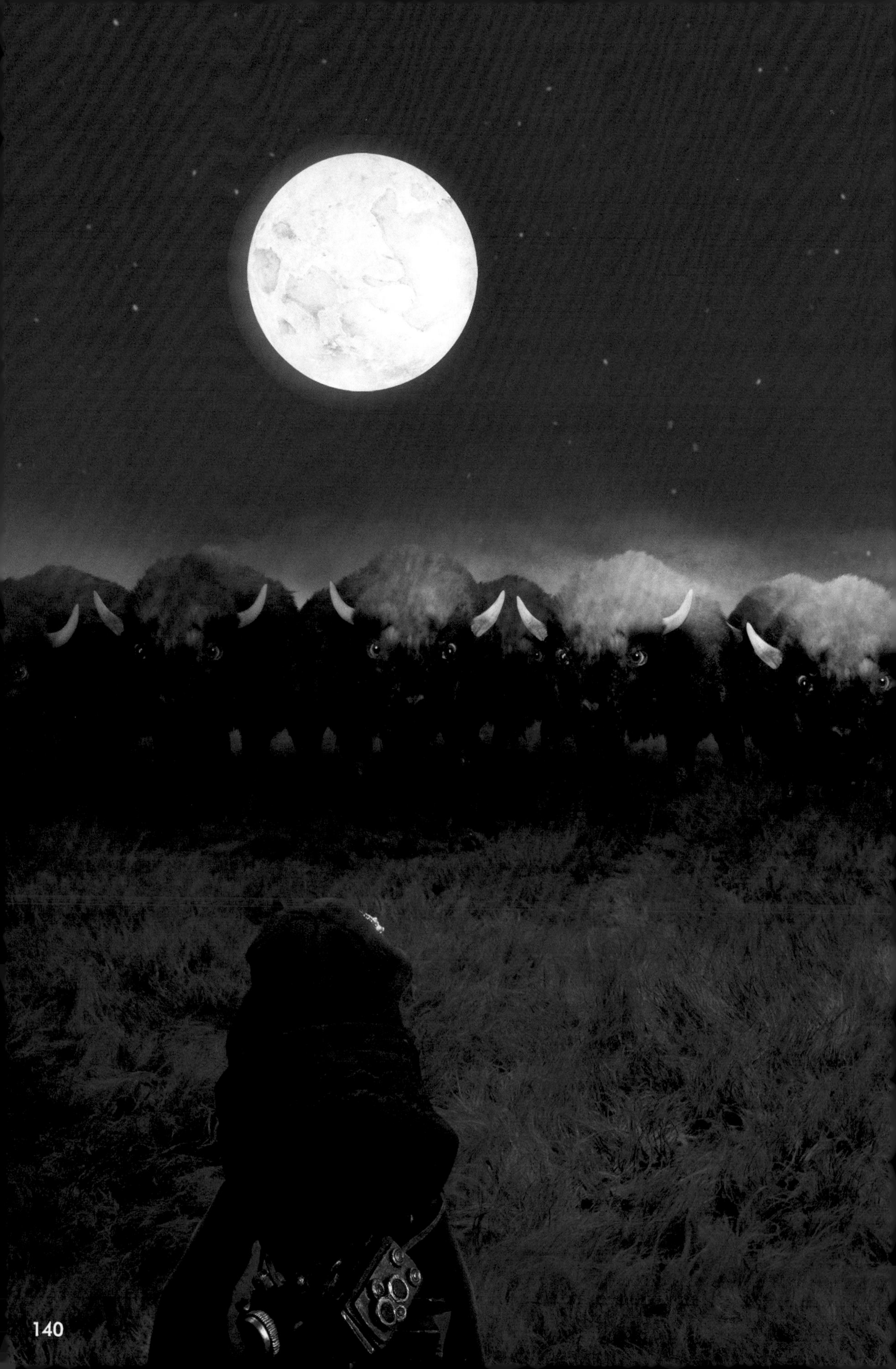

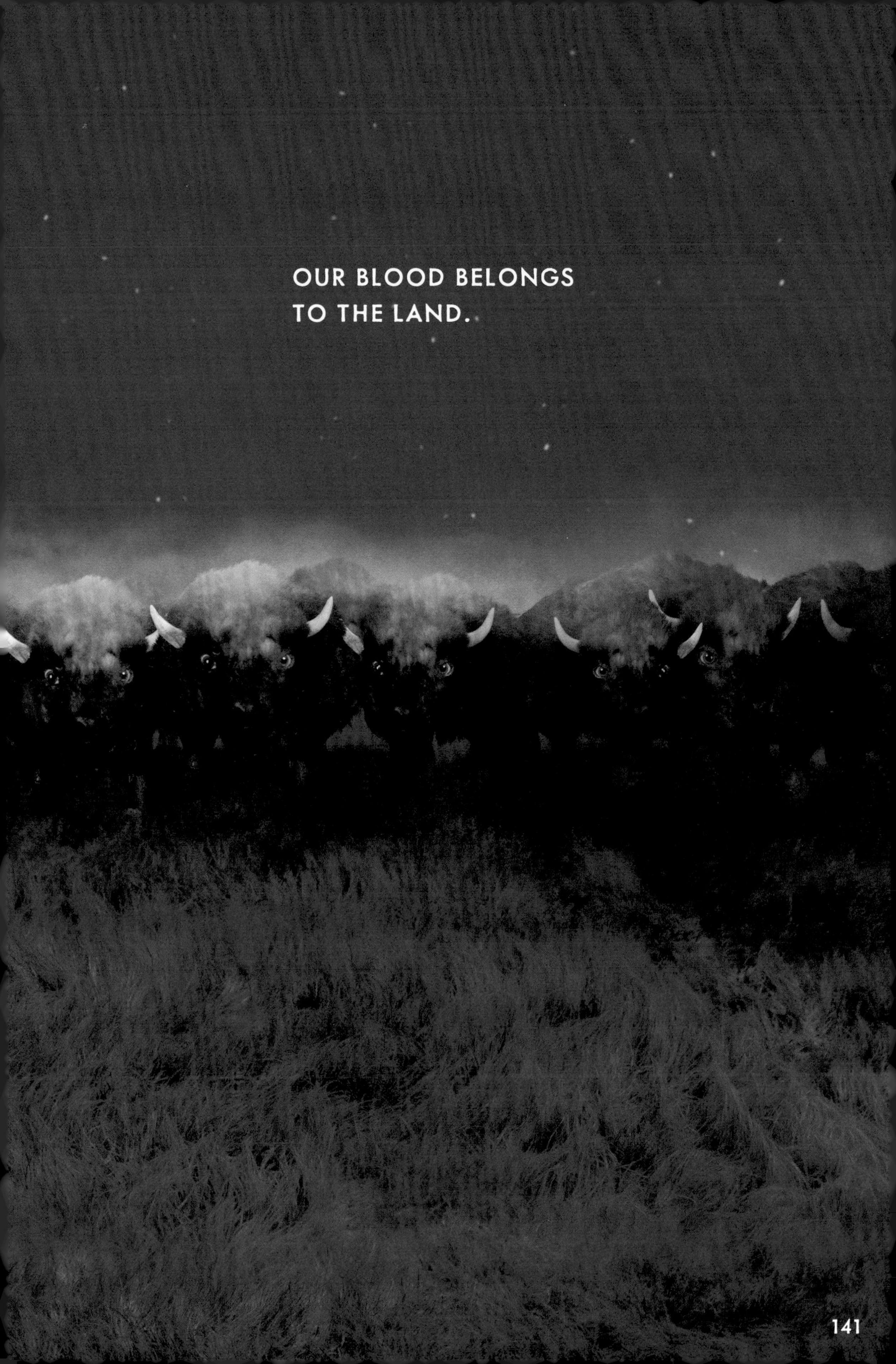
OUR BLOOD BELONGS
TO THE LAND.

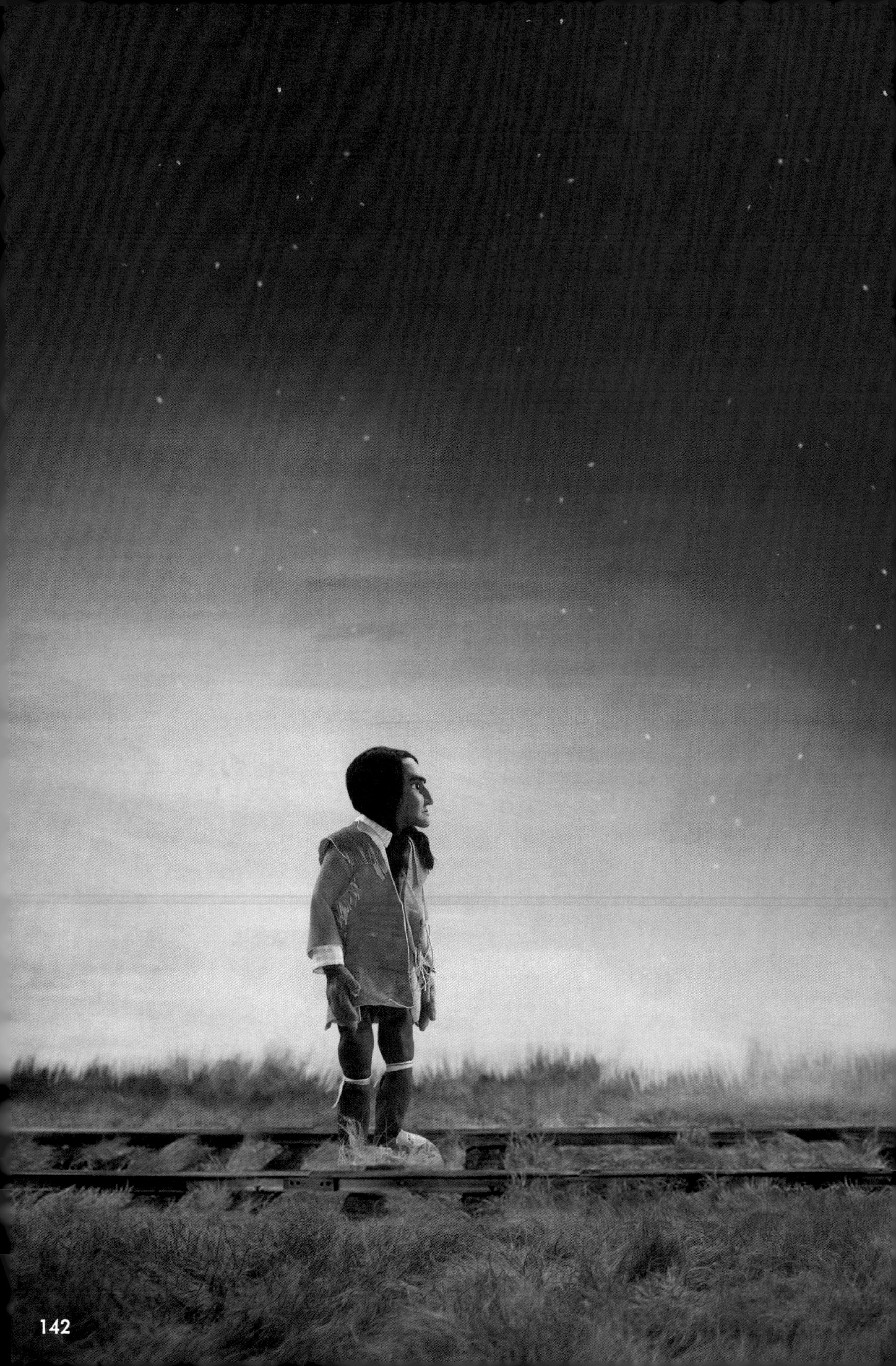

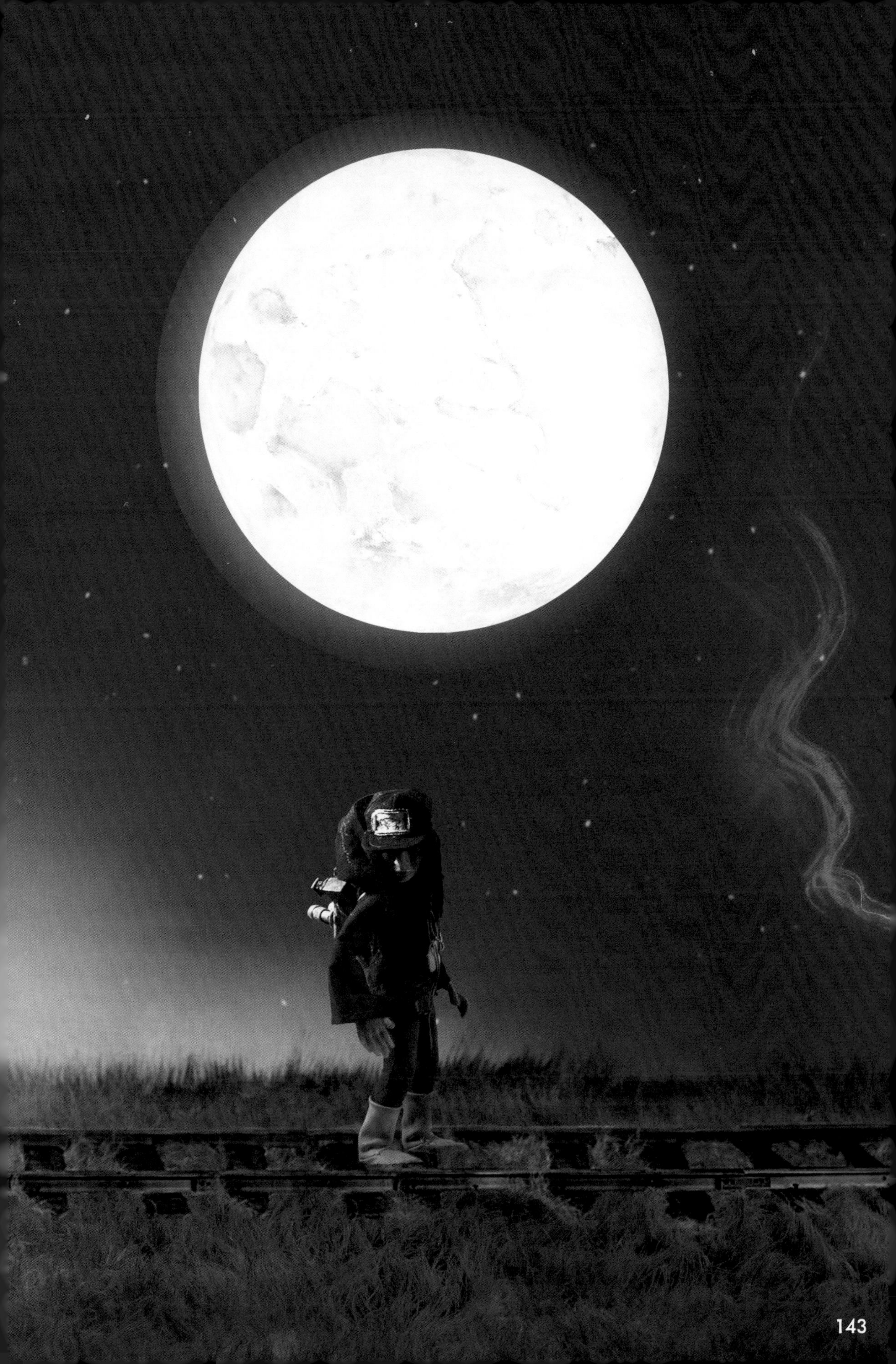

PEMBINA

1850

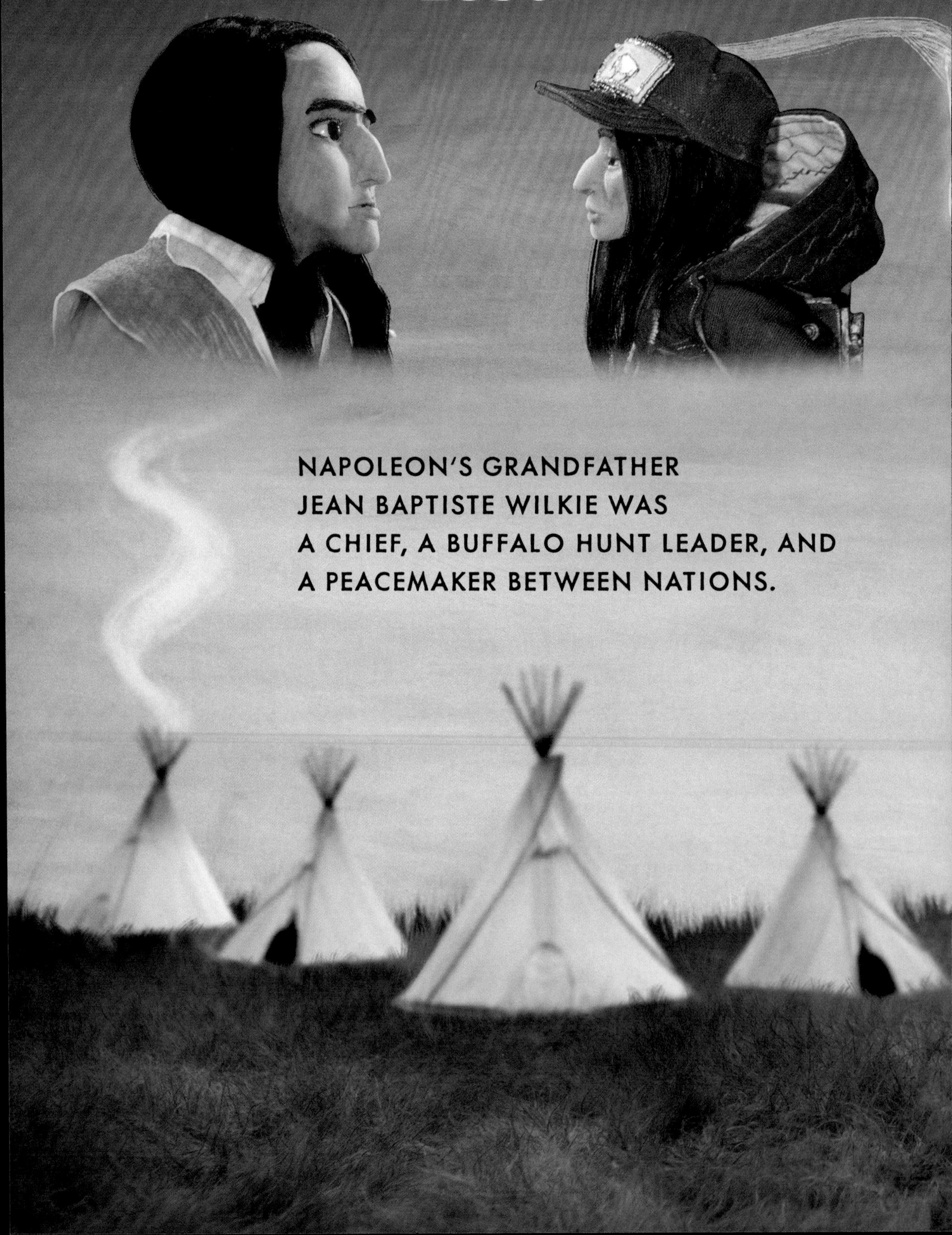

NAPOLEON'S GRANDFATHER JEAN BAPTISTE WILKIE WAS A CHIEF, A BUFFALO HUNT LEADER, AND A PEACEMAKER BETWEEN NATIONS.

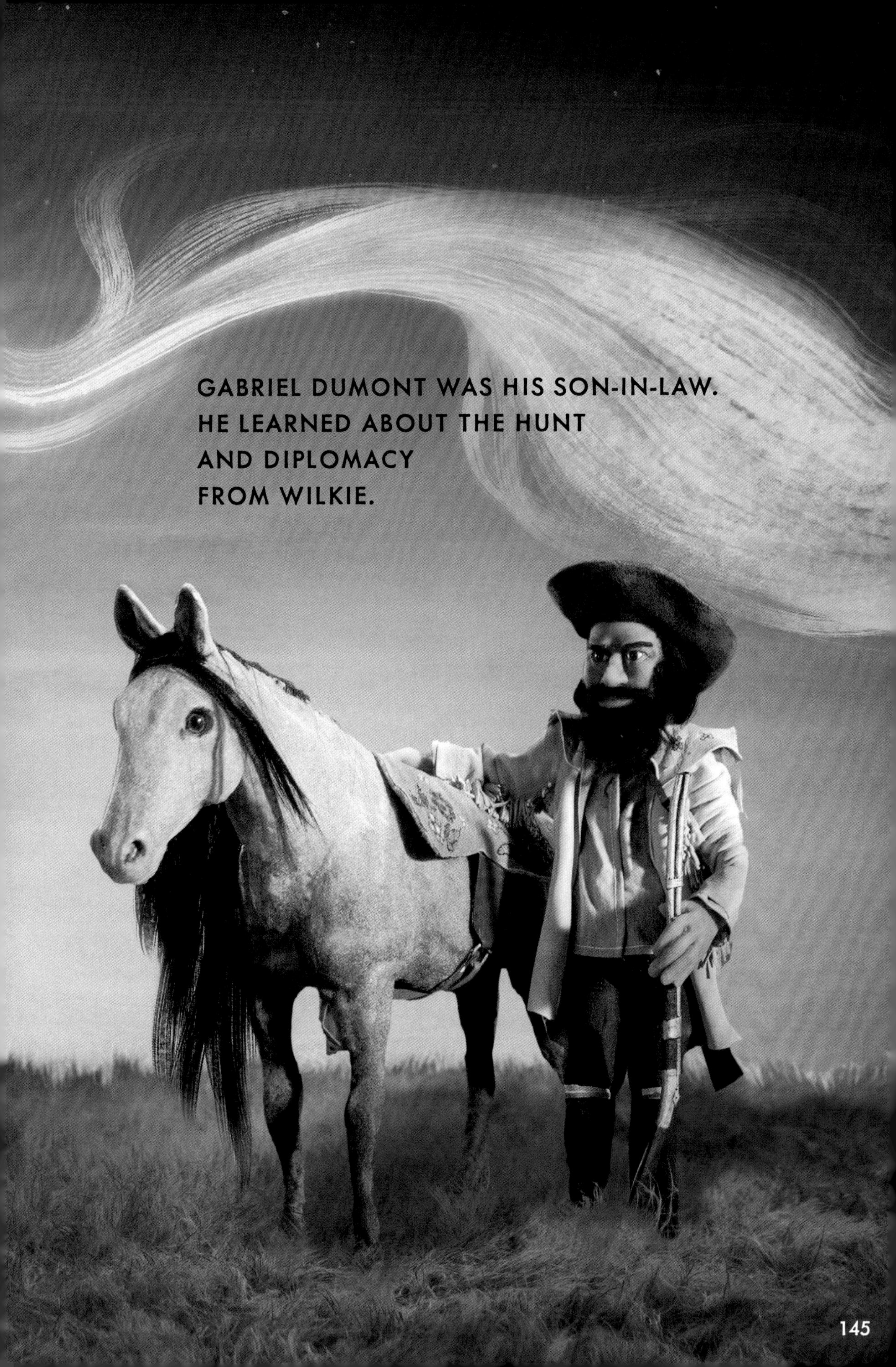

GABRIEL DUMONT WAS HIS SON-IN-LAW.
HE LEARNED ABOUT THE HUNT
AND DIPLOMACY
FROM WILKIE.

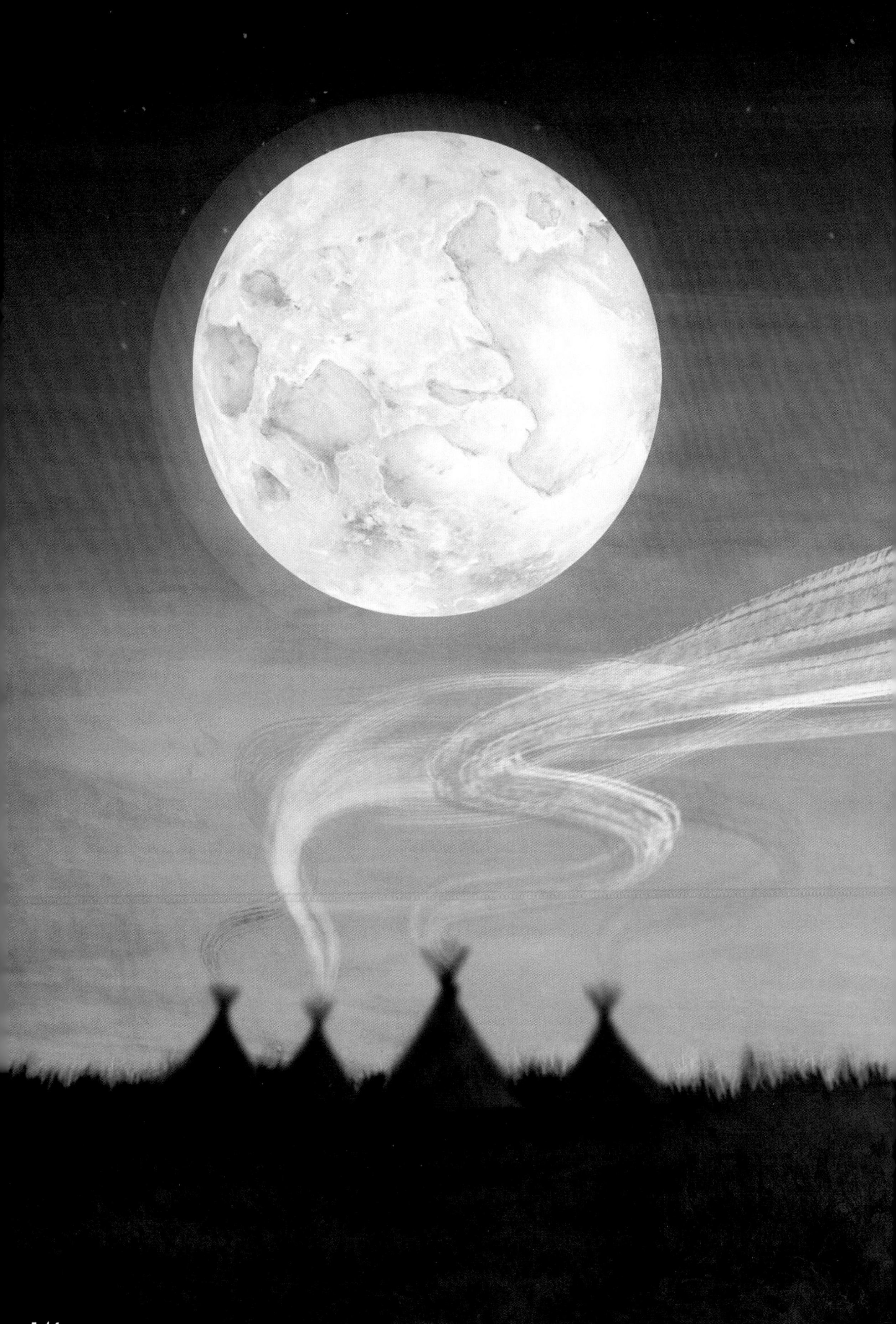

WILKIE SPOKE MANY LANGUAGES AND WAS ABLE TO COMMUNICATE WITH MANY INDIGENOUS PEOPLES AND ENGLISH-SPEAKING SETTLERS.

HE ONCE CAME ACROSS SURVEYORS FOR THE RAILWAY AND SPOKE TO THEM ABOUT THEIR PLANS.

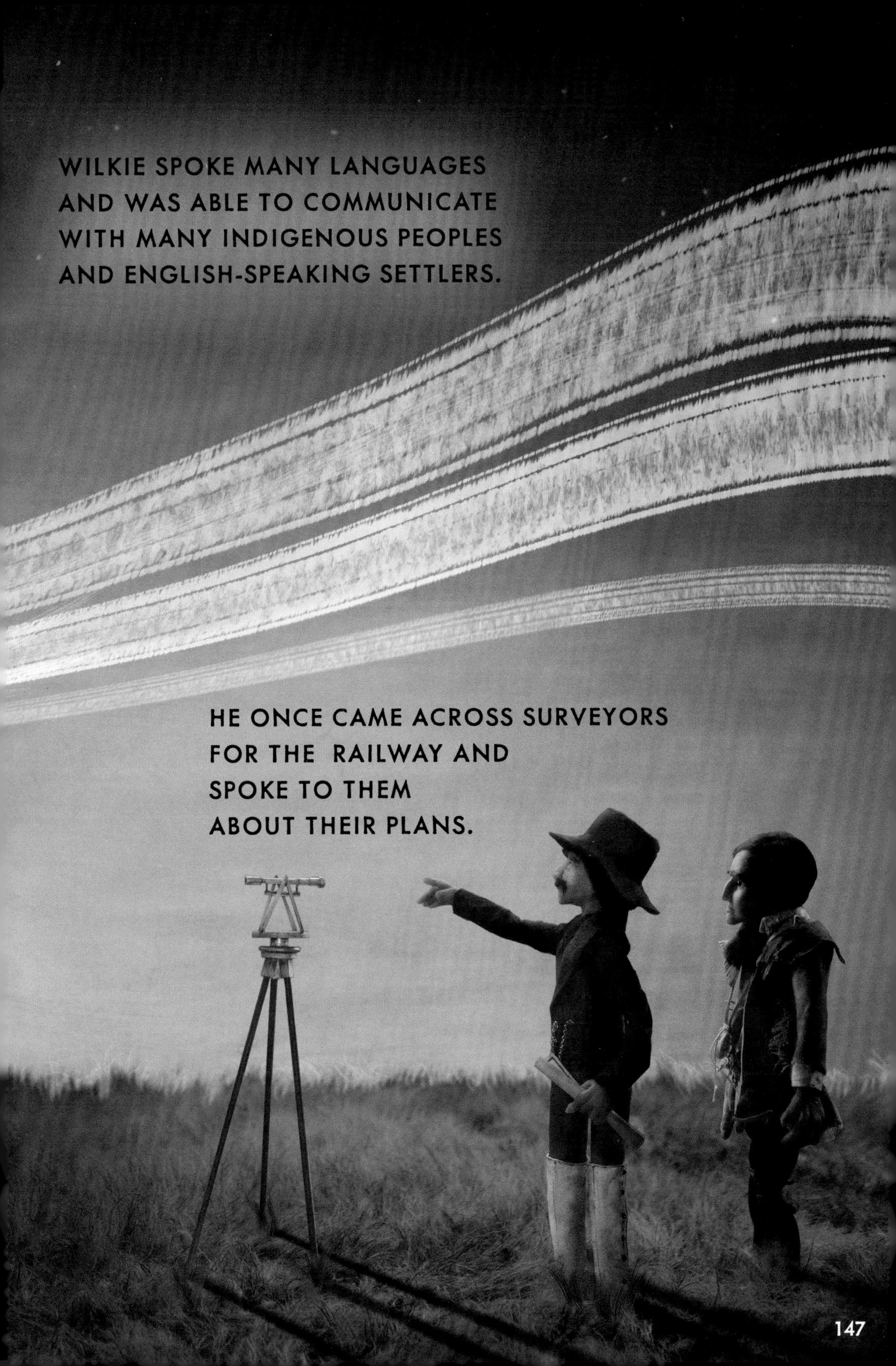

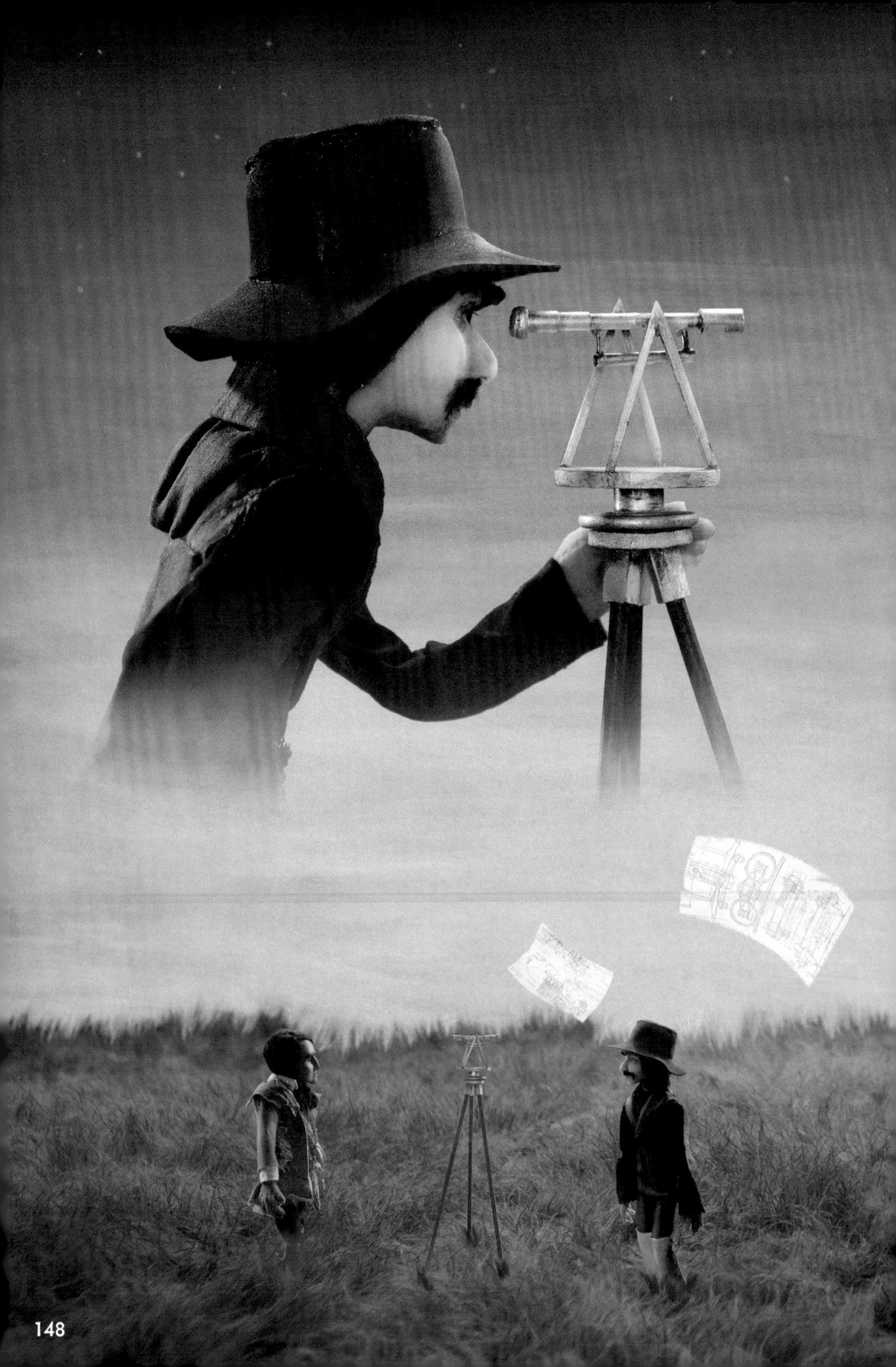

THEY HAD VERY DIFFERENT IDEAS
FOR LIVING
WITH THE LAND.

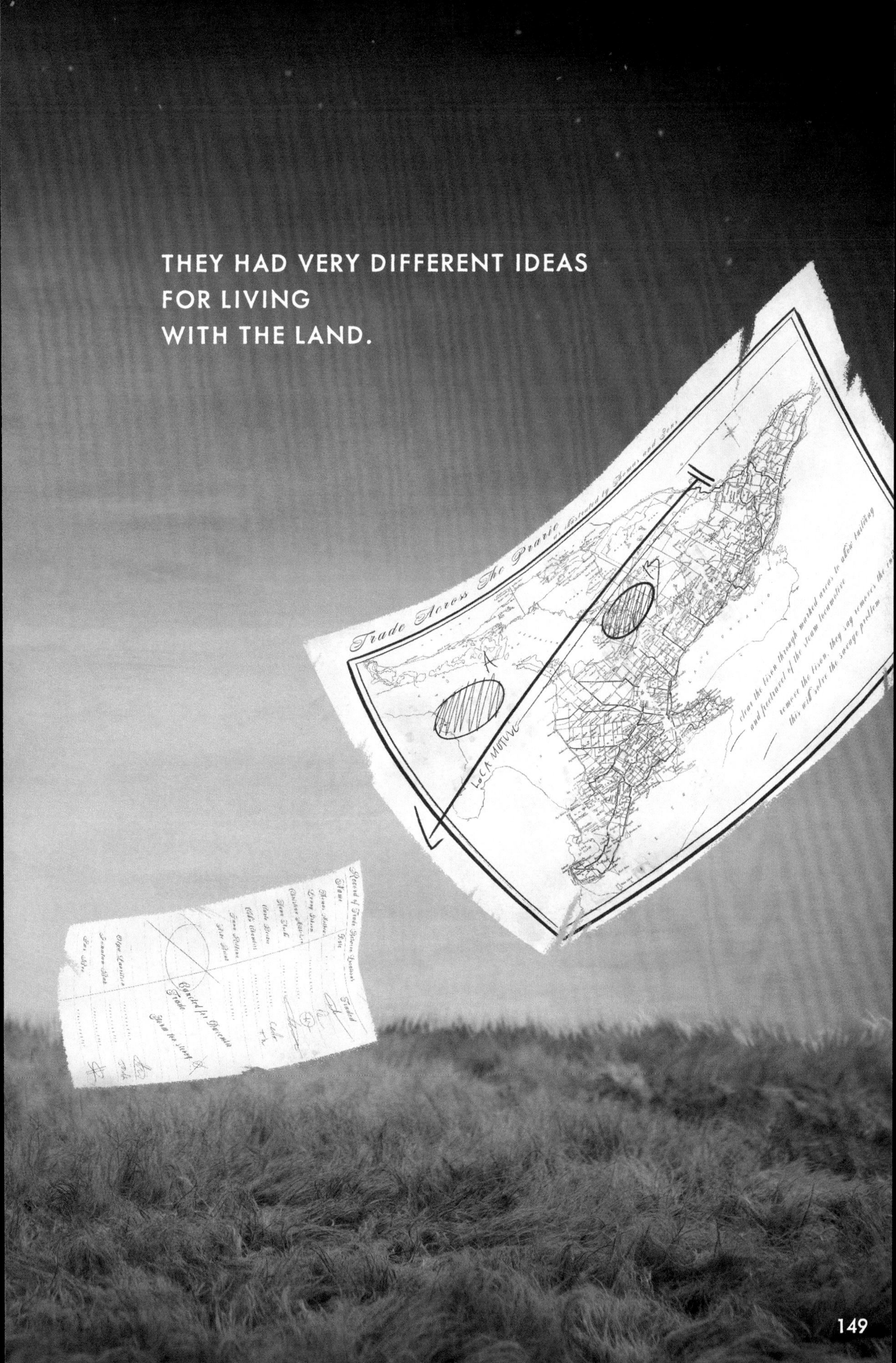

Trade Across The Prairie
LOCAMOTIVE

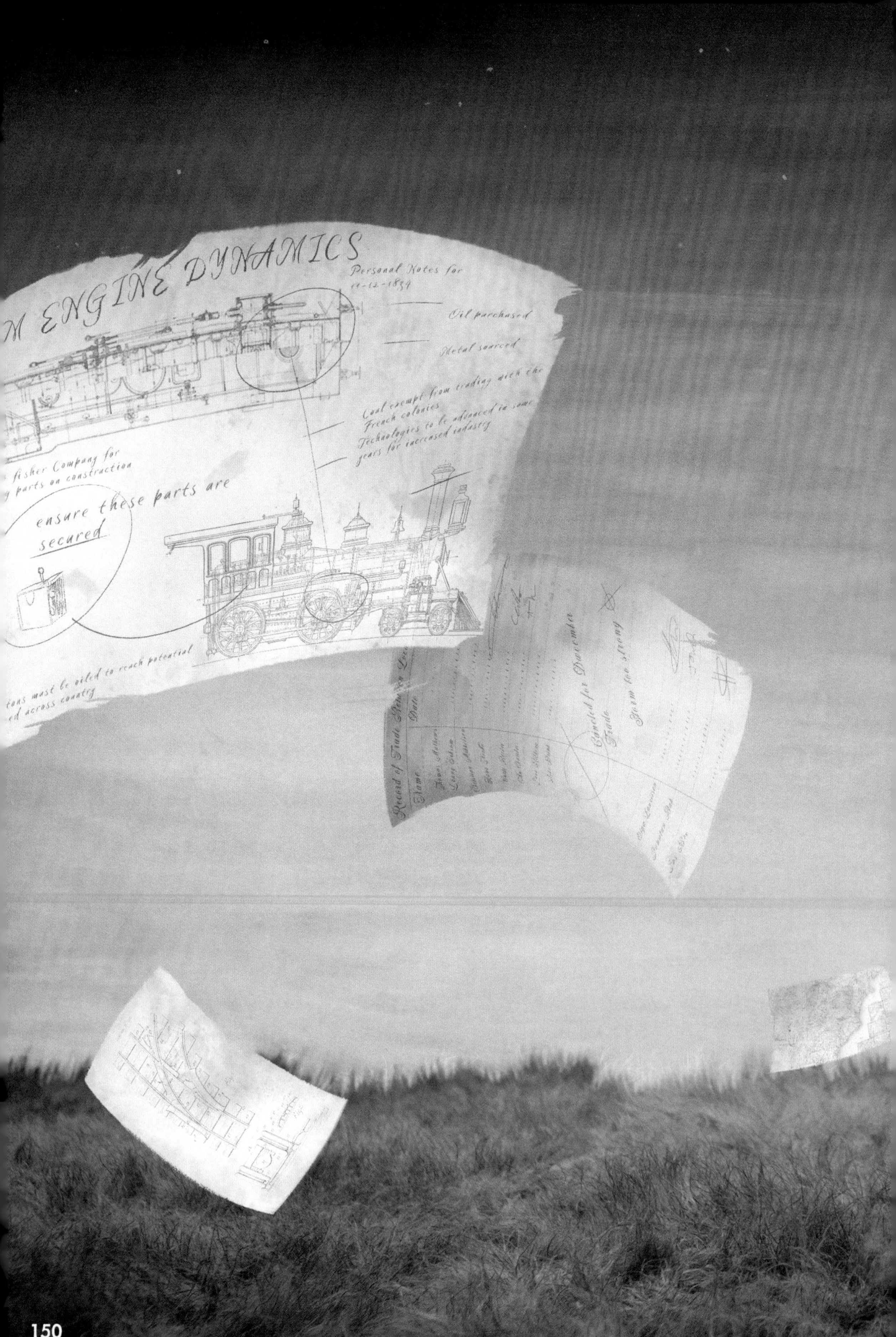
M ENGINE DYNAMICS
Personal Notes for
Oil purchased
Metal sourced
Coal exempt from trading with the French colonies
Technologies to be advanced in same years for increased industry
fisher Company for
parts on construction
ensure these parts are secured
tons must be oiled to reach potential
across country
Record of Trade
Name
Date
Canceled for December Trade
Storm too strong

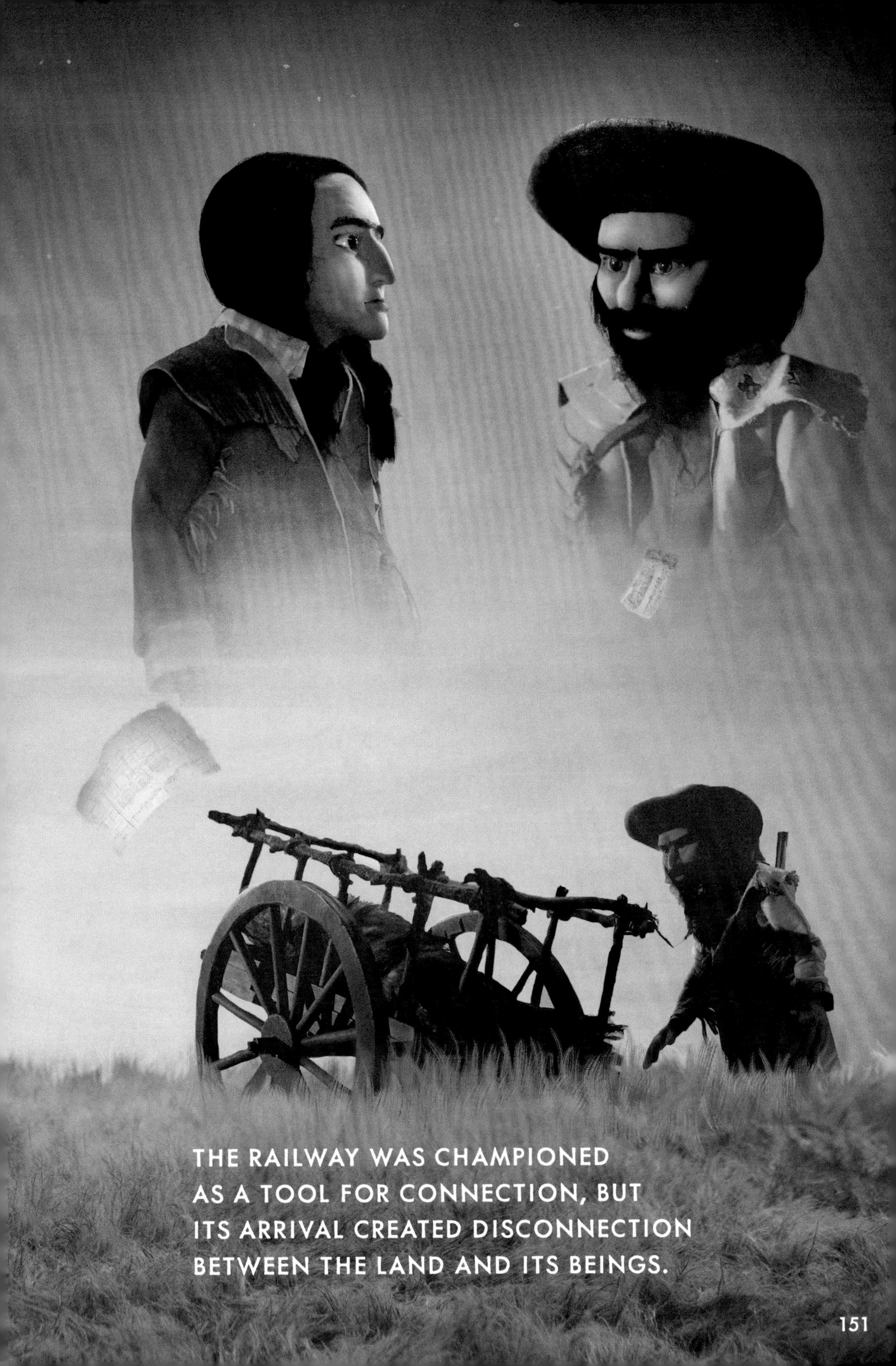

THE RAILWAY WAS CHAMPIONED AS A TOOL FOR CONNECTION, BUT ITS ARRIVAL CREATED DISCONNECTION BETWEEN THE LAND AND ITS BEINGS.

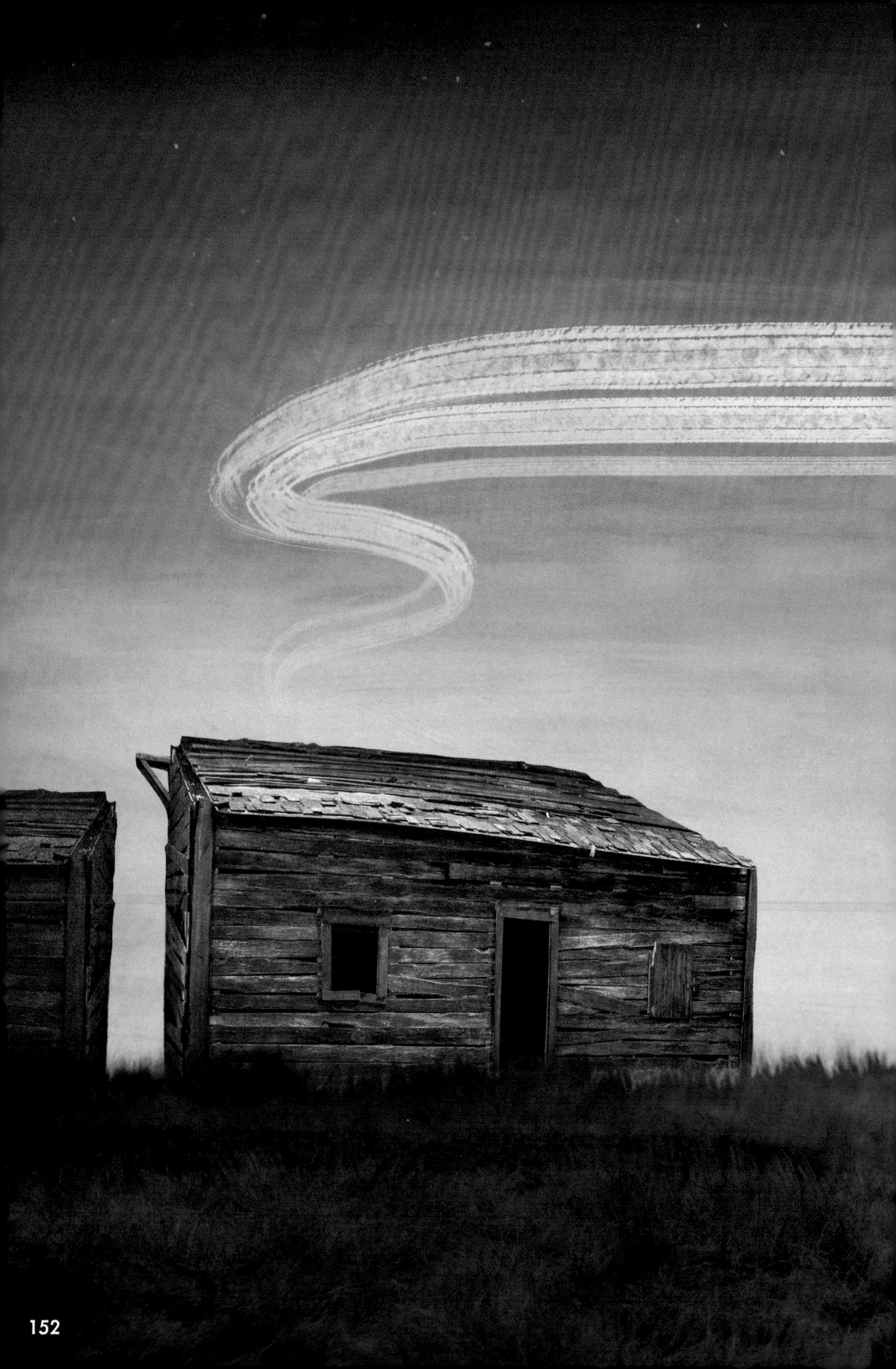

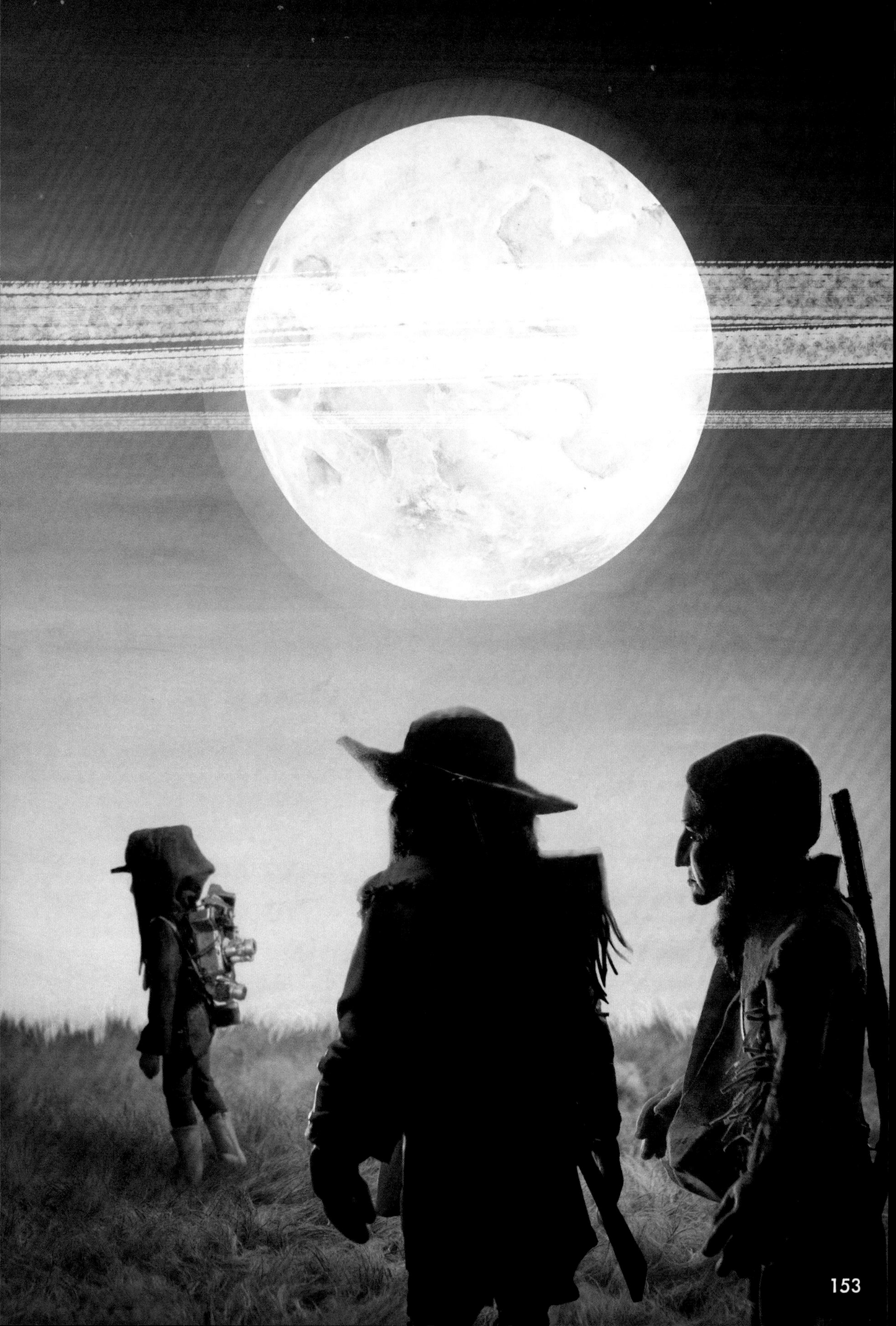

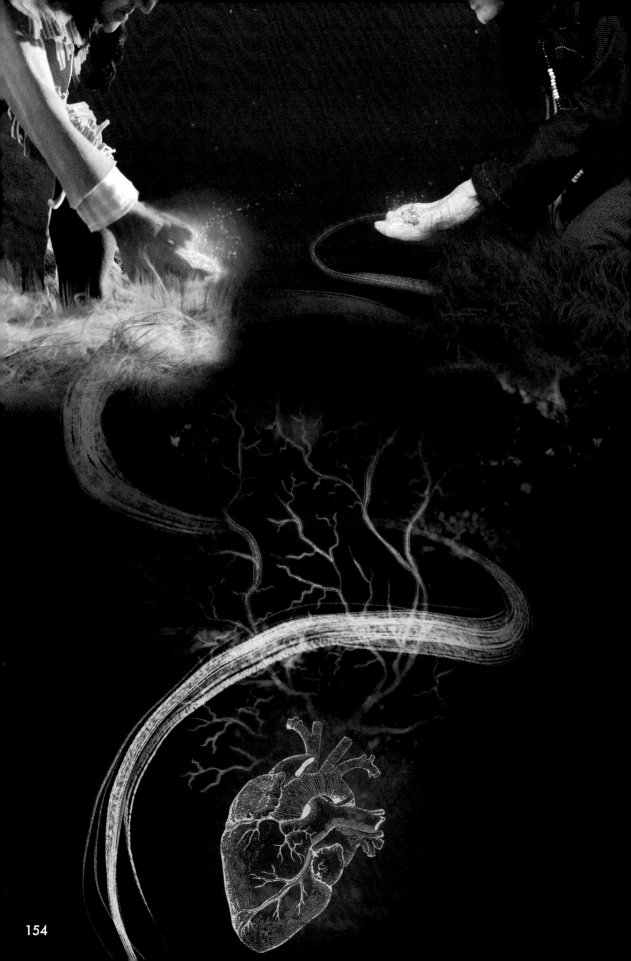

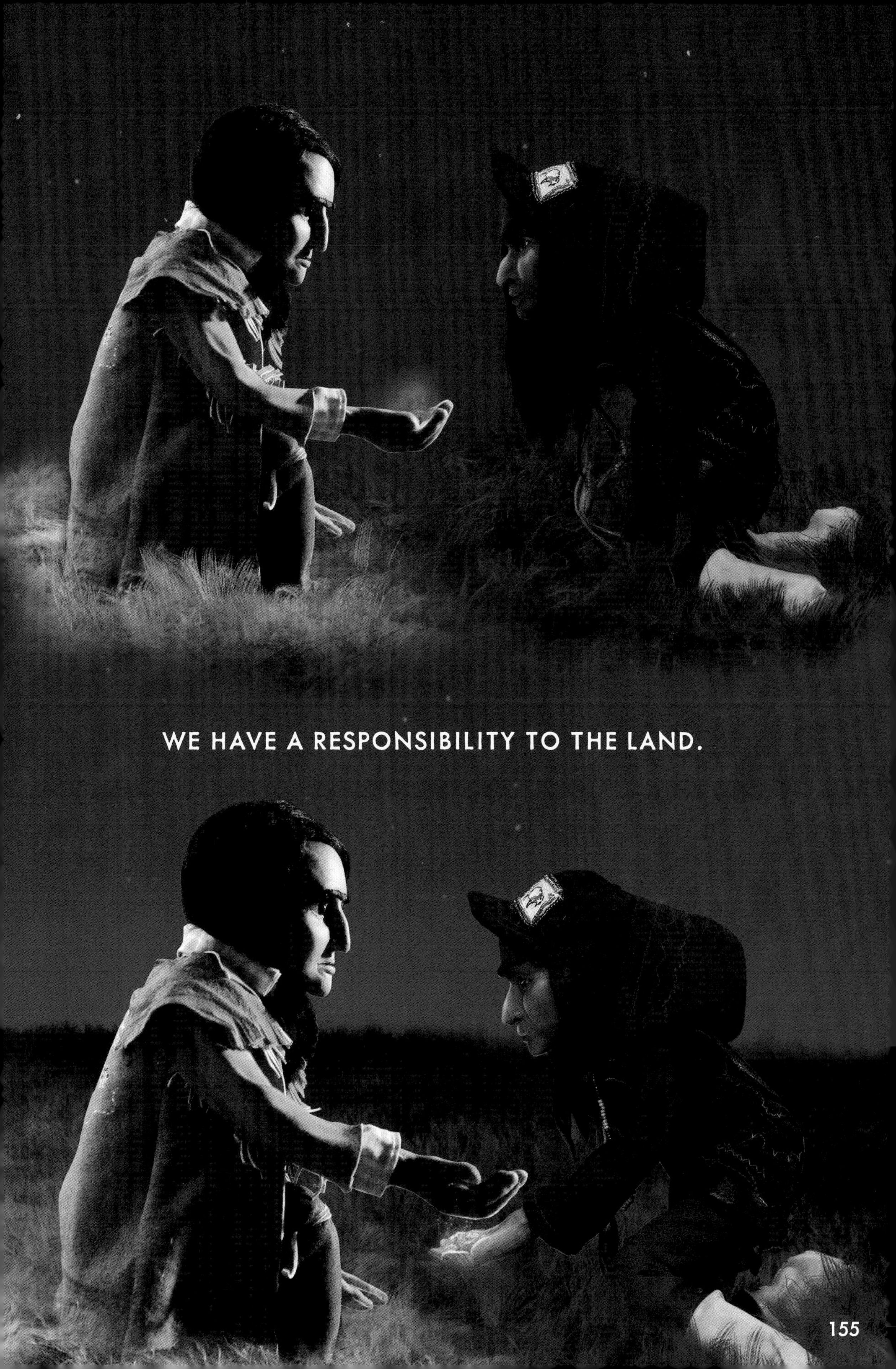
WE HAVE A RESPONSIBILITY TO THE LAND.

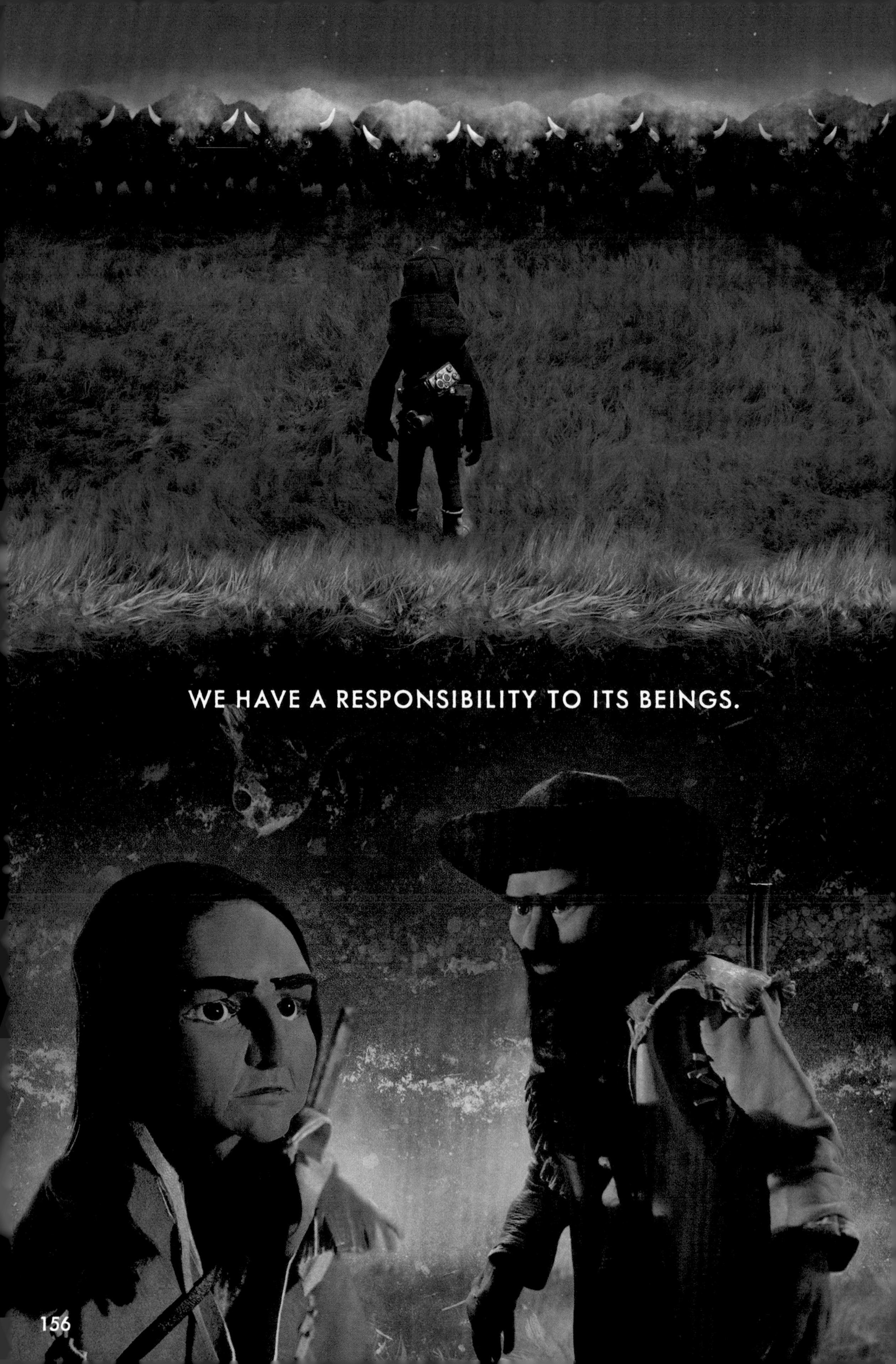
WE HAVE A RESPONSIBILITY TO ITS BEINGS.

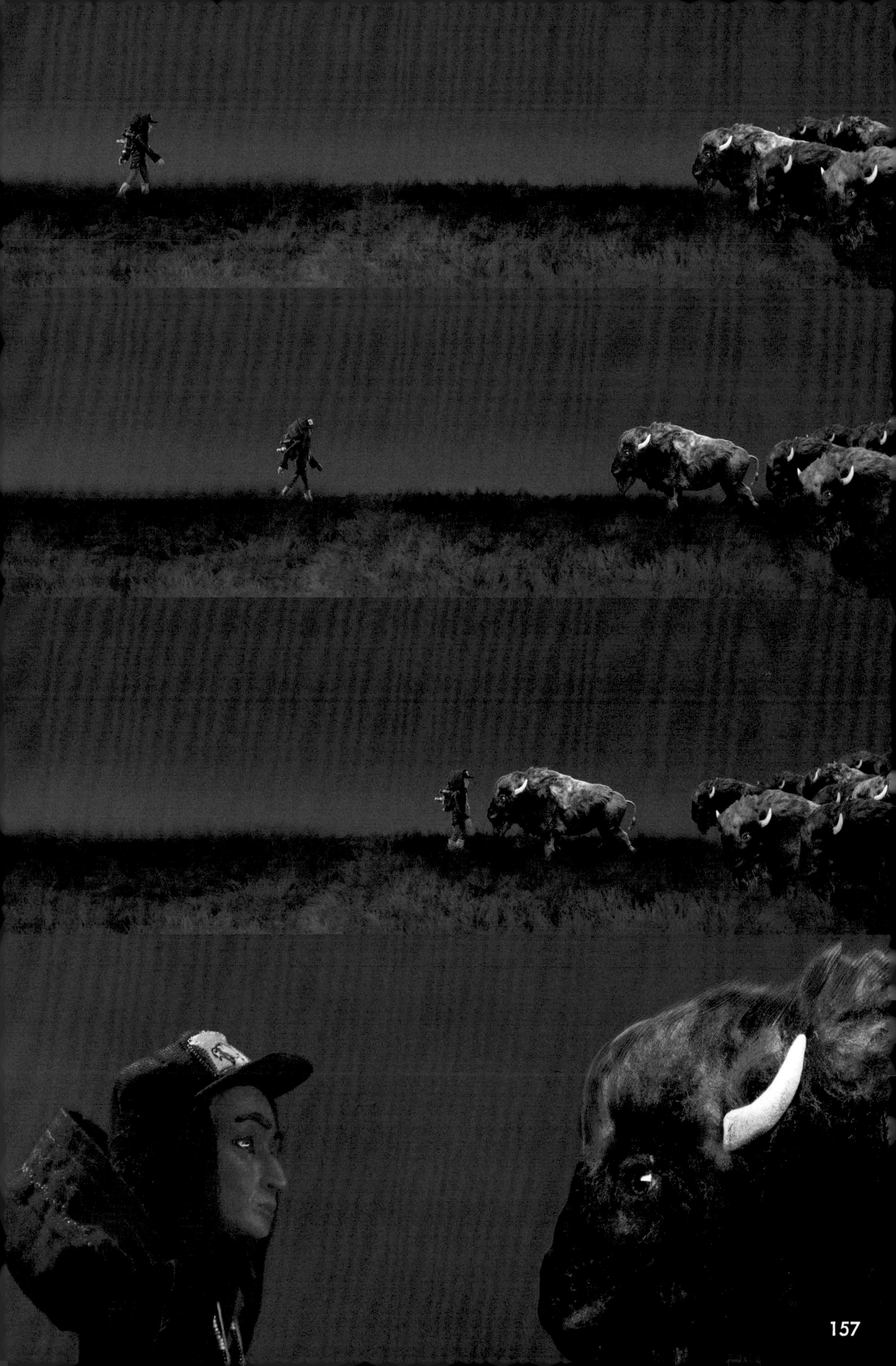

YOUR BLOOD RECOGNIZES
THE SPIRIT OF HOME.
REMEMBER YOUR
SPIRIT'S NAME.

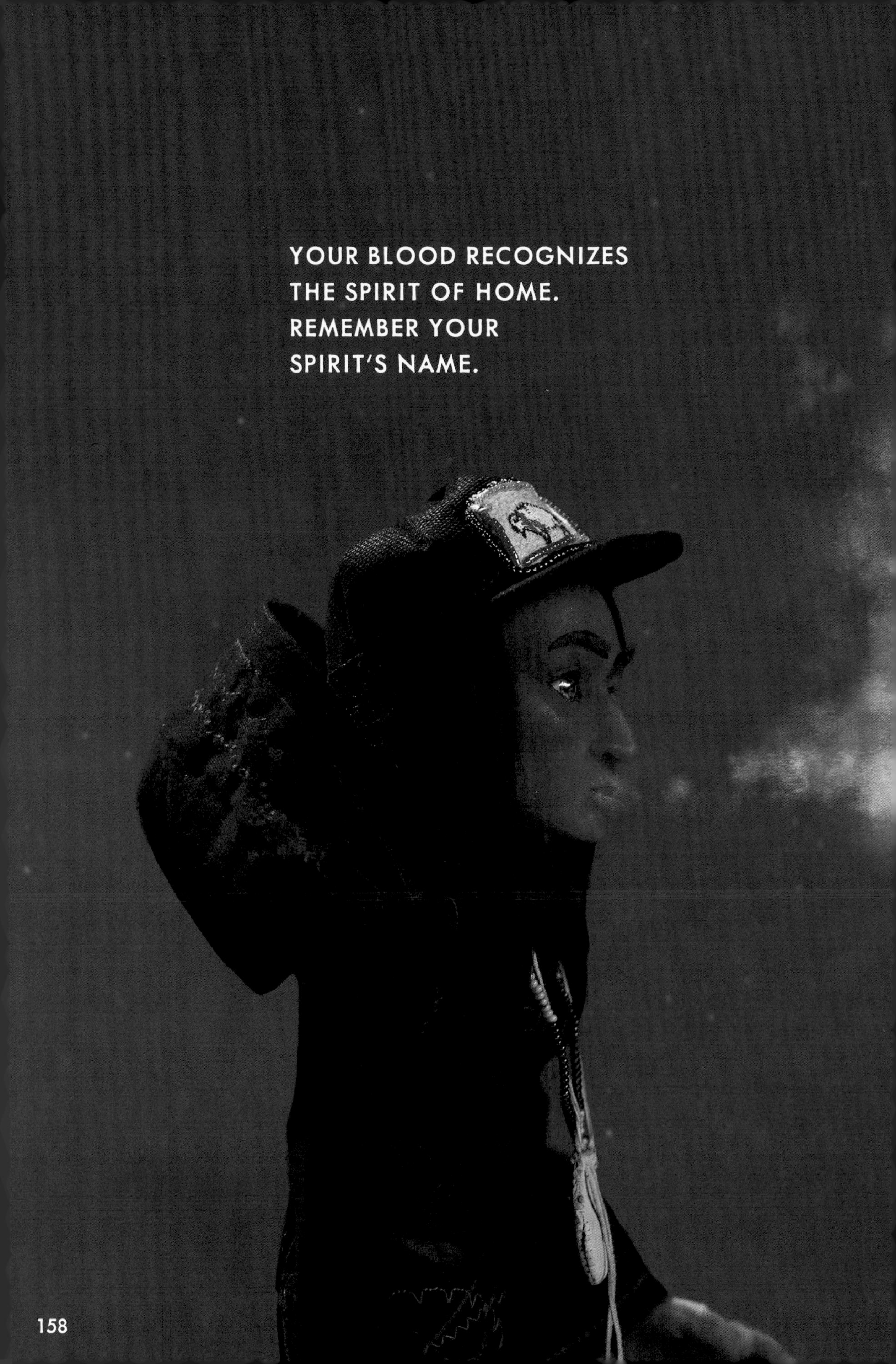

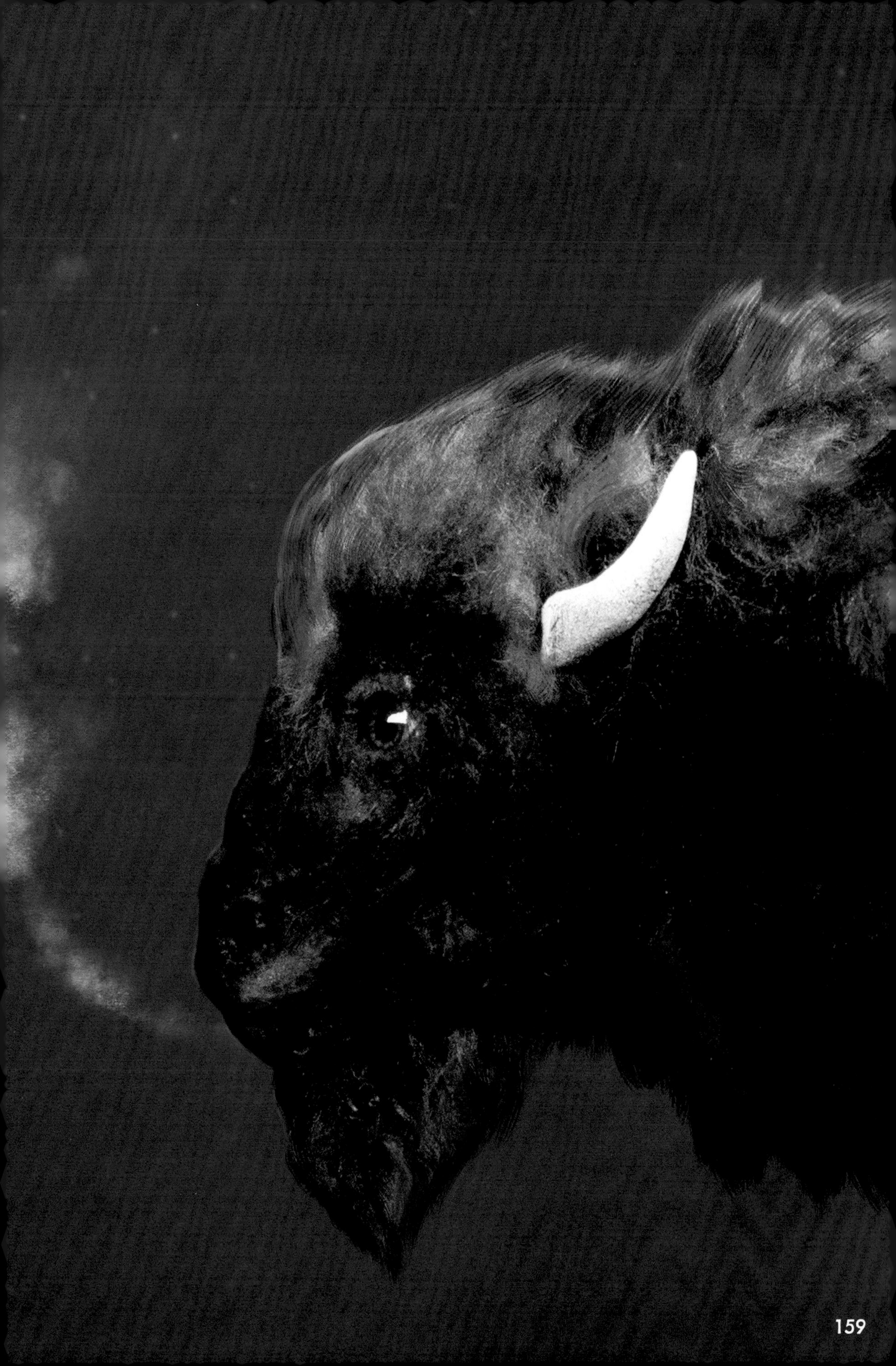

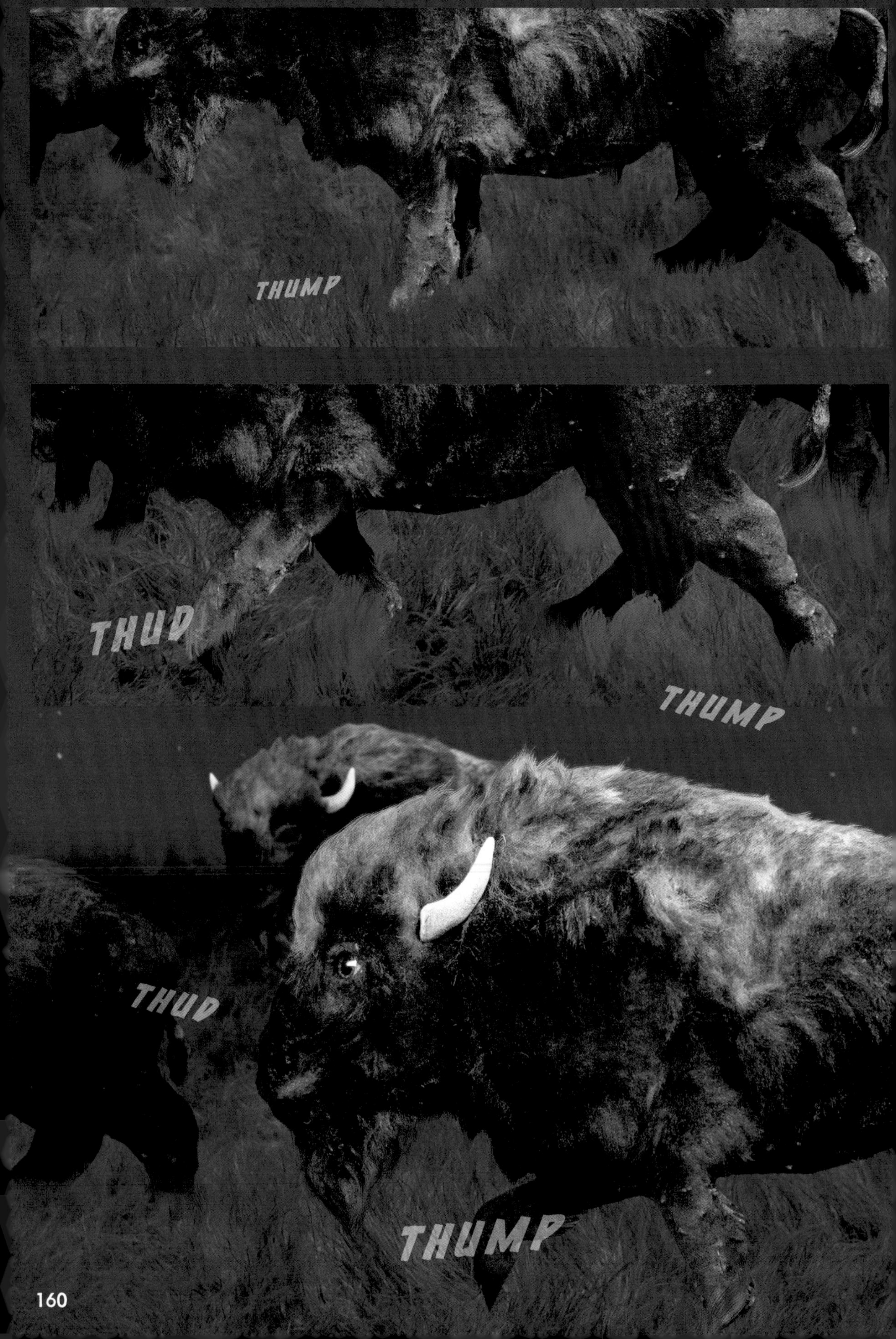
THUMP
THUD
THUMP
THUD
THUMP

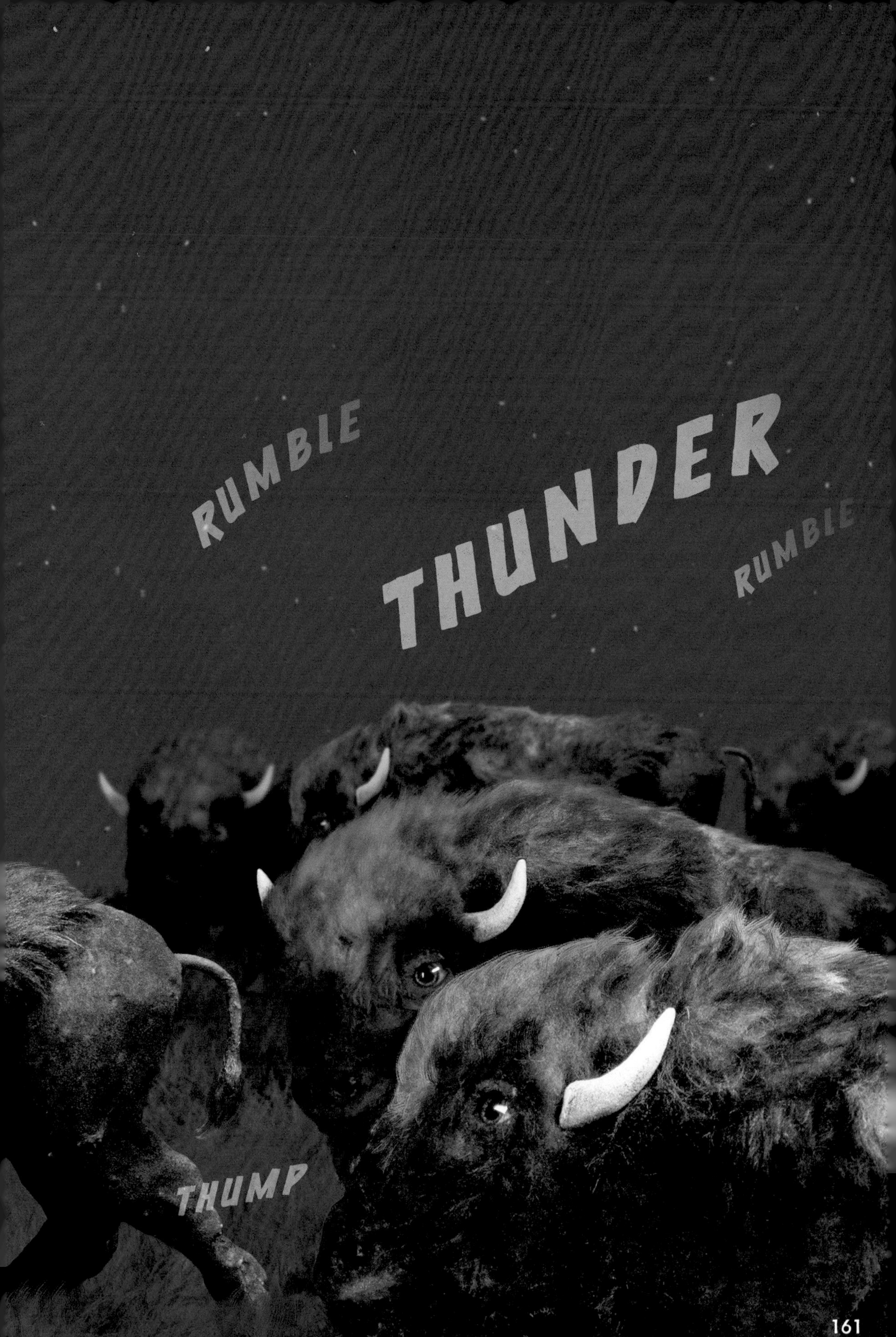
RUMBLE
THUNDER
RUMBLE
THUMP

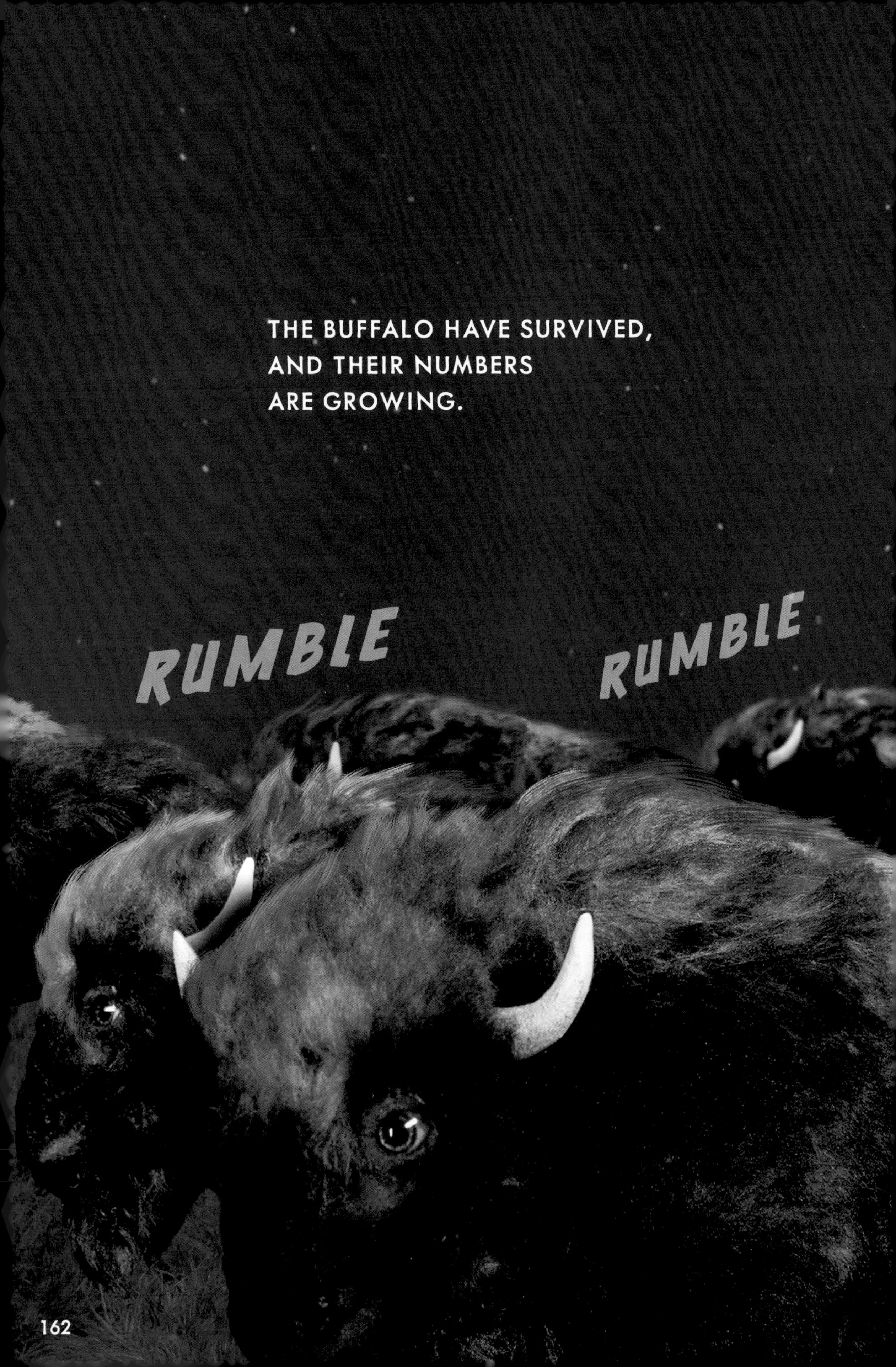
THE BUFFALO HAVE SURVIVED,
AND THEIR NUMBERS
ARE GROWING.
RUMBLE
RUMBLE

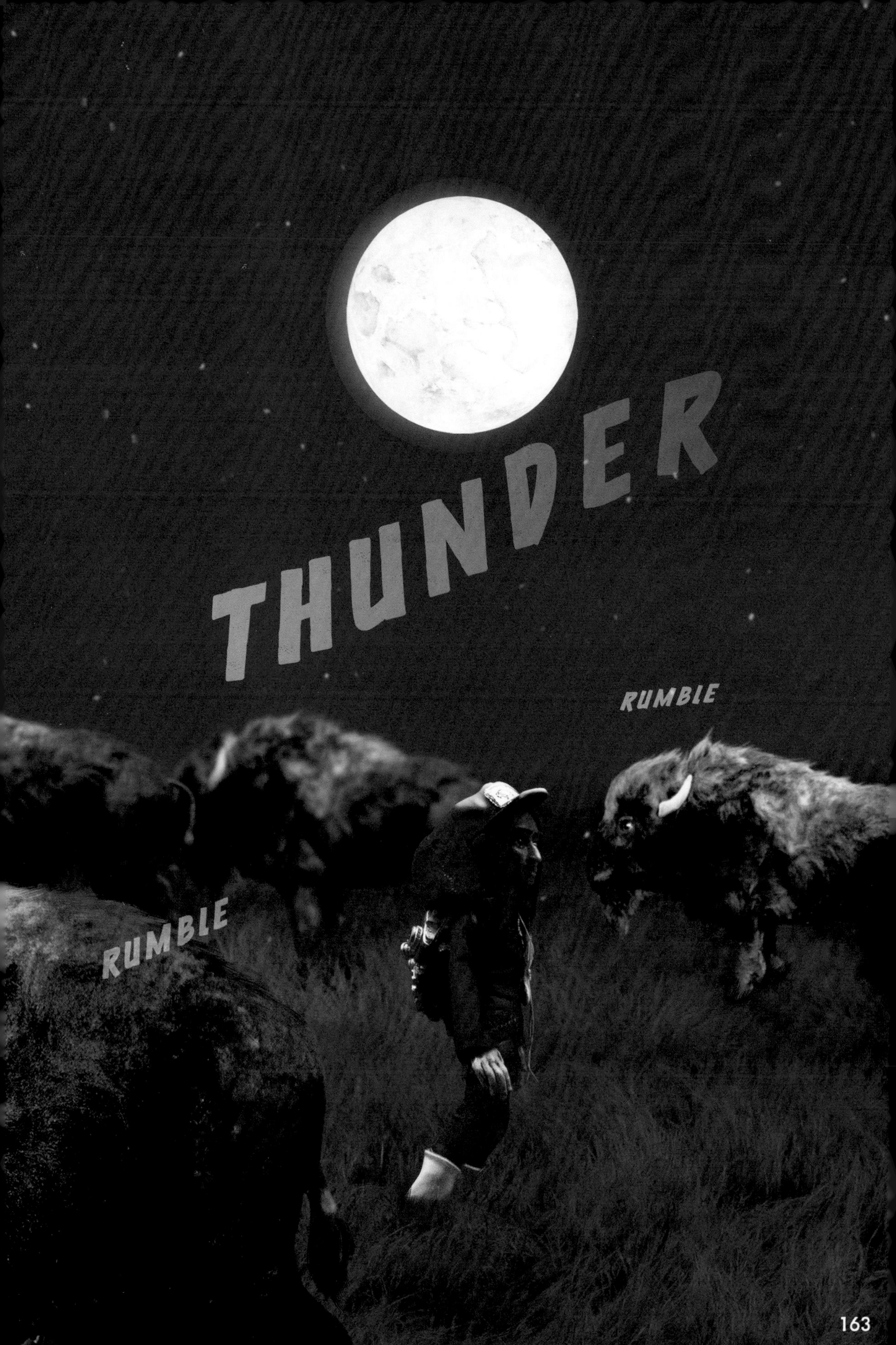
THUNDER
RUMBLE
RUMBLE

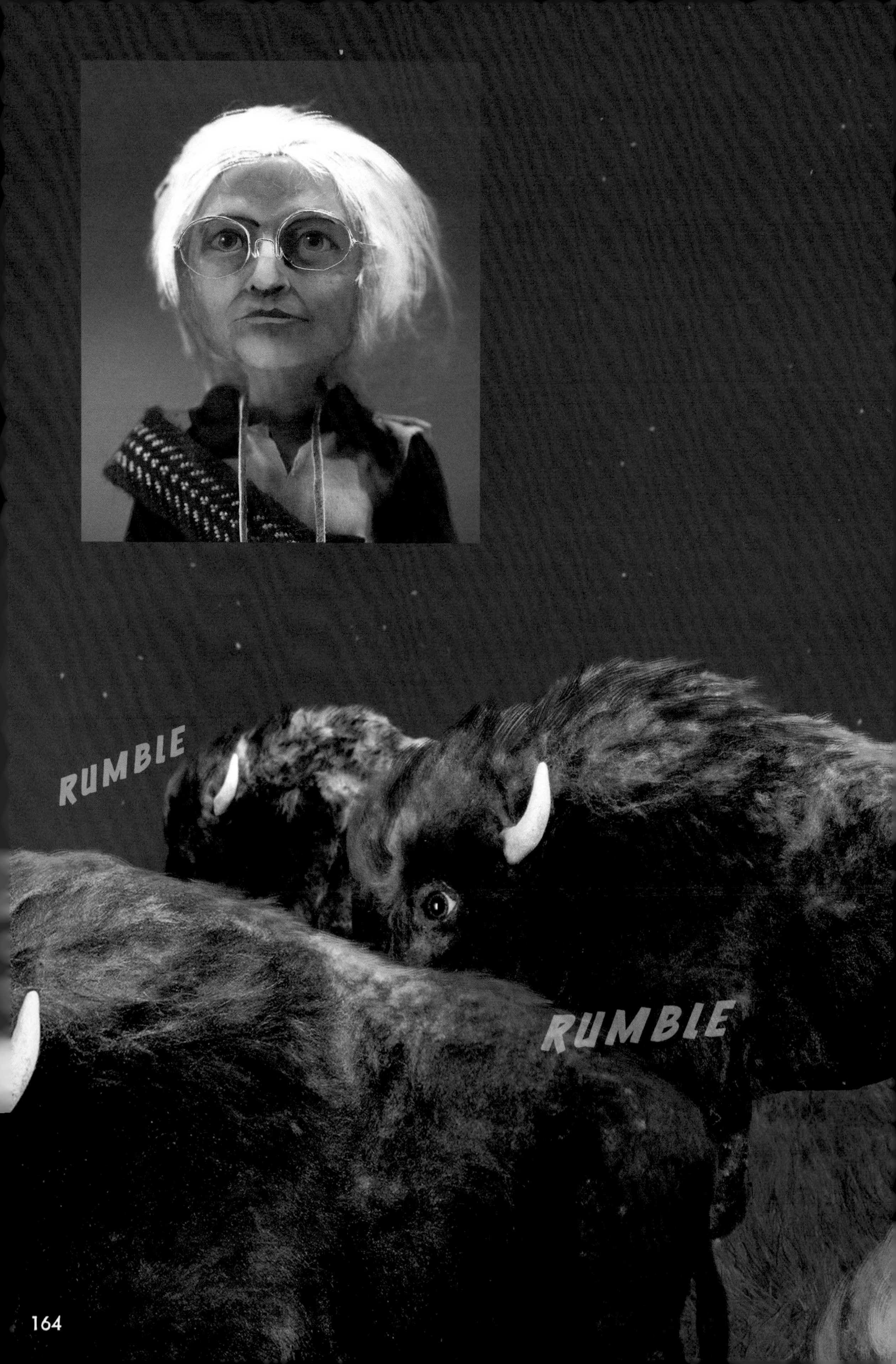
RUMBLE
RUMBLE

MY GRANDMOTHER WAS
A FIGHTER,
A REBEL,
A ROLE MODEL,
A BEAUTIFUL SPIRIT.

SHE LED ME TO MY PATH
AND OPENED IT UP
FOR ME TO TRAVEL.

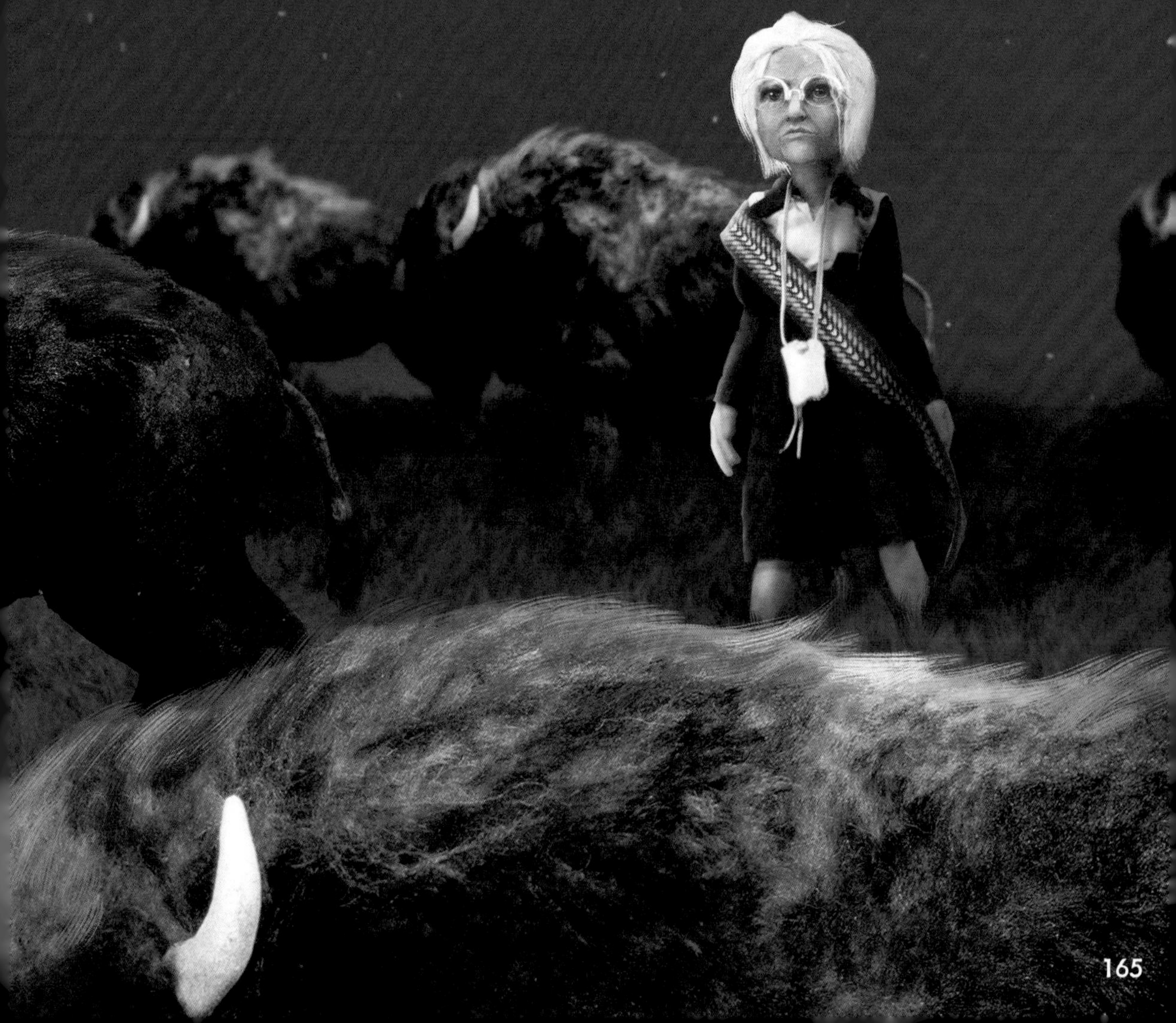

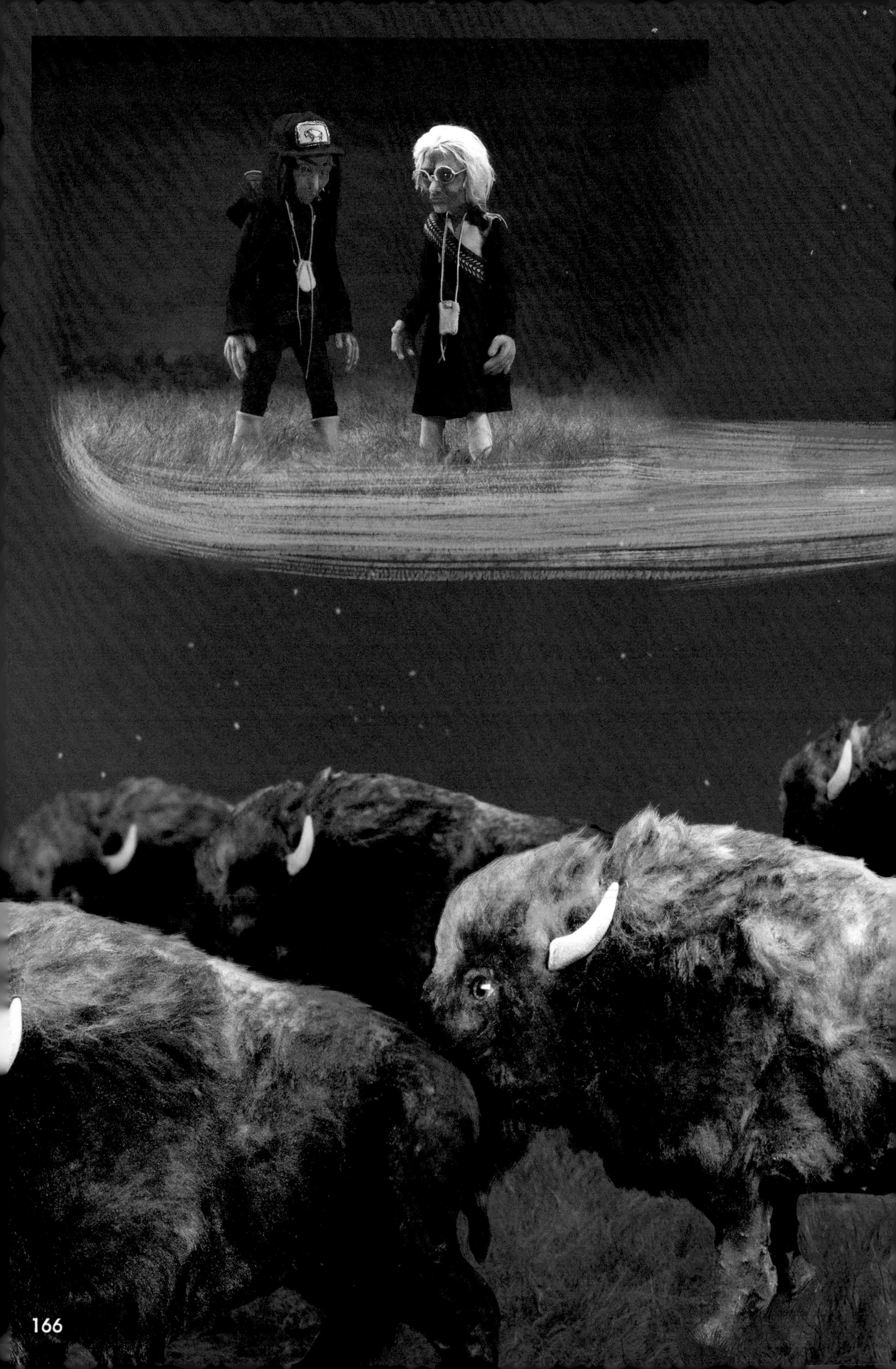

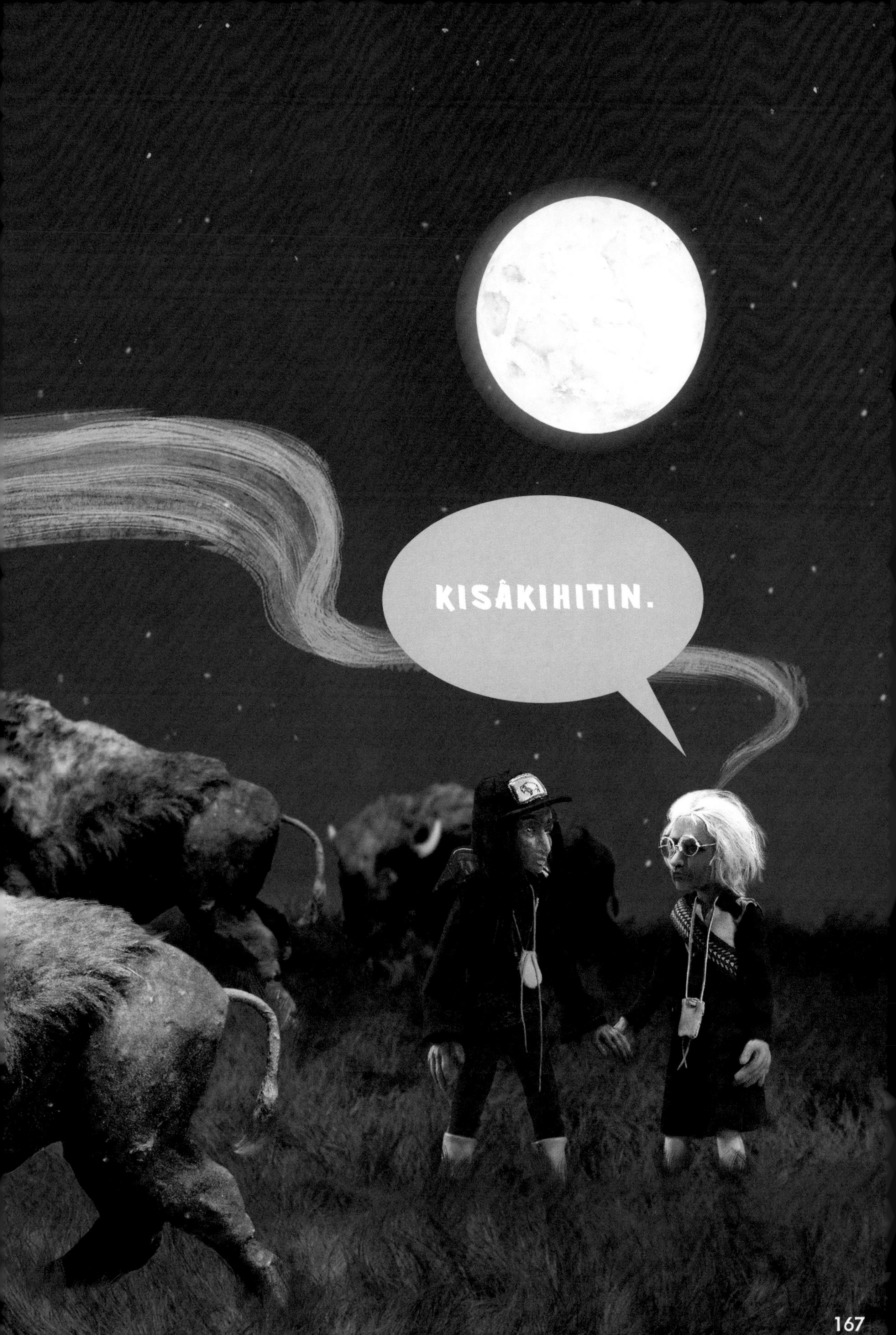
KISÂKIHITIN.

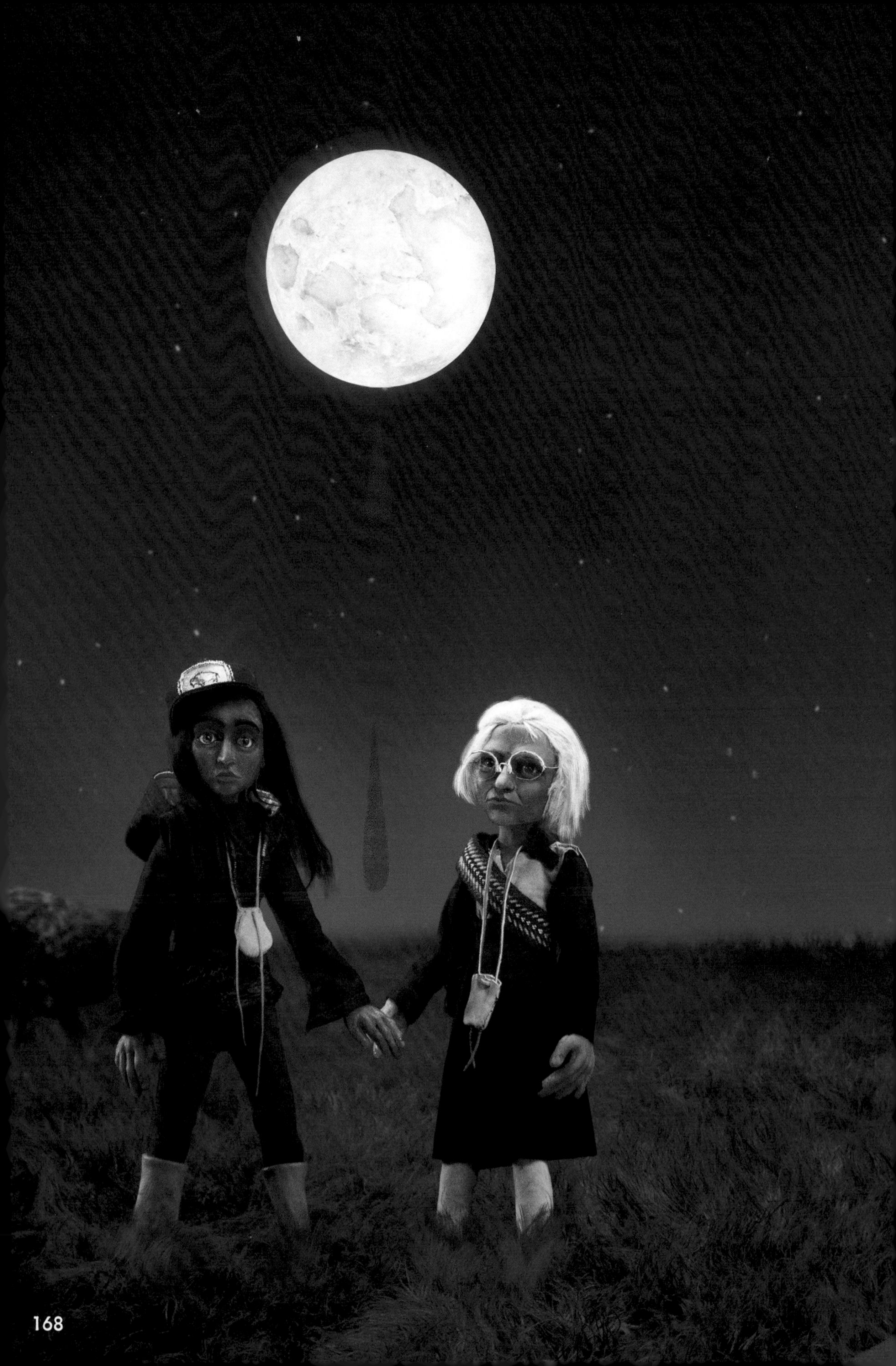

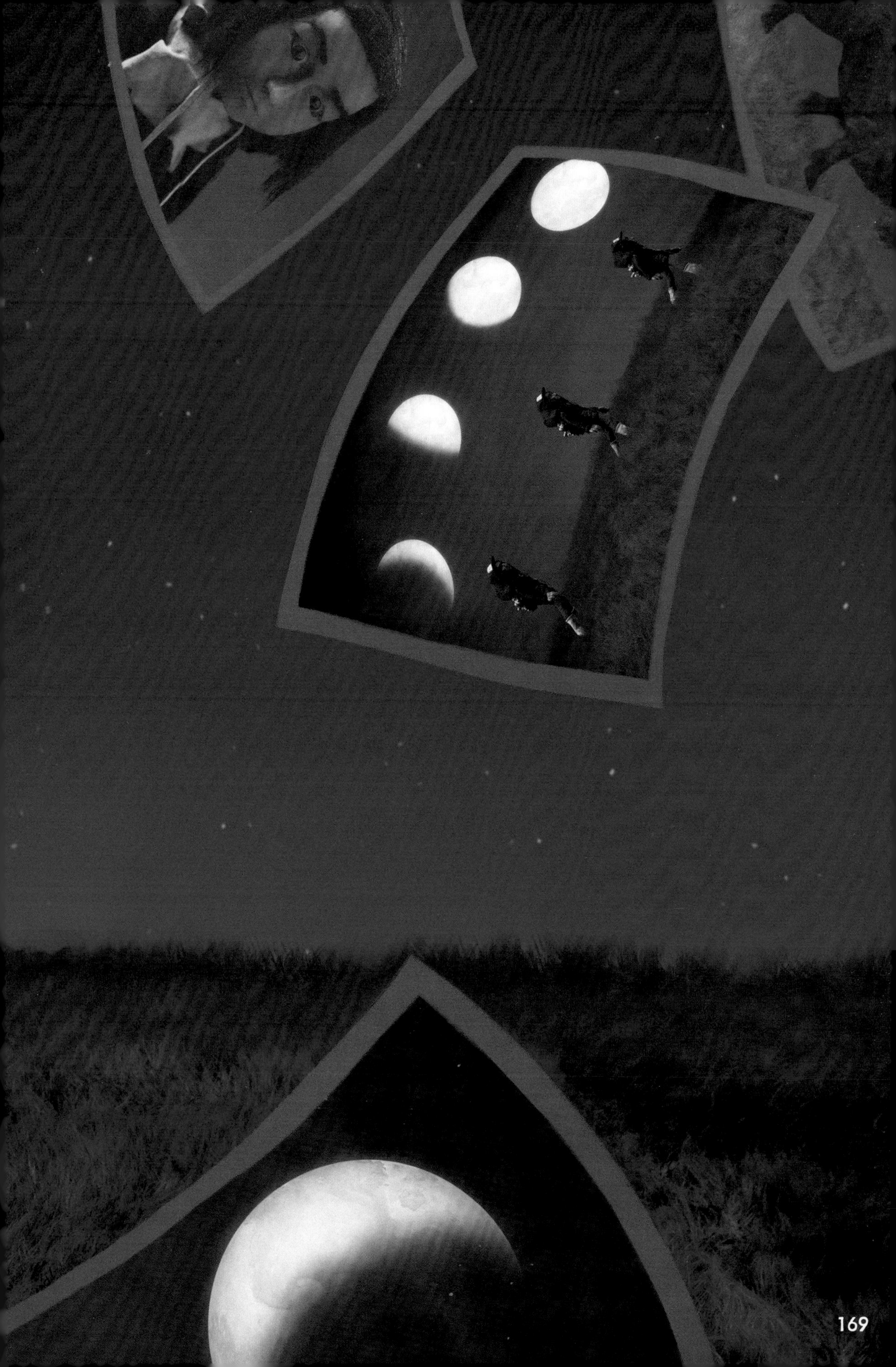

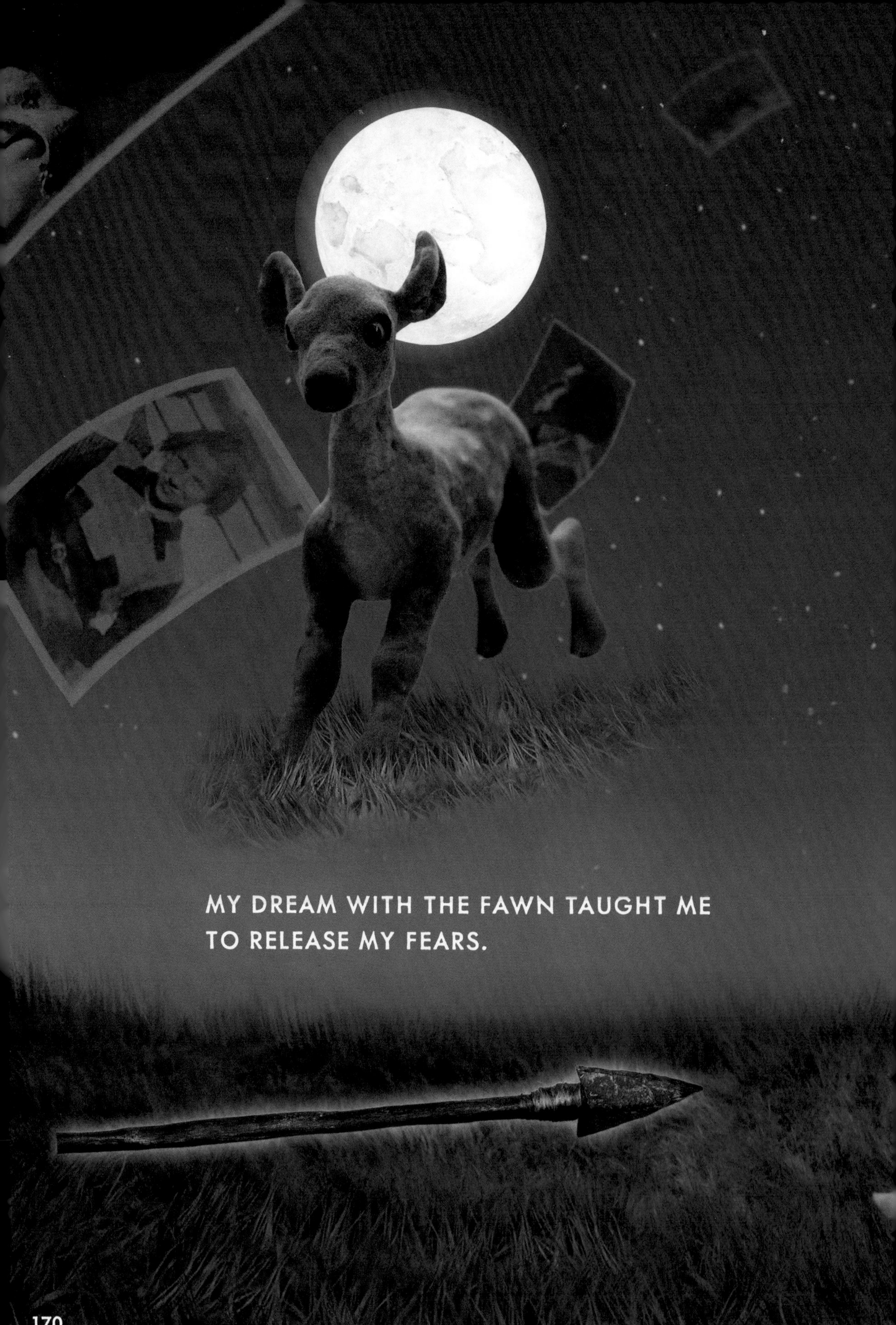
MY DREAM WITH THE FAWN TAUGHT ME TO RELEASE MY FEARS.

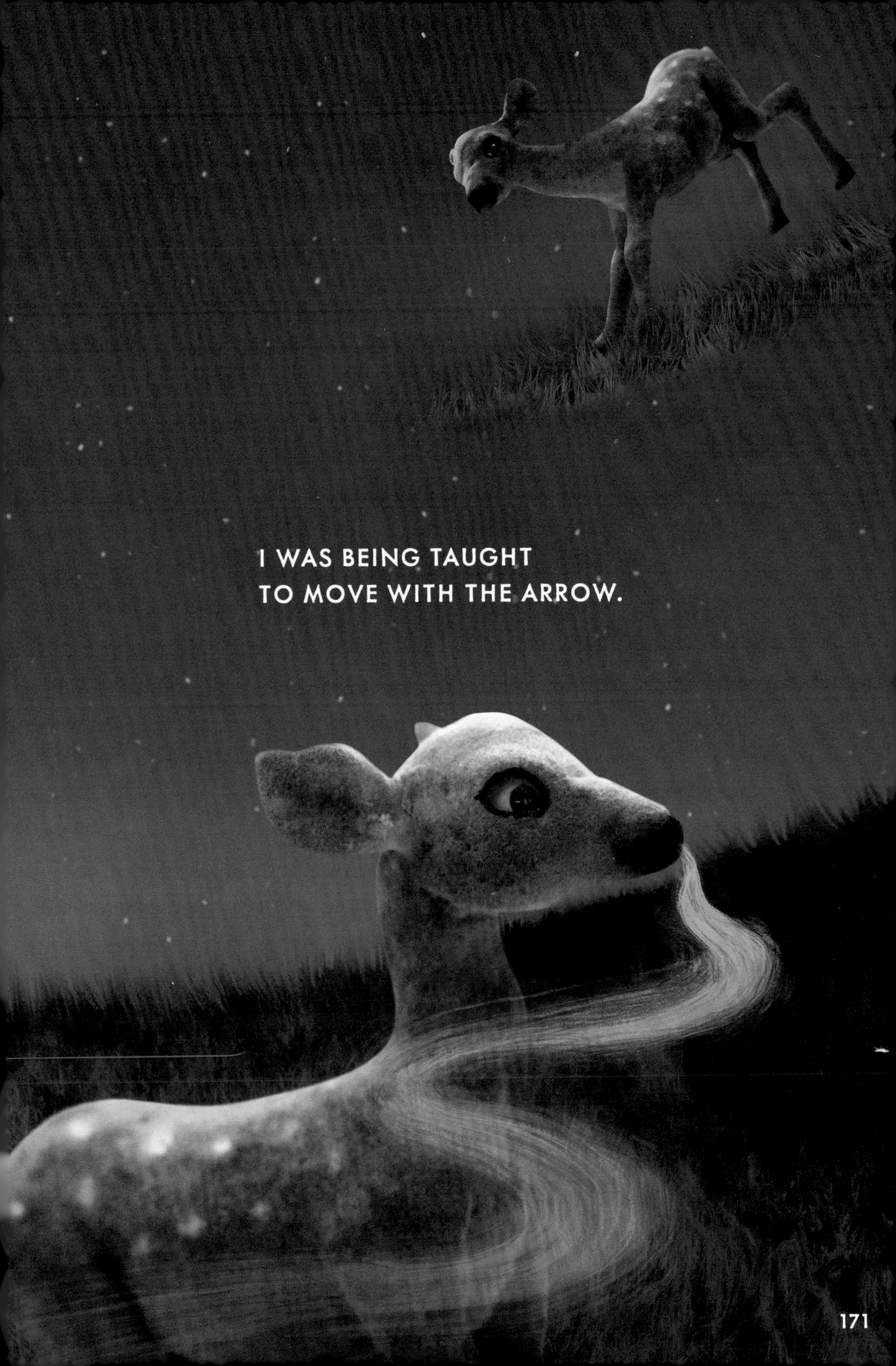
I WAS BEING TAUGHT
TO MOVE WITH THE ARROW.

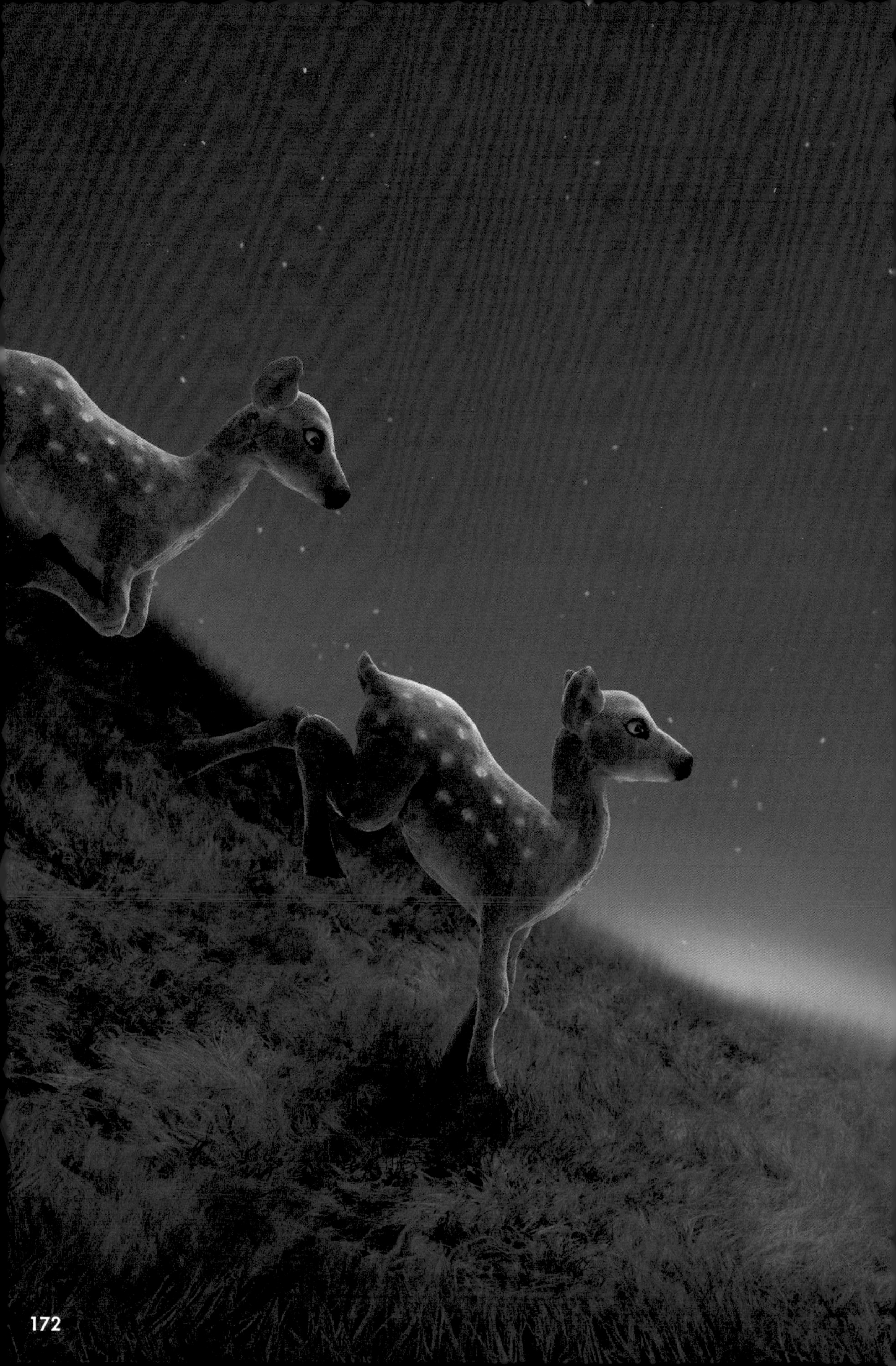

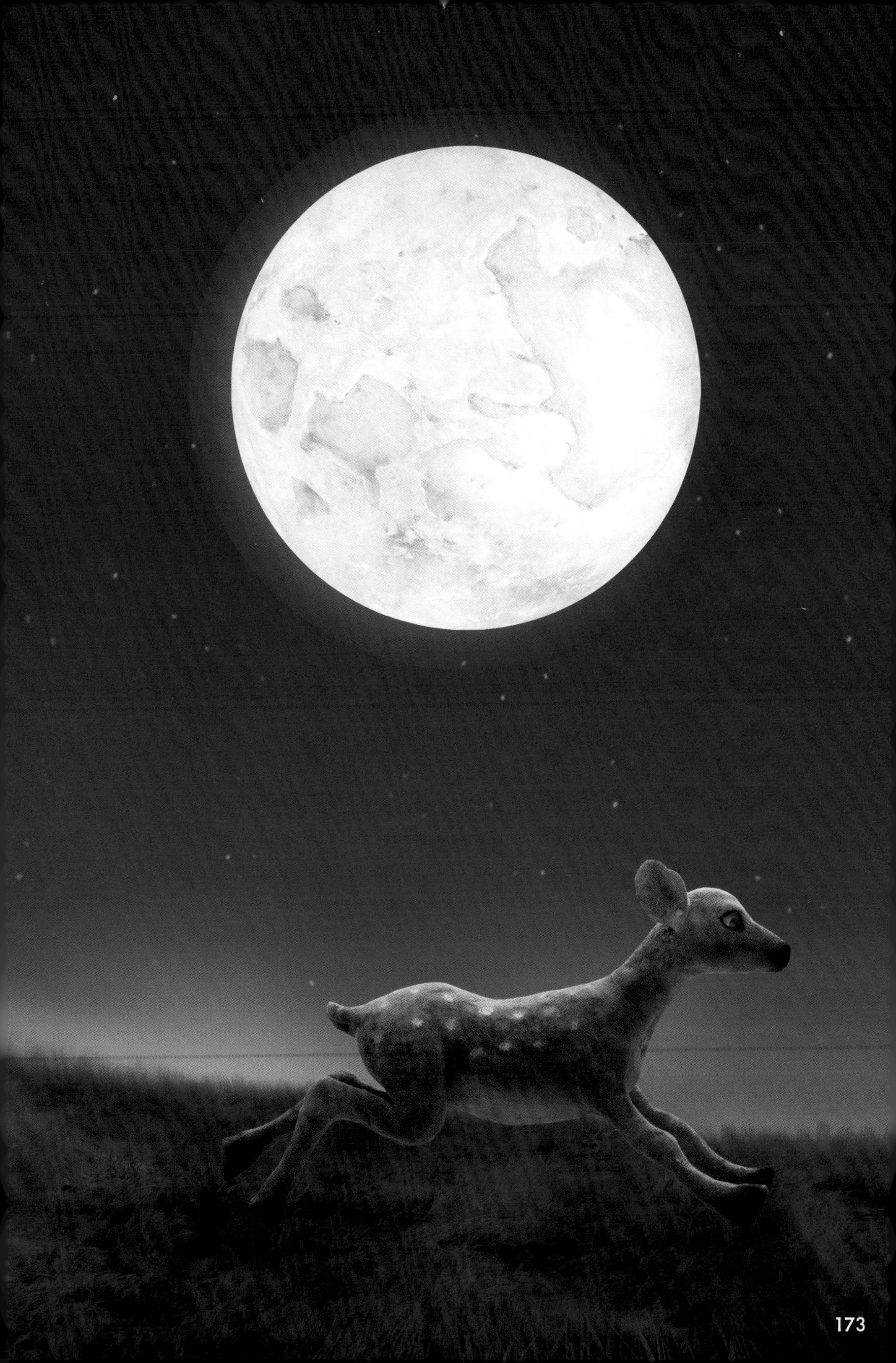

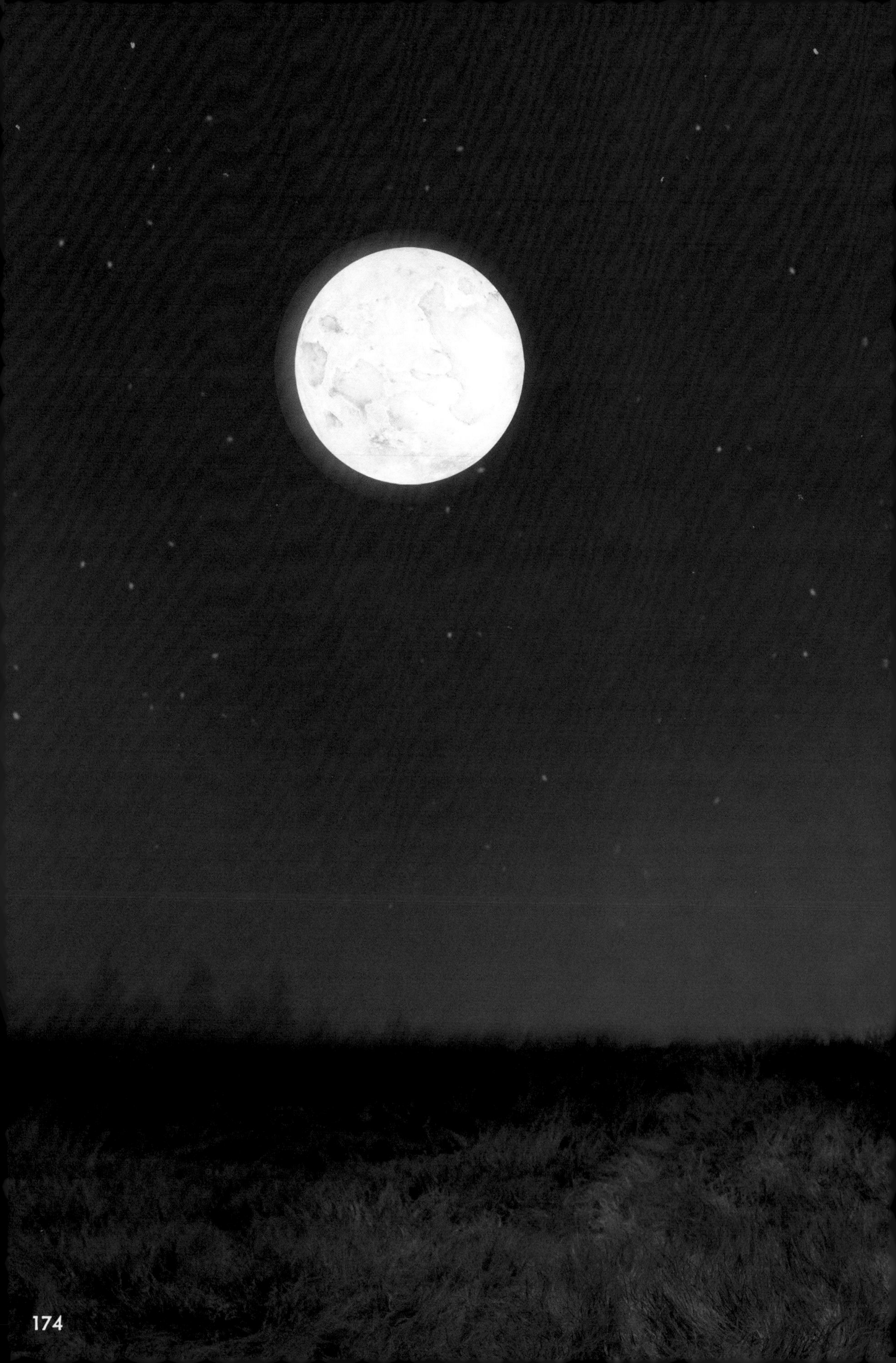

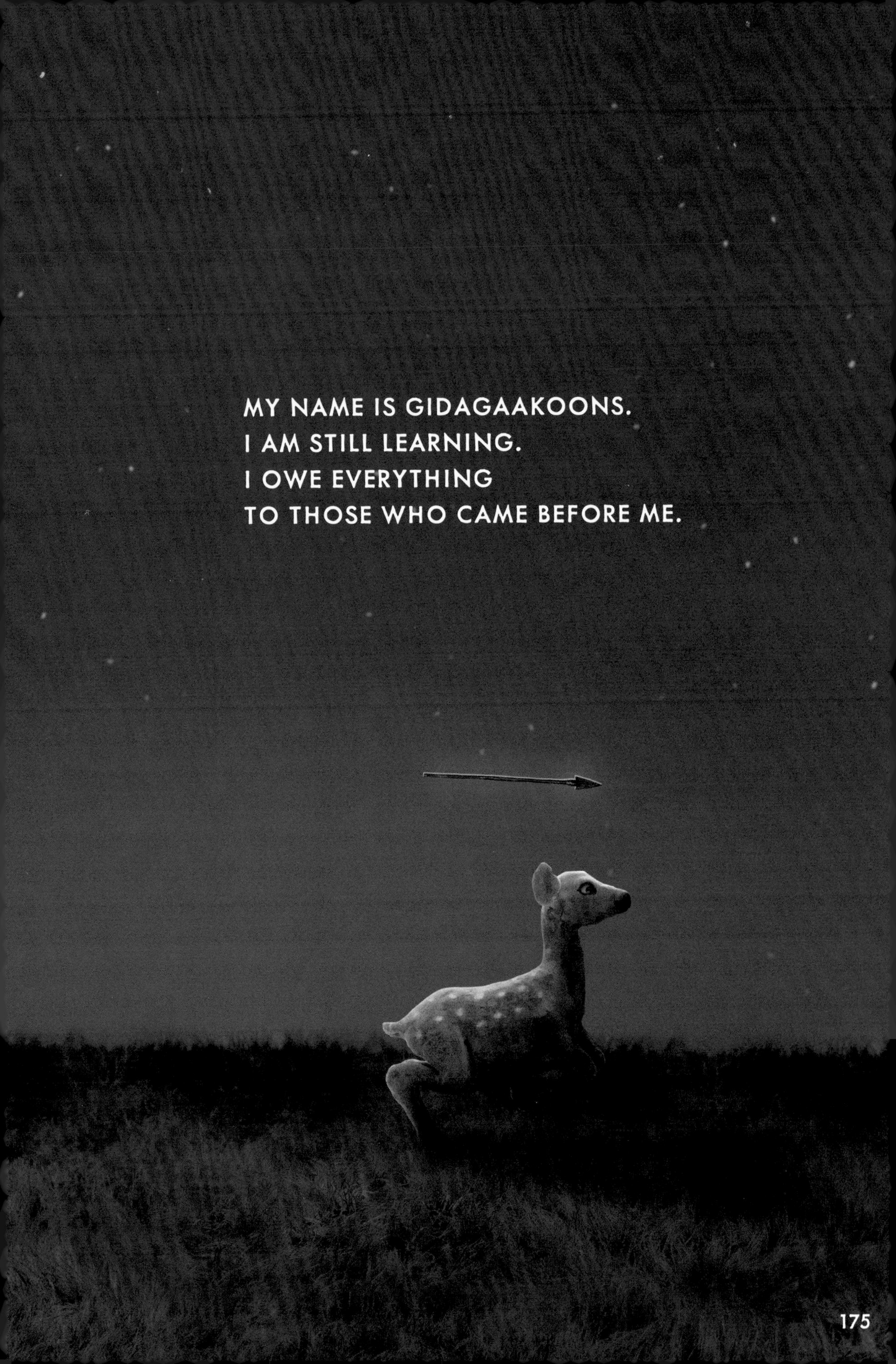
MY NAME IS GIDAGAAKOONS.
I AM STILL LEARNING.
I OWE EVERYTHING
TO THOSE WHO CAME BEFORE ME.

AFTERWORD

Who Are the Métis?

by Sherry Farrell Racette (Métis),
artist, historian, and curator, and
Associate Professor, Department of
Visual Arts, University of Regina

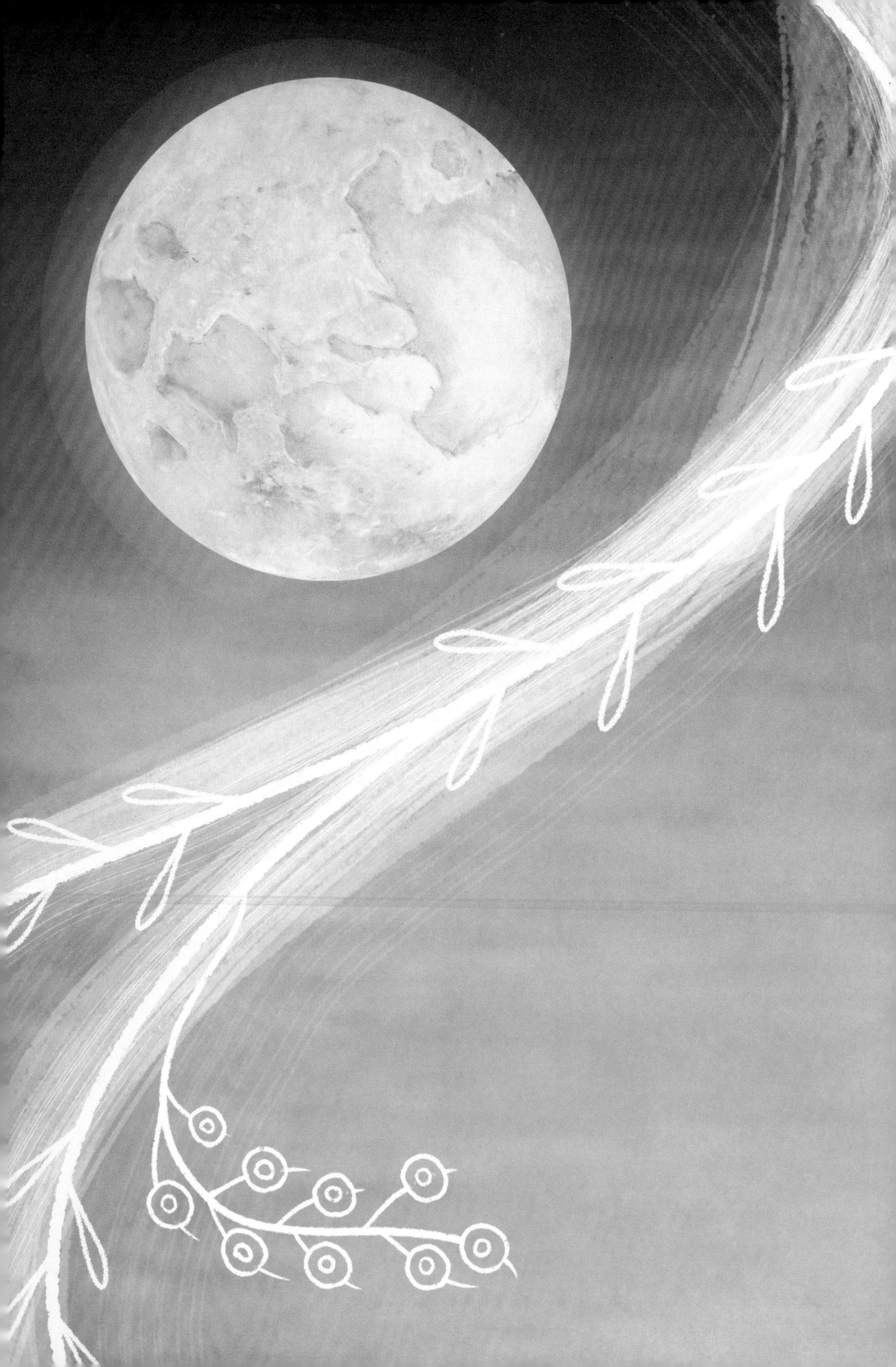

The Story of a Métis Family
Spotted Fawn and Her Ancestors

Métis families are like the interwoven roots of willow trees. They cover vast territories in time and space. Spotted Fawn's Métis lineage, as those of so many, is a window into that complex story with family ties that cross the United States and Canadian border, which from a Métis perspective doesn't really exist.

Her family has deep roots, and, as we see in this graphic novel, they participated in every major historic event in Western Métis history.

Who are the Métis?

The story of the Métis begins with the fur trade, and the (mostly) French and British men who worked as traders, clerks, laborers, and voyageurs. Many married Indigenous women and had children. But the Métis are so much more than this simple origin story.

There are many Indigenous people of mixed descent, and they aren't all Métis. Many children of mixed heritage were welcomed into the nations of their mothers and grandmothers, and their descendants are Nehiyawak, Anishinaabe, Dakota, and Dene. Their fur trade ancestors are often remembered in their surnames, and they acknowledge the Métis as relatives.

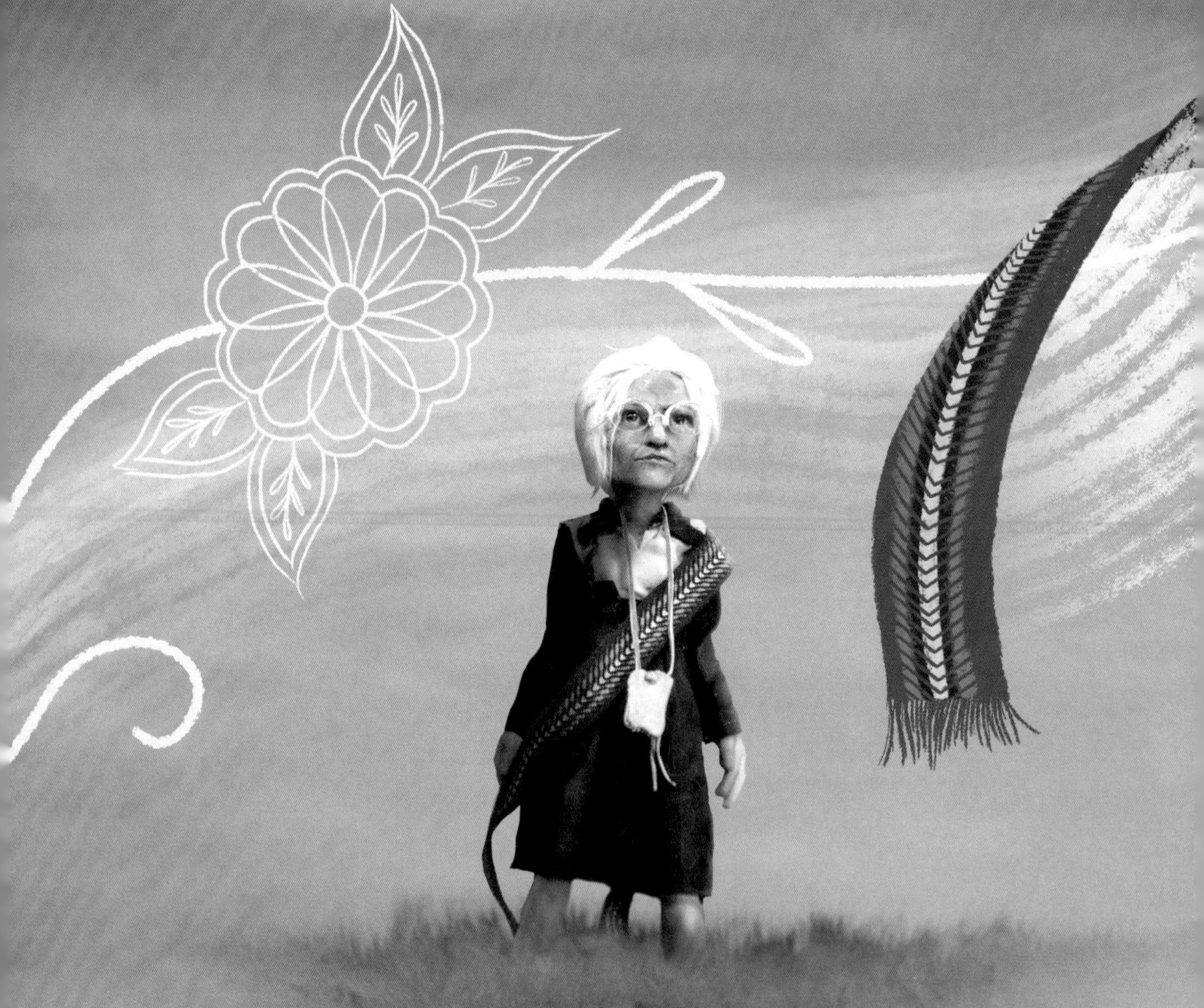

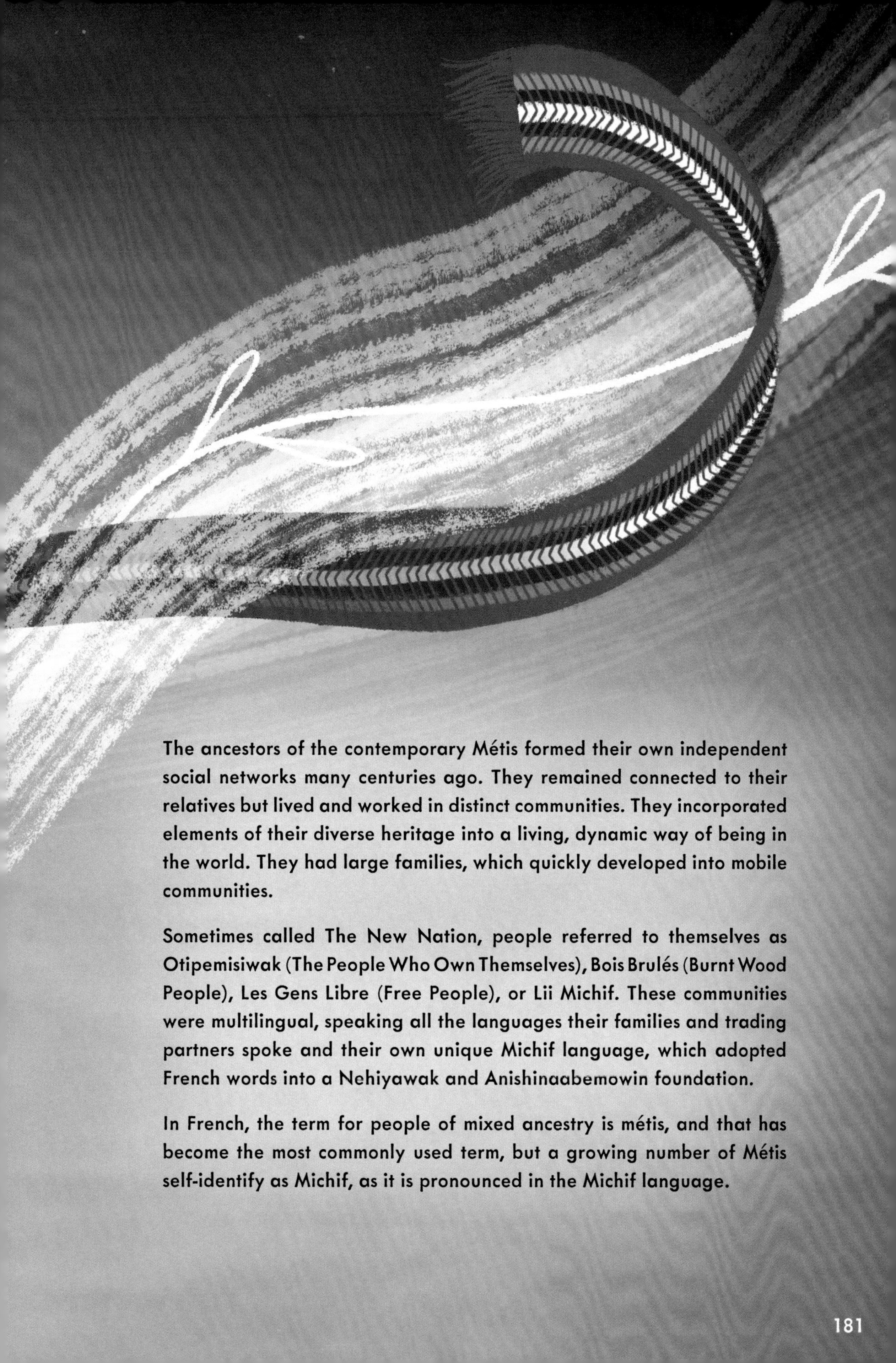

The ancestors of the contemporary Métis formed their own independent social networks many centuries ago. They remained connected to their relatives but lived and worked in distinct communities. They incorporated elements of their diverse heritage into a living, dynamic way of being in the world. They had large families, which quickly developed into mobile communities.

Sometimes called The New Nation, people referred to themselves as Otipemisiwak (The People Who Own Themselves), Bois Brulés (Burnt Wood People), Les Gens Libre (Free People), or Lii Michif. These communities were multilingual, speaking all the languages their families and trading partners spoke and their own unique Michif language, which adopted French words into a Nehiyawak and Anishinaabemowin foundation.

In French, the term for people of mixed ancestry is métis, and that has become the most commonly used term, but a growing number of Métis self-identify as Michif, as it is pronounced in the Michif language.

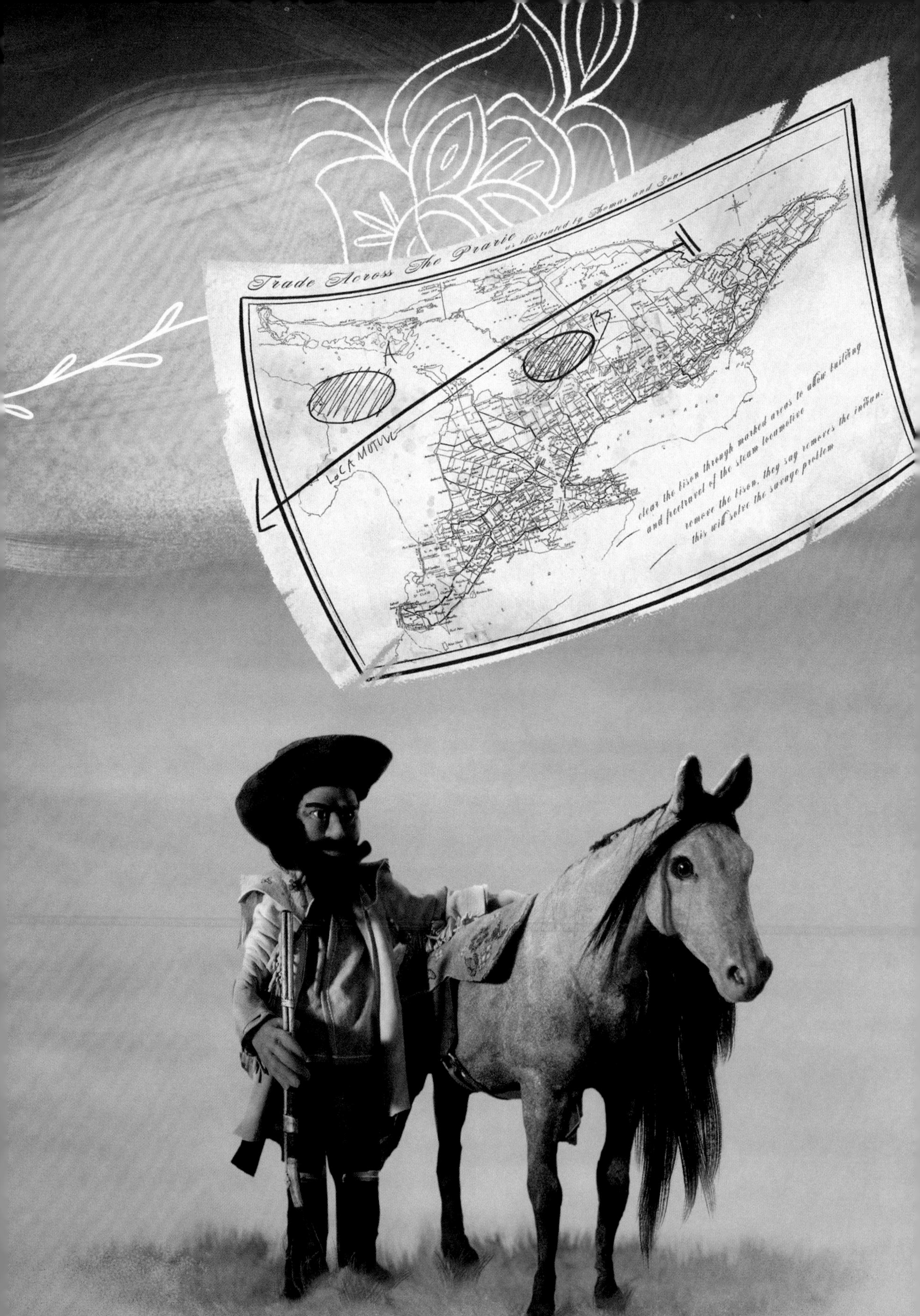
Trade Across The Prarie
as illustrated by Thomas and Sons
LoCA MOTIVE
A
B
LAKE ONTARIO
clear the bison through marked areas to allow building
and foottravel of the steam locamotive
remove the bison, they say removes the indian.
this will solve the savage problem

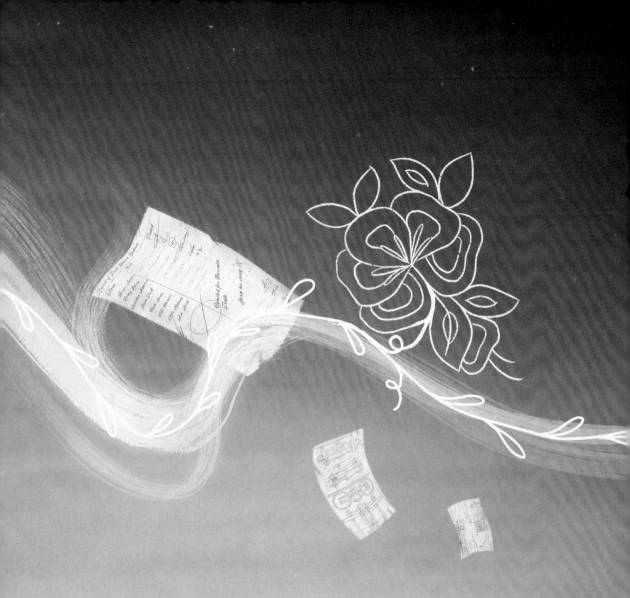

By the early ninteenth century, Métis families began to settle at the forks of the Red and Assiniboine Rivers. They had small farms but continued to travel, hunt, and trade. Fun was an essential part of Métis life. If you know any Métis people, you know how we love to laugh. Fiddle music, dancing, competitive games, and horse races were (and still are) important.

The Buffalo and the Railway

Buffalo provided everything required for life: food, homes, clothing, and tools. Everything came from the Buffalo. They were sacred relatives. The economic and cultural center of Métis life on the Prairies were the great Buffalo camps organized twice a year to hunt. Métis camps were highly organized with a system of councils and headmen. When smaller groups joined to form one large camp, they united into one self-governing community under the man chosen to be Chief of the Hunt.

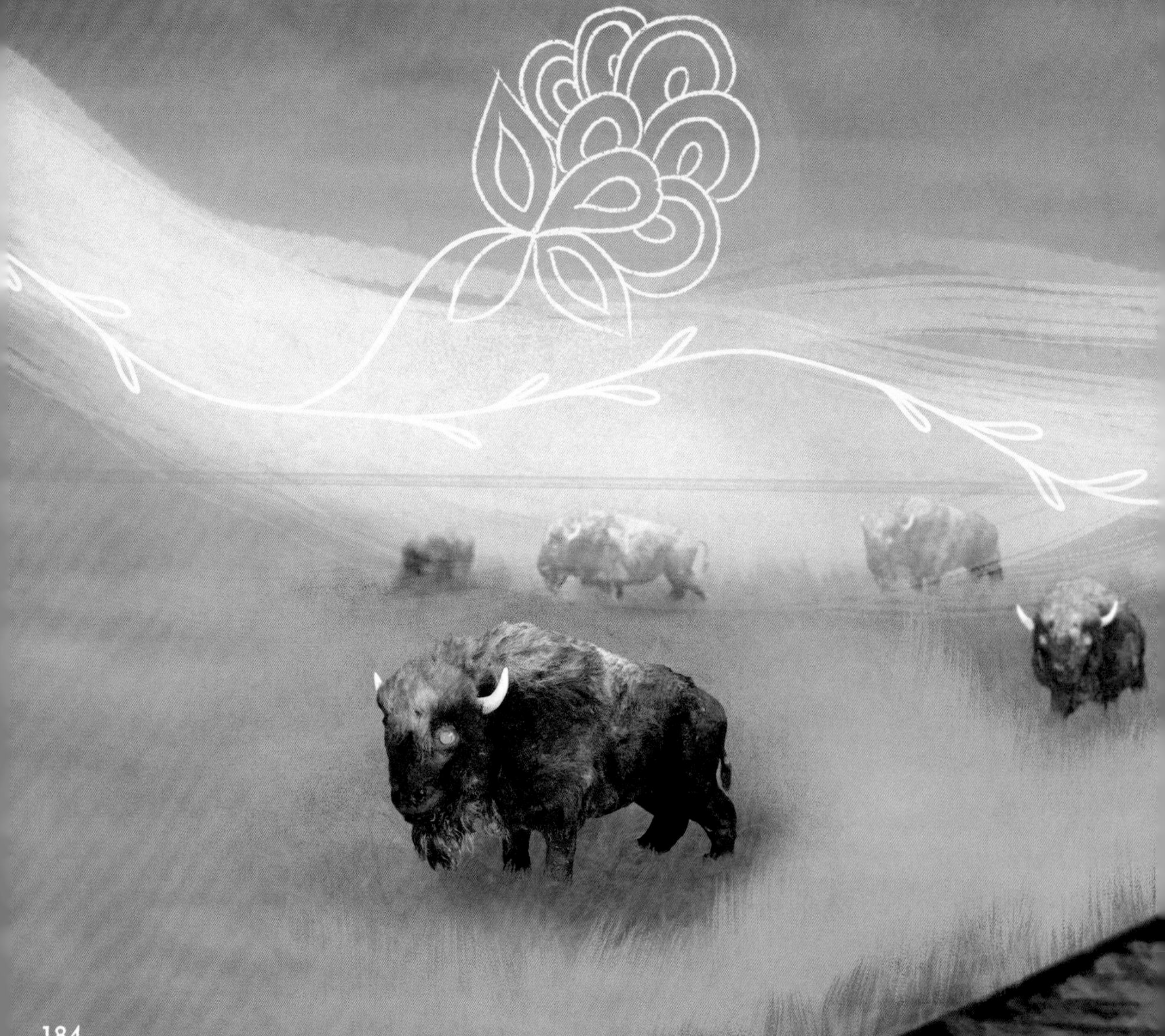

Spotted Fawn's four times great-grandfather Jean Baptiste Wilkie (1803–1886) and his son-in-law Gabriel Dumont (1837–1906) were both community leaders and Chiefs of the Hunt. Wilkie was a trader, hunter, and negotiator. He lived and traded in the Red River region but was primarily based in Pembina in present-day North Dakota.

It is Jean Baptiste Wilkie's spirit who appears to share the teachings of the Buffalo and when Spotted Fawn experiences the extermination of the Buffalo, a strategy used to starve Indigenous Nations into submission.

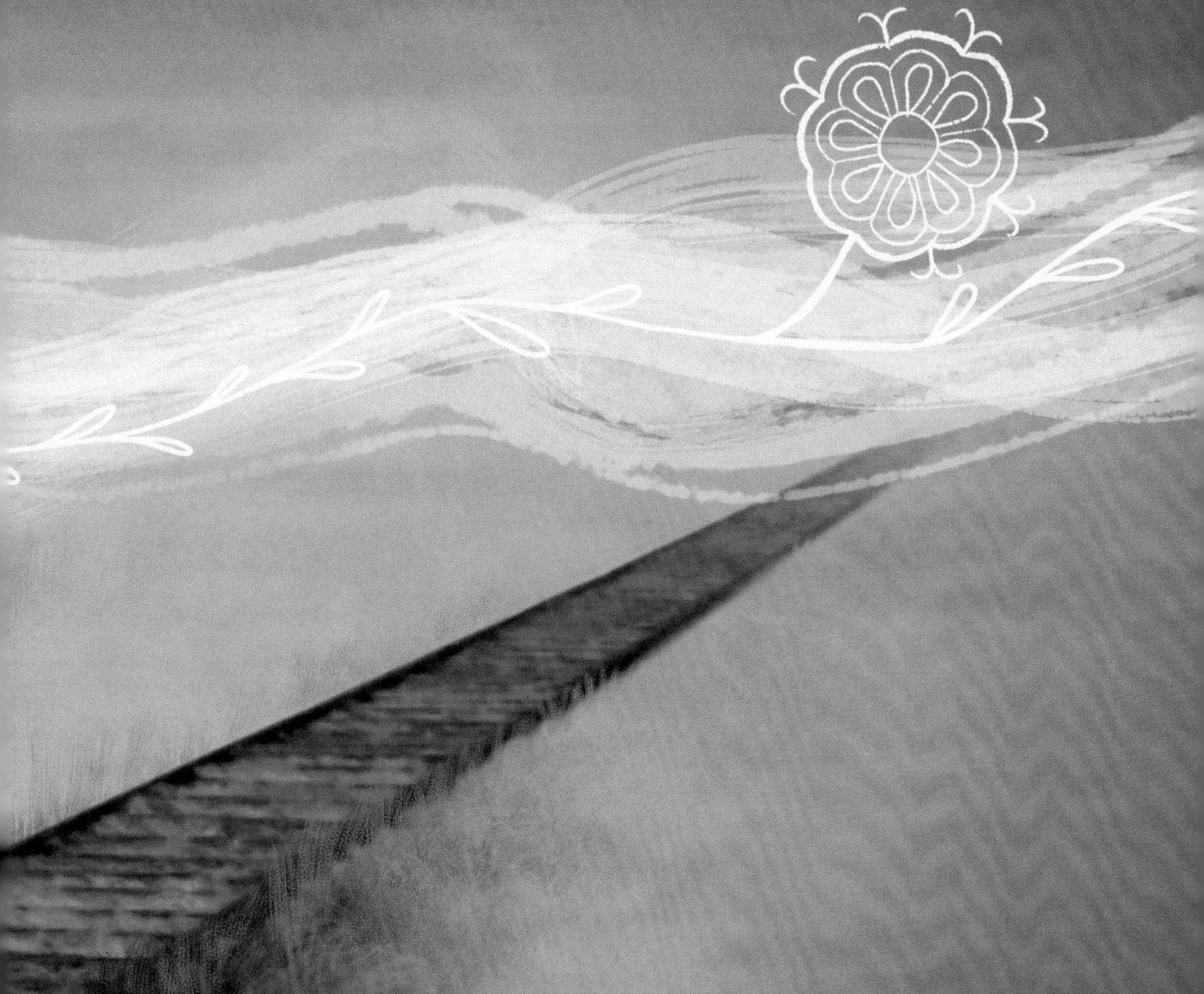

Destroying the great herds was a political act. Millions of Buffalo were killed between the 1860s and 1880s. Building railroads was an important strategy to join settlements on the eastern and western coasts of North America and "open the West."

Railroads running east to west divided the Buffalo and blocked their natural migration flow. Organized lines of hunters' camps along key rivers shot the Buffalo as they came to drink. Thousands were killed for only their hides or tongues.

Most of this decimation was undertaken by the American military, and "sport" hunters enthusiastically joined in. Train passengers shot Buffalo out their windows, leaving the carcasses to rot. While the American government proclaimed this as policy, the new Canadian government (established in 1867) was quietly supportive. The plains were covered with bones. Proud Métis hunters were reduced to gathering bones for a few pennies to feed their families. The piles of skulls haunt the Prairies.

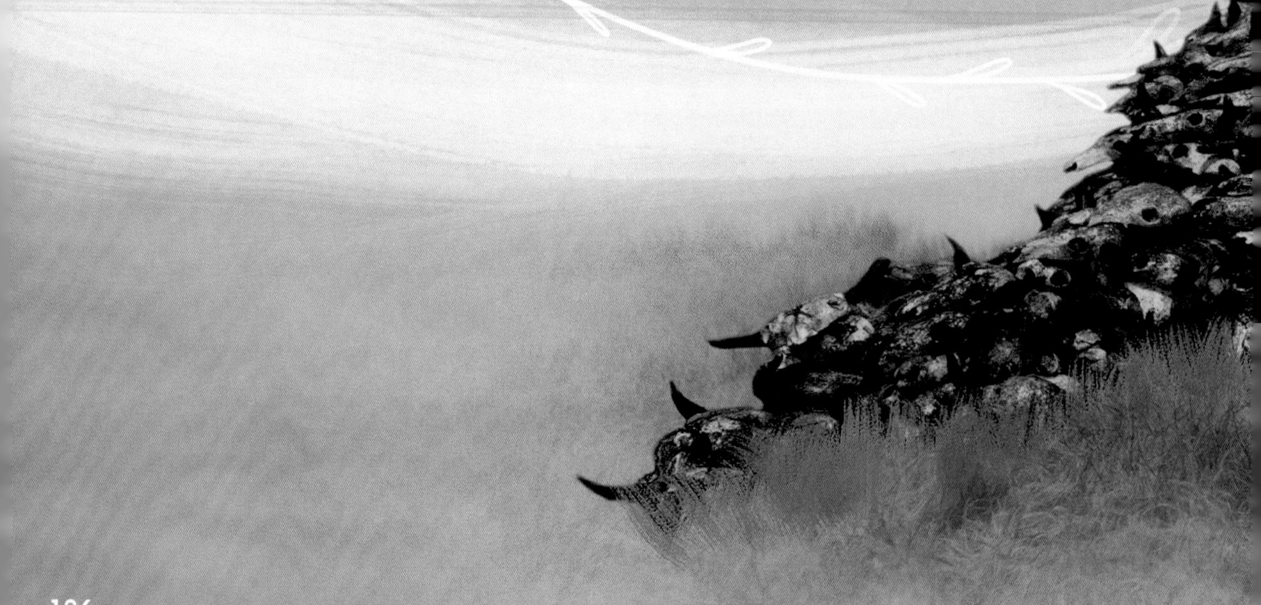

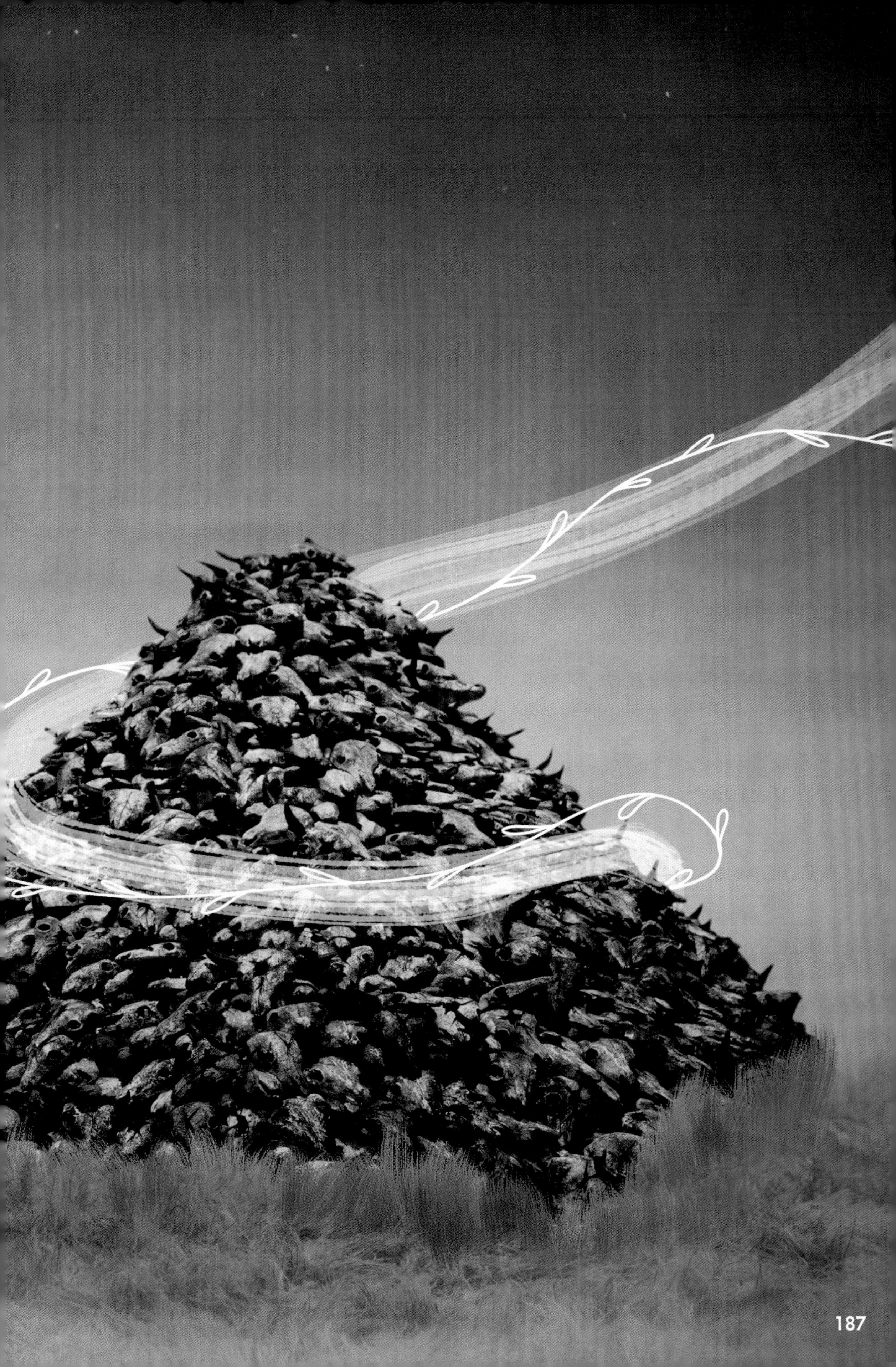

Fighting to Protect Homes, Land, and a Way of Life

The first person we meet in Spotted Fawn's story is her grandmother, the late and beloved Olivine Bousquet (1928–2018), who was not only cherished by her family but was also a very well-respected elder in the larger Métis community.

Elders, like Olivine, are the bridge between the past and the present. Olivine was a dancer, artist, and storyteller who shared her knowledge with many. She fought racism in the school system and the spiritual abuse of the Catholic Church. The Métis of her generation were targeted with messages that they were inferior. Olivine refused those messages. She shared stories of her grandfather Napoleon Bousquet with pride.

We see an image of Olivine's grandfather Napoleon Bousquet offering his paper scrip to the fire. Why would he burn it? To answer that question, we need to consider how Canada was formed. Canada is a very young country, and when it was created in 1867, agreements had to be made with different Indigenous Nations. Most were made by signing treaties, agreements on how we were all to share the land and how Indigenous people's rights and livelihoods were to be protected. However, in 1869, the Hudson's Bay Company transferred a vast territory known as "Rupert's Land" to Canada.

Indigenous people were shocked and angered by the transfer, which was done without their knowledge or consent. The Hudson's Bay Company, a fur trading company established in 1670, had been granted the exclusive monopoly to trade on all the land draining into Hudson Bay. But an agreement to trade is not ownership of land.

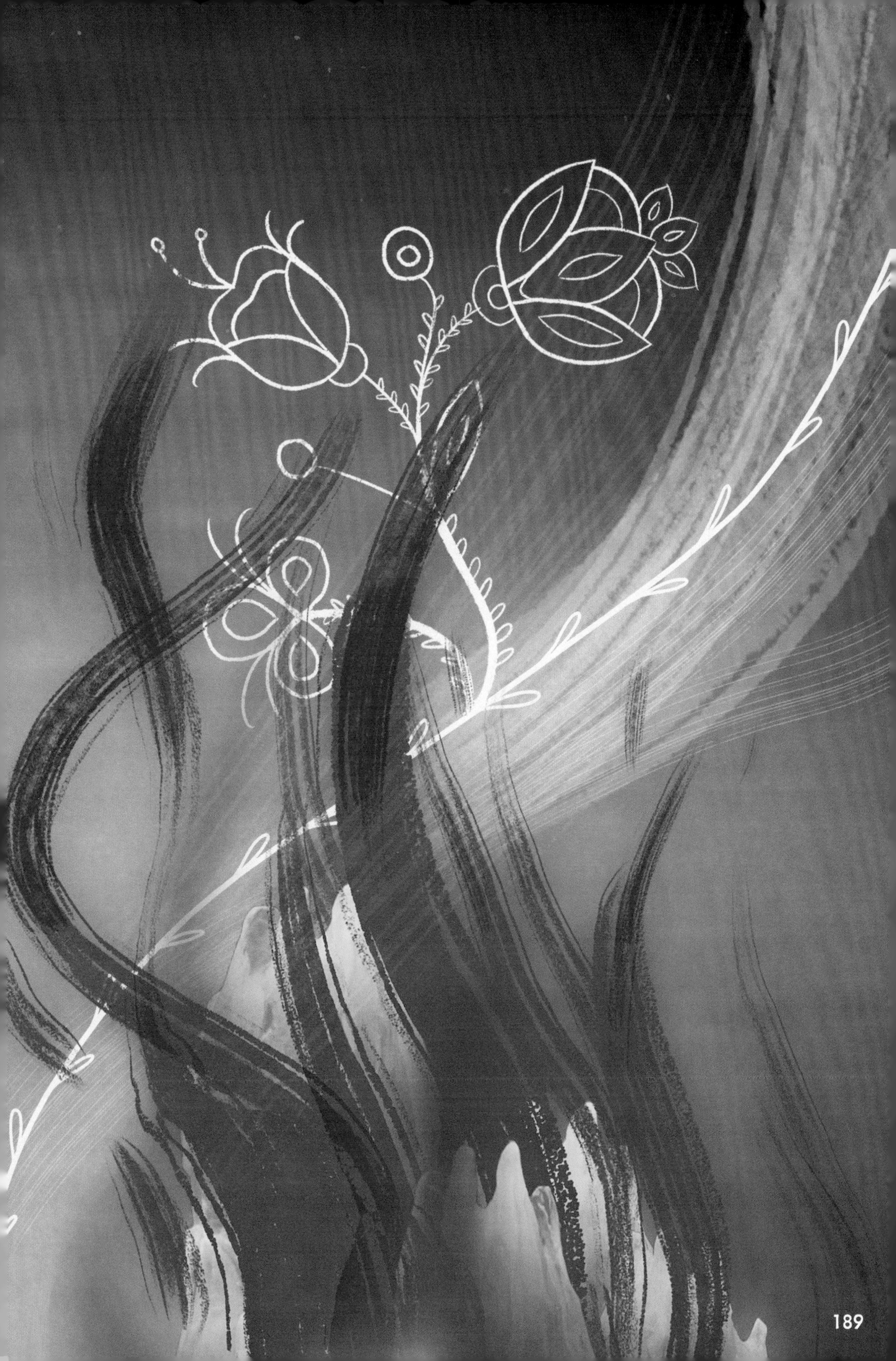

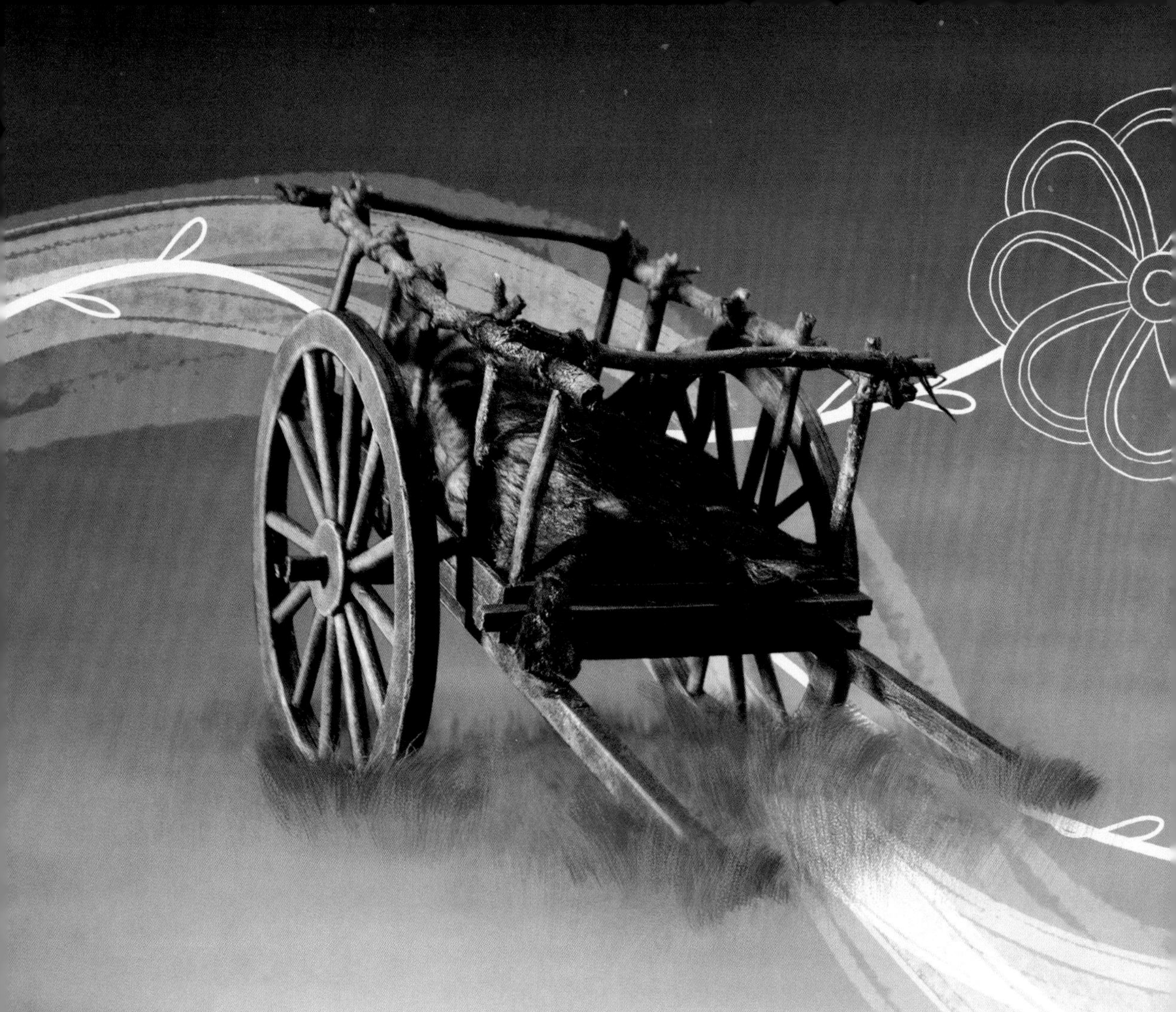

Manitoba, 1870

The Red River Métis organized a provisional government to decide what they wanted to do. They took over the Hudson's Bay Company fort, raised their own flag, and began negotiations. This is sometimes called a "rebellion," but in this case it was not. There were three men with legal training on the provisional government executive (Louis Riel, James Ross, and Thomas Bunn), and they carefully followed international law.

The Manitoba Act, the result of these negotiations, created a new province and guaranteed 1.4 million acres of land be set aside for the children of Métis families. It also protected their homes and way of life, but as we see in this graphic novel, things did not work out as intended.

The 1870 Manitoba census was done to help implement the Manitoba Act and identify children entitled to land. Napoleon Bousquet was enumerated as a four-year-old child. The Canadian government later realized the Manitoba Act did not address individual claims to Indigenous

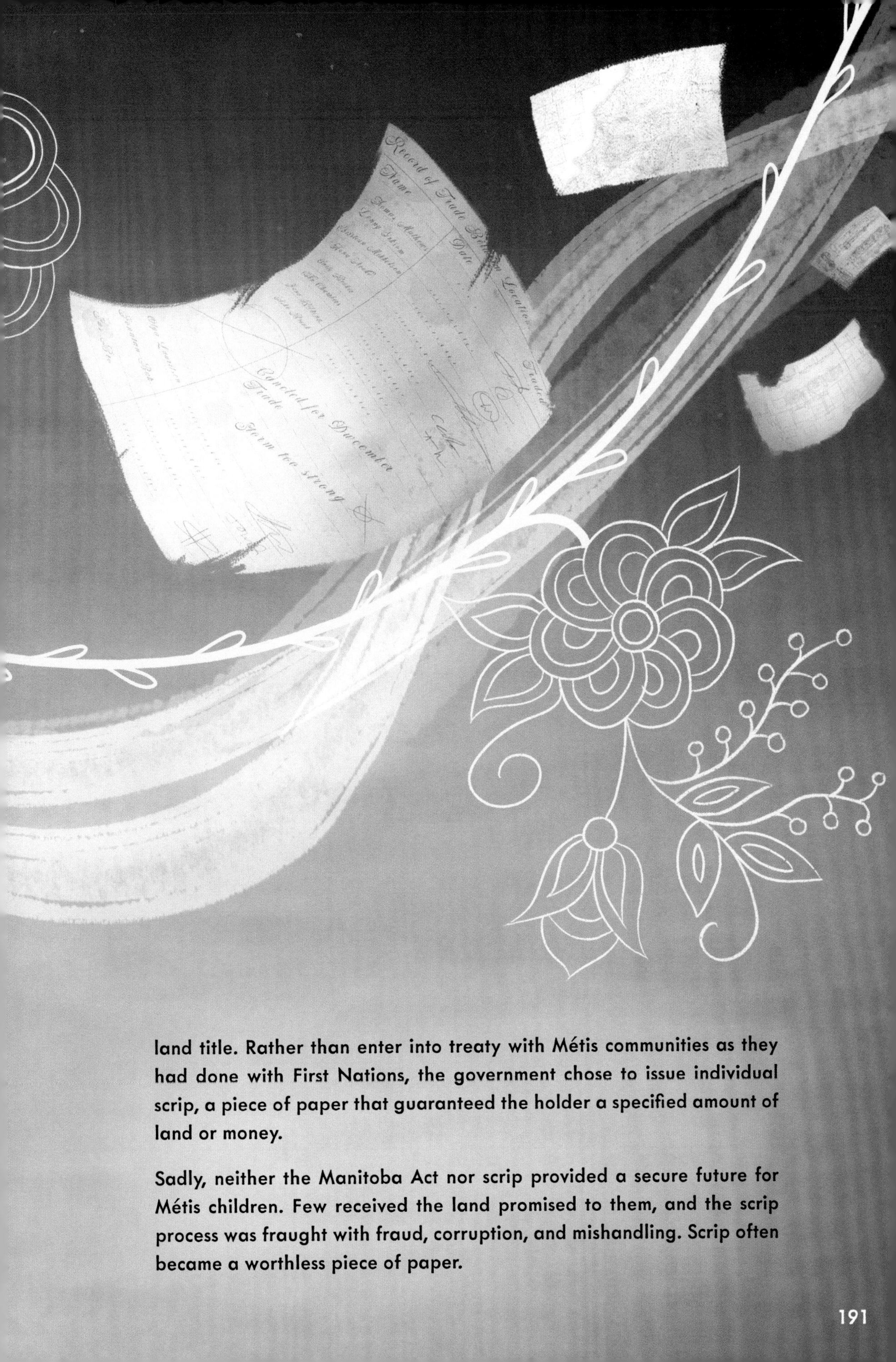
Name
Date
Traded
Canceled for December
Trade
Form too strong

land title. Rather than enter into treaty with Métis communities as they had done with First Nations, the government chose to issue individual scrip, a piece of paper that guaranteed the holder a specified amount of land or money.

Sadly, neither the Manitoba Act nor scrip provided a secure future for Métis children. Few received the land promised to them, and the scrip process was fraught with fraud, corruption, and mishandling. Scrip often became a worthless piece of paper.

The Battle of Batoche

When Canadian surveyors and land companies began to survey land for settlement in Saskatchewan in 1885, the Métis again organized to protect their communities. Many had been pushed out of Manitoba and joined their relatives further west. They did not trust the Canadian government. They had also seen the impact of the treaties and reserve life on their First Nations kin. The Canadian army descended on Métis communities and aggressively silenced their concerns. The Métis at Batoche took up arms to defend their homes. The flag flown during the conflict was a wolf's head, and a hand, with the words "maisons/autels/surtout liberté" (which means "home, altar, especially freedom"). Napoleon Bousquet fought beside his godfather and uncle, Gabriel Dumont. The Métis were defeated at Batoche, and a long, grim time of displacement and poverty began.

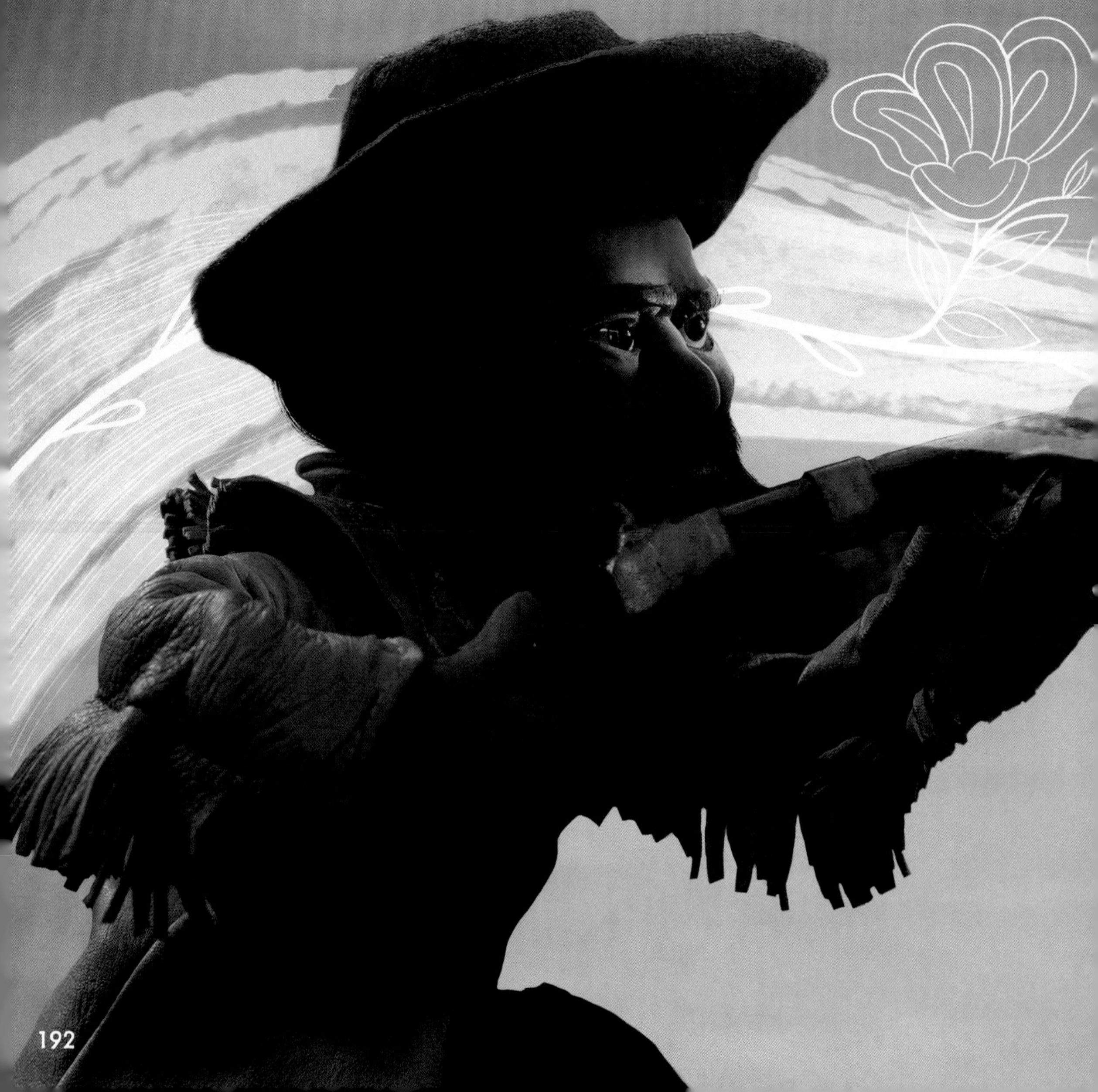

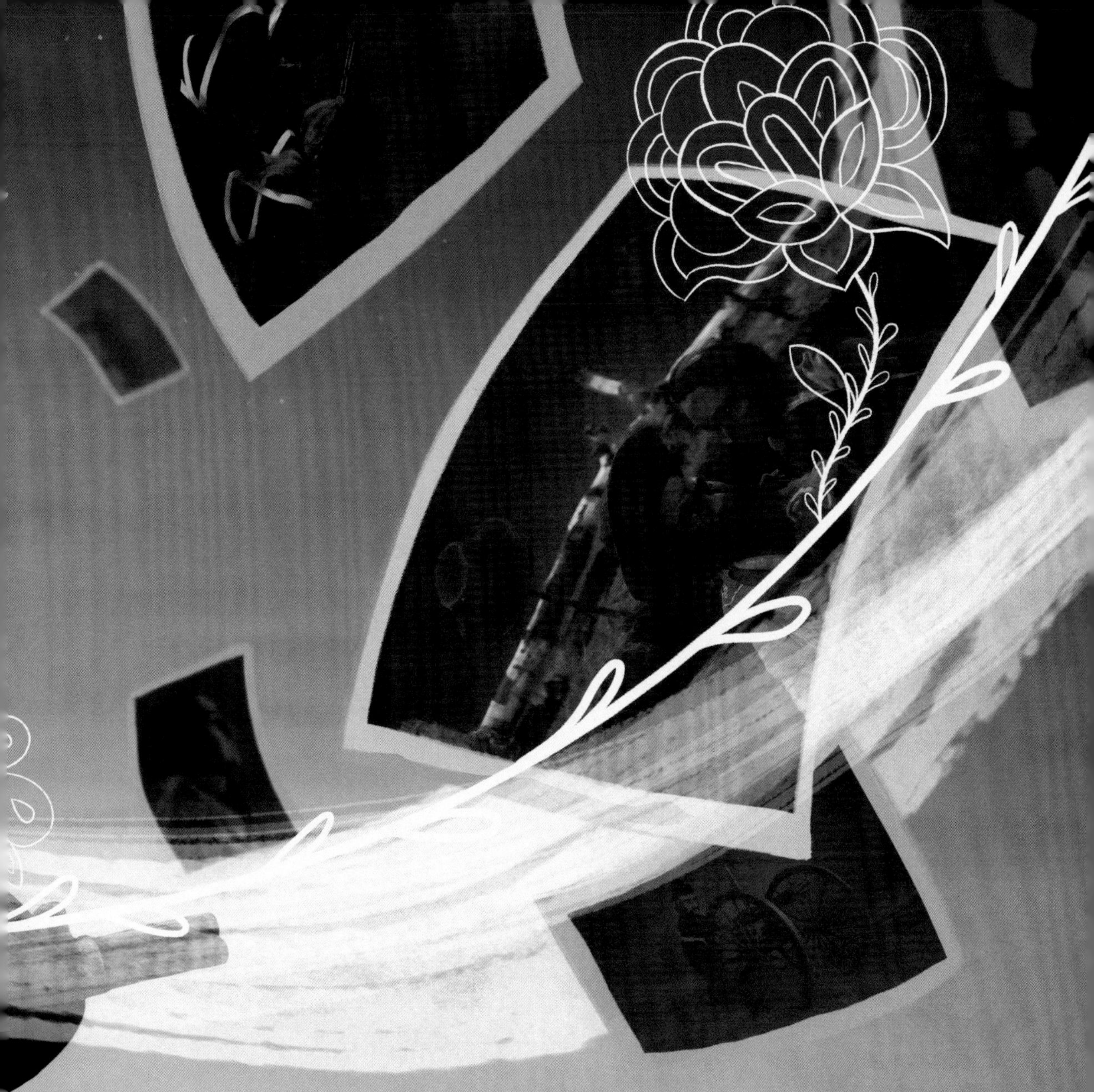

Aftermath

The first half of the twentieth century was a time of great difficulty as Métis families were pushed off their land and struggled to navigate a new system that had no place for them. People often built homes on "road allowance"—land set aside for the development of roads. In these humble communities, Métis families regrouped and supported each other. These small settlements once again became targets. Communities and homes were burned, and people were forcibly relocated to other regions to make way for "progress." Indigenous and Catholic, the Métis were also the focus of Ku Klux Klan campaigns of fear on the Prairies. In addition, children were not allowed into provincially funded schools until after World War II. Catholic missions and residential schools were often the only means to an education. From these challenging circumstances, political movements were born to build a new future for Métis children.

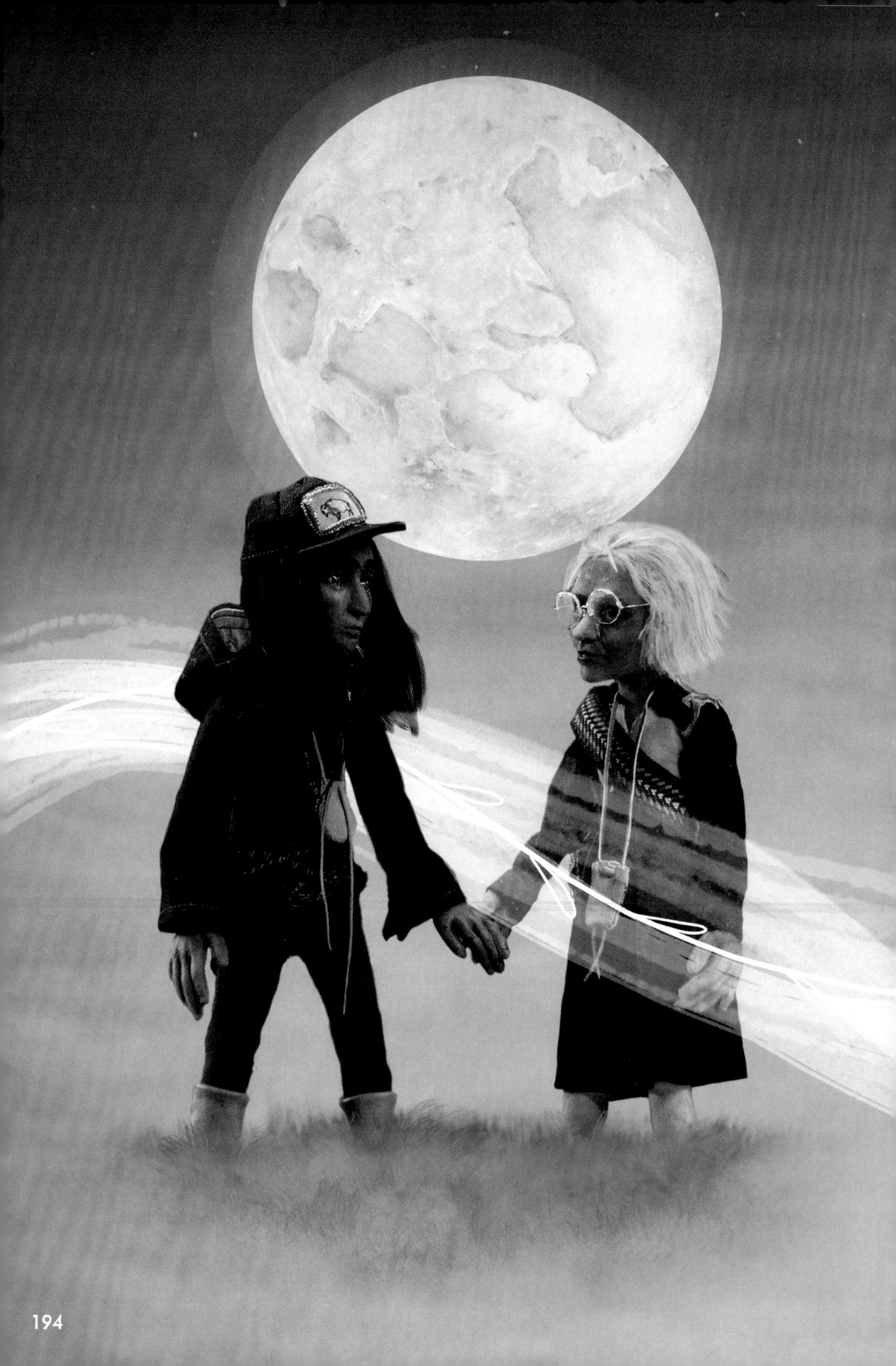

Resilience

Four Faces of the Moon could be read as a story of loss, but it is really a story of courage and resilience. In the midst of the ghost Buffalo herd, Spotted Fawn receives a gift from Jean Baptiste Wilkie and turns to see Olivine Bousquet standing amidst the herd.

She experiences the full circle of her family and makes a commitment to continue and reclaim her family members' knowledge. Like Olivine, we continue to fight, survive, and experience joy in the land, our families, and our traditions.

Timeline

1700

- 65 million Plains Buffalo roam the Prairies.
- British and French fur traders arrive.
- Some Indigenous women marry fur traders and have children, forming new independent communities known as the Métis.

1875

- Construction starts on the railroad.
- The decimation of the Buffalo begins.

1800

- The Métis population grows significantly; some settle at the forks of the Red and Assiniboine rivers.

1869

- The Métis form a provisional government.

1870

- Manitoba is created.
- The Métis claims process begins in Manitoba.

1876

- The distribution of scrip begins in Manitoba.

1890

- Fewer than 1000 Buffalo remain.

1900

- Some Métis build homes on road allowance lands.

1885

- The North West Resistance and the Battle of Batoche take place.
- Post-resistance Métis land loss begins.
- Métis Scrip Commissions visit communities to collect claims and issue Scrip certificates.

1924

- The Métis Scrip Commission ends.

A Note on Language

In *Four Faces of the Moon*, Spotted Fawn honors the heritage languages of her own family, emphasizing a unique aspect of Métis culture. Historically, Métis people spoke many languages and lived in communities of rich linguistic diversity. There were hundreds of distinct languages in North America. During the fur trade, people of many backgrounds gathered to trade, travel, live, and work together. Early observers described a "confusion of languages" or, more kindly, "a medley." But what seemed chaotic to some was familiar to children who grew up hearing the music of many languages.

Métis children would learn languages within their family circle: a Cree grandmother, a Saulteaux aunt, a French father. They would hear other languages spoken around them. Many became traders, either working independently or for fur trade companies. They would learn the languages of their customers, and over time, the Métis developed a language of their own—the Michif language—a unique, blended language that has several regional dialects. Not surprisingly, Métis people became noted as interpreters and translators. They made important contributions creating dictionaries and interpreting at Treaty negotiations. Sadly, in a surprisingly short period of time, that multilingual fluency has all but disappeared. Today there are 70 surviving Indigenous languages spoken in Canada. Many Métis today only speak English, but as with all Indigenous languages, we are making great efforts to revive, teach, and reclaim our languages. They preserve our way of looking at the world. In *Four Faces of the Moon*, language helps recreate the world of the story. Through language, we hear the voices of the ancestors.

—Sherry Farrell Racette, artist, historian, curator, and Associate Professor, Department of Visual Arts, University of Regina

Northern Michif text on pages 2 and 167 as translated by Vince Ahenakew.

Cree text on pages 54 and 85 as translated by Dorothy Visser.

Nakoda text on page 86 as translated by Tom Shawl.

Anishinaabemowin text on page 134 as translated by Lee Benson Nanigishkung.

For Further Reading

Peter Bakker, *A Language of Our Own: The Genesis of Michif, the Mixed Cree-French Language of the Canadian Métis* (Oxford University Press, 1997).

Marilyn Dumont, *The Pemmican Eaters* (ECW Press, 2015).

Rita Flamand and Norman Fleury, *La Lawng: Language Practice* (Pemmican Publications, 2004).

Julie Flett, *Lii Yiiboo Nayaapiwak lii Swer/Owls See Clearly at Night: A Michif Alphabet*, with Grace (Ledoux) Zoldy and Heather Souter (Simply Read Books, 2011).

CREDITS AND ACKNOWLEDGMENTS

GRAPHIC NOVEL CREDITS

Illustrated by:
Maya McKibbin
SJ Okemow
Dora Cepic
Zoë Alexandra
Rayne Burning
Rasheed Banda
Leoni Paul
Katrina Pleasance

Translations by:
Vince Ahenakew (Northern Michif), Dorothy Visser (Cree), Tom Shawl (Nakoda),:
Lee Benson Nanigishkung (Anishinaabemowin)

STOP-MOTION ANIMATION CREDITS

Written, directed, and produced by: Amanda Strong
Story by: Amanda Strong
Screenplay by: Bracken Hanuse Corlett
Executive Producer: Amanda Strong
Produced by: Bracken Hanuse Corlett
Associate Producers: Geoff Manton, Nate Lyman, Dusty Hagerud
1st Assistant Director: Dora Cepic

Artistic Director: Amanda Strong
Assistant Art Director: Femke van Delft
Production Designers: Dora Cepic, William Weird, Daniel Guay, Femke van Delft, Raven John
Director of Photography: Terrance Azzuolo
Grip: Amanda Strong, Daniel Guay
Lamp Operator: Damien Buddy Eagle Bear
Director of Animation: Amanda Strong and Lynn Dana Wilton
Lead Animator: Lynn Dana Wilton
Additional Stop-Motion Animation: Alicia Eisen, Dora Cepic, Amanda Strong

Lead Sculptor: Raven John
Additional Sculptors: Tim Daniels, Ian Nakamoto, Joce Weird
Mould Maker: Raven John
Puppet Construction: Raven John, Amanda Strong, Dora Cepic, Callum Peterson
Animal Puppet Fabrication: Dusty Hagerud
Armature Construction: Callum Patterson, Dora Cepic, Amanda Strong, Raven John
Custom Armatures: Julian Clark
Lead Costume Designer: Chloe Mustooch
Additional Costumes: Natalie Eggerton

Set Construction: Daniel Guay, William Weird, Femke van Delft

Prop Builders: Dora Cepic, William Weird, Raven John, Daniel Guay, Femke van Delft, Zed Alexander, Lydia Brown

Prop Assistants: Danielle Wilson, Rosalie Weeks, Natty Boonmasiri

Concept Art: Zed Alexander

Storyboard Artists: Zed Alexander, Jay White

Story Consultants: Jay White, John Sedore, Daniel Guay, Steve Oka, Luke Sargent

Edited By: Bracken Hanuse Corlett

Compositor: Keith Morgan

Post Effects Supervisor: Bryn Hewk

Online Editors: Serge Verrault, Bryn Hewko

Title Animation: Sahar Homami

Story Editors: Bracken Hanuse Corlett, Jay White

Story Mentors: Sherry Farrell Racette, Leanne Simpson, Cathy Mattes

Studio Coordinator (NFB): Dominique Forget

Studio Administrator (NFB): Rosalina Di Sario

Technical Coordinators (NFB): Steve Halle, Candice Desormeaux, Daniel Claveau

Studio, Executive Producer (NFB): Michael Fukushima

Project Manager: Dora Cepic

Pre-Production Consultant: Alicia Eisen

Technical Consultants: Raven John, Skekemxikst Talu Hanuse

Ground Transportation: Raven John

Legal Counsel: Nathaniel Lyman, Chandler Fogden Aldous Law Corporation

Accountant: Sherryl Sills

Stills Photographer: Daniel Guay

Website Designer: Sebastien Galina

Data Technician: Amanda Strong

Productions Assistants: Daniel Guay, Raven John

SPECIAL THANKS

Olivine Bousquet, Denise Strong and Ed Pryzbylo, Derry and Gail Strong, Geoff and Kevin Strong, Robert and Eve Corlett, Noelle Hanuse and Ken Young, Skekemxikst Talu Hanuse, Glenn Alteen, Tara Hogue, grunt gallery, Cease Wyss, Sherry Farrell Racette, Cathy Mates, Memory Poni - Cappo, Michelle Pichette, Shell Windsor, Turtle Mountain Arts Association, Gabriel Dumont Institute, Museum of Manitoba, Lesley Birchard, Anthony Garber, Boldly Creative Agency, Output Media, Travis Shilling, Daniel Fischer, Mary Beth Leatherdale, Sebastien Galina, Sebastien Aubin, Gordon Smith, Jeneen Frei Njootli, John Sedore, Lucas Sargent, Dominique Forget, Menalon, Cris Derksen, James Gill, Philip Planta, Peter Planta, Craft Cinema, Robin Jaqueline Romansky, Steph Gabriel, CBC Short Docs

All the partners and families of the crew!

Amanda Strong | Author, creator, director

Amanda is a Michif interdisciplinary artist with a focus on filmmaking, stop-motion animations, and media art. She is the founder of Spotted Fawn Productions, an Indigenous-led production studio that provides mentorship and training opportunities for emerging and diverse artists. Her films have screened across the globe, most notably at Cannes and TIFF. She is based out of the unceded territories of the xʷməθkʷəy̓əm (Musqueam), Sḵwx̱wú7mesh (Squamish), and Səl̓ílwitulh (Tsleil-Waututh) Nations.

Dr. Sherry Farrell Racette | Writer, "Afterword: Who Are the Métis?"

Sherry is a Métis, Algonquin, and Irish artist, educator, historian, curator, and interdisciplinary scholar. She was born in Manitoba and is a member of Timiskaming First Nation in Quebec (unceded Algonquin territory). Farrell Racette is an Associate Professor in the Department of Visual Arts, Faculty of Media, Art, and Performance at the University of Regina.

Maya McKibbin | Illustrator and designer

Maya is a 2S multi-disciplinary artist of Yaqui, Ojibwe, and Irish descent. They work primarily with digital mediums including 3D sculpture, digital paintings, and computer animation, experimenting with different forms of narrative in VR, indie games, and illustration to tell layered and emotive stories.

SJ Okemow | Illustrator

SJ is a board-certified medical illustrator who specializes in visualizing unseen worlds. She is of mixed Cree and European ancestry and currently lives in Tkaronto. She has a BSc, an MSc, and is pursuing her PhD looking at visual aesthetics in medicine. As a Nêhiyaw Iskwew, urban Indigenous, mixed identity scientist and artist who has grown up predominantly outside her ancestral culture, she has committed herself to a lifelong journey of reclamation through art, language, and most of all community.

Dora Cepic | Illustrator

Dora is a Serbian-born artist currently living in Vancouver, BC on ancestral Coast Salish land. Her personal work explores themes of displacement and identity in relation to her Balkan heritage.

Bracken Hanuse Corlett | Story editor

Bracken is an interdisciplinary artist hailing from the Wuikinuxv and Klahoose Nations. He began working in theater and performance around 20 years ago before transitioning toward his current practice, which fuses sculpture, painting and drawing with digital-media, audio-visual performance, animation, and narrative. Some of his notable exhibitions, performances, and screenings have been at grunt gallery, Vancouver Art Gallery, the Institute of Modern Art, Three Walls Gallery, Ottawa International Animation Festival, and Toronto International Film Festival.